"I need to take the *Enterprise* out."

Superintendent Chandra studied Kirk patiently from behind the neatly organized desk in his office. "Already?"

"You're aware of the apparent connection of the vacuum flare phenomenon to past *Enterprise* missions," Kirk said. Chandra nodded. "Captain Spock and I believe that a former member of our crew aboard the *Asimov* could provide a vital insight, and it would be faster to rendezvous with them in the *Enterprise* than to call them back to Earth."

"Hmm." Chandra nodded as he thought it over. "That sounds reasonable. Sending the *Enterprise* under Captain Spock is a sensible approach." The senior admiral's gaze pierced him. "But why do *you* need to be there?"

Kirk hesitated, which Chandra took as an answer. "I have accepted the nature of your arrangement with Admiral Morrow. I understand your position that your skills are still useful in the field. Some of us take more comfortably to administration than others." Chandra gestured around him at his office, adorned with paraphernalia of his family, the Academy, and San Francisco, all conveying the sense of a man securely nested in his place.

"But I accepted it with the understanding that you would find a reasonable balance between your Academy responsibilities and your occasional special assignments. I am not convinced you have been sufficiently dedicated to that balance, Jim. You are taking field assignments that do not require your presence, when you should be back here concentrating on your commitments as commandant.

"So I ask again, Jim." Chandra leaned forward. "Does the *Enterprise* actually *need* James Kirk aboard it on this mission?"

STAR TREK™

THE ORIGINAL SERIES

LIVING MEMORY

Christopher L. Bennett

Based on *Star Trek*
created by Gene Roddenberry

GALLERY BOOKS
New York   London   Toronto   Sydney   New Delhi

G

An Imprint of Simon & Schuster, Inc.
1230 Avenue of the Americas
New York, NY 10020

This book is a work of fiction. Any references to historical events, real people, or real places are used fictitiously. Other names, characters, places, and events are products of the author's imagination, and any resemblance to actual events or places or persons, living or dead, is entirely coincidental.

This book is published by Gallery Books, a division of Simon & Schuster, Inc., under exclusive license from CBS Studios Inc.

First Gallery Books trade paperback edition June 2021

GALLERY BOOKS and colophon are registered trademarks of Simon & Schuster, Inc.

For information about special discounts for bulk purchases, please contact Simon & Schuster Special Sales at 1-866-506-1949 or business@simonandschuster.com.

The Simon & Schuster Speakers Bureau can bring authors to your live event. For more information or to book an event, contact the Simon & Schuster Speakers Bureau at 1-866-248-3049 or visit our website at www.simonspeakers.com.

Manufactured in the United States of America

10 9 8 7 6 5 4 3 2

Library of Congress Cataloging-in-Publication Data is available.

ISBN 978-1-9821-6589-5
ISBN 978-1-9821-6590-1 (ebook)

For Nichelle Nichols

Remember thee?
Ay, thou poor ghost, while memory holds a seat
In this distracted globe. Remember thee?
Yea, from the table of my memory
I'll wipe away all trivial fond records,
All saws of books, all forms, all pressures past
That youth and observation copied there,
And thy commandment all alone shall live
Within the book and volume of my brain,
Unmix'd with baser matter.

—William Shakespeare
Hamlet

Historian's Note

The events of this story take place in the summer and autumn of 2279, approximately six years after the reunited crew of the *U.S.S. Enterprise* saves Earth from a powerful machine life-form called V'Ger (*Star Trek: The Motion Picture*) and six years prior to Khan Noonien Singh's escape from exile on Ceti Alpha V (*Star Trek II: The Wrath of Khan*).

Prologue

Passenger Transport *Ballou*
Iota Leonis system

Michael Ashrafi leaned against the forward viewport, straining his eyes as if it would somehow bring Argelius II into view sooner. "Ar-jee-lius, here we come!"

Vekal suppressed a twinge of annoyance. "As I have stated five previous times, Michael," the Vulcan youth said, "it is 'Ar-*ghee*-lius.' A voiced velar plosive as opposed to a voiced palato-alveolar affricate. How illogical that your alphabet employs the same symbol for both."

"It's perfectly logical," countered Zirani Kayros with an impish tilt to her hairless head. "Alphabets evolve over time and must adapt their existing symbols to new or foreign sounds." The Tiburonian tapped one of her broad, elaborately contoured ears. "Sometimes they lack enough symbols to cover them all."

"Then they could simply add diacritical marks to clarify the distinction."

Michael scoffed, crossing his arms over his bright red shirt. "You're one to talk about logic, Vekal. How logical is it for a Vulcan to sneak off on a pleasure trip to sample the hedonistic wonders of Ar-*jee*-lius?"

Vekal fidgeted in his seat. "Respect for infinite diversity requires study and understanding. I am simply here to . . . observe how Argelian civilization has managed to achieve two centuries of peace while freely indulging emotional desire, as opposed to restraining it. If I am to work with emotional beings once we begin our term at Starfleet Academy—"

Kayros chuckled. "So you thought you'd sample a few of those 'indulgences' for yourself, right? Strictly in the name of immersion anthropology." She leaned closer, affecting a pretense of seductive behavior. "Admit it, Vekal. Vulcan teenagers are as curious about sex as the rest of us. Aren't you?"

Vekal had never expected to be so relieved by the sound of a navigational hazard alert. Reflexively, he turned to look out the forward port, where brilliant pinpoints of light were flashing briefly into existence, almost blinding him before the port's filters engaged to dim the view. As the *Ballou* began to decelerate and turn, the pilot's voice emanated from the intercom. *"Passengers, please return to your seats. We're encountering some kind of gravimetric and EM turbulence. I'm bringing us briefly to a relative halt while I assess— Aahh!"*

Suddenly the blinding lights were *inside* the ship, just for a moment or two as it passed through the edge of the effect, despite the pilot's efforts to avoid it. The result was akin to a lightning strike inside the compartment, the heat searing Vekal's skin and the shock waves in the air deafening him.

When he gathered himself afterward, he noted that the engines had shut down and the display screens were dark. The overhead lights flickered and the air carried the scent of burned circuits and vaporized metals. Glancing at the viewport, Vekal saw that the *Ballou* was in a slow rotation.

He looked toward the cockpit, but Kayros had already recovered and was climbing the gangway leading up to it. Sliding the door open, she looked inside and gasped. Vekal strove to make out her words over the ringing in his ears. *"Get the medkit! I think he's been shot!"*

It was an illogical assumption; more likely, one of the pinpoint energy anomalies had passed through the Argelian pilot's body, as they presumably had with the engines. "Send a distress call!" he said loudly as Michael went for the medical kit.

Kayros checked the console and shook her head. "*The power's down!*"

It was reasonable to surmise that the craft had an automatic distress beacon with independent power, but there was no way to be certain. Vekal put that matter aside for now; the pilot was the first priority.

Michael gave him a wry look as he handed over the medkit. "See? This is what you get when a Vulcan tries to have a good time."

U.S.S. *Reliant* NCC-1864
Approaching Iota Leonis system

"Any luck yet, Mister Chekov?"

Commander Pavel Chekov frowned at the radiometrics display on his science console, making one more attempt to refine its scan settings. "Negative, Captain," he told Clark Terrell, who hovered over his left shoulder. In his months aboard *Reliant*, Chekov had learned that the burly, bearded captain was the populist type, often found pacing the outer ring of bridge stations to get his crew's reports at close range rather than holding court from the captain's chair in the center. Chekov appreciated Terrell's personal touch most of the time, but having his commanding officer looming over him when answers were slow in coming was not his favorite sensation.

"We are not quite close enough to separate out the source of the sensor interference," Chekov went on, looking up into Terrell's broad, brown face. "Radiometric readings are still blended in with the flux from Argelius's sun, while gravimetric and subspace readings are intermingled with the heavy warp traffic around the planet. It is a popular tourist destination, of course."

"Which is exactly what worries me." Terrell strode forward two stations, allowing the tension in Chekov's shoulders to ease slightly. "Any luck cleaning up that distress signal, Lieutenant Kyle?"

The fair, goateed Englishman looked up from the communications station. "Nearly there, sir. The interference is rising and falling in surges, but it seems to be diminishing overall, and of course the gain increases as we get closer. I'm getting fragments now—I estimate another minute or two."

Terrell nodded. "Do your best, John." He turned to the helm. "Stoney, any chance of gaining a bit more speed?"

"We're maxed out already, sir," Lieutenant Commander Ralston Beach replied in his pronounced New York accent. "In fact, I don't like going this fast into a high-traffic area with low sensor visibility."

"Needs must as the Devil drives, Stoney."

"Even the Devil would slow down if he were driving into that mess, Captain."

Terrell chuckled. "*Touché.*"

The talk of the Devil brought Chekov no reassurance. His first visit to Argelius II had been a dozen years earlier, on shore leave from the *Enterprise* after a series of stressful missions. The visit had been very . . . well, "relaxing" was hardly the word, but quite pleasant and fulfilling for a twenty-two-year-old ensign on his first visit to a hedonistic society. He had gone down to the surface in a shore party including Lieutenant Uhura, who had promptly lit out on her own pursuits, as they had not yet become more than casual friends. It had been a rewarding but blurry few days—at least for Chekov. Uhura had also seemed highly satisfied when he had seen her again at the transporter station, but he had respected her privacy. However, once they returned to the *Enterprise*, they had been shocked to discover that the vessel had been invaded in their absence by a murderous incorporeal entity calling itself Redjac, which claimed to have been Jack the Ripper and other infamous serial killers from history—or rather, to have possessed and controlled their bodies, as it had possessed a local administrator who had killed several Argelian women as well as Karen Tracy, a medical technician Chekov had been rather fond of. Naturally, Captain Kirk and Mister Spock had managed to save the day, beaming the entity's deceased host body into open space on wide dispersal. Chekov hadn't been sure if he was glad or sorry to have missed it, given that most of his crewmates were still coming down from the tranquilizer high Doctor McCoy had put them on to starve the entity of the fear that sustained it. Lieutenant Sulu seemed to have had nearly as good a time at the helm station as Chekov had on the planet.

But who could really say what it would take to kill an incorporeal entity that had survived for centuries? Chekov knew from his recent experience with the Spectres that it was possible to kill such an entity while it was joined to a humanoid host, but Redjac had evidently been able to jump between hosts far more readily—even possessing the *Enterprise* computer for a time. What if dispersing its transporter beam had only weakened it temporarily? Could these disruptions affecting multiple ships near Argelius be a sign of its restoration?

Chekov reined in his imagination. He was *Reliant*'s chief science officer; his job was to formulate hypotheses based on evidence, not speculation and old fears. Soon they would have more information about the nature of the disruptions, and Chekov could practically hear Spock's voice in his head reminding him to take the time to fill the gaps in his knowledge with data rather than hastening to fill them with conjecture.

Indeed, it was only moments more before Kyle was able to clear up the signal interference. "Argelius II Orbital Control coming through now, sir," he reported.

Terrell nodded. "On screen." He turned to the main view-screen.

"*. . . ontrol to Fed . . . essel, do you read?*"

"Argelius Orbital Control, this is Captain Clark Terrell of the *U.S.S. Reliant*. We read you."

The dark-eyed humanoid woman on the screen gave a sigh of relief. "*Oh, thank the . . . trying to reach you for hours!*"

"Is your situation urgent?"

"*Not . . . ad as we feared, Captain. But multiple ships ha . . . damaged by some sort of gravime . . . ic and electromagnetic discharges in proximit . . . the planet. Multip . . . ges coming and going unpredictably. They're coming less often n . . . eem to be growing weaker, but several ships req . . . assistance.*"

"We stand ready to assist, Argelius Control. Where are we needed most?"

The Argelian looked down, evidently checking her displays. "*That would be the* Ballou, *a passenger transport. We . . . ceived their distress signal, but the interference keeps us from getting a precise fix. But with Starfleet sensors . . .*"

"Please transmit their last known course and position, Control. We'll get right on it."

Kyle efficiently caught the transmitted data and passed it over to the science station. Chekov directed sensors to the indicated area and soon got a hit. "Got it, sir. It's adrift, power almost gone." He worked the controls to refine the dynoscanner read-ings. "Three . . . no, probably four life signs, one weak."

"Then we've got no time to lose," Terrell said. "Stoney, time to play Coast Guard."

"It was the weirdest thing I ever saw," Michael Ashrafi told Terrell as he sat on the edge of his bed in sickbay. Beside him, Nurse Matsuda was applying a salve to Zirani Kayros's radiation burns, as she had already done to Ashrafi. Doctor Wilder was in surgery tending to the *Ballou*'s pilot, while Doctor Valentine was treating the Vulcan youth, Vekal, for his more severe burns and hearing loss.

"There were these really bright flashes of light—just pinpoints, just for a split second, but blinding, like lightning. Unpredictable, like . . . like distant fireworks." He rubbed a hand through his shaggy black hair. "Except not so distant. The pilot tried to stop short and ease around it, but he didn't quite make it. We brushed the edge of the—the storm, or whatever, and the pinpoints started to pop up *inside* the cabin. They didn't burn through the hull, mind you—they just *appeared* right there in midair."

"The way the pilot's wound looked," Kayros said with a squeamish expression, "it was like something had burned a hole in him from the *inside*."

"Probably what happened to the engines too," Ashrafi said. He peered at Terrell. "Starfleet's probably seen weirder things than this, right? You know what this was?"

Terrell patted his shoulder. "We're working on it, son. But for now, at least the phenomenon seems to have subsided. Hopefully it won't repeat."

"From your lips to the Great Bird's ears," Ashrafi said. He tilted his head, grinning wryly. "I came to Argelius to have a blast, but this isn't the kind I had in mind."

The captain chuckled. "You three are all enrolled in Starfleet Academy?"

Ashrafi nodded. "We start in the fall."

"But you're already friends?"

Kayros nodded. "We met at a three-week pre-Academy program on Alpha Centauri."

Terrell nodded. There were various preparatory and affiliate programs offered on different worlds for aspiring Academy entrants, or for accepted cadets seeking a head start. Starfleet had demanding educational standards, and even commissioned officers were expected to continue studying and learning throughout their active service. Therefore, any additional learning that cadets chose to pursue beforehand was welcome and encouraged.

Terrell turned at the sound of the corridor door, which opened to admit Commander Chekov. "Captain, I have the analysis of the sensor readings from Orbital Control."

"Have you been able to identify the phenomenon?"

Chekov hesitated. "Up to a point, sir. The outbursts appear to be . . . well, essentially, they are extremely large vacuum fluctuations."

Ashrafi stared at him. " 'Wacuum fluctuations'? What the hell are those?"

"Oh, come on, Michael," Kayros said. "Elementary quantum physics, remember? The Uncertainty Principle—energy can spontaneously be created as long as it's destroyed in a brief enough time that it doesn't unbalance the books."

He stared at her blankly. "I'm a communications student, Zirani. I barely got through that course."

The young Tiburonian frowned. "But that's not supposed to show up on a macroscopic scale, beyond special cases like the Casimir effect."

Chekov smiled at her. "Very good, miss. You're right, as a rule. But it's a matter of probability. There's always the infinitesimal chance that a spontaneous quantum fluctuation could produce a massive amount of energy. It's incredibly unlikely, but in a vast universe . . ."

Terrell stared at him. "I could buy that happening once, but this was numerous outbursts over hours."

"I'm not saying it's the answer for certain, sir. But it's theoretically possible. The bursts appeared to have the gravimetric signature of quantum wormholes. A single burst of sufficient energy could churn the cosmic foam, so to speak, enough to cause spontaneous tunneling events, possibly a cascade of such wormholes. The energy arising in one spot could spill out through those wormholes, displaced around it in space and time, and those other bursts could produce a chain reaction, until it eventually died down."

The captain crossed his arms. "So you think this was a one-time freak event. We don't have to worry about it happening again."

Chekov straightened. "I am not saying that, Captain. Russians always plan for the worst. And I cannot yet rule out the possibility that some outside influence triggered the event. But at the moment, we have no data to suggest that. And it is within the realm of possibility that it was a unique natural event."

Terrell nodded. "All right. We'll stay in the system for a few more days, just in case." He smiled. "If nothing else happens, we might as well take advantage of the opportunity for some R and R."

Ashrafi hopped off the bed. "Sounds good to me! When do we go?"

"Ah, yes, about that," Chekov said. "Once Doctor Wilder reported your names, our communications officer notified your families." He crossed his arms, taking in both Ashrafi and Kayros. "It seems that your parents have been wondering where you snuck off to. They're on their way to pick you up."

The mop-headed boy groaned and sank back onto the bed. "This is the worst vacation ever."

Terrell caught his gaze. "Look at it this way, son: at least you get to go home from it."

Chapter One

U.S.S. *Enterprise* NCC-1701
Kaleb sector

"Admiral," Captain Spock observed, "the work bee crews *have* been thorough in their inspections."

Admiral James T. Kirk flushed slightly at his old friend's words, a gentle reminder that his aimless fidgeting to distract himself could be taken as a criticism of the *Enterprise*'s diligent cadet crew. "Of course, Spock," he said, abandoning his pretense of looking over the work bee bays' charger connections. Returning to the Vulcan captain's side, he gazed out across the landing bay's wide floor, toward the open hangar doors at the rear and the stars gleaming through the nigh-invisible shimmer of the force field that held in the bay's atmosphere. "I'm just eager for the *Lemaître* to return, so we can get this mission over with. It'll be good to get back to the Academy."

Spock threw him a skeptical look. "If your concern is for your duties at Starfleet Academy, then may I recommend that you employ more selectivity regarding which special missions you choose to accompany personally? The professor, the commander, and I could have easily completed this task without your presence."

"I know, I know," Kirk reassured him—not that Spock needed

reassurance. "But for a sensitive mission like this, given what's at stake . . ."

"Understood."

Kirk smiled. "Besides, how could I pass up a reunion with my two favorite former science officers?"

As if on cue, Cadet Lawler's voice sounded over the landing bay intercom. *"Shuttlecraft on final approach. Stand clear."*

"Punctual as always," Kirk said warmly.

A glint of light moving against the starscape soon resolved into a boxy, wedge-shaped shuttlecraft that slid smoothly through the pressure curtain. The *Georges Lemaître* settled on the deck in front of Kirk and Spock, who stepped toward it as it powered down, its hull creaking and popping slightly as it warmed in the bay's atmosphere.

The side hatch opened, and a distinctive cane, its handle carved in the likeness of an Andorian *atlirith*, preceded its owner onto the deck. "Break out the good stuff, Jim," Professor Rhenas Sherev said. "I feel like celebrating."

Kirk smiled at the small but strongly built Andorian *shen* who had been his science officer before Spock, on the *Sacagawea* an embarrassing number of years ago. "Glad to see you back in one piece, Rhen. I take it the handoff went well?"

Sherev strode toward him easily. With the upgrades to her part-bionic leg over the years, her cane was no more than an affectation, but she liked the air of dignity it lent her—not that Kirk would ever consider her dignified after all the barhopping, poker hustling, and womanizing they'd done together on shore leaves over the years. "With minimal tension, considering the stakes. Nyota was a great help making sure there were no unfortunate mistranslations."

Kirk glanced over her shoulder to where Commander Nyota Uhura, dressed in a stylish civilian jacket and skirt, had now stepped down from the *Lemaître*'s hatch after securing the shuttle. "Commander. Welcome back."

"Glad to be back, sir. It was an intriguing opportunity to see another side to Romulan culture. I'm grateful that you and Captain Spock called on me."

"It has been agreeable to work with you once again, Commander," Spock said. Uhura flashed him a brilliant smile. Kirk was reminded that the two of them had always seemed to have a natural rapport, one that had begun to form under Christopher Pike before Kirk succeeded him as captain of the *Enterprise*.

"So the Sword of Renz Verus is on its way back where it belongs?" Kirk asked as he and Spock led Sherev and Uhura toward the starboard gangway.

"Only about twelve decades late, but yes," Sherev answered. "It would've been sooner without all this diplomatic tiptoeing and pretense."

"You understand why that was necessary," Spock pointed out. "Given the heightened tensions of the past two years, direct involvement by the military on either side—"

"Yes, yes—no need to prove Bones right about your tendency to state the obvious," Sherev told him, not without affection. She had known Spock almost as long as Kirk had, though only intermittently.

"You know patience isn't my strong suit," she went on as they passed through the door onto the gangway that ran along one side of the cavernous cargo bay. "I wish we could get to a point where we and the Romulans could just *talk* and work together, like Doctor T'Lesevek and I did down on Bright Tree."

"It has traditionally been easier for the scientific communities of rival powers to trust one another than it has been for their governments or militaries," Spock observed. "Hence the value of back channels."

"I know. But if that kind of trust could've been extended much sooner, maybe we wouldn't still be rivals today."

Kirk pondered Sherev's words as he led the group into the turbolift whose freestanding shaft pierced the three-story volume of the cargo bay. It had been Sherev who had brought this mission to him at the Academy weeks ago, after the Sword of Renz Verus had been discovered in the estate of a deceased Andorian whose *thavan*—father, approximately—had been a veteran of the Battle of Cheron, in which the Andorian Imperial Guard had finally joined the fight alongside Earth's Starfleet in the engagement that had ended the Earth-Romulan War. A number of the ships on the opposing side had been constructed at the historic Renz Verus Shipyards of Romulus, whose director had personally joined in the battle, bringing along the ancient sword that had been the traditional symbol of the shipyards for centuries. In the aftermath, an Andorian crew had found wreckage from the director's ship and boarded it for salvage, and once the Romulans subsequently reclaimed what was left, they had found the iconic sword missing. During treaty negotiations, they had accused the Andorians of taking it and demanded its return, but the Imperial Guard insisted that no sword had been found; if it had existed, it must have been vaporized or lost to the vacuum of space. The Romulans had protested, but ultimately it had been incidental; their war had been with Earth, and accepting Earth's terms of peace had been their best option to prevent further losses after their decisive defeat at Cheron. Still, according to recent Starfleet Intelligence reports, the clash over the sword had left many Romulans with a profound distrust toward the wartime allies and the Federation they had subsequently formed.

Once the Andorian government had discovered that a member of their fleet had indeed plundered the sword and kept it as a family heirloom, the suggestion had been made to repatriate it to Romulus as a gesture of goodwill. Tensions between the two powers had been rising of late, a delayed side effect of the collapse of the brief Klingon-Romulan alliance earlier in the decade. In the years since the bloody Battle of Klach D'kel Brakt, the two empires had become bitter enemies, making the already warlike Romulan government even more paranoid and defensive and provoking a major buildup of the Romulan military. It had only been a matter of time before that spilled over into renewed hostility toward the Federation as well, and there had been several tense border incidents over the past two years. The hope was that returning the Sword of Renz Verus might improve diplomatic relations with Romulus and defuse further conflicts.

But the mistrust between the two powers was still too strong, so Rhenas Sherev had suggested using the back channel Spock had mentioned, the universal fraternity of scientists that transcended politics. She had worked with Kirk to arrange a meeting between civilian representatives, including herself, at a neutral site unclaimed by either power. She and a leading subspace physicist employed at the Renz Verus Shipyards, a descendant of the wartime director, had met at the Selvidge Archive on the neutral planet Bright Tree in the sparsely populated Kaleb sector. Despite its human name, the archive was a multispecies research institute and library comparable to the Federation's Memory Alpha, but pointedly independent of any state and open to all.

Of course, both parties had been escorted by military vessels as a precaution, with both governments' full knowledge. But maintaining the pretense of neutrality had been important, so the actual handoff had been performed by civilian representatives, with supporting military personnel attending unofficially in civilian attire (Kirk had no doubt that Uhura had had her own counterpart at the handoff). It had been a symbolic gesture, but then, the sword had been a powerful symbol to the Romulans. With luck, its repatriation would help build new trust between the powers, even if neither side openly admitted how the sword had come back to Renz Verus. The Romulans' official story would be that Selvidge Archive researchers had discovered the sword drifting in space.

This had been a straightforward mission, but perfect for the *Enterprise* in its current capacity. Kirk had accepted his second promotion to the admiralty and the position of Starfleet Academy commandant with the proviso that he would be assigned the *Enterprise* as his personal flagship under Spock's command, occasionally taking it out on special missions to ensure that Kirk's talents in the field were not squandered behind a desk. Between such missions, the vessel served as an Academy training vessel and test bed for technology upgrades. Thus, as it was no longer active on the front lines, the *Enterprise* had been a suitably nonprovocative choice for this tentative peacemaking gesture.

As much as Kirk had enjoyed the reunion with his old friend Sherev, he felt envious that she had been the one in the thick of things instead of him. He valued these special missions as a chance to keep his skills honed, yet this one, for all its political sensitivity, had been little more than a milk run from his perspective. The admiral knew he should be grateful that it had proceeded so smoothly, but he still wished he'd gotten to do more.

Sherev, it seemed, felt differently. "Well," she said, stretching languidly beside him, "I'm glad that's all over. I'm eager to get back to my students."

Kirk met her eyes and smiled. "There's still a place for you at the Academy, you know. We'd love to have you."

Her smile in return was patient and apologetic. "You know I have my own projects I can't abandon. And I left the Starfleet part of my life behind a long time ago. Besides, you've already got a solid archaeology department under Scott Saslow."

"Solidity isn't everything. You could shake things up in interesting ways."

She peered at him. "This isn't just about you getting bored behind a desk again, is it? I thought this whole flagship gig was supposed to keep that from happening."

"Of course not. I enjoy my work. Guiding young minds, shaping the officers of tomorrow, shepherding research on the cutting edge . . . it's all the best parts of starship duty without the danger and loneliness of the frontier."

"I'm sure it's me you're trying so hard to convince."

Kirk directed an affectionate glare her way, then decided to change the subject as the turbolift deposited them on D deck, housing the ship's VIP and senior officers' quarters. "And how about you, Commander?" he asked Uhura as they exited the lift. "Back to the *Asimov*?"

"That's right," she said with a smile. "The work isn't as varied or unpredictable as it was on the *Enterprise*, but I'm enjoying the chance to pursue a long-term research project."

"What was it again?" Sherev asked. "Charting subspace density anomalies?"

"Yes, Professor. And using them to amplify sensor and communication beams through a form of gravitational lensing. We're learning a lot about multidimensional subspace topology."

"If I interpret your results correctly," Spock told her, "they suggest methods for predicting the locations of density variations that could be used to optimize effective warp velocities as well."

"I don't want us to get ahead of ourselves, Captain. I've learned the value of being patient with long-term research like this." Uhura gave a sigh that struck Kirk as slightly melancholy.

"Of course. Still, the potential is intriguing."

Kirk envied the ability of the three scientists around him to find contentment in the slow, meticulous routines of their research. He did derive fulfillment from guiding the next generation of Starfleet officers, more so than he had as Chief of Starfleet Operations during his last stint on Earth. But he had to admit, it was a quieter life than what he'd become accustomed to on the *Enterprise*. These special missions helped keep things interesting, but in some ways they just sharpened the contrast with his everyday routine; when he returned home, he found himself wondering how long it would be until the next mission.

He quashed those thoughts. It had been less than a year since he took the post; maybe he just needed a little more time to find his equilibrium. A new term would begin before long, bringing a whole new crop of students. That could provide interesting challenges of its own.

Starfleet Academy
San Francisco, Earth

Leonard McCoy leaned casually against the side of the desk in Admiral Kirk's office. "So as it turned out, your entire contribution to the mission was to hover over Spock on the bridge and sit in your quarters doing paperwork. You could've done that back here."

"It was a sensitive situation," Kirk countered, scrolling idly through the list of proposed course catalog revisions on his desk monitor. "While it was best to maintain the pretense of a civilian exchange, it was important to show the Romulan government that we took the peace gesture seriously—that it had the attention and support of officers at the highest level."

McCoy scoffed. "Most convoluted excuse for a mission I ever heard. I'm just trying to decide if you did it to get out of trudging through that course catalog, or to get out of your blind date with Rosemarie Yeun."

"Rosemarie seems like a perfectly charming lady. I told her I'd be happy to reschedule."

"You knew she was shipping out this week to do a geological survey on that new colony world. Buzzelle or whatever."

"Basel. Like the one in Switzerland." Kirk furrowed his brow, glancing up at the doctor. "Wasn't Buzzelle your grandmother's maiden name?"

"Stop trying to change the subject. You can't keep making excuses to get out of having a social life."

"Bones, you know as well as I do how unpredictable Starfleet life can be." He glanced at the chronometer. "Although I do have a meeting scheduled with Commander Rakatheema from Starfleet Security in about two minutes. So can we talk about this later?"

McCoy grew pensive. "Now that you mention it, there is a very attractive genetics researcher at Starfleet Medical who's been dying to meet you, Jim. If you can find an evening free this week—"

"Bones, just stop. I was being polite before. This obsession of yours with my romantic life has—"

"Or your lack of one."

"Has got to stop. It's not as though I've ever needed help connecting with women."

McCoy crossed his arms. "You're starting to believe your reputation from the vid dramas. I know you better than that, Jim. Getting women interested in *you* has never been the problem. The problem is prying you away from your obsessive work ethic. And I don't mean the occasional casual fling in the heat of a crisis. I mean opening yourself to the possibility, now that you're settled down on Earth, of finding someone worth settling down *with*."

Kirk's aide signaled from the outer office. *"Admiral? Commander Rakatheema has arrived."*

"Excellent, Lieutenant," Kirk said with feeling. "Send him in, please."

"That was not two minutes," McCoy said.

"Some officers pride themselves on punctuality," Kirk said. "You should try it sometime."

"Ha, ha. If I have to be insulted, I'll just go find Spock so I can get it from an expert."

"Bones," Kirk said, stopping him on the way out. "I appreciate your concern for my happiness. But it's for me to work out on my own. All right?"

McCoy's expression showed his understanding, but not his surrender. "Like you said—we'll talk about it later."

The doctor politely greeted Commander Rakatheema on the way out. *The first time I can remember him showing politeness in this office,* Kirk thought. The admiral wondered what the Arcturian commander would think if he knew how a younger, even less tactful McCoy had once described the people of Arcturus IV in Kirk's hearing: "They look like half-melted waxwork sculptures of some other species." Arcturians were pale, hairless humanoids whose heads, and to a lesser extent the rest of their bodies, were draped with irregular flaps of reddish-gray skin. Their sagging, jowly features were often perceived by other humanoids as somber or slothful, but Kirk knew them to be quite an energetic people, with a disciplined, military bent to their culture, but also an inquisitive, artistic nature.

Rakatheema, who wore the dark green turtleneck of the security division under his brick-red uniform jacket, greeted Kirk with a smile and a firm handshake once the door closed behind McCoy. "Admiral Kirk. It's an honor to meet you."

Kirk was never quite sure how to respond to that kind of praise, but the commander delivered it in such crisp, matter-of-fact tones that it didn't feel obsequious. "Ah, thank you, Commander. Have a seat. Coffee? Tea?"

"No, thank you, Admiral. I am adequately hydrated, and I know your time is finite."

Kirk nodded. "Very well, then. What can I do for you?"

Despite his words, Rakatheema hesitated. "How much do you know about Arcturian history, sir?"

The admiral thought it over. "I know the basics. Your distant ancestors migrated out from the first to the fourth planet of Arcturus when the star entered its giant phase. On first contact, you were interested in Earth's experience dealing with climate change, because your own sun is still gradually warming."

Rakatheema smiled. "We were also quite taken with Earth

poetry and music. Captain Shumar of the *Essex* introduced us to Shakespeare in that first exchange. The rhythms of the Bard of Avon's language entranced us even before we understood it."

"I've heard it said that you were the first nonhuman species who mastered Elizabethan English before the modern variety." Kirk kept his tone light, declining to mention that he had once seen the Karidian Players perform an Arcturian-designed production of *Hamlet*. He associated that performance with the real-life tragedies that had surrounded it, and he did not think the commander would appreciate hearing that his people reminded Kirk of the crimes of Kodos the Executioner.

"I trust, then, that you know something of our experiences in the years between first contact and our application for Federation membership."

"Yes," Kirk said. "'Maltuvis's Folly.' The retaliation he provoked when he tried to invade your world proved critical to his undoing."

"More specifically, it was our Warborn who proved critical to Arcturus's defense against the Saurian invaders, as they have in other times of crisis over the past several thousand years."

Kirk hesitated. "I admit my knowledge of the Warborn is limited. Some sort of . . . clone soldiers, weren't they?"

Rakatheema's already wrinkled brow shifted downward into a frown. "Not clones, Admiral. A common misconception."

"My apologies."

"The Warborn are . . . a legacy of our ancient beginnings. As you say, our ancestors migrated from the innermost planet. They reengineered their genes to breed and mature rapidly to facilitate the settlement of our new homeworld. I, for instance, enrolled in Starfleet at the age of eight standard years.

"However, our genome was also modified with the ability to accelerate our breeding even further in times of exceptional need, as a safeguard against colony collapse. Using certain pharmaceuticals and hormone boosters, we can induce the parthenogenetic breeding of large numbers of offspring that are born within weeks and mature within as little as sixteen months.

"At times over our history on Arcturus IV, once our population grew and fragmented into nation-states, we would use this capability to breed vast armies, developing rapid learning techniques to educate them in the ways of war. We also invented religious traditions to teach them warfare as their sacred duty, and to instill that same sense of duty in their mothers so that they would willingly bear the strain and disruption of such accelerated multiple childbirth—and so they would be philosophical about mothering a whole race to die in our wars." He looked down, his tone abashed.

Kirk stared. "No wonder Maltuvis wanted your world."

"Yes. He dreamed of turning our Warborn into his shock troops to sweep across the galaxy. But he did not understand us. Nor was he the first in our history to invade us with similar intentions. Once we grew sick of our wars millennia ago and united as a people, the Warborn became our defense. Our religion evolved along with our culture: The Warborn, and we, came to see it as their sacred duty to fight only in defense of Arcturus against that which threatens it, for no other cause was sufficient to justify such a sacrifice. We would never have submitted to being used by another in that way. Once Maltuvis had fallen, we retired the Warborn who had survived. Nor did we consider joining the Federation until your diplomats convinced us that you had no interest in exploiting the Warborn in your own defense."

"We never would have asked for that," Kirk said. "Even aside from the ethical quandary, our laws about genetic engineering are firm."

"Yes. Though technically all Arcturians are the products of ancient genetic engineering, the enhanced abilities of the Warborn arguably qualify them as a type of Augment. Plus, the notion of creating a race of people specifically as expendable troops was . . . incompatible with Federation ethics." Rakatheema's hooded eyes took on what seemed to be an embarrassed expression. "We had wrestled with the ethics of it ourselves for countless generations, but the custom was entrenched in our culture and traditions. It is an irony that our shorter generations compared to other humanoids make us slower to change as a society, for we mature so quickly that we have little time to question or challenge convention before we must take on the adult responsibility to carry it forward.

"It took an outside nudge—the prospect of Federation membership—to make us finally act on our ambivalence and outlaw the creation of the Warborn."

Kirk leaned back in his seat. "Commander, while I find this history lesson fascinating, I assume you're going to make it relevant to the present at some point."

"Yes, Admiral. You see, we thought we had finally put the Warborn in our past . . . until about two decades ago, when the Klingons invaded the Federation. I trust you know that history quite well, sir."

The observation required no reply. It had been twenty-three years before, when Kirk had been a young lieutenant on the *Farragut*. Ironically, that ship had come through the war intact, then lost its captain and half its crew to a gaseous alien creature barely a month after the armistice. Yet more than a few of Kirk's friends and mentors from the Academy had died in the war or survived with something broken inside them. It was not a time that many in the Federation enjoyed reminiscing about.

After a moment, Rakatheema went on. "As the war worsened, some in Starfleet and the Federation government came to our leaders and proposed breeding a new generation of Warborn to fight the Klingons. Their argument was that, as Arcturus had been a Federation member for nearly a century, fighting in the Federation's defense would be merely an extension of the Warborn's purpose. But our leaders did not agree. The tradition handed down over the centuries was that the sacred purpose of the Warborn, the only cause that could legitimize creating them to fight and die, was the defense of our own hard-won world. That we could not cheapen their sacrifice by allowing it for any other cause, lest we end up throwing their lives away as profligately as our ancestors did in the ancient wars."

Kirk studied him. "You don't seem . . . entirely convinced."

The tips of the commander's skin flaps flushed slightly in embarrassment. "Our traditions exist for good reason, sir, but I can see the merit in the Federation envoys' argument. Indeed, their warnings were borne out. As the Klingons gained more and more ground over the months, our leaders began to fear that Arcturus was in danger of invasion. It seemed likely that the Klingons would either wish to exploit our Warborn as Maltuvis had tried to do . . . or simply exterminate all life on Arcturus to eliminate the threat.

"Though the debate was fierce, the hawks won the day. With Federation officials choosing to look the other way, the ban was suspended and a new wave of Warborn was bred—tens of thousands in all, with the facilities readied for hundreds of thousands more if it came to that."

"But then the Klingon War ended," Kirk prompted. "Chancellor L'Rell took power and declared a truce."

"Yes—before the Warborn had even reached full maturity. We had not needed them after all.

"But what could we do with them? They were living, sentient beings. We could not simply dispose of them. Yet the rapid learning they had been given was oriented solely toward combat. How could we integrate them into a peaceful society? What purpose could they serve without the one they were born for?

"Ultimately," he continued wryly, "our leaders chose to defer the question until after their terms in office had ended. The young Warborn were placed in cryogenic stasis, and ever since, their little lives have been rounded with a sleep."

Kirk folded his hands before him. " 'If you be pleased, retire into my cell,'" he recited, "'And there repose. A turn or two I'll walk / To still my beating mind.'"

Rakatheema beamed. "Well quoted, Admiral! Although their minds lay stilled for more than a turn or two. For twenty-two years, they have reposed in their frozen cells." His smile swiftly faded. "Which is longer than the technology was designed to handle."

Kirk was taken aback. "The stasis has started to fail?"

"Yes." The commander's voice was grim. "We lost over a hundred before we revived the rest. Now we have more than twenty thousand Warborn awake among us, with no war to fight, no purpose to fulfill. Military life is all they know, yet they are forbidden to fight except in defense of Arcturus IV."

"We are a disciplined people, Admiral. We had to be in order to win our world, and that legacy has stayed with us. To live without purpose is no life for an Arcturian, least of all for a Warborn."

The admiral straightened in his chair. "I think I can guess what you came here to propose, Commander."

Rakatheema nodded. "Starfleet has military discipline, yet is primarily peaceful in its goals. I think that might be what the Warborn need: an education that embraces that military mindset yet redirects it toward constructive ends. Starfleet Academy could be the ideal outlet for them."

Kirk frowned. "But even if we employ every satellite campus in the Federation, the Academy can't accommodate twenty thousand new recruits added to the existing student body."

"I don't ask for that many, Admiral. I propose only a pilot program—a dozen or so Warborn to start, as proof of concept. If it proves viable, we bring in more. The rest can be returned to those stasis pods that remain viable, then gradually enrolled over the years ahead."

Rakatheema stood. "I know this is a large thing to ask, Admiral Kirk. I know there will be controversies, objections to admitting the equivalent of Augments into Starfleet. I've already met with such objections back home when I proposed this, as many fear that it might lead to Warborn serving in defense of the Federation instead of Arcturus."

"Is that where you wish it to lead, Commander?"

The pale, hairless man fidgeted. "I wish merely for these people to find a home and a purpose in Starfleet. I hope that purpose remains peaceful . . . but there is merit to the idea that the defense of Arcturus and of the Federation are one and the same. Potentially, the Warborn could be a great benefit to both." He held out his hands, palms forward. "Of course, I do not propose reactivating the program to *create* more of them. Merely to give the ones who now live a way of being useful. Of fulfilling the purpose they were born for in a way that is beneficial to everyone.

"These are innocent people, Admiral . . . orphans of circumstance, needing a place where they can belong and feel useful. They are not expendable, no matter why they were created."

Kirk was quiet for several moments, absorbing it all. "You've given me a great deal to think about, Commander. I'm willing to consider it, but I'll have to discuss it with Superintendent Chandra and the Academy board . . . probably with Starfleet Command as well. There's a lot to sort through in this. I trust you have a more detailed written proposal . . . ?"

"Yes, sir." Rakatheema handed Kirk a data card. "The specifics are on there. Admiral, I greatly appreciate your open mind."

"I'm always willing to listen, Commander. But make no mistake: this was the easy part."

Kirk residence
San Francisco

"An intriguing question," Spock said as he perused the 3-D chessboard in Kirk's fireplace nook, still set up as it had been when they had left off their last game. It was too warm for a fire this time of year, but the nook had quickly become their traditional place for chess, to accommodate the half-Vulcan captain's dislike for cold. It also had the advantage of being away from the wide, curved row of windows that gazed out across San Francisco Bay toward the Marin Headlands, so that the lights and sounds from outside intruded less on the players' concentration.

"Certainly the Warborn's plight is one I can comprehend," Spock went on, projecting so Kirk could hear him clearly from the kitchen over the clinking of the china. "Outsiders to their culture by the nature of their birth . . . of their world, yet apart from it . . . seeking a place where their otherness will not be a hindrance."

Kirk came back into the living room, carrying a tea tray. "Then you think we should admit them to the Academy."

"I did not say that," Spock replied as Kirk set the tray down beside the chessboard. "Empathy does not compel partisanship. It merely provides insight into all sides of a question." Kirk finished pouring Spock's cup and handed it to him. "Thank you, Jim. In this case, I can easily empathize with the other side as well. A race of soldiers that can be swiftly bred by the millions is a dangerous temptation. The potential for abuse is enormous."

"The Arcturians have managed to resist that temptation for over a century," Kirk countered as he lifted his own teacup. "With one notable exception."

"Resisting temptation means nothing if the temptation is not present. The one time they were offered a justification, they took it."

"After resisting it as long as they could."

"True resistance does not yield." Spock set down his cup. "In the *Kolinahr* ritual, there is a phase where one must remain completely silent for several months, acknowledging no others, even in their immediate presence. There is a phase where one must go with no more than the barest minimum of food and water for six weeks, even when meals are provided daily. There is a phase—"

"I get the idea."

"There were many times while undertaking these rituals that my need grew desperate. I became convinced that I would not remain safe or even survive if I did not break the stricture. I felt certain that the cause was justified, that anyone would comprehend my need, that anyone would yield in the same circumstances."

Kirk sipped his tea. "But you didn't yield."

"I understood that those feelings were the very temptations I needed to overcome. So I released them, and did not succumb." The corner of his mouth turned up ever so slightly. "At least until I sensed V'Ger's mind calling out. There, at the point of no return . . . I wavered."

"I think the entire population of Earth is grateful that you did. Along with the crew of the *Enterprise*."

"Still, it proved to me that my commitment to *Kolinahr* was not as absolute as I had believed."

"And you don't think the Arcturians' commitment to peace is as great as they believed."

"On the contrary—I am convinced it is as sincere as the Federation's." He lifted a brow. "And yet, when the temptation was sufficient, they yielded."

"You're saying we could yield too. That having the Warborn in Starfleet would create too great a temptation to use them as they were bred to be used." He reached toward the chessboard, fingers hesitating above one of the smallest pieces. "As pawns to be sacrificed."

"It is a risk that must surely be addressed. Starfleet's martial drives are rarely as far from the surface as we would like to believe." His eyes darted across the antique guns and armor pieces that adorned the walls of the nook. Kirk liked to think he collected and displayed them as a reminder of how far humans had come from their barbaric past, that such things were now seen only as historical curiosities and works of art rather than functional tools of destruction. Yet he understood how Spock could read a mixed message into his fascination with military history.

"However," Spock went on, mercifully leaving that question aside, "it would be no more fair to the Warborn to disregard their need for guidance—for a place where they can lead lives of purpose and fulfillment rather than being cast aside.

"I found such a place in Starfleet. It is entirely possible that the Warborn could do so as well. But we must be certain of our own ability to resist temptation."

Setting down his teacup, Spock steepled his fingers before him and turned his full attention to the chessboard. "Shall we play, Jim?"

Starfleet Academy

Following his discussion with Spock, James Kirk decided to endorse Commander Rakatheema's proposal regarding the Arcturian Warborn. The matter came up for debate at the next meeting of the Academy's senior administrators, held in the office of Admiral Nensi Chandra, a white-haired, round-faced human who had served as superintendent of Starfleet Academy for the past eight years. Also present were Chandra's subordinates: Kirk as commandant of cadets, responsible for the day-to-day supervision and discipline of the student body; Professor Blune, the full-figured Denobulan female who served as the civilian academic dean, overseeing the faculty and academic programs; and the lean, narrow-faced Captain T'Vari of Vulcan, Chandra's chief of staff, who advised on daily operations and administration.

Rakatheema was also on hand to make his case to the board, but Kirk was surprised to see the Arcturian commander joined by his direct superior, Admiral Lance Cartwright, the former captain of *U.S.S. Ark Royal* who now served as the head of

Starfleet Security. "I'm here to add my endorsement to the commander's proposal," the tall, mahogany-skinned admiral had explained to Kirk in his rich, booming voice. "Since it relates to questions of Federation security and defense, I asked to be included."

Kirk had a fairly clear idea where Cartwright's thoughts were headed, for he had been considering similar possibilities. However, it would first be necessary to make the more basic case for the Warborn to Admiral Chandra and his other advisors.

Chandra was an accomplished Starfleet veteran with more than fifty years of experience, having served as a science officer, captain, starbase commander, and Academy instructor and administrator. His path had crossed with Kirk's a few times when the older man had been captain of the *Kongo*, most notably when he had sat on the board of Kirk's court-martial for the negligent homicide of Lieutenant Commander Ben Finney. Kirk had never held that against him, of course; it was simply by chance that Chandra had been one of the command-rank officers available at Starbase 11 at the time, due to the *Kongo* being in for repairs. Indeed, once Spock had deduced that Finney had faked his death, the court-martial had been disbanded before Chandra or the other panelists had needed to make a decision. Over Kirk's months as Academy commandant, he had found Superintendent Chandra to be a capable superior with the reliable judgment and breadth of perspective that came from decades of wide-ranging experience.

As Commander Rakatheema stated his case to the panel, Chandra sat patiently with his hands resting on his hips, arms slightly akimbo—a familiar sight to Kirk from his court-martial, and more recently from numerous Academy meetings. Chandra was a contemplative man, not prone to speak unless he had something worth saying. When the Arcturian commander returned to his seat, however, Chandra folded his hands before him on the tabletop. "You have made an excellent case regarding what Starfleet service could do for the Warborn, Commander. However, the question remains: What could the Warborn do for Starfleet? By your own acknowledgment, their education to this point has been limited to knowledge and skills deemed necessary for combat. The ideal Academy candidate has a far more eclectic education."

"Absolutely," interposed Professor Blune, tapping a meaty finger on the table. "Starfleet officers are explorers, scientists, and diplomats first."

"Which is the goal of this undertaking, Professor—to give the Warborn an opportunity to broaden their range of abilities," Rakatheema replied. "Their training to date may have emphasized combat, but their innate capacity to learn goes beyond that. Their rate of cognitive development and assimilation of new knowledge surpasses what is normal even for my people, and the rapid learning techniques we Arcturians invented for their training have already been successfully adapted by the Federation for medical rehabilitation, for language acquisition in circumstances where computer translation is unavailable, and so forth.

"Naturally," Rakatheema went on, "we would expect the Warborn to meet the same qualifications as any other cadet. The sponsorship requirement is taken care of thanks to Admirals Kirk and Cartwright. Our candidates are already undergoing rapid remedial training on Arcturus, and any further catching up can be done during the summer preparatory program. They would hardly be the first entrants who drew upon the preparatory program to compensate for a lack of conventional educational achievements, due to coming from small colonies, emigrating from non-Federation worlds, or having otherwise exceptional backgrounds."

"Their very exceptionality is a concern," Captain T'Vari put in. "In stressing their learning speed, you remind us of the Warborn Arcturians' augmented physical and mental capabilities.

Starfleet cannot be seen to embrace the recruitment of Augments, least of all those engineered for military purposes."

"By a strict interpretation of those rules, Captain, I would be forbidden from service, as would Professor Blune. Both of us are from species that have undergone genetic engineering in the past."

"On a species-wide level. The restriction regards those beings who are artificially enhanced beyond the general optimum for their species, granting them an unfair advantage."

"Advantage?" Rakatheema countered. "The Warborn have little advantage over other Arcturians. Their accelerated growth gives them shortened lifespans. They are outsiders among our people—placed on pedestals for their sacred role in our defense, yet viewed with discomfort in peacetime, for they have no place in our everyday lives. They are strong and skilled in combat, yes, but little more so than a natural-born Arcturian in peak condition. After all," he added, lowering his head, "they were bred for their numbers and speed of reproduction above all else." He declined to put the cruel calculation into words: parts designed to be disposable and easily replaced did not have to be especially durable.

"Still, Captain T'Vari has a point," Superintendent Chandra put in. "Aside from the ethical concerns, there are political considerations as well. The Klingons would see it as an abrogation of treaties and agreements going back to the Augment Crisis of 2154. Given the current . . . deteriorating nature of our relations with the Klingons, it would be unwise to provoke further mistrust."

Kirk frowned and shifted in his chair, reminded of his own unease at the consequences of the Federation's Augment policy. It had been more than a dozen years since he had exiled Khan Noonien Singh and his fellow Augment leaders to Ceti Alpha V following their attempted takeover of the *Enterprise*. He had recommended to Starfleet Command that the planet be made an official, supervised penal colony, expecting that a legion of historians would descend on the lush, untamed world to fill in the extensive gaps in the recorded history of the Eugenics Wars through interviews with the very men and women who had waged them.

Instead, Starfleet Intelligence had classified the entire incident, not wishing to let the Klingons learn of the existence of dozens of human Augments under Starfleet supervision—least of all the direct progenitors of the genetic line that had caused the Augment Crisis. War had broken out regardless barely a month later, but at the time, there had still been hope of staving it off. Even after the brief conflict, Starfleet had not wished to jeopardize the Organian-imposed peace by revealing the secret. SI had assured Kirk that Ceti Alpha V would be monitored, so Kirk had moved on, not without regret that military secrecy had required censoring one of the greatest historical finds of his career.

Kirk noted Admiral Cartwright's gaze upon him; no doubt he had noted Kirk's reaction to the mention of Augments. Once Cartwright was satisfied that Kirk intended to keep his silence, the older admiral turned back to the superintendent. "It's precisely because of the state of Klingon relations that we need the Warborn in the fleet. Ever since Chancellor Kesh figured out that the Organians can't stand interacting with corporeals and won't intervene in our affairs as long as we leave them alone, he's been testing our defenses more and more, or tacitly encouraging rogue captains to do it. It's easy for you sheltered Academy types to focus on the peaceful ideals of the Federation, but out there in the field, it's getting more dangerous. It's only a matter of time before the Klingons invade us yet again." He glanced at Kirk. "And things aren't much better on the Romulan front, even after the Renz Verus business. With enemies testing us on two fronts, we need every advantage we can get."

"That's not what this is about, Lance," Kirk interposed. "The commander made that clear. The Warborn see it as their sacred duty to fight *only* for Arcturus. We don't have the right to try to subvert that for our own interests."

Rakatheema raised a wrinkly hand. "That is essentially true, Admiral. Of course, it is always possible that some Warborn might feel that they protect Arcturus by fighting for the Federation. But that should be for them to decide as individuals."

"My point exactly," Kirk replied.

Cartwright nodded. "All right, yes, I grant you that," he said, though he did not sound humbled. "I merely meant that the Warborn recruits could substantially bolster our numbers. As for their skills in combat, their mere presence might be seen by the Klingons as a deterrent."

"Or a provocation," Professor Blune said, "as the superintendent suggested."

"Pardon me," Rakatheema said, "but in all this talk about the broader astropolitical or military ramifications of the Warborn as a group, you are forgetting what really matters: who they are as individuals. These are *people* who seek a place to belong, a constructive purpose to fulfill. I admit that even we Arcturians tend to perceive the Warborn as a faceless, interchangeable mass. They can be difficult to tell apart visually. But I have met them, spoken with them, and even with their collective upbringing and training, they are as unique as any of us.

"Yet the one thing they have in common is a yearning to serve. To contribute. All I ask is that you give them that chance."

"He's right," Kirk said. "When has it been Starfleet's way to judge potential applicants by their race, or by the circumstances of their birth? All we have ever judged any applicant by is their merit." He looked around the table at the others. "At least, that's what we tell ourselves. This is our chance to prove that we mean it.

"Will it lead to challenges, to complications? No doubt it will. There have been many challenging, complicated students in the Academy's history, from almost every member species. I'm sure a number of you are dying to point out that I was one of them." That generated a few chuckles. "But more than one of my instructors told me something that I've now learned for myself from this side of the equation: There is nothing more satisfying for a teacher than a student who challenges us. Who makes us question what we thought we knew. Who makes us *better*, in the same way we strive to make them better.

"We don't know what new challenges we'll face if we admit the Warborn. But we don't know what challenges we'll face if we go out to explore other planets, meet other cultures. And that is exactly *why* we do it. That, to us, is the very thing that makes it impossible to pass up."

Kirk stopped himself from saying anything more. These were fellow Starfleet veterans, after all—officers who had lived for discovery and challenge as long as he had, or considerably longer. There was no need to oversell them—simply to remind them of what they already knew.

Chandra looked around the table, sizing up the thoughtful looks on the others' faces. "It appears to me that Commander Rakatheema and Admiral Kirk have both made their points persuasively. Do any of you still wish to object to admitting the Warborn?"

Only Professor Blune spoke in response. "I still don't know how well they can adapt to our curriculum, or how we might need to adapt the curriculum to them. But I suppose that's something we'll just have to figure out as we go."

"As it so often has been," Chandra replied. "Very well. The motion carries unanimously." He smiled and looked around again. "Shall we break for tea?"

Chapter Two

Sulu residence
Lower Pacific Heights, San Francisco

Demora Sulu was annoyed when Uncle Pavel got a call on his communicator right in the middle of dinner. The Starfleet people who called Uncle Pavel and Dad always seemed to do it in the middle of something like dinner or a trip to the park or some other time when Demora wanted them all to herself. Demora thought that was very rude and had made up her mind never to join Starfleet.

At least, not unless they learned to stop interrupting people when they were doing other things. Then she might consider it.

When he came back into the dining room, Uncle Pavel had a look she knew all too well. "Oh, no," Demora said. "They want you to go away again, don't they? You just got back a week ago!"

"Just for a little while, Demya," Uncle Pavel assured her. "They want *Reliant* to look into something, but it's not very far."

"What's up?" Dad asked, glancing in Demora's direction. "Or can you talk about it?"

"No, it's fine, Hikaru. There was an unexplained eruption of energy in space in the Altair system. The readings are similar to what *Reliant* encountered at Argelius a few weeks back."

Dad frowned. "The, what did you call it, vacuum flare?"

"A vacuum energy flare-up, I think I said." He pursed his lips. "I like yours better, though. Vacuum flare it is."

"Whatever it's called, I thought you said it was a one-in-a-trillion fluke."

"Much less likely than that, even—*if* it was what I thought it was. Clearly I was wrong."

He smiled, which made Demora frown. "You're happy to be wrong?"

"Yes, because I am a science officer," Uncle Pavel said. "Now I have something new to investigate—a new puzzle to solve. It would be boring to have all the answers already."

"You don't sound worried," Dad said. "I take it nobody was hurt this time?"

"No, it was in empty space. But you know how delicate the Altair situation is. The native Altairians now suspect the colonial government of doing a weapons test, and they aren't convinced by their denials. Luckily, they sent their readings to Starfleet, and the computers matched the signature to the, ah, vacuum flare at Argelius. They're sending us there to make sure, and to convince the Altairians there's nothing to go back to war over."

"War?" Demora asked. "Who would they go to war with? And why?"

"Well, Demy," Dad began, "there are two main inhabited planets there. Altair VI was settled by humans over a hundred years ago, though it never joined the Federation. There's also a native humanoid people on Altair III. At first, they seemed like they didn't have space travel, so the colonists mostly avoided them."

"The Prime Directive?"

"No, that was before the Directive. They just didn't think the Altairians had a lot to offer them. But then they found ancient ruins on Altair VI, and eventually they figured out that it was the original homeworld of the people who migrated to Altair III thousands of years ago."

"Why did they leave?"

Uncle Pavel fielded that one. "A lot of smart people have been trying to figure that out for a long time. What we *do* know is that when the native Altairians found out that aliens had settled their ancient homeworld, a lot of them weren't happy about it."

"So the two planets have been fighting for a long time," Demora's father went on. "They've been at war on and off for the past hundred years. The Federation's stayed neutral, tried to broker peace and give medical aid, but the instability on our border was dangerous for the whole region. The Klingons even tried to back the natives, hoping to gain a foothold close to the heart of the Federation."

"But then our diplomats finally convinced them to make peace," Uncle Pavel said. "That was, oh, about a dozen years ago. And it was a solid treaty too, with real solutions. Things have finally stabilized, and there's even talk of both worlds applying for Federation membership."

He sighed. "But that sort of thing always gets a reaction from people who prefer to stick to themselves, so there are new tensions on Altair III. Luckily," he finished with a smile, "Captain Terrell is very good at defusing tensions."

"I hope so," Dad said. "Altair's a beautiful system." He turned to Demora. "Pavel and I were there for the inauguration of the new president of Altair VI, after the last wartime president resigned to secure the peace."

"Well, we were a little late," Uncle Pavel said. "We had to make an emergency detour to Vulcan."

"But we were there for the end of it. Luckily there was a lot of celebrating. Even in wartime, Altair VI always had excellent recreational facilities."

Uncle Pavel tilted his head, looking puzzled. "Now that you mention it, it's quite a coincidence that both flares happened at popular shore leave destinations."

"Do you think it means anything?"

"How could it? I still don't know how it could even happen more than once in a billion years. Let alone in consecutive months."

"Maybe somebody's trying to ruin people's vacations!" Demora said, alarmed. "That's terrible!" Demora took vacations seriously. If not for the vacation on which her father and mother had briefly met, she wouldn't exist.

Uncle Pavel stepped closer and put a comforting hand on her shoulder. "Don't worry, Demya. I promise that Captain Terrell and I won't let any more vacations be ruined."

She knew Uncle Pavel was humoring her. After all, she was almost seven and three-quarters, and thus she was not easily fooled. Still, she appreciated the gesture. It was his way of saying he wouldn't forget about her while he was gone.

If there were more people as considerate as him in Starfleet, she *might* just consider joining.

U.S.S. *Reliant*
Altair system

"As you can see, the signatures of the vacuum flares from Argelius and from your system have numerous commonalities," Pavel Chekov told the parties assembled in *Reliant*'s briefing room. Seated on opposite sides of the table were Gon Curi, the ornately robed and hooded ambassador from Altair III's indigenous nation, and Yoko Sasaki, Altair VI's current defense minister. Captain Terrell sat at the head of the long table, which was at an angle to the wall screen by which Chekov stood, so that the captain's large frame did not obscure the view.

"*Reliant*'s own scans confirm the accuracy of the initial measurements, and thus the similarity," Chekov went on. "As the flare at Argelius was judged to be a natural phenomenon, there is no reason to suspect anything different in this case."

Curi's head shifted emphatically, though Chekov could barely make out the ambassador's features under his voluminous hood. "How can your ship have made scans? You were not yet here. It's highly suspicious that you have your own separate readings of a phenomenon you *claim* not to have anticipated."

Chekov strove to remain patient, looking to Captain Terrell's calm as a model. "Naturally, you are aware that light travels at a finite speed. Though starships generally rely on faster-than-light subspace sensors for instantaneous detection, we can sometimes use the speed of light to our advantage. Since the phenomenon occurred twenty-eight hours before our arrival, we simply made observations with conventional optical and gravitic sensors when we reached a distance of twenty-eight light-hours from the site of the outburst. Thus, in a sense, we were able to watch it as it happened, just as the astronomers of history did on both your world and mine. I was personally able to confirm the same electromagnetic and gravimetric signatures I scanned at Argelius several weeks ago."

Minister Sasaki smiled. "And tell me, Commander, was there any hint that the Argelian incident involved any form of weapons testing?"

"Not at all, ma'am. The Argelians are well known for their pacifism."

Curi crossed his loose-sleeved arms. His dark blue-gray hands were his only visible skin. "Very well, then. If this was not a test of some new weapon, what was it?"

Chekov shrugged. "We . . . are still attempting to determine that."

The Altairian scoffed. "You expect us to be satisfied with that? You simply don't know? Do you think we're so gullible as to simply take your word for it?"

Terrell leaned forward, finally speaking in relaxed, reasonable tones. "If I may, Ambassador . . . if we'd come here to lie to you, don't you think we'd have prepared a better story?

"The fact that science doesn't pretend to have all the answers is the very thing that makes it such a powerful tool to search for the truth. It's easy to see a gap in what you know and fill it with your own beliefs or preconceptions—or your own fears. But if you really care about the truth, then you simply step back and let the universe speak for itself. If it doesn't hand you the answer right away, you just keep looking until you find it, however long it takes."

The captain crossed his arms, his tone growing stern. "No, Ambassador, we can't yet tell you what this phenomenon is. But you know what? You can't tell us what it is either. You don't know any more than we do.

"If this *were* some kind of weapons test, there'd be evidence of that, surely. Physical debris, a satellite in the vicinity, a recognizable power signature in the readings. Your own scientists would have been able to spot something, and you'd be here with specific evidence. Instead, all you have are questions. The same questions that we have."

Terrell smiled. "I can certainly understand how not having the answers can be a source of fear and discomfort. But it can also be a source of wonder and optimism. Because not knowing the answers means that you get to go and look for them. It means the universe still has mysteries and uncharted spaces— and there's as much room in those open spaces for hope as there is for fear. You just have to be willing to seek it out."

Once Captain Terrell had said his farewells to the Altairians and summoned a yeoman to escort them to the transporter room, Chekov stared at him in appreciation. "That was quite a speech, sir. It really won the ambassador over."

"Oh, he was just putting on a show of confrontation to appear strong," Terrell said. "I doubt he ever seriously believed it was a weapons test. All he needed was a credible excuse to let us defuse the situation, so he can say he addressed the fears of his public back home and convince *them* it's all right."

Chekov thought that over. "I hope you're right, Captain. This is a beautiful system. I'd hate to see it fall back into war."

"I don't think there's any risk of that. The Altairians are a proud, contentious people, but they're better off now than they were during the wars, and they know it."

The science officer frowned. "I just wish we could be equally sure that these vacuum flares won't be a problem. Two of them in close succession, less than ninety light-years apart . . ." He shook his head. "They may not have been an Altair VI weapons test, but what if there is some artificial cause behind them? Some alien force making it happen?"

"To what end?" Terrell asked. "So far they've both happened in open space. The flare at Argelius only damaged a few nearby ships, and that was in a crowded spacelane. This happened in an empty part of the system, millions of kilometers from anything, and would've been totally harmless if not for the political tensions. If you're suggesting these are some kind of attacks, then their aim is so bad that we may have nothing to worry about."

"Unless they're still trying to find their range."

Terrell shook his head. "It isn't even that destructive. A photon torpedo barrage would do far worse. I still think it's more likely that this is a natural phenomenon. Maybe some kind of . . . storm moving through subspace, occasionally surfacing. Maybe it popped up between systems too, but nobody was around to notice it. If there are more of these, we'll soon find out if they're following any kind of path."

"We should notify Starfleet Command. Advise all vessels to scan for these signatures."

"I'll do that. In the meantime, let's continue forward on the vector it would have followed from Argelius to here. Maybe we can pick up some trace of whatever it is."

Chekov gave him a rueful look. "So no shore leave this time?"

Terrell grimaced. "I never did develop a taste for Altair water."

Chapter Three

Arcturus IV

Horatio stood proudly at attention alongside his fellow War-born. They were a small cohort, only a dozen strong—one of the smallest gatherings of his kind that Horatio had ever experienced in his two years of conscious existence. Yet as Commander Rakatheema of Starfleet stood before them and gave his address, the natural-born Arcturian spoke of their small number as a victory in itself.

"I commend all of you. The Starfleet Academy Preparatory Program is normally a course of six standard weeks, yet you have completed it in half the time." Rakatheema smiled. "Of course, such rapid learning is in your nature. But the subject matter was not. I recognize how challenging it must be for you—to be trained from childhood for war alone, yet now be asked to lay all that aside and learn the ways of peace. Yet you few, you happy few, you band of brothers—and sisters—rose to that challenge and mastered it, as I knew you could."

Horatio recognized the paraphrase from *Henry V*, Act IV, Scene 3. Shakespeare's canon had been part of the Warborn's curriculum over the past months, both before and during the Preparatory Program. Most Arcturians learned it from childhood as an entry point for understanding the minds of humans and other Federation cultures, for it explored psychological drives shared by nearly all species. Yet it was a universality in which the Warborn had not been expected or asked to participate until now.

No wonder that most of the other Warborn in the program, like Horatio, had chosen to adopt their new names from the characters in Shakespeare's plays. Some of them, like Bertram, Viola, and Titus, had done so grudgingly, insisting their serial numbers were good enough identifiers, but Horatio had adopted his name with pride. His lot was to serve Arcturus, as Horatio had loyally served and supported Prince Hamlet. And he would do so by learning of the many things in heaven and earth that had hitherto been undreamt of in the Warborn's philosophy.

"Soon," Rakatheema went on, "you will travel to Earth and join this year's new class of cadets at Starfleet Academy. You will be working and living alongside classmates from many other species—human, Vulcan, Andorian, Saurian, and numerous others. Much like the Arcturian nations of the past, these peoples set aside their historical conflicts and joined together for the mutual good. The Federation is one people, one nation, as Arcturus is one people and one nation. I trust that you will all serve that greater whole in the same spirit that guides you in your service to Arcturus."

Horatio found his words puzzling. The lapse in his discipline must have shown, for Rakatheema turned to him. "Yes, Horatio? You have a question?" At his hesitation, the commander continued. "It's all right. Starfleet cadets are encouraged to ask questions and engage in dialogue with their instructors. You may all speak freely."

"I merely sought to clarify, Commander." Horatio chose his words with care. "When you say to serve the Federation in the spirit of our service to Arcturus . . . that is . . . our service to Arcturus is in the spirit of warriors."

Rakatheema nodded. "I understand your concern, my friend.

Rest assured that Starfleet officers serve in many capacities, most of them peaceful. You are already skilled in the ways of war; you go to the Academy to learn other ways to serve."

"But if we should be called upon to do battle . . ." Horatio shook his head. "We will not fight for anything but our home-world. Will Starfleet honor that sacred commitment?"

"Starfleet would not force its members to act against their beliefs, Horatio." Rakatheema looked around the group. "Yet Starfleet also encourages its members to think for themselves, and to open their minds to new possibilities. I admire your commitment to peace, Horatio. But such a commitment is truer when it comes from informed choice and conviction rather than unthinking dogma. Give yourself a chance to learn."

The commander's answer did not clarify Horatio's confusion. But that did not matter. It was enough to know that Starfleet would respect his beliefs and commitments.

Once they returned to their barracks and disrobed for the showers, the Warborn named Portia moved toward Horatio. Portia was female, though that was only obvious to the eye at times like these when she was undressed. Historically, few War-born lived long enough to procreate, so they did not develop secondary sexual characteristics.

"You didn't like what the commander said about new pos-sibilities, did you?" Portia asked him. "You think Starfleet may want us to fight for them."

Horatio met her eyes evenly. They were approximately equal in height, like most Warborn. "He says Starfleet will not force us to defy our oath."

"You do not wish to fight?"

His gaze sharpened, as did his voice. "We were made to fight for Arcturus alone. That is our sacred calling."

Portia looked annoyed by his response. "We were made to die for Arcturus. Should we hold sacred what was decreed by those who made us only to die?"

Another male, Bertram, laughed loudly. He was not like most Warborn; his head rose higher than the others' and his highly developed musculature was clearly displayed as he turned within his sonic shower chamber. "You object to fighting, Portia? You're the fiercest warrior among us."

She turned her sharp gaze upon him. "I never said I had a problem with fighting. Test me anytime."

"Then what are you saying?" Horatio asked.

Portia turned away. "I don't know. I just don't see the point of all this."

Bertram nodded. "Nor do I. I studied as I was ordered, I passed their tests, but what is the use of it all? We're not scholars or diplomats. We were made to protect Arcturus. And, yes, to die if we must, in the name of its peace."

"A peace we don't get to be a part of," Portia interjected.

"Nor should we. It's not our purpose."

The group moved out of the showers into their dormitory, where they began to don their nightclothes. Bertram continued his thought. "They should never have revived us. They should have kept us frozen until we were needed to fight."

Portia stared at him. "Or until our pods failed and we died!"

"That's our purpose—to die for the peace of Arcturus. Warborn in peacetime are a threat to the peace. So I say let us die."

"In battle, yes. I'm not afraid to die fighting. But to lie down and let it come to you? Do nothing to fight against it? Is that what we were made for?"

Horatio interposed himself between them, catching both their eyes to stem their dispute. "You're both right!" He paused just long enough to ensure they were listening. "We do not serve the peace of Arcturus as we are. That is why we must leave it to learn another way.

"I know it is difficult, what they ask of us. It is not what we expected. But were we not taught that the unexpected is a given in any battle, no matter how well we train?"

Horatio's gaze widened to take in the whole group. "My friends—we are still going into battle for the peace of our home-world. But this time . . . our battle will be with ourselves."

U.S.S. *Asimov* NCC-1652
Approaching Kappa Fornacis system

". . . And Peter stood right up to him," Montgomery Scott declared with avuncular pride as he cradled his cooling coffee mug. "Even though the other lad was twice his size and he didn't have a prayer of winning—still, he stood up for his friend."

Nyota Uhura smiled, having recognized the story from the moment she entered the *Asimov*'s officers' lounge. Yet it was new to Erin Blake, the tall, striking, dark-haired captain of the *Malachowski*-class starship. She leaned forward eagerly, her bright eyes glinting. "So what happened?"

"Oh, he lost, of course. It was over in seconds. But then his friend stood up and said he'd take on the leader next. And then all the other smaller kids stood up too, united against him, and it finally sank in that he'd become the very kind of bully he thought he was protecting them against."

"Your nephew is a brave boy," Blake told him. "Separated from his family for weeks, yet he never lost his cool."

After getting her own coffee and a pastry from the food slot, Uhura joined them. "His parents were worried sick, though."

"Ach, they should've had more faith in the backbone of a Scotsman—even one without the accent." The engineer gri-maced, wrinkling his bushy salt-and-pepper mustache. "That blasted Yankee father of his should never have taken him on that expedition to begin with. Let alone let himself get separated from his boy."

Uhura put a calming hand on his arm. "You know it was

beyond his control, Scotty. And Thomas knew he'd be in good hands with Doctor Varian."

"Well, anyway, it sounds like a fantastic journey," Blake put in, trying to ease the tension. "But then, your tales about your family are always colorful. I sometimes wonder if you're embellishing a little, but I enjoy them too much to care."

Scott crinkled his eyes to emphasize the gleam in them. "Aye, well, that's the storyteller's prerogative, Captain."

Blake turned to Uhura. "You never seem to talk about your family, Nyota. In fact, we've been serving together more than six months and I hardly know anything about your past—aside from your time on the *Enterprise*, of course."

Uhura hesitated. "Well . . . there isn't much to tell. I'm from Nairobi, in the U.S. of Africa."

Blake's brows drew together. "Doesn't your file say Kitui?"

"Oh, yes. I was *born* in Kitui, because my mother, M'Umbha, was working in the area at the time. Her work with elephants entails a lot of travel."

"She's a biologist?"

"A lawyer, actually. She's a judicial liaison for Africa's elephant communities. They're intelligent, of course, but not civilized. They saw what human civilization did to their ancestors, and they have long memories."

An embarrassed silence fell. Humans rarely liked to be reminded of how brutally they had treated their fellow sapient species on their own planet, such as elephants, great apes, and whales, before they ever encountered an alien intelligence.

"Still," Uhura went on, "they need someone who can speak for them in the halls of power—make sure their interests are represented." After the arguably misnamed First Contact, once Vulcan telepaths had confirmed what most human scientists had already come around to accepting even before the Third World War, humanity had striven to achieve communication and peace with the surviving wild intelligences of Earth.

"Like a Council advocate for a Federation protectorate."

"Exactly." After a thoughtful pause, Uhura went on. "It seems my mother's work with the elephants was what inspired my own interest in language and communication, my own interest in contacting new life-forms."

"'It seems'?" Blake chuckled. "You sound like it happened to someone else."

Uhura fidgeted. "Well . . . it was a long time ago. In many ways, none of us are who we were as children. And my family moved around so much—sometimes in Nairobi and central Africa for my mother's work, sometimes in Mombasa for my father's."

Blake opened her mouth and paused. "I was going to guess he did something space-related, but my last guess fizzled."

"No, this time it's the obvious. My father, Alhamisi, was a star pilot. He worked for a couple of Mombasa's major interstellar shipping and transport firms before going freelance with my uncle Raheem."

"So space travel's in your blood too. Do you see your family often?"

Uhura cleared her throat. "My father . . . he was lost in deep space in my third year at the Academy."

"Oh, I'm sorry. I understand if you don't like to talk about it."

She caught the look in Scott's eyes, expressing his truer understanding. "No, it's all right," she said. "I just feel more defined by my career, my accomplishments in Starfleet. I've come to think of my shipmates as my family."

"Aye, in all my years, I've never seen a closer bunch than we became on the *Enterprise*," Scott put in, trying to change the subject. "It was a rare blessing that we were able to bring the entire command crew back together for V'Ger and afterward. Ah, now, V'Ger, that was a mighty—"

The intercom interrupted him. *"Bridge to Captain Blake."*

Blake tapped her wrist communicator—an older model, but

one still in use on second-tier ships like the *Asimov*. "Blake here. Go ahead, Tarha."

"*We've just received a navigational advisory from Deneva traffic control,*" came the voice of the communications officer. "*We only just received it due to signal interference. Some sort of anomalous energy bursts have been detected in interplanetary space. A series of sporadic, intense EM and gravimetric eruptions causing interference and subspace turbulence. All ships advised to divert around the phenomenon.*"

"Does it affect our course?"

"*Mister Chung says no, but they match a recent Starfleet advisory pertaining to a newly discovered type of energy anomaly called a vacuum flare. Any vessel that detects one is requested to investigate.*"

Uhura exchanged a look with Scott. "That's the phenomenon Chekov's been telling us about in his letters. The one the *Reliant* encountered at Argelius and Altair."

"Aye," Scott said. "But they were probing outward along that path, last I heard. Deneva's practically in the opposite direction."

"So either this is something different—"

"—or they've been chasing a wild goose for weeks now," Scott finished.

Blake was already on her feet. "Then I suggest we get to the bridge and find out." Raising her communicator to her mouth, she ordered, "Have Chung set an intercept course."

"*Captain, there are two other Starfleet ships already en route,*" Lieutenant Tarha replied. "*The* T'Viri *and the* Meitner."

"Great, then we'll have multiple readings we can compare." She smiled wryly. "I know you were looking forward to leave, Tarha, but this shouldn't take long."

It was a two-deck turbolift ride to the bridge, so they arrived in moments. Uhura noted that the main viewscreen already displayed a long-range sensor scan of the target area, showing the mysterious display of brief, blinding pinpoint flashes spread over a wide swath of space. After a few moments, the flickers slowed and faded, but then another surge of them began in the corner of the screen, with the vantage adjusting to compensate. "It's like a mob of old-time photographers is taking flash pictures of us," Blake said.

"Or like a fireworks show," Uhura said. "There's a similar rhythm to it, bursts of high activity with rests in between."

"Commander Uhura, do you remember the lights of Zetar?" Scott asked. "They looked a little like what's out there."

"The entities that attacked Memory Alpha back in the late sixties?" Blake asked.

"Yes, Captain," Uhura said as she relieved the officer at the science station. "But they weren't quite like this. Not as widespread or blinding, and persistent rather than intermittent. And their effects were neurological, not EM or gravimetric."

"So don't judge a storm by its flicker," Blake said. "That covers what it isn't. George," she said to Chung at the helm, "bring us in closer so we can try to narrow down what it is."

"Ah, Captain," Chung advised, "the way the flare-ups are jumping around unpredictably, I'm not sure how close we can safely come."

"Feliki," Blake told the Ithenite navigator, "plot their positions up to now and draw up a probability curve. George, stay outside the three-sigma line." Both officers acknowledged her order. Uhura found her reasoning sound; the probability of an outburst forming more than three standard deviations from the mean position would be less than one percent.

"Preliminary readings track with *Reliant*'s," Uhura reported. "Signatures consistent with microscopic quantum wormholes produced by anomalous spikes of vacuum energy. Except . . ."

"Commander?" Blake asked.

"The data from Deneva show that the outburst began three hours ago. The previous vacuum flares had begun to subside by then. This one is persisting—no, more than that. It's still expanding!"

Blake turned to the helm. "George, slow us down. How close are those other two ships to three-sigma?"

"*T'Viri* is well clear," Chung reported. "*Meitner* is cutting it close, but it should be— No, belay that! Her shields just went up."

Uhura could only watch with concern as a new surge of actinic pinpoints began to form directly in *Meitner*'s path. The small science vessel attempted evasive maneuvers, but not soon enough; it passed through the outer fringe of the still-expanding field of micro-wormhole bursts. The ship's momentum carried it beyond them soon enough, but its running lights guttered and its nacelle heat sinks began to dim.

"Distress signal coming in," Tarha said a moment later.

"On audio," Blake ordered.

"*. . . requesting assistance. We have sustained significant internal damage and multiple injuries. But keep clear of the flare at all costs! Shields had no effect. Repeat, deflector shields had zero effect on the phenomenon. The bursts formed directly inside the ship.*"

"*T'Viri* is closing on them," Chung said. "They're nearer than we are—and that thing is between us and them."

Blake grimaced. "Then we'll trust them to do their part and we'll do ours. Keep studying the vacuum flare. Learn everything you can."

"It's finally starting to subside, Captain," Uhura reported.

"That's good. But if this one got so much bigger and more dangerous than expected," Blake wondered, "then what about the next one?"

U.S.S. *Reliant*

By the time *Reliant* made it back to the Federation's core sectors nearly three weeks after the Deneva incident, two more vacuum flares had occurred, in the Cygnet and Makus star systems. Both had been in empty parts of the respective systems, doing no damage except to a passing comet in the latter, but both continued the pattern of growing larger and lasting longer than the previous ones.

"Starfleet is taking this as a serious threat," Captain Terrell told the assembled command crew in the main briefing room. "Every one of these vacuum flares has occurred in a major Federation or allied system. At this point, it's unlikely that it's random."

Terrell's first officer, Rem Azem-Os, flexed her green-and-gold wings thoughtfully. "Every one we know of," the venerable Aurelian replied in her fluting voice. "If it's happening in uninhabited or precontact systems, we might simply be unaware of it."

Chekov shook his head. "The major Federation observatories have been scanning for similar bursts. The gravimetric surges would be detectable on subspace bands, but there's been nothing, except from these five systems."

"So *is* it some kind of attack after all?" asked Lieutenant Mosi Nizhoni, the chief of security.

Commander Beach spread his hands. "Not necessarily," the helmsman told the younger Navajo woman. "For all we know, this could be some kind of natural phenomenon resulting from repeated warp travel in those regions. Maybe we've worn potholes in subspace."

"There's been far more warp travel around Earth, or Vulcan or Andoria," Chekov countered.

"What is it that these five systems *do* have in common that others don't?" Terrell asked, impatience tingeing his voice. "Argelius, Altair, Deneva, Cygnet, Makus. What's the common denominator? How can we predict the next system to get hit?"

Chekov opened his mouth, but hesitated. Azem-Os caught it. "You have a thought, Commander?"

"It's . . . tenuous."

"That makes it no different from anything else about this situation, Pavel. Tell us."

"Well . . . I couldn't help but notice that all five of these systems have been visited by the *Enterprise*."

Beach shrugged. "They're major ports. Hundreds of Federation vessels have visited them."

"In reverse order?"

That got everyone's attention. "Care to clarify?" Azem-Os asked.

"Here." Chekov moved to the wall console and called up a listing of the *Enterprise*'s ports of call from 2266 to 2267, scrolling backward in pace with his commentary. "We took shore leave on Argelius on stardate 3614. About six weeks before that, on stardate 3378, we attended the inauguration on Altair VI. On stardate 3287, we rescued Deneva from the neural parasite infestation." He faltered. "Well, not 'we'—I was still on my engineering rotation, not yet part of the bridge crew. The fourth was just before I came aboard, when the ship laid over at Cygnet XIV for computer maintenance on stardate 3109. And finally—or rather, first—the *Enterprise* visited Makus III on a medical supply run on stardate 2826."

Beach shook his head. "Okay, that's pretty wild. But it's still not much to go on."

"There is more," Chekov said, working the controls to call up orbital charts of the five systems, subdividing the screen into multiple windows. "Here are the current positions of the systems' planets, and the locations of the vacuum flares." He superimposed the latter.

Azem-Os peered sharply with her raptor's eyes, no less piercing for her age. "I see no pattern."

"But here are the orbital positions of those planets at the time of the *Enterprise*'s visits twelve to thirteen years ago." He linked the windows to the dates he'd highlighted in the itinerary chart, and the planets realigned themselves to their earlier positions. While none of them aligned exactly with the vacuum flare positions, all five now came near enough to make the pattern evident.

"They aren't bull's-eyes," Nizhoni said, "but at least now it looks like they're actually aiming at the dartboard."

Beach frowned, rubbing the back of his neck. "But if there is a pattern there, why would it be backward?"

"And why target places the *Enterprise* has been?" Terrell added.

Nizhoni shrugged. "We always were popular. Even before I got there."

"More to the point, why only those places?" Azem-Os asked. "Major interstellar ports visited by the *Enterprise*. Why not its other destinations? The frontier worlds it charted, the research outposts it resupplied? Why not Organia or Cestus III?"

"Not only that," said Chekov. "There are other major ports the *Enterprise* visited during that period that have not experienced vacuum flares. Just before Altair, we were at Vulcan. Shortly before Deneva, we were at Starbase 12. Just after Cygnet, the *Enterprise* had a two-week layover in the Sol system, to repair damage after a close call with the Black Star. That's when I joined the crew, in fact. And between Makus and Cygnet, the ship visited Starbase 11 twice."

Terrell stroked his beard. "So we need to find some common ground uniting those five systems specifically. Something we can use to predict the next potential target. Either to get there ahead of time, or just to disprove this hypothesis. Chekov, can you think of anything the *Enterprise*'s visits to those systems share that the others don't?"

Chekov gave a feeble grin. "The only connection I can think of is that I took shore leave on the last two. But I had leave on Starbase 12 too."

"At least," Azem-Os said, "the *Enterprise*'s itinerary narrows the list of candidates down to a finite number that we can monitor."

"Possibly." Chekov consulted the list, reading the brief notations of the ship's activities at its ports of call, since they were all from before his time now. "Maybe the Benecia colony, or Alpha Proxima II . . ."

"Compile a list," Terrell instructed, "and we'll forward it to Starfleet. It's thin, but at least it's a possibility."

"Aye, sir."

Terrell dismissed the briefing, and the crew began filing out of the room. Beach caught up with Chekov on the way out. "What is it with you *Enterprise* guys? You always have to be at the center of everything, don't you?"

Chekov took the teasing in good humor, as it was intended. "Just when I thought I was out."

Chapter Four

Starfleet Academy

Zirani Kayros had a hard time looking away from the Warborn Arcturians as she and the other first-year cadets filed out from the assembly hall. From the chatter her large Tiburonian ears picked up, she wasn't the only one. Admiral Kirk and Commander Rakatheema had introduced the twelve parthenogenetically bred cadets during the opening assembly that had just ended, explaining their unusual situation to the student body and encouraging the other cadets to welcome and bear with them as they adjusted to Academy life. So far, the process seemed to be off to a slow start.

Some of the cadets looked as though they wanted to approach the Arcturians and say hello; but the twelve of them stayed clustered together as they strode from the hall with military precision, their gaze straight ahead. It was hard to see an opening for an approach.

Maybe they're just nervous, Kayros thought. *You'd be too if everyone was staring at you. Give them time.*

Michael Ashrafi's thoughts as he strolled alongside her were less generous and rather more audible. "No wonder people mistake them for clones," the shaggy-haired, tan-skinned human remarked. "I don't want to sound like . . . you know . . . but aside from the big muscley one, I can hardly tell them apart."

"Don't worry about it." The speaker was Targeemos, a natural-born Arcturian female who was also in their class. "To be honest, even we have trouble telling the Warborn apart. It's the nature of their special genetics, or their fast development, or both. That's why they wear those bandoliers and epaulets on top of their uniforms." Kayros had wondered about those embellishments to the standard cadet dress code. The metallic pieces hadn't struck her as very functional; the bandoliers in particular appeared to be merely loops of cable draped around the neck and right shoulder.

"The color patterns show their regiments and serial numbers, which is how you tell them apart," Targeemos went on. "At least until you get to know them well enough to recognize them, I suppose." The ruddy, hairless humanoid fidgeted. "Not that I've ever met any before. They're not even supposed to be created anymore. But my family has passed down stories about the Maltuvian invasion. My great-grandmother treated some of the Warborn who survived."

On Kayros's other side, Vekal clenched his jaw; she could hear his muscles tensing and his teeth clicking together. "Breeding a whole subspecies purely to serve and die in combat is deeply unethical," the young Vulcan said. "The Warborn program should never have been revived, no matter the provocation."

Targeemos looked offended. "I never suggested otherwise."

"I was not implying that you did. I was expressing my own objection."

Kayros stared at him. "So, what, you're saying you don't think those guys over there should ever have been born? What, do you think they should've been euthanized or something?"

His brows shot up. "That was not my intent. I simply mean that their presence here raises questions."

"Like what?" Ashrafi asked.

"The Warborn program was revived during a time of conflict with the Klingons, in the belief that they would be of value in the war. Now, relations with the Klingons again grow tense—the Romulans as well—and the Warborn are revived and enrolled in the Academy."

Ashrafi laughed. "You think this is some conspiracy to turn them into Starfleet infantry or something? Come on, you heard the admiral. They're here to learn stuff *other* than fighting."

Kayros tapped the side of Vekal's head. "Logic, remember? They already know how to fight, so if that were all they were needed for, they wouldn't be at the Academy."

Vekal squirmed away from her touch. "It need not be their only role in Starfleet for it to be a potential role. And if Starfleet is open to it, then that suggests Starfleet's emphasis may be shifting toward greater militarization. I do not wish to see it move in that direction. I joined to become a scientist, like Captain Spock."

"You don't need to worry about that," Targeemos said. "The Warborn . . . They're a piece of our past we're ambivalent about. We honor them for their sacrifice in defending the homeworld, but we see them as victims of an unenlightened practice, created to be exploited for our benefit. We've grown past that now." She cleared her throat. "Or we like to think we have. I can't believe the Arcturian government would have let them join Starfleet if they thought it would lead to them being exploited again. The people back home would never stand for it. We wouldn't force them to fight."

Vekal gazed at the Warborn, who had taken up positions in an open plaza and begun performing martial-arts exercises with strict, regimented precision, ignoring the wary spectators who gave them a wide berth. "Perhaps. But do *they* know that?"

It had made Portia uncomfortable to be paraded before the Academy's other first-year cadets at the opening assembly. Ever since she and the others had been revived from cryosleep, the citizens of Arcturus had looked on them as outsiders, anomalies with no place in their world. She had longed to have an enemy to fight, a battle to be sent to so that she would not feel so purposeless. Now she finally had a mission—to attend the Academy, to integrate with the Starfleet community, to learn the ways of exploration and diplomacy. Yet being sent here had only worsened her sense of being out of place and unwanted.

Not that she could blame that entirely on the cadets who scrutinized them warily, keeping an uneasy distance. In some ways, she felt just as out of place among her own group, unsure if she saw their mission the same way the others did. That became clear when she downloaded her course schedule and texts onto her Academy-issue data slate and began to look them over. Horatio was standing beside her, doing the same with his own slate, but he had always been inquisitive, so he looked over hers as well. What he saw made him frown, and he turned to confront Portia.

"You are registered for Tactics 101? That is a combat course!"

She stared at him. "Why shouldn't I be? This is the core curriculum. We must take all its courses, regardless of the order we take them in."

Bertram stepped forward, facing down Horatio. "I'm in that course as well. Why not? It's what I know."

Horatio was unimpressed. "We're here to learn what we do *not* already know. Diplomacy, history, science."

Another male, Benedick, moved in alongside Horatio, nodding eagerly. "That's right. There are so many fascinating new subjects here to learn, so many exciting new challenges. I had a hard time choosing among them. I want to master them all!"

Portia chuckled. Benedick had gestated at the same time as the others, yet he always seemed more youthful and innocent.

"Give it time, comrade," she told him. "Better to start with the familiar, then expand from there. You want them to accept us, yes? Let's impress them with what we can do. Maybe we can teach *them* a few things about combat."

Horatio clasped her arm. "We wish them to accept us, not fear us. They question the rightness of our being here, when we were made only for war. We must prove to them that we will not fight, except to defend Arcturus."

Portia was growing weary of his self-righteousness. "It's only unarmed combat, Horatio. Barely more than exercise. You worry too much about how others will view us."

"And you don't? To many of these people—especially our own people—we are a mistake that should never have happened. We do not want to convince them they are right."

She pulled away from his grip. "Maybe I'm tired of worrying how others define me. If it was wrong to create us to serve others . . . then maybe we should start thinking about how to serve ourselves."

Starfleet Medical Center
San Francisco

Leonard McCoy pulled up short in the doorway to his office. In his absence, the desk had been converted into a makeshift picnic table, the traditional checkered cloth covered with a luxuriant spread of sandwich fixings, baked beans, cornbread, fresh fruit, and the like. "What the hell is this?"

As he spoke, he spotted Jim Kirk standing at the window to his right. It came as no surprise; he'd concluded already that Kirk must have been behind this. Spreading his hands, the admiral answered, "We've been having trouble scheduling lunch lately, so I thought this would save you some time."

McCoy peered at him. "How much time did it take *you*?"

"Only as much as it took to order a yeoman to do it." He winked. "Rank hath its privileges."

"Speaking of rank, if the Head hears about this—"

"Oh, she encouraged it. Says you've been working too hard and forgetting to eat."

"Tell that to the Icorians who'll die of *Synthococcus novae* if we don't find a vaccine for this new strain!"

Kirk chuckled, then affected a gruff voice. "'Jim, you'll be of no use to anyone if you collapse from hunger in the middle of a crisis!' Sound familiar?"

McCoy grumbled, but he was already helping himself to some sandwich fixings. That smoked turkey smelled really good. "So what is it you want from me?"

"What makes you think—"

"Now, you know that wide-eyed innocent act doesn't work on me, Jim. You wouldn't have gone to this trouble if you didn't have something important to talk about." He furrowed his brow at his old friend. "But not something official where you can just haul me in and issue an order. You want my help with something else—or you want to talk me into something."

Kirk nodded. "There is a matter where I might be able to use your . . . intercession. Or rather, introduction." The admiral picked up a data slate that had been resting next to the cole slaw, displaying a paused vid file. "This is from a protest rally that was held near the Academy a couple of days ago."

The file showed a slight, black-haired woman addressing a multispecies group of civilians in a public square, though the angle didn't give McCoy a clear look at her face. He tapped the screen to resume the video and hear what she had to say.

"*Over the past several years, we've expressed our concerns about the increasing militarization of Starfleet. As tensions with the Klingons and Romulans have worsened, Starfleet has adopted measures that seem to be anticipating war rather than de-escalating. Shipbuilding has increased. New designs and refits are more heavily, more visibly armed, as if intended to intimidate or provoke. New combat simulations have been added to Academy training. Even the uniforms have become more martial.*

"But the admission of the Arcturian Warborn to Starfleet Academy sends a particularly troubling message. Ever since first contact, the Federation has denounced the archaic Arcturian practice of breeding a race to serve as cannon fodder. Arcturus IV was required to abandon the practice in order to join, and aside from a single lapse during the First Klingon War, they have abided by that commitment to peace and sentient rights. Yet now, the admission of these Warborn students, with more to follow if the program succeeds, appears to be a Federation endorsement of this immoral practice.

"They say the Warborn will be taught like any other cadets, but isn't that the problem? What does it say about Starfleet's intentions for our human youth, our Vulcan and Andorian youth, our Tellarite and Rigelian and Caitian youth, if the Academy's teachings are now seen as compatible with the practice of breeding a servile race to die in battle?"

As the speaker paced the stage to take in the whole crowd, McCoy got a better look at her face—an oval face in its midforties, with a strikingly beautiful blend of Chinese and European features. It only took him moments to realize why her voice sounded so familiar. Once he'd heard enough (and finished half his sandwich), he paused the playback. "That's Doctor Ashley Janith-Lau. We worked together on a research project seven or eight years back." It had been during his all-too-brief return to civilian life, between resigning from Starfleet after his first five-year stint on the *Enterprise* and being drafted back in by Kirk and Admiral Nogura for the V'Ger crisis. Janith-Lau, a pediatrician, had sought his help in developing a treatment for a congenital developmental disorder causing cognitive defects in children on Terra Nova.

"I know," Kirk said. "I was hoping you could arrange an introduction."

McCoy stared at him, grinning. "I thought you didn't want my services as a matchmaker anymore."

The admiral glowered. "I never wanted them in the first place. And my interest is professional. What she's saying about the Warborn could stir up trouble."

That was a sobering choice of words. "She has a right to protest."

"Of course she does. But with every right comes a responsibility. In this case, a responsibility to get her facts straight about her subject. Her misrepresentation of Starfleet's intentions toward the Warborn could undermine the program before it has a fair chance to succeed."

The doctor narrowed his eyes. "And that's your only intention? Just to share your side of the story with her?"

"Naturally." Kirk glanced down at the image on the slate. "I admire her passion for her cause. It's obvious that she believes strongly in peace. Naively, perhaps, but I can't fault her principles. I just want a chance to show her we're on the same side. This is about remaking the Warborn in Starfleet's image, not the reverse."

McCoy thought it over. "All right. I'll contact her and see what I can do about arranging an introduction. But there's a catch."

Kirk looked at him warily. "There usually is. What did you have in mind?"

"Make sure the listening goes both ways. Don't close your mind to the possibility that she could have a point." He glanced down at Kirk's heavy maroon jacket. "She's certainly onto something about the uniforms. They make me feel like I'm dressing up for a reenactment of the Battle of Trafalgar."

Ignoring the crack, Kirk studied him. "Do *you* think she has a point?"

"Let's just say I can sympathize with her opinion about the military side of Starfleet. But it's not my reaction that matters here. Just go in with an open mind."

Kirk tilted his head in acknowledgment. "Only fair, since that's all I want from her."

"Is it?" He gestured at the still image of Janith-Lau's lovely, passionate face. "You're slipping."

"Are you going to finish eating?" Kirk asked, annoyed.

"Okay, okay."

As the doctor resumed his lunch, he mulled over the possibility. Ashley was smart, beautiful, close to Kirk's age, and a firebrand activist with a deep commitment to peace and compassion, not unlike Kirk's lost love Edith Keeler. McCoy might have made a play for her himself eight years ago, but she had been too driven by her work to have room for romance, and he'd been looking for something more relaxed and low-stress at that point in his life. But a woman like her could be the perfect match for Kirk after all.

U.S.S. Asimov

Uhura was running an analysis of vacuum flare sensor readings at the *Asimov*'s science station when Lieutenant Tarha addressed Captain Blake. "Captain, a new advisory from Starfleet. Latest vacuum flare outburst: the Vega system."

Erin Blake's face showed concern as she turned toward the communications officer, whose long, straight blond hair was tied back in a severe ponytail. "That's a busy system. Any damage?"

Tarha's voice was heavy. "Two ships sustained damage, ma'am. A civilian freighter out of Rigel, the *Norman Mallory*, and a Starfleet scout, *U.S.S. Xuanzang*. Multiple injuries on both. Three fatalities on the *Xuanzang*."

Blake gritted her teeth, fist striking the arm of her command chair. "Damn it! The first fatalities. And we still have no idea why."

She rose from her chair and stepped up to the railing by Uhura's station. "Commander, was Vega on the list of candidate worlds visited by the *Enterprise*?"

Uhura had already called up the records on an auxiliary screen, which she consulted now. "Yes, Captain. We had a brief layover at the Vega Colony on stardate 1502, before commencing a star-mapping tour."

"Aye, I remember," Montgomery Scott said from the engineering station. "Not long before we had that run-in with Balok and that oversized Christmas-tree ornament he called a ship." Uhura gave him a slight nod, acknowledging the reminder.

"Which would seem to support *Reliant*'s theory," Blake said.

"So far," Uhura cautioned. "One confirmed prediction isn't enough to be sure."

Blake stroked her chin. "But what is it about the *Enterprise* that could be connected to this phenomenon?"

"I've been investigating that," Uhura said, gesturing to the analysis running on her screens. "I've compiled all the sensor readings taken from the first five incidents, scanning for any pattern matches to the *Enterprise*'s engine signature, its shields, phasers, anything."

Scott moved over to stand by her station. "We didn't use ship's phasers in any of those systems, though. They're friendly ports."

"I know, but I don't want to rule anything out."

"Aye."

Blake turned to Tarha. "Lieutenant, relay the readings from Vega to the science station, please."

"Aye, Captain." She worked the transfer controls on her station.

Moments later, the data downloaded onto Uhura's board, and she set to work integrating it with the previous data sets. After letting the analysis run for a few moments, the commander shook her head. "Still no evident pattern matches."

"So what *did* the *Enterprise* do at those ports that it didn't do elsewhere?" Blake wondered. Her eyes locked on Uhura's. "Can you remember anything that stands out about those particular visits?"

Uhura hesitated, unsure how to answer. Scott moved forward, almost shielding her, and fielded the question. "Argelius will always stand out for me, thanks to that demon Redjac and those poor women it tried to frame me for killing. And Deneva was a terrible time, what with the captain—Admiral Kirk losing his brother and sister-in-law to the damned parasites. Compared to those, though, the others were pretty routine. Aside from the hash those Cygneti pranksters made of our computer, thinking it needed 'more personality.' Took us two weeks to overhaul the system after that." He chuckled. "Although the inauguration parties on Altair weren't what I'd call routine. I wouldn't expect anyone to remember much of what they did on that visit."

"Scotty's right, Captain," Uhura said. "There's nothing obvious setting those six visits apart. The systems' stars are of different spectral types, different ages. Four of them have humanoid natives, but the other two are Earth colonies."

"Any commonality in the planets' magnetic fields?" Blake shrugged. "Maybe they had some weird resonance with the *Enterprise*'s warp reactor, or something like that."

Uhura called up the data on the console. "Different field intensities, different inclinations and declinations, different activity levels during our visits."

Blake chewed on her lip. "Well, this is getting us nowhere, and we're near end of shift. I recommend you sleep on it, Nyota."

Uhura smiled. "That sounds like a good idea, Captain."

Nonetheless, Uhura had difficulty taking her mind off the analysis. Something about it stuck in her mind, as if there were some pattern in the vacuum flares just hovering on the edge of her awareness. Something about their radiometric and gravimetric oscillations felt almost familiar to her in some way.

Just before turning in, as she sang to herself in the sonic shower, she was struck by a new idea, a way to analyze the spectrum and structure of the flare oscillations in a manner akin to the analysis of musical patterns. She had already tried a basic Fourier analysis, but what if she tried organizing the data in terms of dynamics, texture, and articulation?

Setting sleep aside, Uhura threw on a kaftan and sat at the computer station in her quarters, setting up the new parameters for the flare analysis. Before long, she felt she was starting to tease out a recurring pattern hidden in the noise. Her hands moved on the controls, guided by some intuition she couldn't articulate, and the pattern began to emerge. She began a computer search for similar patterns in the Starfleet database. On a strange impulse, she tied in her personal database as well.

When the result came up, Uhura stared in disbelief for a long time.

It was impossible, surely. She had done the analysis wrong, her assumptions leading her down a blind alley.

She rechecked her methodology, reran the analysis. The same conclusion emerged.

"I must be too sleepy to think straight," she murmured. "I'll look again in the morning."

She lay awake the whole night, afraid she was going mad.

Chapter Five

Starfleet Academy

"I'm not here to give you the answers."

Portia observed Commander Anjani Desai as the human woman paced slowly before her students, taking care to make eye contact with every member of this study group. The Starfleet Academy ethics professor was a physically unimposing figure, her frame modest in height and displaying soft, pronounced curves rather than firm muscle, her black hair impractically long and carefully styled. Her bronze skin was as unnervingly smooth and taut as an infant's, a characteristic shared by most non-Arcturian humanoids until they reached advanced age. Still, beneath Desai's soft-spoken manner, Portia sensed a strong, commanding will that easily held the attention of the students present.

"Starfleet officers encounter many situations that have no precedent in our experience," Desai continued. "Defining 'right' and 'wrong' in those situations is something you'll have to decide for yourselves when you face them. Or at least something your commanding officers will have to decide, with your input as advisors. So what I'll try to teach you in this course is how to ask the right questions—how to learn the habits of ethical judgment that will guide you in shaping those decisions, or making them for yourselves."

Like Bertram, Portia would have been more comfortable sticking with the subjects she knew she could do well, like unarmed combat, survival training, or piloting. Yet she had succumbed to Horatio's insistence that all twelve Warborn should take Ethics 101 at the earliest opportunity. She did not share his eagerness to become tame and docile; like it or not, she had been bred to fight, and she accepted that as her nature. Yet the boyish Benedick's eagerness to learn new things had helped her realize that a warrior should welcome being challenged. Thus, she had accepted Horatio's challenge to enroll in Ethics and prove she could master the subject as well as he, if not better.

Due to the nature of the subject, the class as a whole had been broken up into these smaller study groups that would meet once a week to discuss ethical questions in depth, led by the professor's teaching assistants or by Desai, schedule permitting. This group had fourteen students; aside from Portia, Horatio, and Benedick, there were five humans, two Vulcans, an Andorian, a Tiburonian, a Caitian, and an Escherite, a large arthropod whose long, multilegged silver body sat curled up on the floor alongside the others' seats.

As Desai encouraged the group to put forth hypothetical scenarios posing ethical conundrums that Starfleet officers might face, it was not long before the male Vulcan, a young, lean one named Vekal, peered intensely at the three Warborn and asked, "Can it be considered ethical to create an entire race of people purely to fight and die in wars?"

Horatio faced the pointed-eared youth with an even, calm gaze. "I would ask the opposite: Is it ethical to force ordinary people to sacrifice their homes, their families, their careers, and even their very lives in order to transform them into warriors? If wars must be fought, should they not be about protecting the lives and freedoms of ordinary people, rather than taking them away?"

Next to Vekal, his Tiburonian friend Zirani Kayros tilted her head quizzically. Kayros looked slightly more like an Arcturian than any of the others here, for her scalp was bare and she had large, scalloped outer ears bearing a faint aesthetic resemblance to an Arcturian's skin folds. "I thought the whole reason you were here was to learn to live like ordinary people," Kayros said to Horatio. "You don't think you have a right to that?"

Horatio smiled at her. "I believe my purpose is to serve others. To protect my homeworld and its people's well-being. That is the sacred calling I was created to serve."

Vekal lowered his upswept eyebrows mistrustfully, taking in all three Warborn with his gaze. "You were created to fight and kill. Do you believe that's your calling now? Are you here to fight?"

Portia locked eyes with him and smiled. "Are you offering?"

Horatio touched her arm to still her. "What matters is the end, not the means. Our ancestors kept the people of Arcturus safe and free to live their lives by defending them against invaders. We do the same by removing ourselves from Arcturus and learning to follow a new path." He shook his head. "And no, that path cannot include combat. Not unless the motherworld herself is threatened."

"So, what if you're on a ship that's attacked?" Kayros asked. "If you're part of the crew and your captain orders you to fight? Will you disobey?"

Horatio looked uneasy. "Not all posts in Starfleet are combat-oriented, or even starship-based. There are ground postings. Administrative tasks. Communication and clerical work. Research asteroids."

Benedick grinned. "I would like to serve on one of those. Imagine—a whole asteroid, and all they do is research!"

"Even those can come under attack," Kayros countered. "A

crew needs to depend on all its members to work together to defend it."

"Our faith does not allow it," Horatio insisted. "Starfleet would not force anyone within it to violate their beliefs."

"Then how do you expect to make this work, if you don't think you can fulfill your duties to Starfleet?"

"She has a point." Portia was surprised to hear herself speak up, preempting Horatio's reply. "Our calling is to protect our world, our people. If we become part of a Starfleet crew, don't they become our people? Don't we have a responsibility to fight for their safety?"

"Ohh." Benedick blinked at her, his mouth open and rounded. "That *is* a good point."

Horatio remained adamant, shaking his head. "That's not what doctrine says."

"The doctrine wasn't written to cope with this situation," Portia countered. She gestured toward Desai, who was listening silently but with intense interest. "It's like the professor said—we'll face situations without precedent. We'll have to decide what's right as we face them." Portia looked around at the group. "And what feels right to me is fighting to protect my people. *Whoever* my people are."

After the study group let out, Horatio pulled Portia aside. "What you said in there was unwise."

She pulled her arm away. "That's not for you to say. And the professor said we were free to voice our thoughts."

"Others have that freedom, yes. We have to be more careful." He looked around at the other students filing out, including Vekal, who still peered at them warily as if expecting them to go berserk at any moment. "We are feared for what we represent. We must prove to them that we are not a threat. That we are not here to be warriors."

"You heard Zirani. If we refuse to fight even in defense of our shipmates, that makes us a threat too. We need their trust, not just their lack of fear."

Horatio shook his head. "You're striking a dangerous course, Portia. There have always been those outside Arcturus who wished to exploit us as warriors. Half the invasions the Warborn have defended the motherworld against have happened *because* we existed. Because outsiders wished to corrupt our sacred purpose for destructive ends."

"You think Starfleet is destructive?"

"I think we are a temptation they could succumb to, if we allow them to think it could happen. Please, Portia, do not encourage them to see us as fighters."

"I don't know what else I can be—for them or for myself. If it's right to fight for Arcturus, can't it be right to fight for the Federation?"

"It can be right for others, if that is their choice. It is not a choice we have. It would open a door that might never be closed again."

She held his eyes. "Then how *can* we make this work? What are we even doing here?"

"We are following orders. We're serving our creators."

Portia stared at him a moment more before turning and striding away. She'd been hearing that answer her whole life, and it brought her no more comfort now. There had to be more to her existence than that. Wasn't that the whole point of coming here?

For a couple of weeks now, Hikaru Sulu had been hearing from other faculty members that the Warborn Arcturians were difficult, aloof, at once overly aggressive and resistant to any teaching that even hinted at a combat application. He didn't see it himself. The Warborn cadets in his introductory piloting class were focused, quick, and enthusiastic—particularly the youthful-seeming male called Benedick, whose eager inquisitiveness reminded Sulu of his younger self, and the quieter female Portia, who was quick to show anger or frustration but showed signs of being a natural, instinctive pilot.

If nothing else, the Warborn cadets differed from the rest in one refreshing way: they didn't beg him to jump right to the combat piloting simulations a semester ahead of schedule, or attempt to hack the simulators to call them up. To most young people in the Federation, battle was an exotic abstraction, a fantasy made romantic by its remoteness from their everyday lives, so they were eager to get a taste of it—until the grim realities sank in. But the Warborn had trained for battle their entire lives. If anything, it was the mundane piloting operations that were the novelty to them.

The course work at this early stage consisted mostly of lectures, readings, and simulator time, but at the end of the second week, Sulu took his cadets up with him individually in an Academy aerial shuttle for an introduction and familiarization session, letting them observe his operation of the craft from the copilot's seat. It was admittedly as much about giving himself a chance to do some flying as it was about providing the cadets with experience. But it served both purposes, so why not?

Most of the students he took up, including Benedick, pleaded with him to let them take the controls, however briefly. If he thought highly enough of their learning curve and reflexes, he'd grant the request during one of the easier parts of the flight. He would have readily allowed Portia to try it; indeed, her Warborn training had already included fighter piloting, so she was overqualified.

However, when her turn came, Portia merely sat quietly and watched. For days now, she had seemed distracted. She had always been punctual, completed all her classwork, and done everything required of her, yet no more than that, as though her mind were elsewhere.

Hoping to draw her out, Sulu smiled at her. "If you have any questions, I'm happy to answer."

The young Arcturian ruminated for several moments, then sighed. "I have too many questions. Just not about this."

"Questions about what?" At her silence, he continued. "A distracted pilot is not a good thing. It might help you clear your mind if you talk to someone. Doesn't have to be me, but . . ." He gestured around them at the cockpit. "At least it's private in here."

Again, Portia was slow to answer. "We're trained not to show . . . vulnerability."

"That makes sense when you're facing an enemy. With your friends, it's a bad idea. Even more so with your teachers. How can you fix a vulnerability if you don't admit it?"

That finally seemed to get through to her, though it clearly wasn't easy for her to open up. "I just don't know what I'm expected to be. We're not allowed to pursue the ways of war here, but fighting is all I know. It's who I am. How do I make myself into something else? How do I even choose?"

Sulu chuckled. "Portia, the great thing about your first year of college is that you don't *have* to choose. This is your chance to try new things, to explore all sorts of possibilities and see what you're good at, what captures your fancy. There's no rush to decide right away.

"If fighting's all you know, that's just because you haven't *tried* other things yet. This is your opportunity to do that. Just relax, take your time, experiment. That's what first year's all about."

Portia studied him. "How long did it take you to decide on your path?"

He laughed louder. "Oh, a *long* time. I've always loved piloting, but I also studied astrophysics, security, botany, you name it. I eventually decided to work toward starship command, but I wasn't in any hurry. I felt I still had a lot to learn under Captain Kirk."

She did not seem too pleased with his answer. "I don't have that luxury. Our life expectancy is considerably below yours. The Warborn were not expected to need long lives."

Sulu cleared his throat, unsure how to respond to that. "Look . . . I know it can be hard to adjust to a sudden change in your life. I . . . I only found out last year that I had a daughter. It wasn't planned, and her mother never told me. She raised Demora alone. But last year, she died, and Demora came to live with me. A man she'd never met."

He shifted in his seat. "It was . . . a process of adjustment for both of us. It was hard for her, to be uprooted from the life she knew, to start over somewhere else with no anchor, no direction."

Portia's gaze sharpened. "And have you now . . . adjusted?"

"More or less. I think parents and children getting used to each other might be a lifelong process. But we found common ground, and things are good between us now. She's growing so fast, learning so fast. I see my job as doing everything I can to encourage that, and to give her the space to explore life as widely as I have. To choose whatever she wants to be."

The cadet contemplated that. "But what if she already knew what she wanted to be—knew who she was at heart—and it wasn't permitted? Because the world she was part of wouldn't accept it?"

Sulu considered the question. "Demora and I are lucky to live in a time when we have the freedom to choose to be whatever we want. But there were times in the past when that wasn't the case—when society wouldn't accept certain ways for people to be. The reason we have that freedom now is because of people back then who didn't settle for the limits others put on them. People who embraced what they were meant to be and convinced the rest of the world to change."

Portia absorbed that silently for a time, and Sulu let her. Noting the chronometer on the console, he spoke softly. "Looks like we've used up our flight time—better get back. We don't want to keep the others waiting. But hey—we can talk about this more later, if you'd like."

She turned to face him. "Thank you, Commander. I will consider that, and the rest of what you have said."

She remained silent on the flight back, which gave Sulu the chance to wonder if his advice had been appropriate. It had sounded very much as if Portia was talking about embracing her role as a fighter, despite Arcturian belief and tradition. Did he have the right to encourage her to do that? Did the Federation have the right to exploit her services in that capacity when her whole subspecies had been bred to be exploited? What about the concerns people were raising about the precedent it would set for Starfleet?

All he knew was that this intense young woman was searching for identity and purpose, not unlike Demora—and not unlike himself at various times in his life. She had a right to find her own answer, whatever the larger issues.

And if the course she chose turned out to meet with resistance, he was confident she had the strength to handle it.

Kirk had to wait a week to get his meeting with Ashley Janith-Lau. McCoy hadn't been able to make time for it until he'd succeeded in creating that vaccine for the Icorians. Even then, according to him, it had taken a fair amount of sweet-talking to bring her around.

Once the peace activist finally entered his office, though, Kirk's immediate thought was that she was very much worth the wait. Her beauty was intoxicating in a way he'd begun to fear he'd outgrown. It wasn't just the flawless delicacy of her features; he could sense the intensity and keen intelligence behind her dark, piercing eyes.

He chastised himself, striving for focus as he rose to greet her. He was letting Bones's incessant matchmaking get to him. There might be time for that later, the Great Bird willing, but he had greater responsibilities to concentrate on right now.

"Doctor Janith-Lau." He shook her hand, and it was dainty and refreshingly cool to the touch, but with a strong, decisive grip. "I'm glad you could come in to see me. I've been looking forward to meeting you. Doctor McCoy speaks highly of you."

"And of you, Admiral." The pediatrician gave a small smile; a larger one might have blinded him. "I admit, I find that surprising. The Leonard McCoy I knew eight years ago seemed to have put Starfleet behind him rather decisively—indeed, he seemed to have little use for modern civilization altogether. I never would've expected him to go back to military service, or to remain in it now that he's living on Earth again." She examined Kirk curiously. "He gives me the impression that you're the main reason he chooses to stay."

Kirk returned her smile. "Doctor McCoy and I have known each other for seventeen years, almost all of them in Starfleet. Our friendship began with an argument—one that saved my life when he diagnosed me with Vegan choriomeningitis in the nick of time. It wasn't the last time he'd save my life—and it was far from the last time we argued."

Janith-Lau laughed. "I'm not surprised. My friendship with Len started with an argument too."

"In my experience, most of his friendships do." Kirk gestured her toward the couch to the side of his office, taking the armchair opposite her as she sat. He wished to set a more inviting tone than he could from behind his desk. "I value that as a reminder that people can disagree strongly, yet still work toward a common goal."

She tilted her head. "I see. And you're hoping you and I can find common ground on the Warborn issue."

"I'm hoping I can convince you that we already share it."

"Oh? How so?"

"The goal of enrolling the Arcturian Warborn in the Academy is to help them find a peacetime role. Arcturian law and tradition forbid them from participating in combat except in defense of their homeworld. Naturally, Starfleet respects that prohibition."

"I have read the press release, Admiral. But surely you can see there are gaps in its logic." She leaned forward. "Starfleet may call itself an organ for diplomacy and research, but you are also the Federation's military. You're the group that fights our battles, that patrols our borders, that enforces our laws on the frontier."

"There's room in Starfleet for both soldiers and scholars. We boast some of the finest research facilities in the Federation. We attract many of the best scientific minds."

"Yes—and it saddens me to see so many great minds subverted to the cause of military readiness. Len McCoy included."

"McCoy serves as a healer. His responsibility is to save lives, not to take them."

"Exclusively? Can you really say that Doctor McCoy has never fired a phaser, never participated in a battle?"

"Only when he's had no other choice. I told you he's saved my life a number of times. More than once, he's done it with a phaser, saving me from predatory creatures."

"That's just it, Admiral," Janith-Lau said. "However much you profess your benevolent intentions, being in Starfleet forces people to become fighters. Trying to be both scientists and soldiers at once—it keeps you from doing either one as well as you should."

"Out on the frontier, there's no telling what a ship and its crew may be called upon to become at any time. It's best to be prepared for every possibility."

"Exactly. How can you guarantee that the Warborn will not have to fight if they join Starfleet? It doesn't make sense."

Kirk pondered his reply for a moment, and decided to go

for honesty. "I admit we don't have all the answers. That's the reason for this pilot program—to explore whether we can make it work. This is new ground for us, as well as for the Warborn cadets. But I believe that if anyone can help them integrate into peacetime society, it's Starfleet." He leaned closer. "You see our blend of martial and peaceful aspects as a weakness. I see it as a strength, a source of adaptability. Who better to guide a people trained solely for war to redirect their abilities for peace?"

Janith-Lau folded her hands on her lap, considering his words. "That might be a more convincing argument, Admiral, if not for the timing. It doesn't seem accidental that you attempt to bring a specially bred warrior subspecies into Starfleet at the same time that Starfleet is turning toward a more martial footing."

He blinked. "I don't believe that it is, Doctor. It's the galaxy that's growing more dangerous. Renewed Klingon aggression, our turbulent relations with the Romulans, unpredictable outside threats like the Naazh or these vacuum flares. Starfleet is merely responding to those threats."

"The way to respond to a threat is to de-escalate, not to heighten tensions still further."

"I assure you, Doctor, Starfleet's policy is always to use force as a last resort when peaceful options have failed. But there are many cultures out there that respect strength, or that see any weakness as an opening to be exploited." He smiled. "If you make it clear that you have teeth but *choose* not to use them, that demonstrates your peaceful intentions more effectively than going unarmed."

She did not look convinced. "So do you think this conversation would go better if I'd come in here brandishing a phaser? Would I even have been let onto the grounds?"

Kirk gestured between them. "You and I are members of a single society with established norms and expectations. If we were from different cultures meeting for the first time, then yes, we might both need to be armed to establish the ground rules of the exchange." He chuckled. "It's not so different from how Doctor McCoy makes friends."

She lowered her head, stifling a laugh. Then she met his gaze again. "I guess you do know how to de-escalate after all."

"I try my best." He spread his hands. "Look . . . we've wandered off-topic. We aren't going to settle the larger philosophical questions about Starfleet's existence in this office. I just want to convince you that our intentions for the Warborn are beneficial—to guide them toward a constructive purpose, not to exploit them for combat. If you can be persuaded of that, then you can take that message to the public and assuage their fears about the program.

"Maybe what you need is to meet them for yourself. Talk to them. Get to know them as individuals."

Janith-Lau nodded thoughtfully. "That is only fair. I suppose . . . I have been reacting to the threat I feel they represent, rather than who they are as people. And maybe I've been unconsciously feeding those prejudices in my speeches. I should do better than that if I want to be true to what I claim to stand for."

Kirk smiled, very impressed by her admission. He'd always believed that true morality began with questioning oneself, not just others. That she believed the same spoke well of her.

He rose, and she followed. "Very well, Doctor. The students are in class now, but we can schedule a time when you can speak to them as a group."

"I'd like to do more than just speak to them," she ventured. "If you don't mind, perhaps I could shadow them for a day. Observe them in their classes, see what they're learning and how they're interacting with their fellow students. I'd try not to be too intrusive—"

"No, that's quite all right, Doctor. Full transparency is important if we're to reassure the public about the value of this program. I'm sure it can be arranged."

"All right, then, Admiral Kirk. I look forward to it. For now . . ." She held out her hand. "This has been . . . very interesting. And more agreeable than I thought it would be."

He smiled as he clasped her hand. "I feel the same, Doctor. It's been a pleasure."

His gaze followed her as she left his office, and lingered on the door for some time after she left. "That is quite a woman," he murmured. Maybe for once, McCoy's matchmaking instincts were onto something.

Chapter Six

U.S.S. *Enterprise*
Earth Spacedock

The day after his meeting with Ashley Janith-Lau, Kirk beamed up to Spacedock to welcome the *Enterprise* back from its flight, a brief training cruise for the second- and third-year cadets. "It was not necessary for you to greet us in person, Admiral," Captain Spock said once the bosun had piped him aboard at the main gangway hatch.

The admiral shrugged. "The end of the first training cruise of the semester? I think that warrants a little ceremony."

The two *Enterprise* veterans began walking through the saucer corridors they both knew so well. "It was merely a familiarization exercise," Spock replied, "as one would expect this early in the term. It proceeded within expected parameters."

"Good, good."

Spock hesitated, which was unusual for him. "However unnecessary, it is convenient that you are here. I trust you have heard of the most recent vacuum flare event?"

"Near Delta IV, yes. Fortunately harmless, but it disproves Chekov's theory about a link to past *Enterprise* missions. It looked promising after Vega Colony." The *Enterprise*'s itinerary for the preceding several years had never included the Deltan star system.

"In fact, Admiral," Spock replied, "I believe this new datum not only supports Commander Chekov's hypothesis, but allows refining it to identify the exact common factor unifying the events." Again he showed that odd hesitation. "If you will accompany me to my quarters, Admiral? Until I am more certain, it would be best to discuss this in private."

Spock led the admiral up one deck to the captain's cabin. Spock kept his quarters softly lit and sparsely furnished, the better to facilitate quiet contemplation. The primary decoration was a large mural of the Vulcan IDIC emblem assembled from hundreds of small metal disks; Spock had told Kirk once that he mentally associated each disk with a specific person from his past, meditating on each in turn to reflect how their diverse influences had combined to shape the course of his life. Next to it, the small cylindrical dining nook had been converted into a meditation alcove, for Spock rarely entertained guests or took elaborate meals.

Spock did, however, respect human conventions enough to offer Kirk a beverage. Kirk brushed it off and said, "Just tell me, Spock. What have you figured out that's so sensitive?"

The Vulcan captain sat at his work desk in the corner and steepled his fingers. "As you are aware, Jim, we had not been able to determine a single common factor among the previous systems struck by vacuum flares. Though they were all visited by the *Enterprise* in reverse sequence, and all contain relatively advanced worlds in regular contact with the Federation, the list excluded numerous worlds that fit those same parameters. Therefore, any hope of predicting future flares relies upon identifying some additional variable shared only by those systems. Yet the ones we could discern appeared trivial: all entailed layovers of several days, all entailed vessel maintenance and resupply, all entailed shore leave for at least a portion of the crew."

"All routine matters." Kirk stopped there, resisting the impulse to insist that Spock get to his point. He knew Spock well enough by now to understand that the captain wished to restate the parameters of the problem clearly as the first stage of his methodical analysis.

"So it would seem," Spock said, "but that creates a dangerous temptation to dismiss data that could be significant. Consider, Jim: Though the *Enterprise* is the unifying variable in all these incidents, the vacuum flares appear to be aimed instead, however imperfectly, at the *planets* the ship visited—never at any point in interstellar space, even ones where the *Enterprise* spent a considerable amount of time.

"It stands to reason, therefore, that the key lies with something that occurred on those planets *while* the *Enterprise* visited them."

"I see what you're getting at, Spock." Kirk began to pace the room. "If some . . . cosmic force is sending these flares . . . then it's not targeting the ship, but one or more of its *crew*. Somebody who left the ship at each of those ports, and did something to attract its attention."

"Or did something that triggered some form of natural outburst as a delayed reaction," Spock countered. "It is still too early to make assumptions regarding the causal factor; I am merely proposing a correlation."

"Of course. But it does narrow it down. It's not about the *Enterprise*, but about the people aboard her." He snapped his fingers and pointed. "That's why the Deltan system is significant. The *Enterprise* didn't go there, but one of the crew did."

Spock nodded. "Upon having this insight, I reviewed the duty rosters to compile a list of personnel who went ashore at every one of the systems affected by the flares. I was able to narrow it down to eleven people, including you and myself, but no further."

"How many had previously visited Delta?"

"Within a year prior to the *Enterprise*'s visit to Vega Colony, records show only two." He worked his console, bringing up a personnel file displaying a familiar square-jawed face. "Lieutenant Vincent DeSalle made a layover in the system in late 2265, only long enough for a brief sightseeing tour."

The next file he displayed featured a far more familiar and stunning face. "And Lieutenant Nyota Uhura spent a week on Delta IV in early 2266, while the *Enterprise* was undergoing repairs and refitting following its return from the galactic rim."

Kirk leaned forward. "Uhura? How could this have anything to do with her?"

"I have no hypothesis at this time, Jim. However, the records do show that Uhura spent at least several hours on the surface of every affected planet, often more than a day—during which her activities were unaccounted for."

The admiral threw him a look. "Spock . . . it's shore leave. Your activities are *supposed* to be unaccounted for. What Uhura does in her free time is her own affair."

Spock raised a brow. "It seems unlikely that the type of activity you implicitly refer to would have any connection to the vacuum flare phenomenon—despite colorful human metaphors pertaining to fireworks and seismic upheavals."

Kirk flushed. "I only meant that we have no business assuming anything untoward from the simple fact that she acted in private."

"Again, no assumption is intended." Spock inflected the word "assumption" as if referring to something vile. "I am merely defining what is known and what is still unknown. Uhura is the one variable shared by every vacuum flare incident to date, as is the fact that she was on each planet for a significant amount of time with her activities undocumented. Therefore, it is plausible that something she did during that unaccounted time is connected in some way to the vacuum flares—most likely in some way she is unaware of, or she would have recognized the pattern herself and notified us."

"Then we need to contact her. Find out if she can remember anything she did during those leaves."

"Certainly that is the next logical step. As is compiling a list of her previous shore visits to worlds that fit the parameters, so that we may predict future flare sites and have advance warning—or at least rule out this hypothesis if its predictions prove incorrect."

The admiral shook his head. "I'm not sure whether to hope it's right or wrong. We need a way to predict future flares, and ideally to learn what causes them, before they start doing serious damage. But if it turns out that they have some connection to Uhura, what could that mean to her? Or about her?"

Spock held his gaze. "Now you understand why I did not wish to publicize this until we can be sure. The natural human temptation is to speculate, to imagine dire possibilities to fill the gaps in our knowledge. Commander Uhura deserves the benefit of the doubt as we seek more information."

"Of course, of course, Spock. You're right."

Still, as he thought about it now, it struck Kirk that there had always been something mysterious about Nyota Uhura. For all her outward warmth, she was a very private individual. He had come to think of her as a trusted colleague, even a friend, though more casually than he was with Spock or McCoy, or than she was with Sulu and Chekov. Yet on reflection, there was still a great deal he did not know about her personal life.

His first reaction had been disbelief that Uhura could be involved in anything connected to the vacuum flares—anything on the level of a cosmic mystery this great. But was that simply because he had always taken her for granted? What depths might she possess that he had never discovered?

Starfleet Academy

"I need to take the *Enterprise* out."

Superintendent Chandra studied Kirk patiently from behind the neatly organized desk in his office. "Already?"

"You're aware of the apparent connection of the vacuum flare phenomenon to past *Enterprise* missions," Kirk said. Chandra nodded. "Captain Spock and I believe that a former member of our crew aboard the *Asimov* could provide a vital insight, and it would be faster to rendezvous with them in the *Enterprise* than to call them back to Earth."

"And this can't be done over subspace?"

Kirk paused. "It could be . . . involved. We have a tentative idea of a connection, but it might take extensive discussion and analysis, working together, to determine what it means."

"Hmm." Chandra nodded as he thought it over. "That sounds reasonable. Sending the *Enterprise* under Captain Spock is a sensible approach." The senior admiral's gaze pierced him. "But why do *you* need to be there?"

Kirk hesitated, which Chandra took as an answer. "I have accepted the nature of your arrangement with Admiral Morrow. I understand your position that your skills are still useful in the field. Some of us take more comfortably to administration than others." Chandra gestured around him at his office, adorned with paraphernalia of his family, the Academy, and San Francisco, all conveying the sense of a man securely nested in his place.

"But I accepted it with the understanding that you would find a reasonable balance between your Academy responsibilities and your occasional special assignments. I am not convinced you have been sufficiently dedicated to that balance, Jim. You are taking field assignments that do not require your presence, when you should be back here concentrating on your commitments as commandant.

"Particularly now, with the tensions surrounding the Warborn cadets. It was largely at your urging that we accepted them, after all. You have an obligation to see this through."

"I understand that, sir. But this shouldn't take more than a few days—"

"To reach the *Asimov*, perhaps. But if your consultation with your crew member does produce a useful insight, it will probably be best to act on it promptly. This could be an open-ended venture. So I ask again, Jim." Chandra leaned forward. "Does the *Enterprise* actually *need* James Kirk aboard it on this mission?"

Kirk tried to think of a reply that wouldn't seem self-serving. The very fact that he needed to try told him the answer. He lowered his head. "No, sir. You're right. I'm needed here. And I have full confidence in Captain Spock's ability to fulfill the mission on his own."

Chandra nodded, smiling a bit to ease the tension. "Very good. Have Captain Spock contact me about the mission parameters. If he deems it safe enough, he can select a senior cadet crew and make it a training mission."

"I don't see why it shouldn't be, sir." Kirk stopped himself. "But I'll leave that to Spock to decide."

Chandra smiled wider, a bit wistfully. "Get used to saying that, Jim. A flag officer has to learn to delegate. You've been on the other side of that often enough, I'm sure. You don't want to become the stereotype of the imperious admiral getting in the way of the captains trying to do their jobs."

"Fair enough, sir. I'll keep that in mind."

Kirk found he did not feel too disappointed as he left the superintendent's office. To be honest, part of him was grateful for being grounded. Tomorrow was the day Ashley Janith-Lau was scheduled to meet the Warborn Arcturians and observe them in their classes. It was a relief that he would not have to miss her second visit. He was very much looking forward to spending more time in the peace activist's charming company, even if they did disagree on quite a few issues.

If anything, Janith-Lau's arguments in favor of pacifism reminded Kirk of a number of his past debates with Spock over the years—debates that had helped him temper his own martial impulses and stay true to his aspirations to be a better man. He and Spock had formed an enduring partnership based on their differences. Perhaps that could be possible with someone else as well.

The next morning, Kirk and Commander Rakatheema met Ashley Janith-Lau outside a common area in Hernandez Hall, the Warborn students' dormitory. The peace activist had come with two other members of her organization, a diminutive Vulcan woman named T'Sena and a portly Argelian man named Rogo.

"They're all waiting inside, Admiral, as you ordered," Rakatheema reported. He directed a glare toward Janith-Lau's group, his jowly features making it seem especially lugubrious. "I'm still not convinced this is a good idea, sir. These cadets are having a difficult enough time feeling accepted. I've seen the doctor's speeches stirring up fear and mistrust toward them."

Doctor Janith-Lau lowered her gaze, not attempting to dispute his characterization. Kirk answered in her stead. "Then you should welcome her visit, Commander. The best antidote to fear is understanding. That's what we're here to build."

Rakatheema frowned at the doctor again. "I hope you're right, Admiral. All these cadets want is the chance to prove themselves, the same as any other cadet. And that means to prove what they can *do*—not to constantly justify their very existence."

This time, Janith-Lau didn't look away. Her tone was calm and relaxed, but there was steel behind it. "In that case, Commander, we should let them speak for themselves, shouldn't we?" She moved past him, offering a courteous smile. "Shall we go in?"

Kirk hastened to follow her inside the lounge, concerned at how the Warborn cadets would react to the sight of her. Indeed, he found them already facing her tensely. As Rakatheema and the other two activists came in behind Kirk, one of the Warborn stepped forward and circled Janith-Lau, sizing up the slighter woman as if she were an opponent in a sparring match. "So you're the peace doctor." Kirk recognized her voice and manner—it was the female called Portia. He was still learning to differentiate the Warborn by their identifying decorations and subtle differences of face, build, and body language, but Portia's intensity made her stand out from the pack. "The one who doesn't think we have the right to exist."

The largest Warborn, Bertram, shrugged. "Our existence isn't a right. It's an accident. If she's afraid of us, she's not wrong."

"Both of you, stand down." The speaker was the one called Horatio, memorable for his charisma and the de facto leadership role he seemed to have adopted. Kirk saw command potential in him, and that perception was reinforced as Horatio stepped forward, greeting Janith-Lau with an extended hand. "Doctor. I'm Horatio. I appreciate your willingness to meet with us and gain our perspective on this pilot program. I want you to know that I admire your commitment to peace. Protecting the peace of our people is the purpose we were created to serve. There is no higher calling."

"I appreciate it, Horatio." Janith-Lau shook his hand, then turned to take in the others. "I want you all to know that it isn't your existence we object to. Our concern is merely that you not be exploited—that your lives not be devalued or jeopardized in service to others' agendas."

"Many in the Federation are uneasy with the apparent trend toward militarization in Starfleet," T'Sena added. "There is concern that your recruitment may have a hidden agenda behind it."

Janith-Lau resumed the thread. "Admiral Kirk assures me that the goal is just the opposite—to help you find a peaceful, constructive way to contribute your skills. I certainly want to believe that's true, and I and my colleagues look forward to seeing what your classroom experience is like. I hope that over the day, we'll be able to hear from you about your experiences here so far, and your expectations and goals for what lies ahead."

Many of the Warborn cadets looked skeptical, as did Rakatheema—and both of Janith-Lau's colleagues. But class time was drawing near, so the group headed off to their various courses, with the activists splitting up accordingly.

Kirk went with Janith-Lau to observe Horatio's first course of the day, Federation History 101. By accident or design, Professor Sunderland's lecture today was about Surak's Reformation on Vulcan, one of the known galaxy's most successful and enduring peace movements. Once the dark-bearded historian finished summarizing the turbulent process by which Vulcan had embraced peace (for the sheer number of planets whose histories were covered in this overview left little time for in-depth examination), he looked over the class and asked, "Why do you suppose it is that Surak's philosophy of logic has endured planetwide for nearly two thousand years, while other peace movements in other worlds and times have failed?"

Most of the students were reluctant to speak first, as was common in elementary courses. But Horatio wasted little time filling the gap. "I believe it was the power and clarity of Surak's message. The fact that he committed his whole existence to his cause, that he laid down his own life to save his people, showed the depth of his faith, and inspired others to follow."

One of the Vulcan students, a young male named Vekal, bristled in that cool, disciplined way that Vulcans bristled. "Surak's philosophy is not a religion."

Horatio met his eyes evenly. "I did not say 'religion.' I said 'faith'—a pure, unshakable commitment to one's purpose, a certainty so absolute that it outweighs one's own life in importance. He did not just *say* that the needs of the many outweighed the needs of the one—he demonstrated it through self-abnegation."

Vekal only appeared more disturbed. "It sounds as if you intend to liken Surak's sacrifice to your own people's created purpose to die for Arcturus. It is not comparable. First, you were made to kill, which Surak would not do under any provocation. Second, you did not choose to sacrifice yourself; you were engineered for that purpose by others."

"And I have faith in that purpose, because it was done in the name of Arcturus. That is my choice." Horatio continued before Vekal could reply. "And that purpose is not to kill, certainly not as an end in itself. It is to protect—in whatever way we must."

Sunderland brought the debate to a halt to continue the lecture, but Kirk studied Janith-Lau as she pondered the exchange. She noted his scrutiny and smiled. "He's an interesting fellow. There's something very familiar about his passion for his ideals, even if I don't agree with his methods."

The next class they visited was an introductory engineering course. The instructor, Lieutenant Commander Longo, assigned the class to break into several groups, each of which was given a standard kit of components and a randomly drawn card specifying what kind of device they needed to build from them. This was a test of the cadets' creativity and problem-solving skill as well as their engineering knowledge.

The youthful-seeming Warborn cadet called Benedick threw himself into the exercise with enthusiasm, meshing smoothly with his study group. It seemed to Kirk that he was more outgoing than the other Warborn, possessing a guileless openness that made him easy to get along with. He experimented gamely with the components and went along readily with the suggestions of other group members. He didn't seem to have much insight into the principles behind the components, but he was eager to explore the possibilities and learn from their outcomes. Kirk found himself reminded of a young Pavel Chekov.

Conversely, the other Warborn cadet in the class, a female called Viola, struggled with the assignment, appearing frustrated and lost. She contributed no useful suggestions, though she followed instructions gamely when the others encouraged her to contribute her dexterity and steady hands to the work. Still, she made mistakes, struggling to understand how the components should fit together. When Janith-Lau spoke to her afterward, seeking to understand her perspective, Viola replied with stiffly controlled frustration. "Give me instructions to follow and I'll do it. I can field-strip and reassemble any weapon you put in my hands. I'm trained at that. I understand that."

"It's more of a challenge to create than to destroy," Janith-Lau told her gently. "But that means it takes more strength, more courage. Don't you think so?"

Viola scoffed. "I'm not a hero. I just do my duty. That's my place." She looked around. "But this duty, this place . . . I may be the wrong choice for it."

When Janith-Lau returned to Kirk's side, she bore a wistful smile. "One thing this visit has made clear—the Warborn are as individual as anyone else. I'm embarrassed at myself for expecting otherwise."

Kirk was not able to accompany the doctor to every class she visited, for other Academy duties intervened for much of the day. He had to meet with Professor Blune and several faculty members to finalize the parameters for next semester's starbase work-study program for the second-year cadets; afterward, he needed to attend a disciplinary meeting to determine punishment for a trio of third-year cadets who had attempted to revive an infamous, long-banned hazing practice known vernacularly as "the Finnegan." Kirk struggled to compartmentalize his humiliated memories of falling prey to it in his own first year, so as not to penalize them more harshly than they deserved. Admiral Chandra would surely frown on keelhauling.

Eventually, he was able to rejoin Doctor Janith-Lau for a rather different classroom experience: Unarmed Combat under Lieutenant Commander Vandenecker. Kirk arrived in time to see the two Warborn cadets in the class, Portia and Bertram, engaged in a fierce, ruthlessly efficient sparring match against each other while the rest of the class looked on with expressions of admiration and intimidation. Even knowing that these Arcturians had been bred and raised as soldiers, Kirk was startled by their display of skill and aggression, having become accustomed to the notion that their studies at the Academy would be oriented toward peace. Bertram had a clear advantage of size and bulk, but the leaner Portia made up for it with her agility and sheer drive. It was a truly impressive sight, and if anyone had been taking wagers (and if he had been willing to overlook such a violation of Academy rules), he would have put his credits on her.

This time, Janith-Lau was not impressed. "This is just the sort of thing my people are concerned about," she said to Commander Rakatheema, who bore a proud look on his face as he observed the combatants. "Shouldn't the Warborn be exempt from the requirement to take combat-oriented courses? Isn't that against Arcturian belief?"

"They *are* exempt," Rakatheema told her. "These two chose to enroll anyway. Who are we to forbid them? After all, it's only training."

"The purpose of which is to prepare cadets to do the real thing. Will you train them in phasers too? In shipboard weapons and combat maneuvers? Will you teach them these things and then not expect them to use them?"

"Starfleet officers are never expected to use force, except as necessary in defense of self or others."

"Yet you keep finding situations where it is 'necessary.' So tell me, Commander, what is the real goal here? I'm having trouble seeing just where you're drawing the line between Starfleet responsibilities and Arcturian doctrine on when and why the Warborn can fight."

Rakatheema answered slowly. "Finding a balance between

doctrine and a changing reality is not simple. A healthy doctrine may need to evolve to remain relevant."

Janith-Lau's eyes narrowed as if her suspicions had been confirmed. "That sounds very much like you're hoping the Warborn will fight for the Federation after all."

"I just think it's important to be open to all possibilities. One can fairly argue that defending the Federation *is* defending Arcturus. And it hardly seems fair to ask these young people to remain passive if their very lives are threatened, or those of their comrades for whom they feel responsible."

The peace activist's expression showed very little peace. "This is what I was afraid of. You're just trying to do what the Arcturians have always done—use the Warborn to serve the interests of their leaders, no matter the cost to themselves."

Portia and Bertram had stopped their match some moments earlier, and they and the whole class were focused on the argument. Noting this, Janith-Lau turned to address the two Warborn. "Are you really okay with being used like this? Defined as living weapons with no other purpose than to fight and die for a higher power?"

Portia took a couple of loping paces toward her. "Is that what you see? Us being asked to fight?" She shook her head. "We're being asked to do everything *but* that. Everything but the one thing that makes us who we are. And now you ask us to deny that last bit of ourselves."

Janith-Lau shook her head. "You don't have to be bound by the role your creators designed you for."

The lanky Warborn female scoffed. "Them? I have no loyalty to people who made me to die."

"Then why cling to this warrior role?"

"Because why they made me this way doesn't matter. It's mine now, and I do what I choose with it. I will fight to be who I am, whether it's with words or with weapons. We have the right to fight for our existence, on our *own* terms."

The two strong-willed females faced off, silently sizing each other up. Bertram just looked confused and troubled, as if he'd rather not face these complicated questions.

Finally, Janith-Lau spoke. "I respect your conviction, Portia. I was wrong to assume you were blindly following. But I hope in time you'll learn that there are better things to live for than fighting."

Portia smirked, but respect showed in her eyes. "Take a look at yourself. You're more of a fighter than you admit."

Kirk was uneasy as the tour came to an end. He had hoped that observing the Warborn at their studies would assuage Janith-Lau's concerns about their possible exploitation and the increased militarization of Starfleet. Instead, it seemed to have deepened her concerns—and raised some questions in Kirk's mind as well. Was Janith-Lau right that Rakatheema hoped to loosen Arcturian doctrine to allow the Warborn to fight for Starfleet? And if so, how did Kirk feel about that? As a military man, he was keenly aware of the potential advantages for Federation defense. But he was not blind to Janith-Lau's arguments, or Spock's, about the sentient-rights issues it raised or the dangerous precedent it could set.

The other cause of Kirk's unhappiness was simply that his time in Janith-Lau's company was coming to an end. His admiration for her had only grown as he had watched her demonstrate her compassion, her openness to learning, and the strength of her convictions. He would welcome the chance to spend more time in her company, with or without a professional reason.

As he escorted Janith-Lau to the edge of the Academy grounds where her colleagues awaited, Kirk contemplated whether to invite her to dinner. Normally he wouldn't hesitate, but under the circumstances, he was concerned that she might misconstrue it as an attempt to influence her stance on the War-born. He considered what the best way would be to broach the offer.

Yet Janith-Lau broke the companionable silence first. "Admiral . . . I've been meaning to ask you something. It's . . . not a professional question."

Kirk turned to her, his pulse quickening. Was she going to beat him to it? "Certainly—if you call me Jim."

She smiled. "All right, Jim. And you can call me Ashley."

"I'm honored, Ashley. Ask away."

"Well . . . I was wondering . . ." She took a calming breath, then girded herself. "Jim . . . Do you know if Leonard McCoy is seeing anyone?"

Kirk stared at her. Even as his hopes sank, he felt laughter at his own expense rise up and burst from him.

"What? What's so funny?"

He controlled himself. "Nothing. Sorry. I'm just . . . pleased on Doctor McCoy's behalf. He's very lucky to have such a re-markable woman interested in him."

"So is he available?"

"Oh, definitely. If you want to ask him out, I say go right ahead."

"Great! I'll do that." She clasped his hand warmly. "Thank you for everything. I appreciate your openness and your efforts on my behalf. I wish we could've come to a more satisfactory resolution."

Kirk raised his eyebrows wistfully. "So do I."

She gave him one last smile and headed off. He watched her go, letting out a heavy sigh and then a chuckle. It was a good feeling to turn the tables on Bones in the matchmaking game.

More seriously, though, he hoped it would work out for McCoy. As much as he would have liked to pursue something with Janith-Lau himself, he'd be content to see his old friend find happiness with her.

Chapter Seven

Starfleet Academy

Zirani Kayros frowned at Vekal in disbelief. "You're kidding," she said over the background chatter of voices in the dining hall. "Rakatheema didn't really say that, did he?"

"I was present at the time," the Vulcan youth replied. "The commander did indeed indicate that he was open to broadening the traditional role of the Warborn to include combat on behalf of the Federation as a whole."

Nearby, Targeemos shifted uneasily in her seat, glancing across the room at the tables where the Warborn sat, still keeping apart from the other students. "I can't believe that. It would defeat the whole purpose of them being here."

"Or perhaps you were misled about what that purpose was."

Next to Kayros, Michael Ashrafi smirked and peered at Vekal. "What were you even doing in a combat class? I thought you were this committed Vulcan pacifist."

Vekal narrowed his eyes in annoyance that was not as well contained as he probably thought it was. "The core curriculum is mandatory. Taking that course in my first semester happens to be part of the most efficient allocation of the core courses for my purposes."

"Nah—if you ask me, you wanted to keep watch on the big

Warborn and his scary lady friend. You've been giving them the evil eye from the start." Ashrafi chuckled. "Or maybe you're interested in Portia for another reason, huh?"

"I will not dignify that sophomoric insinuation with a reply."

"Sophomoric is next year. I'm just freshmanic." He shrugged. "And if I flunk my exams, I'll be freshmanic-depressive."

Vekal ignored him. "We should file a protest. Recruiting the Warborn to serve in combat is incompatible with Starfleet ethical principles. They should be expelled before this goes further."

"Hey!" Kayros protested. "Don't blame them for it. If Rakatheema does want that, it's on him."

"She's right," Targeemos said. "This is meant to be for their benefit, to offer them a constructive role. At least that's how Rakatheema sold it to the public back home. We wouldn't have agreed to it otherwise."

Kayros stood. "In which case, I say we go over and hear their side. This is about their future, so their opinions matter more than ours."

Vekal was skeptical. "They will follow where they are ordered to go. That is their conditioning."

"You assume. Where's the logic in refusing to find out?"

Not waiting for his reply, the Tiburonian cadet strode over to the Warborn's tables, ignoring the stares that followed her. Ashrafi hopped up from his seat and tagged along behind her, and Vekal grudgingly followed a moment later. Targeemos stayed in her seat. Kayros was aware that she preferred to avoid the Warborn, for their existence reminded her of uncomfortable truths of her people's history.

The youthful-seeming Warborn, Benedick, rose to greet Kayros with a smile, seeming oblivious to the surrounding tension. "Zirani! Good. I was hoping you could go over my physics notes with me." He greeted the others amiably as well. "Michael. Vekal."

Portia sized Kayros up with a clinical gaze. "She's not here for a study session, Benedick. She's here for the same reason as everyone else."

Horatio, who seemed to have appointed himself the leader of the group, stood as well, taking a mediating pose between the groups. "I understand that many of the students have concerns about the dialogue last night between Commander Rakatheema and Doctor Janith-Lau. I'm happy to help assuage your concerns."

Vekal raised a skeptical brow. "So Rakatheema did *not* say he was open to a combat role for the Warborn?"

Portia scoffed. "Of course he did. He's just like all the other Arcturians—they made us to fight and die so they don't have to."

The Vulcan's confrontational gaze shifted to her. "You sounded perfectly willing to go along with that yesterday."

"I'm willing to fight—but for *my* reasons." Her tone sharpened as her eyes held Vekal's. "I'm done being defined by others—the commander *or* you. We have a right to define our own path."

"I don't know." The big one, Bertram, looked upset and confused. "How could we know better than our makers? We're their tools. They made us to fight for the motherworld. That's as valid a reason to exist as any." He shook his head. "All the rest . . . We shouldn't even be here. This isn't our purpose."

Horatio put a hand on his burly shoulder. "It *is* our purpose to protect Arcturus. From ourselves, if necessary. That is why we are here."

He turned to take in Portia and Vekal, who still faced off tensely. "I'm sure Commander Rakatheema didn't mean what either of you imagined. From the start, he's only had the best interests of the Arcturian people in mind—the Warborn included."

"Has he told you that?" Kayros asked. "Or are you making assumptions the same as the rest of us?"

"I have faith in his commitment to our principles, and to our welfare. Remember, we have known him much longer than you have. He has guided us through this process from the start. I know where he stands."

Vekal looked the others over. "Not all of you agree with that assessment, however."

Horatio smiled. "I'm sure we will all find common ground and understanding in time. That is what Starfleet is all about, after all."

Neither Vekal nor Portia seemed mollified by his diplomatic efforts. Deciding there was no point in further confrontation, Kayros sighed and grabbed Benedick's arm. "Come on, kid. Let's go review those physics notes."

"Gladly!" Benedick deftly snatched up his data slate while allowing himself to be led away from the table. "I've been following up on the discussion we had in class about the vacuum flares. I'm still confused about how quantum fluctuations work. I'd love to hear more from someone who witnessed the very first documented flare."

Oh, boy. Kayros wondered what she'd let herself in for. "Witnessed" was an overly mild word for that harrowing experience. She'd be perfectly happy if she never had to think about a vacuum flare again.

Midoren City, Denobula
Iota Boötis system

Daibak-oortann-daruum had always been fond of offworlders. His mother, Vaneel, and his first-tier grandfather, Phlox, had raised him with an appreciation of diversity and a fascination for exotic cultures and points of view. Daibak had not inherited their wanderlust—the desire to leave the homeworld was a rare trait among Denobulans—but luckily, he had lived most of his hundred and two years in a time when Denobula had been a member of the Federation and a welcoming port for travelers from dozens of different species.

Most of those species were unlike Denobulans in that they needed to sleep during the night. Which meant they needed a regular place to stay while on-planet. Hotels for offworlders, equipped with the beds, hammocks, nests, or other sleeping facilities that they required on a regular basis, had been a lucrative industry even before Federation membership, and xenophiles like Daibak were a natural fit for it. The mature, pale-haired, round-bodied Denobulan had been one of the more successful hoteliers in Midoren City for several decades, and he had generally found it an enjoyable, educational profession.

Part of the charm, though, was that most visitors stayed only a few days or weeks at a time, long enough that the novelty of their company didn't wear off, and that they stayed by choice, as interested in what Denobula had to offer as Daibak was in the stories they had to tell. These past two days, things had been different. Starfleet had somehow managed to predict that Denobula was the next probable target for the space storms they were calling vacuum flares, and so the planetary government had imposed a no-fly order, grounding all nonessential space travel within the system. Not only had the hotel's guests been forced to prolong their stays, but a number of other itinerant travelers had found themselves unexpectedly in need of rooms, filling the hotel nearly to capacity and putting an unexpected demand on its staff and resources.

Still, Daibak was trying to make the best of the situation, reassuring the nervous or impatient guests that they shouldn't have long to wait. Most of these flare events had been harmless, and they only seemed to strike each system once, so as soon as the current one was over, it would not come again. And they might get a marvelous fireworks display out of it if the flares came close enough.

So it was that Daibak was hosting a stargazing party on the

roof of the hotel. Midoren was one of the younger, smaller cities in the interior of Denobula's single vast continent, on the fringes of the enormous desert at its heart, so it suffered less from light pollution than the vast, never-sleeping capital of Gronim City. At this time of year, when the distant but bright companion star of Denobula's sun was absent from the nighttime sky, you could get a fine view of the galaxy at night when the weather was clear (as it usually was this far into the interior). Right now it was only a couple of hours past dusk, not yet prime stargazing time, but Denobulan nights were long, so there was plenty of time. Daibak was happy to keep the party going for as long as it took.

"Hey." Daibak tapped Orat, the young concierge, on the shoulder as he passed by. "They collide without making a sound, and never break no matter how often they collide. What are they?"

Orat sighed. "You already did that one. It's your eyelids."

"Oh. Really? Oh, well." He thought for a moment. "They always look down when moving forward—"

"Your nostrils."

Daibak sighed. "It's this lockdown. No new guests, no new inspiration."

"Or you just ran out of body parts."

"Not *all* my riddles are about body parts."

"But too few are about the interesting ones."

Daibak scowled at Orat's sly grin. "Oh, go refill the ice buckets."

A minor outcry from the other side of the rooftop caught his attention. It was the Kanums, a monogamous Antaran couple on their honeymoon, pointing out to the sky above the desert that stretched beyond the city edge. Following their gestures, Daibak spotted an effervescent flicker of light over the horizon. He followed the other guests as they congregated around the Kanums to ooh and aah at the sight. Even Daibak, who had seen plenty in his life despite not traveling far from home, was impressed by how close and vivid the flickers appeared for something far out in space.

But as successive clusters of flashing pinpoints came and went, as the phenomenon rose higher in the night sky, the flickers seemed to draw even closer, growing more painfully bright. Daibak imagined he could almost hear a distant rumbling, as if they were a thunderstorm over the horizon. It had to be his imagination, surely. Even a lifelong planet-lubber like him knew that sound didn't travel through space.

Then the rumbling became clearer, louder. It was more than a sound—the ground was trembling. Still the intermittent clusters of pinpoint flashes grew nearer and brighter, spread higher and wider across the sky.

Then they erupted out of the desert sands with geyser-like columns of vapor. The Kanums screamed. They weren't the only ones. Daibak realized the lights weren't just rising from behind the curve of the planet—they were rising *out of* the planet itself!

And they were spreading out to engulf the whole city.

The crowd's paralysis at the inconceivable sight finally broke as the crackling thunderclaps grew ever louder and nearer. The quaking of the ground grew worse, and a hot wind began to blow across the rooftop. Tenants pushed each other aside in their rush for the stairwell, and Daibak called out, urging them to stay calm and lie flat on the roof.

But few of the guests listened, instead crowding against the stairwell door and trying in vain to force their way inside. When Daibak tried to intervene bodily and drag them apart, he ended up succumbing to the press of bodies, falling to the roof beneath the feet of the panicked crowd.

After what seemed like ages, a strong hand caught his arm and pulled him free. He looked up to see Orat staring at him solicitously. "Are you all right, boss?"

"Oh, Orat, thank you! I promise, I'll never tell another riddle."

"We've got to get away!"

"No, we've got to get through to them before they crush each other to death! They're our guests, our responsibi—"

Then the entire rooftop bucked, and he was almost blinded as a surge of lightning-bright pinpoint bursts rose straight up through the roof.

U.S.S. *Reliant*
Orbiting Denobula

"The flare's coming *out* of the planet?" Captain Terrell cried in disbelief.

Pavel Chekov looked up at the bigger man who loomed over the science station. "It emerged inside the planet, yes, sir," he said. "The planet's orbital motion is carrying it past the emergence zone. It should be clear within a few minutes."

"But what's it doing to the planet in the meantime?"

"The micro-wormholes are quite small, sir. The energy they release is intense, but brief." Chekov studied his scans. "There are some seismic and meteorological disruptions, but mostly in the uninhabited interior. Luckily most of the population is concentrated around the capital region, well away from the affected area."

"I don't understand," said Rem Azem-Os. The Aurelian flexed her wings as she stood behind the vacant command chair. "I thought the vacuum flares centered around the positions the planets occupied in the past."

"Relative to their stars' positions, yes," Chekov said, "with a degree of uncertainty. But it's been almost exactly twenty-eight Denobulan years since the *Enterprise*'s visit, so the planet's roughly back in the same spot. Or close enough to fall within the margin of—"

He broke off at an alarm from his console. "*Bozhe moi.* There's a small city, Midoren, on the edge of the emergence area. One of the wormhole clusters has passed through it!"

"Damage?" Terrell asked.

Chekov tightened the scan, adjusting the frequencies and detection protocols. "Extensive disruption to the power grid. Electrical discharges and blowouts. Vehicle crashes. It's night there, but Denobulans rarely sleep." He looked up at Terrell. "A few building collapses. The wormholes must have caused structural damage, or the thermal shock to the atmosphere may have—"

"It doesn't matter why," Azem-Os interrupted. "We need to help those people. Can we transport the injured?"

"There's heavy interference," Chekov told her. "We'd have to get within . . . approximately eight hundred kilometers."

The Aurelian stepped forward to the helm station and leaned over Beach. "Stoney, can you get us in closer?"

"Up to a point, Commander, but there's no predicting where a new surge might pop up."

"That's a risk we have to take," Terrell told him, backing up his first officer. "Just stay alert." He descended to his command chair and activated the comm switch. "Terrell to sickbay. Doctor Wilder, stand by to receive casualties. And we're going to need medical and rescue teams on the ground."

While the captain coordinated with sickbay, Chekov studied the worrying seismic readings from Midoren. A thought struck him, and he ran some quick computations to support it. Once the captain was done speaking, he called out across the bridge to the weapons station. "Nizhoni! I think we can damp the ground tremors with a tractor beam. I'm sending the parameters to gravity control, but you'll need to ride them manually."

"On it," the long-haired tactical officer said, crossing the front of the bridge to the stand-up gravity control station just starboard of the main viewscreen. Within moments, she had locked *Reliant*'s powerful tractor beams onto the surface near Midoren, spreading out their focus and fine-tuning their gravitational energies to damp the tremors endangering the city. Chekov saw her smile, and as a former tactical officer himself, he understood her pleasure at being able to use her targeting skills to protect lives rather than take them.

"In transporter range," Beach called out.

"Transporter rooms report evac underway," Kyle announced a moment later.

Terrell's eyes were on the vast field of quantum fireworks that filled the space above the planet surface. "I don't like being this close to that thing. The faster we get those people out, the better."

"The planet should be clear of the effect in another minute or so," Chekov said. "Barring aftershocks, we'll be able to focus on putting out the fires in its wake—literal or otherwise."

"It's lucky it didn't hit the main population center," Terrell said. "Nearly twelve billion people packed over such a small percentage of the planet."

"If anything, Captain," Chekov replied, "it's very *un*lucky that it hit a populated area at all, with most of the planet's surface being empty. Not to mention all the volume of space around the planet where it could've—"

The alert klaxon sounded. "New surge, directly below us!" Beach called.

"Evasive!" Terrell barely had time to get the word out before the microflares penetrated the ship. The lights flickered and consoles sparked, and a clatter of loud bangs went off inside the bridge like firecrackers as the tiny but ultrahot pinpoints flash-heated the air like lightning bolts.

Chekov screamed as a microflare passed through his right shoulder. Through the agony, he vaguely noticed a number of the science station's displays and control panels sputtering and blowing out. A keening eagle cry pierced his already ringing and popping ears, and he realized Azem-Os must have been hit as well.

It took a few moments for Chekov to rally his focus through

the pain. Fortunately—or unfortunately—he was no stranger to dealing with pain and injury. Sulu and Uhura joked that he was the unluckiest man in Starfleet, getting injured with alarming frequency—though he countered that the unlucky ones were those who didn't survive. He wasn't sure he agreed with the saying that the things that didn't kill him made him stronger. But at least they no longer surprised or overwhelmed him.

Still, he found himself wishing for a Deltan empath to ease his pain right around now.

Once he refocused outside himself, he found the bridge in a sorry state, ruddy under the emergency lighting, with multiple holes burned in various surfaces and the majority of the consoles damaged or inoperable. Azem-Os's left wing hung limp from her back as she struggled to raise herself from a crouch, while Terrell comforted her and tried to keep her from overstraining herself.

Still, the captain's primary focus was on the viewscreen, which was awash with static, but in its clearer moments showed the planet surface drawing closer than it should. Chekov should have seen that coming. *Reliant* had been keeping station above Midoren at well below synchronous orbit, so with propulsion no doubt disrupted by the flare impact, they were moving too slowly to maintain altitude.

"Beach, stabilize our orbit!" Terrell called, clearly recognizing the same thing.

"Impulse engines won't respond, sir! Trying to reroute!"

"Thrusters?"

"Partial thrusters only."

"Use the gyros, then. Try to get our nose up. Skip off the atmosphere like a stone."

Beach stared. "You sure, sir?"

Terrell grinned and clapped his shoulder. "We had a few memorable crashes on the *Sagittarius*. I've thought about this kind of thing a lot."

"If you say so, Captain. Computing new attitude."

The ship began to judder as it passed through density variations in the thin outer atmosphere at high speed. Then it jostled sharply as it made its first "skip." Chekov was knocked sideways, and the pain in his shoulder blacked him out for a moment. His perceptions were a blur of noise, jostling, and shouting voices, and he wondered if his luck had finally run out.

Chekov awoke to find himself on a couch in the officers' lounge. Turning his head gingerly, he saw Azem-Os and the navigator, Ensign Sarhin, on adjacent couches. Azem-Os's wing had been treated and placed in a sling, and a nurse was tending to Sarhin's burned thigh. Chekov looked down at his shoulder to see it had already been treated and dressed.

He spotted Captain Terrell standing nearby. "Captain . . . ?"

The big bearded man moved toward him and helped him sit up. "It's okay, Pavel. Obviously we made it. But sickbay's full of evacuees from Midoren. Plus we're closer to the bridge here."

"Casualties?"

"Up here, twenty-seven injured, but we didn't lose anyone. Down there, our team and the Denobulan authorities are still searching, but there are dozens of dead already accounted for."

Chekov grimaced. "Is *Reliant* in any condition to help them?"

The captain offered a reassuring smile. "I think you already helped a lot with that tractor beam idea. It could've been a lot worse. Midoren isn't in an earthquake zone, so the buildings weren't designed to handle them.

"On the other hand, since Denobulans rarely sleep, most of them don't have permanent homes, so at any given time you'll find more of them outdoors than on most planets, even at night. That kept the toll from being higher." He tilted his head. "You might be interested to know that one of the people we rescued is the grandson of Doctor Phlox, the CMO of Jonathan Archer's

Enterprise. He was very concerned about the guests and staff in his hotel. Luckily, we managed to rescue them all, and he's down in sickbay now, regaling them all with riddles. But others weren't so lucky," he finished with a heavy sigh.

Chekov was too worried to appreciate the historical trivia. "I feel so useless. We finally know where the flares will strike next, but have no way to prevent or contain them. And they keep getting bigger and more destructive."

Terrell grew somber. "Well, I'm afraid *Reliant* is out of the game, Pavel. We took heavy damage. It'll take weeks in dry dock to get us back in action."

"Damn. We've been tracking this from the beginning. We can't be taken out now."

The captain sat down next to him. "I've been thinking about that. We know these things are connected somehow to Federation or allied planets the *Enterprise* has visited."

"Yes?"

"Well, think about it, Pav. If you trace the *Enterprise*'s course back far enough, where will the trail eventually, inevitably, end up?"

Chekov's eyes widened. "Earth."

"Earth."

"We need to get back there."

Terrell tugged on the hem of his uniform jacket. "*Reliant*'s going to be under repairs here for some time. I need to stay with my ship, and to help with relief efforts. But this is your baby, Pavel. I'm willing to authorize your temporary transfer back to Starfleet Command on Earth, if that's where you feel you need to be."

Chekov smiled at him. "Yes, sir. Thank you, sir."

The captain grimaced. "Don't thank me. If there's one thing we learned today, it's what can happen when you deliberately head *toward* one of these things."

Chapter Eight

U.S.S. *Enterprise*

"Captain on the bridge!"

As Spock stepped out of the turbolift alcove, he turned to Cadet Marar Ferat, who had announced him from the communications station. "At ease, Cadet. For future reference, that ritual is not required aboard the *Enterprise*. I am aware that some commanding officers prefer it, but I have always found it redundant. If bridge personnel are properly alert, they may discern for themselves whether or not I am present. And I expect all bridge personnel to comport themselves with equal professionalism in either circumstance."

The curly-haired Cygnian flushed in abashment. "Aye, Captain Spock. Understood."

Lieutenant Ledoux rose from the captain's chair as Spock approached. "I relieve you, Lieutenant."

The dark-complexioned woman, a veteran of the *Enterprise* crew from its second five-year tour, nodded. "I stand relieved."

Spock took her report, then circled the outer deck of the bridge, checking the performance of the cadet crew one by one. Pryce-Jones at engineering, Suarez at tactical, and Nadel at sciences gave their reports crisply and efficiently, though they had little to report beyond the commonplace routine of a starship in the second day of a four-day journey.

When he reached the helm console, however, he frowned at the readouts and addressed Cadet T'Lara. "Warp velocity has diminished by zero point eight percent relative to power expenditure."

The young Vulcan woman looked up at him calmly. "I am aware of the discrepancy, sir. Our course is transverse to a subspace gradient. Maintaining course against its pull requires diverting a portion of warp power."

The problem was commonplace enough; a human would probably analogize it to crossing a river perpendicular to its current and being pushed downstream. But T'Lara's response to the problem provoked a raised eyebrow. "I see. As I recall, you studied helm operations under Lieutenant Commander Grodnick. Correct?"

"Affirmative, sir."

"Had you studied under Commander Sulu, he would most likely have informed you of a more efficient method of compensating for such a gradient. Adjust the relative timing of the warp nacelles in proportion to the fourth root of the displacement rate, with the bias in favor of the nacelle opposite the direction of the gradient. This will cancel the lateral displacement with no added power demand."

T'Lara raised both her brows. "Understood, sir. An elegant solution. Why is it not in the standard texts?"

"Perhaps because Commander Sulu has not yet written one. However, I shall speak to Professor Grodnick upon our return. Carry on, Cadet."

Before Spock could take the command chair, Ferat spoke up. "Captain Spock? Priority transmission from Admiral Cartwright of Starfleet Security."

Spock nodded. He had expected such a call for the past hour, since the news of the destruction on Denobula reached the *Enterprise*. "Have it relayed to my quarters. Lieutenant Ledoux, you have the bridge."

Once seated at the desk in his quarters, Spock leaned back and steepled his fingers as Cartwright's stern features appeared on his screen. *"Captain Spock."*

"Admiral Cartwright. I believe I already know why you have contacted me."

The admiral glowered. *"Why don't you tell me, then, Captain?"*

"No doubt Starfleet Security has arrived at the same conclusions I have regarding the possible correlation of vacuum flare outbreaks to locations visited by *Enterprise* crew members during shore visits. As only two members of the *Enterprise* crew from the period in question are aboard the *Asimov . . ."*

Cartwright nodded. *"We suspected it had something to do with Nyota Uhura. What just happened at Denobula clinches it. Only she was present at every location struck so far, and in reverse order."*

"Indeed." Spock recalled the *Enterprise*'s visit to Denobula Triaxa, which had occurred late in Christopher Pike's tenure as captain. It had been a period of rest and recuperation for the crew after a turbulent mission, taking advantage of Denobula's advanced medical facilities as well as their extensive leave facilities. Though most Denobulans preferred not to travel beyond their world, their society was unfailingly welcoming to visitors.

"I understand why you and Admiral Kirk were hesitant to bring her name into this without solid evidence. But over a hundred people died at Denobula, Spock. This is no natural phenomenon—this is a targeted, ongoing attack on Federation worlds. And Commander Uhura is involved somehow."

"Admiral, I have known Commander Uhura for the vast majority of her Starfleet career. I can state with confidence that the probability of the commander having any voluntary involvement with any force or entity hostile to Federation security is effectively zero."

"*Spock, you'd be surprised how many times I've heard that from the friends and colleagues of people who turned out to be enemy agents. Or at least assets, through extortion or neural conditioning. It's possible that the side Uhura presents to the public is not her true face.*"

"It is premature to derive that conclusion from the available evidence, sir."

"*Don't give me the Vulcan runaround, Spock! You're trying to protect a friend, the same as anyone else would.*"

"I assure you, Admiral, I am able to retain my objectivity. I will follow the evidence where it leads—but as yet, we have too little evidence to act upon."

Cartwright reined in his temper. "*Which is why your orders are to bring Nyota Uhura back to Earth for questioning. We need to find out everything she knows, whether she's an active part of this or an unwilling dupe.*"

"Or to clear her if the correlation is determined to be spurious."

"*Yes, yes, of course. All we want is to get to the truth.*"

Spock raised a brow. "In that case, Admiral, you and I are already committed to the same goal. If that is all, sir?"

The admiral glared. "*You have your orders, Captain. Starfleet out.*"

Golden Gate Park
San Francisco

Leonard McCoy frowned on Ashley Janith-Lau's behalf as the two of them strolled together in the park. "It sounds like your Academy visit didn't ease your concerns."

The activist doctor sighed, watching a group of children run past in the middle distance. It was a warm, clear Saturday afternoon, the first chance she and McCoy had gotten to touch base since her visit. "In some ways it did. Most of the Warborn seem genuinely committed to the goal of finding a peaceful purpose."

"But in other ways?"

"I'm more concerned than ever that Starfleet could succumb to the temptation to use them as soldiers. Commander Rakatheema as good as said he was hoping for that." Her lips narrowed. "As for Jim Kirk, I'm not sure which side of the question he's on. Though I give him credit for listening with an open mind."

McCoy smiled at her. "So . . . you're calling him Jim now, eh?"

She smiled back, a bit quizzically. "Sure. That's what you do when you make friends with someone."

His face sank. "Just friends?"

"What else would you expect? I mean, heaven knows, the man has a reputation, and I can see why women fall for him. But come on, did you seriously imagine I'd ever pair off with a military man?"

"Oh." He furrowed his brow. "I guess I've gotten so used to associating with Starfleet people that it didn't occur to me."

Janith-Lau finally registered his disappointment. "You were *hoping* something would happen! Is that why you set up our meeting? Some kind of matchmaking ploy?"

McCoy cleared his throat. "I set it up because Jim asked me to, like I told you. But, well . . . Jim's a lonely man. And you're quite the catch, my dear. You can't blame me for hoping two of my friends could find happiness together."

She stared at him. "Really. Is that why you haven't made a play for me yourself?"

He stared back, stunned into silence. "W-well," he finally stammered, "I'm certainly not the type to poach on another man's . . . I mean . . ."

Janith-Lau scoffed, arms akimbo. " 'Poach'? What is this, Capella IV? I'm not a possession, Leonard."

"No, of course not. That's not what I . . ." He sighed. "I'm sorry. That was a stupid thing for me to say. I just meant that I wanted Jim to have a shot at being happy."

She relaxed and gave him a beautiful smile. "You know what? Jim said something very similar about you." Her expression sharpened again. "And he was rather quicker to accept that I had a say in the matter."

McCoy didn't trust himself to reply. He was feeling lost. Was she angry at him or flirting with him? "I . . . thought you weren't interested in military men."

Her head tilted in confusion. "Then why did you think I'd be interested in Jim?"

"Well . . . because he's Jim! I don't know. Maybe I figured he could win you over. I never expected you to make the first move. Least of all with me."

She stepped closer. "You, Leonard McCoy, are the least military Starfleet officer I've ever met. You're a healer, a man of great compassion. The fact that you tolerate being in Starfleet at all is my greatest source of reassurance about its intentions." She smirked. "Even if you do act like a relic of a less enlightened age sometimes."

"I do fancy myself an old-fashioned gentleman," he admitted. "But that means always letting a lady set her own pace. So . . . what *would* your say in the matter be, Doctor?"

Her features became more approving. "I say I know an excellent vegetarian restaurant in the Mission District, and I'd like to take you to dinner there tonight. Are you game?"

The first thing he thought to say was *If I wanted a vegetarian meal, I'd go to dinner with Spock.* The second thing he thought, mercifully, was *What the hell are you thinking? Say yes!*

He gave her a courtly smile and bow. "I would be honored, my dear."

McCoy began to wonder why he'd devoted so much of his attention lately to Kirk's romantic life instead of his own. Perhaps, given his record of failed relationships, he'd assumed he was a lost cause.

Yet now that he finally saw what was in Ashley Janith-Lau's eyes as she looked at him, he felt renewed hope that maybe he was worth pursuing after all.

U.S.S. *Asimov*

When Captain Spock had come aboard the *Asimov* and requested to speak to Nyota Uhura in private, Montgomery Scott had insisted on joining them, his manner making it clear that he would not take no for an answer. After Denobula, Uhura had told him of her concerns, and he was determined to stand in support of her. In a way, he was the only one who could understand, so she was grateful for his presence. Fortunately, Spock had become much more accepting of the human need for such sentimental connections in the years since his encounter with V'Ger.

Captain Blake also insisted on being present, as was her prerogative as Uhura's current commanding officer. As soon as the four of them had taken their seats around the table in the *Asimov*'s briefing room, Uhura spoke. "You must have figured out the same thing I did, Captain Spock—that the one thing connecting every system struck by a vacuum flare is me."

Spock replied slowly. "So it would appear. The correlation has been consistent enough that it is unlikely to be coincidental."

She smiled wistfully at his reluctance to commit, knowing it was a wasted effort. "It isn't, Spock. There's one more connection that I suppose you haven't found yet. It was actually my first clue.

"At first, I was sure I had to be imagining it. That my mind was projecting something onto the data that wasn't there. When I kept getting the same result, I wondered if I was going mad."

Blake's bright eyes studied her intently. "Commander?"

"Here, I'll show you." Uhura moved to the wall screen, working its controls to tie into her personal database. "It started a couple of weeks ago. It occurred to me on an impulse—at least, I thought it was an impulse—to analyze the gravitic and radiometric output of the vacuum flares as if they were acoustical or musical patterns. I thought it might help me tease out some kind of harmonics or structure that could give insight into their origin. But when I tried to match the results to known patterns . . . well, I got more than I bargained for."

She called up two graphics on the screen. "The graph on the left is the harmonic analysis of the vacuum flare event we observed at Deneva. The patterns I could reconstruct out of its noise were fragmentary, scattered . . . but they showed a statistically relevant correlation with the wave pattern you see on the right."

Spock frowned as he studied the indicated wave function. "It appears to be the audiospectrogram of a humanoid voice."

"Not just any voice, Captain." She activated the playback.

"It seems like we've known each other forever / It feels like a billion years and a day . . ."

"My God," Blake said. "That's *your* voice!"

Uhura halted the playback. Spock appeared astonished, his eyebrows climbing toward the sharp edge of his bangs. Scott, whom she had already told, merely furrowed his brow and shook his head in confusion.

"I compared the other flare signatures against my singing too. The echoes are fragmentary at best, massively distorted and rearranged, but it's the same in every case: the one pattern to which they all show a statistical similarity is my own singing voice."

"It's incredible," Blake said.

"I couldn't believe it either," Uhura said. "But it led me to check the records, to confirm that I had taken leave at every one of those ports of call."

The *Asimov's* captain leaned forward. "So . . . what did you do on those leaves?"

Uhura traded a look with her former *Enterprise* crewmates. "I . . . don't know."

Spock leaned back. "Of course. Every incident was prior to our encounter with . . ."

"With *Nomad*," Uhura confirmed, appreciating his reluctance to say the name in her and Scott's presence.

"*Nomad*?" Blake asked.

Spock fielded the question. "On approximately stardate 3450 local time, all life in the Malurian star system was exterminated. Upon investigating shortly thereafter, the *Enterprise* encountered a small but immensely powerful robotic space probe calling itself *Nomad*."

"Like the one launched from Earth in the early twenty-first century?"

"It was, in fact, that very probe. Or rather, a hybrid of that probe and an alien probe with which it had collided and somehow fused. That probe, known as *Tan Ru*, had been programmed to collect and sterilize soil samples, for unknown purposes." Spock frowned. "It seems unlikely that such a mundane mission was its entire purpose, for it possessed truly extraordinary power and sophistication, far beyond anything we possess. However, that was the portion of its mission profile that survived the collision, and that somehow became blended with *Nomad's* programming to seek out alien life."

"Seek out life . . . and sterilize," Blake deduced.

"Yes. The hybrid probe's damaged logic compelled it to exterminate any life it deemed imperfect—which was all life."

"And one probe destroyed Maluria? All four planets?"

Scott finally spoke. "Aye, Captain. That wee floating toolbox wasn't much to look at, but it packed an incredible punch. I would've given anything to crack it open and see what powered it, if it hadn't been a bloody damned mass murderer. If it hadn't . . ." He fidgeted.

Blake looked puzzled. "I remember hearing about the Malurian extinction . . . but I don't recall any connection to the *Nomad* probe."

Spock steepled his fingers. "That aspect of the event was classified. Starfleet and the Federation Council agreed that the involvement of an Earth probe in the annihilation of four planets should not be publicized, lest the facts be . . . misunderstood."

"Okay, I get that part. But how did the *Enterprise* ever survive an encounter with a planet-killer like that?" Blake asked.

"Through a bad pun," Uhura said, not laughing.

"Excuse me?"

"*Nomad*'s creator was Jackson Roykirk. When the hybrid probe heard the name 'Captain James Kirk' in our hails, something clicked in its damaged memory."

"That's . . . odd. Why would a space probe be programmed to know the *sound* of its creator's name?"

"Roykirk was an eccentric and arrogant inventor," Spock explained. "He followed the precedent of the earlier *Voyager* probe series and included a digital recording extending greetings to extraterrestrial life and information about the probe's planet of origin. Due to his vanity, Roykirk recorded the message personally, repeatedly emphasizing his name and his role in the probe's creation. Evidently *Tan Ru* retained enough intelligence after the collision to interpret what remained of this recording."

"That's all beside the point," Scott interrupted. "Begging your pardon, sirs. What matters is, that thing's addled brain decided Captain Kirk was its creator and had to be obeyed. At least until it decided it didn't fancy his orders and started going where it liked on the ship."

"It found me on the bridge," Uhura said. "I was singing to

myself, and it couldn't understand the purpose of music. It . . . probed my mind. Scotty . . ." She reached over and clasped the engineer's hand. "He tried to protect me, and it . . . killed him."

Blake's expression was growing exasperated, as if she were tired of being surprised. Scott shrugged. "It didn't stick."

"To be precise," Spock explained, "*Nomad* possessed sufficiently sophisticated matter reconstruction capability to restore Mister Scott's damaged organs and restart his life processes. Fortunately he was revived in time to prevent the onset of neurological damage." The Vulcan captain's lips narrowed. "However, Ms. Uhura was not so fortunate."

Uhura sighed. "*Nomad* didn't just read my memory—it wiped it. The scanning beam it used was so intense that it disrupted my memory pathways. I suffered near-total amnesia, losing all my episodic and autobiographical memory, and all but my deepest, earliest semantic memories. I remembered Swahili, but not English. I knew how to walk, to feed and dress myself, even how to work a computer, after a little prompting; the procedural memory was still there. But I didn't recognize my crewmates or remember any of my past experiences."

"My God," Blake sighed. "Couldn't *Nomad* replace what it took?"

"It claimed it could not," Spock said. "I would surmise that, as it considered the data it extracted from Uhura's mind to be imperfect and irrelevant, it simply . . . erased it from its own memory."

"I had to be re-educated," Uhura said. "Doctor McCoy and Christine Chapel used Arcturian quick-learning techniques to bring me back up to speed on English, Starfleet procedures, and so on. It helped that . . ." She let out a small, bitter laugh at the irony. "I have an eidetic memory. I only needed to relearn everything once. I was back on duty within two weeks."

Blake frowned. "I understand that on a frontier mission like the *Enterprise*'s, you don't always have the luxury to put off injured crew at a starbase for recuperation. Still, after an ordeal like that, it seems it would've been kinder to let you go home. Rebuild your connections to your past."

"I was given the option," Uhura told her. "But to me, that past didn't exist anymore. All I knew about my life started at the moment I woke up after *Nomad* attacked me. The *Enterprise* was the only home I knew, its crew my only family. It was the only place I felt safe."

"You must have tried to reconstruct your past before then. You must have had personal logs, family correspondence, albums . . ."

"With my eidetic memory, I barely needed them. I searched voraciously through what logs I had, but they were superficial. So much in them was left implicit, because I assumed I'd always remember the things I alluded to. Without those memories, I couldn't piece together what I was talking about."

"All the more reason to go home. Talk to your family and friends, let them remind you."

Uhura blinked away a tear. "I couldn't. I just couldn't.

"You see, what *Nomad* couldn't erase were my feelings. When I thought about my family, when I looked at their faces in old holos, I still remembered loving them. I remembered joy and hilarity and pain and frustration, everything you feel for your family . . . but I couldn't remember *why* I felt those things. I couldn't remember the time we shared, not a single thing we ever did together. I didn't even consciously recognize their faces! I just knew they provoked an emotional response, one I had no context for."

She turned away, unable to face the others' sympathetic gazes. After a moment, she went on speaking. "To put my family through that . . . to go home to them and demand that they give me back my life, when I could give them nothing in return . . . it would have hurt them too much. I couldn't bring myself to face them, not like that.

"So instead, I focused on the family I knew. My crewmates

on the *Enterprise*. They were my whole life now, and I embraced them more than ever before. I built a new life with them, a good life . . . and I kept up a brave front and gave as little thought as possible to the person I'd been before."

When she turned back, she saw tears glistening in Blake's bright eyes. Spock and Scott both looked somber and respectful, though there was deeper emotion smoldering beneath Scott's avuncular features.

"Which creates a problem for us now," Uhura said. "Because whatever it was I did on those shore leaves—whatever I might have done that triggered or attracted these vacuum flares—I have no way of remembering or reconstructing it. Whatever it was, I forgot about it after *Nomad* and haven't done it since. Which must be why the earliest event was at Argelius. That was the last leave I took before Maluria."

Spock furrowed his brow. "If we presume you engaged in a consistent, repeated activity that connects in some way to the flares, then it follows that you were pursuing some project over a considerable span of time—at least two point four standard years. In that time, you must have spoken to someone about it."

"But if I'd told any of my crewmates, Captain Spock, they surely would have reminded me long ago. For some reason, I kept it secret for all that time." She kneaded her hands. "Which, admittedly, does not look good for me. I can't blame Starfleet Security for wanting to question me. I just wish I had something to tell them."

"Perhaps," Spock said, rising, "we will be able to formulate a hypothesis by the time we return to Earth. For now, Captain Blake, I hereby request permission to transfer Commander Uhura to the *Enterprise*."

Blake shrugged. "It's Starfleet Security's orders, Captain Spock. Of course I have to grant your request."

Scott rose as well. "Captain . . . Captains . . . request permission to accompany Uhura to Earth."

Uhura turned to him in surprise. "Scotty, that's not necessary. You have nothing to do with this."

"Yes," Blake said, "and it's bad enough I have to give up my science officer without losing my chief engineer too."

"I'm sorry, Captain, but . . ." Scott turned to Uhura. "Lass . . . I never knew you carried so much pain—so much loss from what that metal monstrosity did to you. You bounced back from it so well. You seemed so strong, so content."

She gave him a wistful smile. "I was—so long as I focused on the present, instead of what I'd lost."

"Still, I should've realized. If I'd paid more attention . . . I mean, we were the only two survivors of *Nomad*. I thought we were both the lucky ones—we got to be put back together, not like the Malurians or the four good security men it vaporized without a thought. But I was wrong. I got back everything I lost, but you . . . Oh, lass, I just didn't think about it. I was too caught up in my own nightmares about that dark day, my own stubborn pride pretending I was fine."

She clasped his hand again. "I can't blame you for trying to put it behind you, Scotty. I did the same."

"Aye, but now those times have come back to haunt us. Not *Nomad* itself, thank heaven, but some secret it took from you. I want to be there to help you figure all this out, lass—like I should've been back then."

"Oh, all right," Blake said after a moment, wiping away more tears. "Just go already, both of you. It's not good for a crew to see their captain get all blubbery."

Despite her words, she gave each commander a warm hug before letting them go. "Good luck, my friends. I really hope you find what you're looking for."

I do too, Uhura thought. *But first we have to figure out what that is.*

Chapter Nine

Starfleet Security Headquarters
San Francisco

"So you admit this doesn't look good for you, Commander."

Admiral Cartwright paced around the table in the sparse, windowless interview room. It was an intimidation tactic, but one that Uhura did not let herself be cowed by. Over her years as a starship communications officer, she'd been shouted at, browbeaten, and threatened by admirals, ambassadors, commissioners, warship commanders, planetary leaders, revolutionaries, pirate queens, and superbeings that defied classification. Cartwright had nothing to throw at her that she hadn't seen before. Still, she drew some comfort from Captain Spock's presence as he stood nearby, a pillar of stillness and serenity to counter the admiral's stormcloud intensity and thundering voice.

"I only acknowledge the truth, Admiral. And the truth is that I have no answers for you."

"But don't you see how that's suspicious in itself?" Cartwright took a breath and went on more reasonably. "Look. I don't question the reality of your memory loss. Your medical records provide ample confirmation. What's strange is the lack of any *other* evidence of your activities on those planets."

"We may make certain deductions, Admiral," Spock interposed. "The echoes of the commander's voice patterns in the vacuum fluctuations imply that she was undertaking some form of communications experiment. Perhaps she was studying a natural subspace phenomenon that reflected the vocal and musical patterns she transmitted."

"Or maybe," Cartwright countered, "she was in communication with some intelligence that's beaming her singing back as a reply."

"That cannot be ruled out, no. Neither can it be supported."

"That's the problem, Captain. A Starfleet communications officer conducting communications research on Federation worlds—why not do it in Starfleet facilities? There's nothing in her records suggesting she's ever conducted any research on vacuum fluctuations, micro-wormholes, quantum communication, or anything of the sort. Not using any Starfleet or official Federation resources, at least."

Cartwright turned back to Uhura. "Which means that whatever you were doing, Commander, it was on your own personal time, and you chose to conduct it at private, civilian research facilities."

"Which is within my rights, Admiral," she said. "Being in Starfleet doesn't prohibit having a life outside it."

The admiral leaned over her. "But you can't remember what that life was. Who were you back then, Nyota Uhura? Do you even know? Do you know what you believed? What you stood for?"

"*I* knew her at the time, Admiral," Spock pointed out. "I never found her to be less than an exemplary officer."

"But what about off duty? What about that life beyond Starfleet she just talked about? Did she ever reveal anything about that to you?"

"I respected her privacy. While she was outgoing and friendly toward her crewmates, she possessed a reserve regarding her personal life that, as a Vulcan, I understood and respected. She spoke freely of her family, evincing great pride in their accomplishments, but on the subject of her own off-duty activities, she was considerably more private. While she occasionally initiated interactions with me in a manner that my human colleagues perceived as flirtatious, I never took them to be seriously intended. After all, I was her superior officer."

Uhura blushed a bit. She had learned from the *Enterprise* crew about the teasing songs she'd infamously regaled Spock with in the rec room in those early years, and she preferred to think they had been the mere amusements that Spock had taken them to be. But how could she ever really know? How different a person had she been before *Nomad*?

"In any case," Spock went on, "she never gave me any reason to question her loyalties to the Federation or her commitment to Starfleet's principles. I would assess the probability of her voluntary participation in anything harmful to innocent lives as negligible."

"People can hide their true selves, Captain. Put on a façade for their crewmates to cover their true goals."

"Theoretically. However, Admiral, if you are proposing that Commander Uhura's younger self was complicit in some act of sabotage against the Federation, I would question why she would do so in a way that would take twelve to fourteen years to come to fruition."

Cartwright crossed his arms. "I've encountered spies and sleeper agents playing longer games than that."

Spock raised a brow. "Logically, any stratagem put into effect so far in advance would be meticulously planned and directed. It is inconsistent with the haphazard nature of the vacuum flares." He continued with what Uhura recognized as a hint of wry amusement. "Not to mention that any such devious spy or saboteur would surely take care *not* to encode her own voice in the disruptions."

The admiral hesitated, clearly unable to answer that. Uhura took the opportunity. "Permission to speak freely, Admiral?"

"That's what you're here for, Commander."

"Then with respect, sir, may we cut to the chase? I can hear in your voice that you don't actually believe I was some kind of saboteur or sleeper agent. You're flailing for answers like the rest of us. You fall back on interrogation tactics like these because it's what you know."

Not letting his glower affect her, she gestured at her longtime shipmate. "But Captain Spock here has been able to give you more answers about my activities and personality pre-*Nomad* than I have. If we want answers about my past, I'm clearly the wrong person to interview."

Uhura hesitated to follow that thought where it led. But Spock followed it through to its inevitable conclusion. "Logically, Admiral, we should consult with Ms. Uhura's former commanding officers and shipmates. Whatever it was she kept from the crew of the *Enterprise*, perhaps she was less inclined to conceal it from previous crewmates, or less successful at doing so."

There it was. The answer was obvious, but it was one she'd resisted for a dozen years now. She had always been too afraid of what she might find—or what pain she might cause.

While speaking to Uhura's former colleagues may have been the next logical step, the results proved that a logical process was only as good as the data fed into it. The interviews proved informative for Uhura, but not in the way Admiral Cartwright would have hoped.

"*No, Captain Spock, I don't remember Uhura doing any personal research projects off-ship,*" said Commander Vheman, a bronze-haired Arbazan woman who had been Uhura's bunkmate on the U.S.S. *Ahriman*, the *Saladin*-class scout that had been her first posting out of Starfleet Academy. On the viewer in the Starfleet Security communications room, Vheman chewed thoughtfully on one tip of her writing stylus. The mannerism seemed vaguely familiar to Uhura, though she couldn't be sure she didn't just *want* to find it familiar. "*Honestly, I don't see how she would've had the time. She was very dedicated to learning the ropes, as humans call it. Mastering her responsibilities, the ship's equipment and protocols, cross-training in science and naviga-tion.*" The commander shifted her gaze to Uhura and smiled. "*Your enthusiasm was stimulating, but it could be exhausting try-ing to keep up with you.*"

"Was I that buried in my work?"

"*Oh, no, Nyota. You and your keen memory—you were such a swift learner that you needed little time to study, so you were able to make plenty of time for me and our other friends. We were pretty inseparable that year on the Ahriman.*

"*That's why I can't see you having any chance to do any major research away from the ship. We generally spent our leave time together as a group—you, me, Tsukasa Komaki, and . . . oh, that Orion girl, what was her name?*" Uhura could only shrug. "*And we were pretty frank with each other about anything we did on our own, if you know what I mean.*

"*Oh, you weren't the type to keep secrets. You loved to talk about your family back home, your Academy friends . . . the only thing I ever knew you to be reticent about was your given name.*"

"My name?"

Vheman chuckled. "*You didn't like to share it with people until they earned your trust. Apparently you were afraid of being teased because it meant 'star' and you were in Starfleet. Also it annoyed you when people mispronounced it.*" The Arbazan shook her head. "*I can't believe you of all people lost your memory. I guess that's why we fell out of touch, huh?*"

Uhura winced. "I'm sorry. It was—"

"*Don't worry about it. People drift apart, even without such a good excuse.*"

Uhura's crewmates aboard her second starship posting, the *Azrael*, gave much the same answers. Yongnian Shen, the retired commodore who had been Uhura's commander during her stint in Starbase 32's communications center, could offer little more despite beaming in personally from Shanghai for his interview. "No, Commander. While you did conduct various research projects under my command, they pertained more to practical matters like improving subspace signal range and clarity, or straightforward probing for subspace communications from uncontacted civilizations beyond known space. All properly logged and on the books, and too routine to warrant pursuing them privately as you've described."

The thin, wizened retiree paused to reflect, and Uhura wondered what he had been like as a commanding officer. When she had mentioned Shen in her personal logs, it had been with an air of disapproval and frustration, but as usual, she had recorded little detail, presuming her keen memory would fill in the blanks. Had she simply been dissatisfied at not being assigned more challenging and varied work, or had there been some more personal reason for her low opinion of the commodore?

"As far as personal leave goes," Shen went on, "Starbase 32 is parsecs away from any inhabited planet. There wasn't really anywhere to go beyond the station's own recreational facilities, or those of visiting ships.

"When you took leave, Commander, you generally returned home to Earth. It was a fairly long trip, but you must have been very close to your family, from the way you spoke about them when you returned." He smiled. "That must have been a blessing for you, to have your loved ones to fall back on after such a trauma. I would have found myself far more alone. But then, I had fewer memories I would have regretted losing."

Uhura was stunned and embarrassed by his words. She regretted having any doubts about his worth as a person.

Something had evidently changed by the time Uhura transferred to the *U.S.S. Potemkin.* "*Yes, I do recall you going off on your own during several shore leaves,*" said Commander

Vintnef nd'Elogat, a bulbous-browed, slender-faced Arkenite who had been Uhura's department head during her time as junior communications officer aboard that ship. *"You did not discuss your activities, but I don't believe they were work-related. On one occasion, I briefly glimpsed you meeting up with a human male, evidently a civilian, with whom you seemed quite familiar. I believe he would have been deemed attractive by human standards."*

Uhura was surprised. Her personal logs and interviews with other crewmates had referenced various shipboard romances and the occasional shore leave fling, but gave no hint of an ongoing affair with a civilian. "Did I ever mention anything about him? Can you describe him?"

Commander nd'Elogat shrugged. *"Moderately taller than you, not significantly older, paler in complexion, though comparable in hair coloration. I recall no other distinctive features. I only glimpsed him briefly."*

Uhura traded a dissatisfied look with Spock. The commander's description would fit a high percentage of adult human males. This was compounded when nd'Elogat added, *"Indeed, I can't be entirely sure he was human. Your physiognomy is so . . . generic as humanoids go. No offense."*

No one else they could reach from Uhura's tenure on the *Potemkin* could add anything further, and that was her final posting before the *Enterprise*. "Whatever I was doing," Uhura told Spock and Admiral Cartwright subsequently, "it apparently began by the time I boarded the *Potemkin*. If that's true, then this might all fizzle out once the sequence reaches that point."

"You still took a fair number of leaves in the interim," Cartwright countered. "With these flare outbursts getting bigger and lasting longer, the odds of serious loss of life are getting greater. We can't just sit back and wait for them to die out."

"Nor can we conclusively state that your actions began at the time," Spock said. "We can only say that is the earliest instance we have been able to track down through interviews with your Starfleet colleagues. There were occasions, during your starbase assignment and in between your early starship tours, when you spent significant amounts of time on Earth. Your activities could have begun there. Indeed, they could have been ongoing for a number of years earlier than we have been able to trace."

Cartwright grimaced. "Which means that we could be heading for a series of *repeated* vacuum surges right here in the Sol system. This *has* to be stopped before that happens!"

Spock raised a scathing brow. "That is axiomatic, Admiral. It would be more useful to discuss *how* that might be achieved." Ignoring the admiral's glower, Spock turned to Uhura. "If the next step of our investigation points toward Earth, then I recommend you contact your family and personal friends, Commander. To all accounts, you were quite close to your family before your memory loss. If anyone knew of any activities you chose not to discuss with Starfleet, it would probably be they."

Uhura had trouble meeting his calm, expectant gaze. What he asked was not as easy as he made it sound.

Sulu residence

"I do not see the problem," Pavel Chekov said as he, Uhura, and Sulu took tea together in the living room of Sulu's dwelling, which they had to themselves while Demora was on a sleepover at a friend's home. "It's not as if you're estranged from your family or anything. Don't I recall your mother helping out Admiral Kirk with an undercover investigation a few years back? Something about smuggling on Mestiko?"

Uhura was glad that Chekov had returned to Earth while the *Reliant* was under repairs, for she could use the support of her closest friends through all this. But for all his good intentions,

Pavel could be blunt and clueless at times. "Oh, yes, we've been in touch . . . at a comfortable distance. Everything's perfectly . . . cordial between us."

Sulu leaned forward in his armchair. "But?"

She shifted her weight uneasily, even though the couch cushion beneath her was quite comfortable. "But . . . I barely know them. All I know is what I've read about them in my logs, what they've said in their letters."

She took a long sip of tea to fortify her, then set the cup back down on the coffee table. "After *Nomad*, they invited me to return home, offered to help me remember. But I . . . I couldn't. I experienced all these emotions when I thought about them . . . about these people who were strangers to me."

Chekov answered slowly. "Because your episodic memory was lost, but not your deeper, conditioned responses such as emotions."

Uhura nodded. "It was terribly confusing. More—it was frightening. Rather than facing all that, it was easier to start over and build a new life with my crewmates." She reached out and touched both men's hands. "You were all I knew. Everything I remembered was aboard the *Enterprise*, with all of you around me. So you became my comfort zone. I came to think of you all as my family."

She leaned back, lowering her head. "But in the process, I neglected my birth family. I sent polite acknowledgments of their letters, their invitations, their pleas. I said I'd come home when it became feasible, and then I kept putting it off. Eventually the requests tapered off. They must feel that I've . . . moved on without them.

"After all that . . . after turning my back on them when they offered to help me . . . now I have to go back to them and ask for their help. And it's because of the very thing that created the rift, that took their close, loving daughter and sister away from them and created this . . . stranger in her place."

She blinked away tears, and Sulu and Chekov both came around to flank her on the couch, their hands on her shoulders. "Hey," Sulu said. "I can guarantee they won't see you that way."

"How? How can you possibly know?"

He grinned. "I'm a dad now, remember? A year ago, I didn't know Demora existed. Now it feels like she's always been part of me.

"That's how family works, Nyota. No matter how long you're apart, no matter what comes between you, that connection is always there. And a parent's sense of responsibility for their child never goes away."

"Besides," Chekov added, "I know that your mother is a kind, compassionate, and understanding woman."

"I didn't think you'd met her."

"I have met *you*. Think about it, Nyota. *Nomad* may have taken away your learning, your experiences—but what remained was who you are at the core. Who you were born to be. And that is a kind, compassionate, and understanding woman. That wasn't learned—it's genetic."

Sulu tilted his head. "I'm not sure it works quite that way. I mean, she retained her ingrained skills. Plus it could've come from her father's side."

"Stop analyzing. I'm trying to be comforting."

Uhura laughed. "And you're both doing a fine job—in your ways."

Neither one of them was a master at this, yet she still drew strength from their willingness to help. As imperfect as it was, she realized, the connection helped. Would reconnecting with her biological family really be that different? She feared the parts that would be awkward and difficult, but didn't those go hand in hand with the more fulfilling aspects of family?

Well, sister, she told herself, *there's only one way to find out.*

Chapter Ten

Nairobi, United States of Africa

Returning to her childhood home felt to Nyota Uhura like visiting an alien planet.

She could have beamed directly to her mother's residence—indeed, she should have, given that this was fairly urgent Starfleet business. However, she had chosen to beam to the local transporter depot and take in the city for a bit, both to delay the inevitable and to see if it sparked any memories. Nairobi was certainly a stimulating environment, a multispecies melting pot of Federation cultures almost as rich as San Francisco or Paris. The Green City in the Sun had always been a place where cultures blended, for better or worse—from its turbulent early decades as an anchor of British colonialism to its post-independence role as a center of tourism and trade. True to its nickname, it was an interface between civilization and nature as well, directly abutting one of Africa's largest nature preserves and blessed with an abundance of parks interspersed among its towering skyscrapers, its elegant museums and churches and mosques, and its colorful shops and restaurants. Many cities on Earth were like that now, but Nairobi had been one of the first.

Still, none of it sparked any recognition in Uhura, any memory of herself as a part of this environment. There was an occasional, subliminal sense of familiarity, but far from bringing comfort, it unnerved her. To someone with eidetic memory, the inability to know *why* something evoked an emotional response was disturbing.

If just the city did that to her, what would it be like going home?

As she walked the streets, Uhura noticed others' eyes following her, reacting to her Starfleet uniform. She was not the only Starfleet officer in town, to be sure, and she wore dark glasses against the bright tropical sun; yet the crew of the *Enterprise* had become well-known in the years since V'Ger, and the Nairobians were presumably aware of their native daughter within that crew. But was that all she saw in their eyes? Or could some of them be old friends surprised to see her home after so long—wondering why her own gaze brushed past them with no recognition?

The more she contemplated that, the more she realized what a mistake it had been to waste time like this. If she had to face this kind of discomfort, she should at least do it in private, to limit the variables.

M'Umbha Uhura's home was located, not coincidentally, in a residential tower overlooking Uhuru Park, one of the city's oldest and most prominent public spaces, next to the central business district and near the University of Nairobi, where M'Umbha's current husband taught. Uhuru—"Freedom" in Swahili—was a popular name in East Africa, though a Western-influenced ancestor of the Uhuras had chosen to "soften" the final vowel a few generations back. Perhaps this had been meant to make them stand out from the crowd, but M'Umbha had chosen to take a dwelling near their namesake park despite that. Had that been out of pride, Nyota wondered, or a legal advocate's appreciation for the ideal the name embodied? Or did it reflect her sense of humor? She wished she could remember.

When the door to the Uhura apartment began to open,

Nyota wondered for a moment if she would even recognize her own mother. They had exchanged brief, often tense correspondence on occasion since *Nomad*, but no more than a cordial, distant acknowledgment for the past several years. Still, she knew immediately that the woman standing in the doorway was her mother, for she looked the way Nyota imagined—or hoped—that she would look in thirty years. M'Umbha was a lean, regal woman in a brightly patterned *kanga* dress, with a cloud of silvery-white hair framing her striking, large-eyed features.

Those dark eyes glistened with tears, and before Nyota could react, she found herself in the older woman's embrace. "Oh, *binti yangu*! Nyota! Welcome home!"

After a moment's hesitation, she relaxed into the embrace and returned it. She had no right to close herself off to this freely offered love just because her memory of it was gone. That absence was artificial, imposed by a heartless, half-alien machine. M'Umbha's experience of their bond was the true one, and she should defer to it if she could.

Besides, being called "my daughter" gave her a sense of attachment she hadn't known she'd been missing.

M'Umbha led Nyota inside the spacious apartment, but the commander hesitated at the sound of activity and male voices from the kitchen. "I . . . I thought it would be just the two of us," she said.

"Oh, I know, dear, but Omar insisted on preparing a feast for the occasion. This is the first time he's actually had a chance to meet you! And as for Malcolm, well, he insisted on beaming in from Kampala. You know how stubborn he can—" She broke off, kneading her hands in embarrassment. "I'm sorry. That just slipped out."

"I understand. It's not your—"

"Well, there you are." A tall, mature man with a neatly trimmed, subtly graying beard, dressed in modern attire that would not be out of place in San Francisco or Utopia Planitia, leaned against the frame of the kitchen door. "The great Starfleet hero finally deigns to grace us with her presence."

"Malcolm, don't start," M'Umbha chided. "You know what your sister has been through."

"Is she? My sister? Or have we let a stranger into our home? She's certainly treated us that way." Doctor Malcolm Uhura held Nyota's gaze, coolly scrutinizing her reaction. "At least until she needed something from us."

"Come on, Malcolm, no getting out of your work," came a deeper voice from the kitchen. "Don't let the sukuma wiki get mushy. It's almost ready."

"Yes, Dad." Malcolm rolled his eyes and went back into the kitchen.

Once her brother was out of the way, Nyota could see the older man who had spoken, a rotund, gray-haired gentleman with a medium-brown complexion, wearing a light-hued dashiki and a cylindrical *kofia* hat. "Hello, Nyota," he called through the door as he bustled around the stove. "I'm Omar Ghalib, your stepfather. I hope you don't mind that I'm too busy to greet you properly, but dinner will be ready shortly."

Nyota smiled at his easy acceptance, a relief after her brother's cold treatment. "That's fine, Omar, thank you. It smells delicious. Nyama choma and ugali?"

"With pilau rice and matoke for dessert. It's your first time home in so long, we thought you might like something traditional."

"It sounds lovely."

"Ah, so do you, my dear. You have your mother's euphonious tones. They were what drew me to her in the first place." As M'Umbha moved past Nyota into the kitchen, Omar's eyes roved up and down his wife's figure and his smile widened. "Many other things followed." The couple shared a lascivious laugh, making Malcolm wince in embarrassment. Nyota found it adorable—and wondered if she should regret that detachment from childhood baggage.

While Nyota had urgent questions to pursue concerning the vacuum flares, she felt it would be inconsiderate not to ask after her hosts'—rather, her family's current affairs. M'Umbha was easily drawn into a discussion of her work with the elephants; Nyota supposed her obvious passion for the subject was what made her a good advocate for their interests. It seemed she had been involved in a lively dispute with a Federation Council committee insisting that the Prime Directive should prohibit any active social work or medical care among the elephants, as that would constitute interference in their natural development. M'Umbha had countered that in a case where humans had already interfered with an alien culture—as they had with elephants to devastating effect over millennia—they had an obligation to take an active role in correcting the harm they had done. She had cited a number of Starfleet missions as precedents, including the *Enterprise*'s interventions on Iotia and Ekos.

The mention of Professor John Gill's twisted experiment with fascism on Ekos left Omar shaking his head. As a fellow historian, he said, he was bewildered that a once-respected scholar of Earth history had embraced such an easily discredited fringe interpretation of the so-called "efficiency" of the Nazi regime, or had believed that it could be divorced from its hateful, genocidal aspects, as if those had been a peripheral element instead of the central driver of the entire ideology. Then he laughed and, apologizing for bringing the mood down, shifted into an amusing anecdote about a Rigelian student whose glitchy translator had led her to mistake a history assignment about the Mauryan Empire for one about a "Martian Empire," leading her to produce a thoroughly researched, highly revisionist essay on the wrong era of history altogether.

Malcolm ate in sullen silence at first, but Omar eventually drew him into a conversation about his research in interspecies medicine at Makerere University Hospital. Her older brother spoke of his ongoing studies into the symbiotic biology of the Pandronian biosphere, which he believed could point the way to new methods of organ transplantation or limb replacement. It was the first time Nyota had seen him brighten all afternoon.

Taking in the mood, M'Umbha smiled. "Well, this is lovely. What a shame Samara's dance troupe is off-world—we could've had the whole family together again."

To hide her embarrassment at failing to ask after her younger sister, Nyota took a sip of chai and said, "Well, this is just a lovely meal, Omar. I don't think I've ever had nyama choma this good."

M'Umbha dropped her fork, and a silence fell over the table. "It . . . it's your mother's recipe, dear," Omar demurred.

Being at a loss for words was another novel experience for Nyota. "I . . . oh, I . . . I suppose that must be why it seems so right. I should have . . ."

"No," M'Umbha said. "No, it's all right." She forced a smile. "It's a pleasure to get to see you discover it all over again, *binti*." She cleared her throat. "Well, we've been monopolizing the conversation too long. I know you came here in search of help with your problem. You believe these space storms popping up all over are connected to you somehow?"

"That's right." She went on to spell out the basics of the situation and the connection she'd found to her own music. "We think I must have been conducting some sort of ongoing communications research, but for some reason, I told no one in Starfleet about it. Yet according to everyone I spoke to, if I had told anyone, it would be . . ." She lowered her head. "My family."

"Yes," M'Umbha said, following suit. "You used to share everything with us."

"I . . . I'm sure I did. So if there's anything you can remember that could help—"

"This is outrageous," Malcolm interrupted. "You don't owe

this . . . this *stranger* anything, Mama. Twelve years ago, she forgot us, and she was fine with doing so."

"Malcolm!" M'Umbha protested. "You know that wasn't her fault."

"Losing her memory, no. But she *chose* not to come back to us after, to reclaim what she had lost. After twelve years of choosing to stay away, she doesn't get to use that robot as an excuse anymore."

He turned to Nyota. "Mama is doing a good job of hiding it, but you need to know the pain you've caused her, coming back here after all these years just for work, for Starfleet. You only come back now that you need some information from us. Not for Mama and Omar's wedding, not for Samara's graduation, not even for Babu Uchawi's funeral!"

She let his anger wash over her, not feeling entitled to challenge it. "I understand your anger, Malcolm. I just hope you can understand how hard it was for me."

He held her gaze, and she saw a deeper compassion beneath the anger. "I can't begin to imagine what you went through. I worked with a few amnesia cases during my residency, but they were usually partial or temporary. And even then, I could barely imagine how it would feel not to recognize your own loved ones.

"Because when members of this family have gone through pain or loss, we have always turned to one another. When our father, yours and mine and Samara's, died out in space, you came straight home from the Academy and we grieved *together*. We helped one another endure the loss, and we helped one another heal from it over time.

"Not that it was easy," he added. "I tried so hard to talk you out of staying in Starfleet. I was so afraid that we might lose another one of us to space, that Mama might have to grieve all over again. We argued so fiercely. But the things you said about the reasons for your commitment to space, the value of the risks you took . . . I never admitted it then, but they helped me forgive Baba for going out there and getting himself killed. As hard as it was, Nyota, we worked through it because we were family.

"So when we learned what had happened to you at Maluria, we couldn't understand why you wouldn't turn to us, wouldn't let us help you with that loss. Instead, it felt as if we'd lost you too—and *by your own choice*." He shook his head. "That was almost worse than if you'd died. At least I would've understood then why you didn't come back."

Nyota was weeping now. "I wanted to, brother. I wanted to know what I'd had taken from me. I still remembered what I *felt* for you all." He scoffed. "I *did*. But what would it have been like for you, to have me come into your home like a stranger and demand you share a relationship with me when I couldn't give anything back? How could I do that to you? What could I have offered you without my share of the history we once had?"

"You could have offered your presence," M'Umbha replied proudly. "Your *participation*. Nyota, you speak of memory as a thing of the past. But memory doesn't end." She took Omar's hand in hers. "When we lost Alhamisi, I felt for a long time that I would have no more joyous memories of my husband. But then I met Omar, and I found I could still build new memories to fill the void."

M'Umbha took her hand. "You could have been part of those memories, Nyota. We would have been happy to have you. In twelve years, imagine how many new memories you could have formed with us to make up for the ones you lost."

Nyota looked at her mother's hand clasping hers, felt her cool, leathery skin . . . and suddenly she was in another time. Her mother's face was younger, her hair still black, and Nyota could feel her own hair lying long and straight against her spine. Malcolm paced nearby, lean and beardless, intense with emotion.

"*I won't insist that you give up your dream,*" M'Umbha said.

"Only you can decide what it's worth. Just consider everything that's at stake."

A flash of the young Malcolm shouting . . . then Samara wailing, fleeing to her room . . . Nyota sitting beside her on her bed, cradling the thirteen-year-old, promising that nothing would take her away.

When she came back to her senses, she was breathing hard, gasping. Tears rolled down her cheeks. M'Umbha was rising from her chair, moving closer. "*Binti*? What is it?"

Her mouth worked, torn between sobbing and grinning. "I remembered something! I . . ." She broke down, unable to say more.

Malcolm was by her side a second later, checking her pulse. "Breathe, Nyota. Slow, deep breaths."

Once she had her breathing under control, she took a long sip of cold chaï, emptying the cup. Omar took it from her, fingers brushing against hers. "I'll get you a fresh cup."

"All these years . . . nothing but vague sensations, emotions . . . usually not even that. This was . . . actual words, images. The experience . . ." She laughed out loud. "Mama, *I remembered something!* It's not all gone. *Nomad* didn't take it all!"

As mother and daughter embraced, Malcolm stood close by. "It makes sense. The brain is too interconnected for any memory to be cleanly, perfectly excised. There would still be a web of associations connecting to other parts of your brain. A strong enough reminder could help reconnect the severed pathways."

Nyota wept freely as his words sank in. All this time, she'd retreated from her past connections to avoid facing the pain they triggered, the certainty that she would never recover what *Nomad* had burned away. If she had sought out her past instead, if she had faced the loss alongside her family, how much more could she have recovered?

Her mother saw all this in her eyes and stroked her hair forgivingly. "It's all right, my love. You're home now. We can begin anew."

The Uhuras moved to the living room and talked well into the night, teaching Nyota about her own life—her formative years in Nairobi and Mombasa, her annual vacations in the country with Babu Uchawi and her cousins, her visits to her mother's family in Zambia, the family jaunts around the Sol system with her father and Uncle Raheem. M'Umbha and Malcolm regaled her with tales of her father, including the embarrassing details of how Alhamisi Uhura had earned his childhood nickname Damu Pua, "Bloody Nose."

Only a few of the tales they told sparked buried memories in Nyota, and then only fragments and flashes—but even that was a blessing she had never expected. She eagerly absorbed everything they told her, amazed to discover her younger self through their eyes—a self at once very familiar and entirely unexpected.

In time, the discussion came around to the purpose of her visit—not without reluctance on everyone's part, for none of them wanted the visit to end too soon.

"You always found subspace radio fascinating," M'Umbha told her, "ever since Alhamisi showed you the radio on his transport. The idea of talking to people all over the galaxy made your eyes glow. You begged me to get you a subspace ham radio of your own, so you could build it and tinker with it and make new friends across the stars."

"Oh, the weird noises that emanated from your room at odd hours while I was trying to study," Malcolm complained. "All that whistling and buzzing and chattering as you tried to tease signals out of cosmic noise, as you rebuilt your set to boost its gain and range and whatever. I thought that as you got better at it, you'd produce less noise and more signal." He threw up his hands. "But you embraced the noise! You listened to it longer and louder. You swore you could hear some kind of pattern in the noise, something almost musical."

Nyota stared at him sharply. "Did I ever sing back?"

He shrugged. "Now and again." After a moment, her intensity registered. "Wait, do you think this is connected to what you came here for? You think you actually *were* talking to something? Or . . . singing to it?"

"That's what I'm hoping you can tell me."

"I'm afraid I tried to pay as little attention as possible. I was trying to get into medical school!"

M'Umbha touched her arm. "I remember your enthusiasm about what you thought you heard—at first."

Nyota turned to her. "At first?"

"As I recall, you eventually decided that you were hearing the patterns from too many different locations all over space, too far apart and random to be connected. You decided it must have been pareidolia."

Omar spoke up for the first time in a while. "Pair-eye what?"

Malcolm answered. "The tendency of the mind to construct patterns out of randomness. Like the Man in the Moon, or seeing palaces in the clouds."

"That's right," M'Umbha said. "You decided that you heard something musical in the noise because it was what you wanted to hear. You were so disappointed—you thought for a few weeks there that you were on the verge of a major discovery."

"In your defense, you were fourteen," Malcolm conceded.

"Still," their mother went on, "I always had the feeling that it was the yearning that experience gave you—the need to hear the songs in the stars—that inspired you to pursue a career in Starfleet. That sense of awe and excitement in your eyes when you were on the track of a discovery—I saw that same look when your acceptance to Starfleet Academy came through."

"So that was how it began?" Nyota asked, awed.

"As far as I believe, yes."

She sighed. "I wish I could remember that. Choosing my path."

M'Umbha took her hand. "It's all right. You have us to re-member it for you."

Nyota squeezed her hand in return, then stood and began to wander the room, taking in its decorations and the abundant photos of family members and elephant herds. "I appreciate all this, but it's not bringing me any closer to understanding my connection to the vacuum flares. Unless there's something in those subspace patterns. Are you sure I gave up on them com-pletely? Did I ever give you any indication that I was researching something like them later on?"

"Like at the Academy?" M'Umbha considered. "You talked about a lot of things you did there—your studies, your gym-nastics, your boyfriends." She chuckled. "I think you tried to continue your own research projects when you could, but they kept you pretty busy."

They spent some time trying to recall details from her sto-ries about Academy life, or showing her letters and mementos she had sent them. She would have loved to take the time to pore through them all in detail, but she strove to focus on what was relevant to her mysterious subspace research. Yet nothing seemed to offer any clear connection to it.

"None of your Academy friends could offer any insights?" M'Umbha asked after a while.

"None that I could contact," Nyota said. "A number of them have died in action over the years." She leafed through the print-outs resting on the table, though after reading them once, she knew them by heart. "Do you remember me talking about this 'Jen' person I mention in some of my correspondence? That one confuses me. I did mention a Jen sometimes in my personal logs, but I didn't have any classmates named Jennifer, or Jendayi, or any likely alternative."

Malcolm looked up. "Jen wasn't a woman. It was . . . Rajen-dra, wasn't it?"

"That's right," M'Umbha said. "Rajendra Shastri. You and he

were good friends for a while. Yes, you told me that he was a fellow subspace ham growing up. You were in several of the same classes and worked together on various communication projects. If anyone knew something relevant, he might."

Rajendra Shastri. The name was familiar, though not from her Academy days. Not long after *Nomad*, she had received several subspace messages from him asking when they could meet again and discuss "everything that happened." She'd had no idea what he was referring to, but she'd felt such intense emotion at the sight of his name that she had avoided responding until she could sort things out.

She had researched him thereafter, determining that he had been a classmate of hers at the Academy, but had mustered out of Starfleet after a brief tenure, moving to a Federation colony world named Penthara IV. Eventually, concluding that anyone she felt so strongly about deserved at least some response, she had sent Shastri a brief message informing him of her memory loss. His response had been terse, angry, and disbelieving. As she had still been in a vulnerable state in the wake of her trauma, she had been deeply hurt and offended at the suggestion that she would lie about it, so she had deleted all his messages, giving him no further thought.

That man was one of my friends? she thought with disbelief. The emotions she associated with his name were too bitter, too fraught with betrayal. What kind of friend would turn on her so readily after learning of such a trauma? How could he just dismiss it as a lie?

"Oh, dear," said Omar, studying her face. "Perhaps that friendship turned sour somewhere."

"I'm sorry," M'Umbha said. "I fear I've upset you."

Nyota shook her head. "No, no, it's all right. I needed to know. Whatever the history is between me and this Shastri, he may still be a lead to the answers I'm seeking. I'm grateful to you for that. If . . . if only I'd come to you a dozen years ago, maybe

I'd already know what was behind all this. Maybe we could even have stopped it sooner."

M'Umbha rose. "Don't you dare blame yourself for this, *binti*. We all respond in our own way to trauma. What you went through was terrible. You coped the best way you knew how." She took her daughter's hands. "I'm just grateful that you had such loyal and caring friends aboard the *Enterprise* to help you rebuild your life. To help you become the strong, wise, dedicated, and caring woman I see before me."

Nyota hugged her. "Oh, Mama. You shaped me too. Even if I don't remember the events, the knowledge, values, and habits you instilled in me remain. You've always been with me—even when I didn't know it."

Chapter Eleven

Starfleet Academy

Commander Sulu wore a heavy expression as he entered the classroom, and Zirani Kayros wondered why he was looking at her. She soon got her answer, once the students in the piloting class had fallen silent in response to their instructor's uncharacteristically somber manner.

"There's been a new vacuum flare," Sulu told the class. "It began a short while ago in the Tiburon system."

Kayros gasped. The aftermath of the Midoren City disaster on Denobula had been all over the news for almost a week, so Sulu's words prompted her to imagine the same calamities befalling her home and family—and her own firsthand experience of the Argelius flare added vivid detail to her imaginings. The rational part of her mind took a moment longer to engage, reminding her of the improbability of two such direct strikes so close together.

Sulu's next words, directed mainly at her, reaffirmed this. "The homeworld is fine. It was a large flare, but well removed from the planet and the lunar colonies." He paused. "However, there were casualties. A civilian transport with twenty-four people aboard was in the vicinity. They were vacationers returning home to Tiburon from a tour of the outer ice giants. They apparently decided to divert closer to the vacuum flare so they could get a better look at it—it's not clear yet whether it was the pilots' idea or if the passengers talked them into it. Either way, they didn't anticipate this flare being larger than the previous ones, so they were caught in a sudden microflare burst. The microflares breached their reactor . . . the transport was lost with all hands."

After a moment, he went on. "The families have already been notified. I guess that means you're in the clear, Zirani."

She nodded, taking it in. There were also friends and classmates to consider, but the odds that two dozen people out of an entire planetary population included anyone she knew were minuscule. Still, she would not truly know until she called home.

Sulu seemed to divine her thoughts—no doubt because a Starfleet veteran like him had extensive experience with disaster and loss. "If you'd like to be excused from class today, I understand."

Kayros cleared her throat. "No, sir. It's okay. Thank you, though."

She did her best to focus on his lesson in celestial navigation, hoping it would make an effective distraction from the news. Still, her mind drifted a few times over the following hour. She thought she'd put her vacuum flare experience at Argelius behind her. It had been three months ago, after all, before the phenomenon had even been named. But this latest incident had struck close to home in more ways than one, it seemed.

After class, several of Kayros's fellow students clustered around her to offer support, including Michael Ashrafi, who rubbed her shoulder kindly. "I'm here if you want to talk, Zee. I . . . probably don't have anything helpful to say, but I can listen." She patted his hand briefly, appreciating the gesture.

Benedick, the outgoing Warborn cadet, was there as well, with Portia hovering beside him like a bodyguard. "I too stand ready to listen, Zirani," Benedick said, a kindly expression on his jowly, drooping face. "I know how it feels to endure deaths among your people. A number of the Warborn that I was raised alongside did not survive the cryogenic process."

Hearing that made her feel guilty. "It's, ah, it's okay, Benedick. I doubt they were anybody I knew. Just a random group of tourists. Probably older people."

Portia grimaced. "Such folly. To die so carelessly, for no reason."

Her words made Kayros bristle. "It doesn't mean their lives were worth any less!"

The tough Warborn female's eyes widened in offended surprise. "That's what I meant. Life is too valuable a resource to squander so frivolously, out of mere unconcern for an obvious risk. Life should be fought for, protected. It should not be taken for granted or thrown away for no purpose. One's own or anyone else's."

Portia strode off before a chastened Kayros could decide how to reply. The Warborn continued to surprise her. She felt she'd hit it off well with a few of them, mainly Benedick and Horatio, but Portia had seemed the most cold and hostile one, the Warborn least likely to find a place in Starfleet.

Now Kayros began to realize what a loss that would be.

San Francisco

When Leonard McCoy invited Jim Kirk to dine with him and Ashley Janith-Lau, the admiral was glad for the opportunity to set aside his worries about the burgeoning vacuum flare crisis for an evening. Granted, Janith-Lau was a reminder of the ongoing controversy around the Warborn Arcturians, but that was a milder crisis, and Kirk still had hopes of finding common ground with the charming activist. Mainly, though, he welcomed the chance to see how his old friend and his new friend (or friendly rival, perhaps) were hitting it off. The two of them had been seeing each other for nearly a week now, and while it appeared to be in a relaxed, casual capacity, McCoy certainly seemed happier than Kirk had seen him in quite a while.

Both Kirk and McCoy were initially a bit awkward with each other in Janith-Lau's company, embarrassed by their mutual former hope for romance between her and Kirk. But the pediatrician proved a deft peacemaker, her easy, comfortable rapport with both men proving contagious. Soon the three of them were chattering and laughing around the table like lifelong friends.

It was inevitable, of course, that the conversation eventually came back around to the Warborn. But this time it was a relaxed and open discourse among friends, and Kirk took heart from that.

"I've been researching Arcturian history a lot lately," Janith-Lau told him. "Trying to get insights into the traditions of the Warborn practice, its specific tenets and how they might have been bent or broken in the past. I'm trying to find out if there are precedents for what I fear Commander Rakatheema is trying to do—to broaden the Warborn's mandate to fight for the whole Federation."

Kirk studied her. "Would it really be so wrong to let them defend the Federation the same way the rest of us do? After all, it's not like we're going to reinstitute the Warborn breeding program. These twenty thousand are the only ones of their kind."

McCoy spoke up in support of his ladyfriend. "That's what they say now, Jim. But a hundred years ago, they said they'd never breed any more Warborn at all. Once you make that first compromise, it gets easier to make the next one, and the next, until you forget there used to be a line you wouldn't cross."

Janith-Lau nodded. "I just don't want to see Starfleet's purpose go through that same erosion. I don't believe you do either, Jim. But other Starfleet officers have crossed ethical lines before."

Kirk kept his silence. He'd certainly known some who fit the bill—Ben Finney, Ronald Tracey, Antonio Delgado—but he had no desire to impugn his fellow officers in the company of civilians.

The activist sighed. "To be honest, I've gained a lot of admiration for the Arcturians. They found a way to achieve peace among their own nations far earlier than Earth did, even earlier than Vulcan, and they've kept it up for an impressively long time.

"But the perpetuation of the Warborn practice is the one major blemish that remains. The peace, prosperity, and equality they built for natural-born Arcturians came at the expense of an exploited class. It was a cultural blind spot that they weren't able to face until Federation contact."

"The Warborn filled what was seen as a sacred role in Arcturian culture," Kirk countered. "That history, that heritage, was woven into their sense of identity. It wasn't an easy thing for them to let go of, because it was interwoven with so many of their traditions."

"I can relate to that," McCoy said. "I'm a proud Southerner, but I don't deny that the history of the American South is rooted in slavery and oppression. There was a time, not too many generations ago, when many Southerners *did* deny it—when they believed that holding on to their heritage meant perpetuating oppression and injustice toward the descendants of former slaves, or living in denial about the oppression that still existed. It was a long, hard struggle to overcome those habits of thought—to find a way to divorce the worthwhile parts of Dixie culture from the parts that deserved to die unloved."

"I don't think the Arcturian situation is quite the same, Bones," Kirk said. "They saw the Warborn as a necessary evil, but one deserving of respect and gratitude for their sacrifice."

Janith-Lau put on a skeptical moue. "The Aztecs felt the same way about the people whose hearts they cut out to appease the sun god."

"The Warborn did help them keep the peace, by defending them against outside threats."

"Many of those invasions happened *because* the Warborn existed! Conquerors like Maltuvis couldn't resist the potential of a quick-bred slave army."

"And it's to the Arcturians' credit that they committed themselves so religiously to ensuring that never happened. Whatever your concerns about Rakatheema, Ashley, I doubt that one man can change so many centuries of conviction."

She considered his words for a time. "I want to believe you're right . . . but it's hard to reconcile a commitment to peace with the perpetuation of such a warlike custom."

Kirk replied slowly, thoughtfully. "I think every culture that pursues the path of peace must struggle with the potential for violence that still remains within their nature, and attempt to reconcile themselves with the ways it's shaped their history and values." He gestured to McCoy. "For Bones, it's the role of slavery in Southern heritage. For me, it's the paradox of American freedom being built on continent-wide conquest and genocide."

She nodded, conceding the point. "I'm Russian-Chinese. Plenty of autocrats and mass murderers in both those histories."

McCoy leaned in. "Then you've got a planet like Argelius. Two centuries of peace, but they've never bothered to repeal the law that murderers are put to death by slow torture. Even Vulcan still has a legal form of ritual combat to the death in . . ." He cleared his throat. ". . . certain rare cases."

"The point," Kirk said, "is that no culture is perfect. No matter how much you strive to be better, some mistakes and bad habits will remain. The Federation's made its share of mistakes too, like Captain sh'Prenni's botched first contact with the Partnership, or John Gill's misguided experiments on Ekos.

"The important thing is to face those flaws, to admit them as part of ourselves. That's the only way we can hope to overcome them. And just as importantly, that ability to acknowledge our own flaws is what enables us to forgive the flaws we see in others. To understand that they might be struggling to improve themselves just as we are, and that they need encouragement for what they do right, rather than just condemnation for what they get wrong."

Janith-Lau smiled at Kirk in appreciation. "You do have a way with speeches, Jim."

"I've caught him practicing in a mirror more than once," McCoy teased.

"You make a good point. It is important not to be too self-righteous. I should talk to Commander Rakatheema again, try to understand his side. If I can relate to his intentions, maybe we can find some common ground when it comes to his methods."

"That's an excellent idea," Kirk said. "I believe in the commander's good intentions. He only wants what's best for both Starfleet and the Warborn. It's just a matter of finding the right balance between the two."

Janith-Lau sobered. "I hope you're right, Jim. But I'm not sure he and I will ever agree on what that balance should be. And only history will be able to say if his vision of the Warborn's future in Starfleet will turn out to be another of the Federation's great mistakes."

U.S.S. *Enterprise*
Earth Spacedock

"But how could you not have known this Jen was a man?" Montgomery Scott asked Uhura as they and Spock sat with her in the officers' lounge, listening to her account of her discoveries on Earth. "When you talked about him in your logs and letters, you must have used a 'he' or 'him' somewhere."

"Those logs and letters were in Kiswahili," she told him. "The pronouns are ungendered."

"Oh." Scott flushed, embarrassed not to have known that.

Captain Spock steepled his fingers. "Now that you know, do your logs provide any further insights?"

"Nothing yet. But I did send a message to his current residence at the Penthara IV colony." She did not let herself show how difficult that had been, given her uncertainties about the state of her relationship with this person. She had kept her communique as objective and calm as possible, focusing on the urgency of the vacuum flare crisis. "The only response was an automated notification that my message had been deleted unread."

Scott rolled his eyes. "Oh, this just keeps getting better. Bad enough you lost your memory of all this—it's like the universe is conspiring to keep you from getting it back!"

"I'm almost tempted to believe you, Scotty, given that the universe itself seems to be generating these flares in response to me, somehow."

Spock addressed them patiently. "It is premature to ascribe cosmic design to what may yet be accounted for by coincidence. We have made some slight progress, and there are still avenues of investigation we may pursue."

He contemplated Uhura. "You said that the emotional stimulus of your reunion with your family triggered the recollection of fragments of memory you had believed were lost. Has your contemplation of Mister Shastri provoked any similar recollection?"

She winced. "I've tried. As much as it . . . roils my emotions just to hear his name, I get no specifics, no matter how much I try to face those feelings. There's just not enough there to latch onto." She paused, thinking it through. "Yes . . . it was the sense memory of my mother's touch, her scent, the surroundings of home, that sparked the connection. With Shastri, I have little more to think of than the name. It's too abstract."

Scott cleared his throat. "Forgive me if I'm crossing a line here, Captain Spock . . . but isn't there some Vulcan mind technique you can use to find those lost memories in Uhura? You brought Admiral Kirk back after that Preserver obelisk thing wiped his memory."

Spock shook his head slightly. "Believe me, Mister Scott, were that a feasible option, I would have proposed it already. In that case, the memories were fully intact, simply blocked from the captain's conscious mind.

"There is a theoretical Vulcan technique that has been proposed for the restoration of memories deeply repressed due to psychological trauma. However, it would require the subject to meld with a close family member—someone who knows their mind and their personality intimately enough to function as a guide and interpreter, in order to assist them in understanding and reintegrating the memory. While Commander Uhura and I have had an excellent professional relationship for many years, we are not as close as family. Nor am I personally familiar with the details of the technique. It might not even be applicable to this type of memory erasure."

His lips narrowed. "It would seem that our best option would be to speak to Mister Shastri. Regrettably, as he is a civilian, as well as a resident of a remote colony, there is little we may do to gain his cooperation if he chooses to withhold it."

Uhura sighed. "You're right. It's not the universe that's to blame for these dead ends, it's me. When my past was erased, I chose to let it stay that way. I thought it would be easiest for everyone to make a clean break and start over." She lowered her head. "I was wrong. I see now just how much I cost myself, and my family. It's no wonder my old friends feel alienated too.

"I've always prided myself on my ability to make connections—to bridge seemingly impassable divides and create understanding. But I cut off my own connections to my old life. I let them wither and die, and now we're all paying the price."

"Hey, hey." Scotty moved to sit beside her on the couch and

put an arm around her shoulders. "Don't beat yourself up, lass. *Nomad* did a hell of a number on both of us, you know that. The only one to blame is that blasted machine.

"And the connections didn't die. You reconnected with us on the ship, stronger than ever. And now you've got your family back too. Give this Shastri bloke some time. If he was really such a fine friend, maybe he'll come around. And in the meantime . . . well, I'm sure he was very far from your only friend at the Academy. So let's talk to the others and find out if they can tell us anything."

Uhura hugged him. "Thank you, Scotty. You're right."

Starfleet Academy

When Uhura tracked down her old Academy classmates to ask about Ravinder Shastri and any communications research she might have done with him, it finally seemed to bear fruit. More than one old friend confirmed that she and Shastri had worked together on some kind of unusual research project. However, they agreed that the two cadets had been reluctant to offer details, telling their classmates that whatever they were investigating was a long shot and they did not wish to commit to anything until or unless they obtained positive results. The interviewees also agreed that both cadets had stopped talking about it early in their fourth year, beyond saying that their research had led down a blind alley and been abandoned. Given the increasing frequency and size of the vacuum flares, Uhura could not afford to believe that assessment.

The next day, Spock and Uhura met with Admiral Kirk in his office. The admiral wasted little time getting to the point. "I had my staff investigate Academy records for any use of the communications or subspace physics labs by Cadets Uhura and Shastri at the time in question. They found nothing . . . or so it seemed."

Kirk handed a data slate of their findings to Spock. "Tell me if you notice the same pattern I did."

It only took moments before Spock responded. "I see. Not merely an absence of evidence . . . but evidence of absence. Something has been redacted. With skill, but a footprint remains if one knows what to look for."

Kirk nodded. "Which suggests that whatever you and Shastri were investigating, Commander, it infringed on a security or intelligence matter. Most likely you were ordered to drop it and sworn to secrecy, and the evidence was classified."

Uhura sagged. "Scotty was right. It's like the universe is conspiring to erase all the leads."

"On the contrary, Commander," Spock said. "This is our most promising lead yet. If Starfleet did order the matter classified . . . then someone in Starfleet knows why. If we can determine who gave the order, we should be able to persuade them that the vacuum flare crisis demands its disclosure."

The admiral rose and came around the desk, addressing Uhura. "I looked a little deeper into your contacts around the time you appeared to abandon the research. There were three visits to the Academy grounds that month by Starfleet Security or Intelligence personnel whose specific activities were redacted. I've determined that one was in connection with a member of the faculty, while another involved a non-Federation exchange student.

"The remaining visitor was a Commodore Conrad Reppert of Starfleet Intelligence." He handed her a second, smaller slate with an image of a light-skinned human male with a broad face, salt-and-pepper hair, and a pug nose. "I don't suppose his face rings any bells?"

Uhura studied the image. "I'm afraid not. But you think he's the one who classified our work?"

"He's the only credible possibility we've found. Unfortunately, Cartwright wasn't able to find any entries in his record confirming it, and Reppert's superior at the time is deceased now. If the commodore did talk with you, the report was buried so deep that even Cartwright can't find it."

"Is Commodore Reppert still alive?" Spock asked.

"He's retired now, living on Kaferia." Kirk paused, shifting his weight uneasily. "But even he may not be able to tell you what you need to know."

Chapter Twelve

Starfleet Headquarters

". . . So that is where we stand." Pavel Chekov tried not to sound too apologetic as he finished his report to the room full of high-ranking Starfleet officers, all of them captains and above. Admiral Cartwright had gathered this group to discuss defense plans for the vacuum flares, and Chekov had been given the unenviable task of summarizing how little they had to work with. "We know that if the vacuum flares continue to backtrack through Commander Uhura's life history, they will soon reach the Sol system. But we have not yet devised a means to predict their onset or shield against them. Nor are we any closer to determining their origin or finding a way to prevent them." He searched for words. "I'm afraid that's all I have to report at this time."

"Thank you, Mister Chekov," Cartwright said, rising to take the floor. Chekov returned to his seat at the meeting room's long, black oval table as the admiral moved behind the podium. "But I have to disagree with you. The fact that we know they're coming is an advantage in itself. It means we have a chance to prepare.

"That's why we're gathered here, people. We know a storm is coming. We can't stop it, can't shield against it, but we can still cope with it. Working alongside civilian emergency response organizations, we can patrol the endangered volume around Earth's orbit and be ready to respond swiftly to any outbreak, with enough ships to provide evacuation and medical treatment in a timely manner."

"Is the risk really that great?" It took Chekov a moment to place the speaker as Lawrence Styles, captain of the *U.S.S. Artemis*. The narrow-faced, high-browed Earthman went on with a skeptical twist to his mustachioed lip. "I mean, it's called 'space' for a reason. Even if the flare hits somewhere around a point in Earth's orbit, the odds that Earth will actually *be* there at the time are one in a hundred thousand, and that's not even counting the margin of error for these things. What happened at Denobula was an incredible fluke. The odds of it happening again here are minuscule."

"If I may, sir?" Chekov asked Cartwright. The admiral nodded. "With respect, Captain Styles, we are not expecting only a single flare. We believe that whatever research these flares are reacting to was underway while Commander Uhura was at Starfleet Academy. We have no idea how long her efforts lasted, but we can safely assume there will be more than one flare in this system. Possibly quite a few.

"Not only that, but the flares last longer and spread over a larger volume of space each time—and we have no idea what upper bound there is on their size and duration, if any."

"There's another possibility." The speaker was Admiral S'rrel, a brown-furred Caitian male who served as a Starfleet liaison to the Federation Council. "The flares so far have been tracking back through years of the commander's life in a matter of months—and they have been accelerating. Aside from the backward order, the only correlation is to place, not timing. So for all we know, every flare aimed at Earth could arrive simultaneously. The whole inner system could be engulfed, and the combined surge of radiation and gravimetric distortion could cause massive disruption to ships and infrastructure even beyond the directly affected areas."

Styles scoffed. "What are you basing that on?"

"That's the point. We don't know enough to make assumptions either way. We must be ready for anything."

Commodore Margaret Song of the Mars Defense Perimeter leaned forward in her seat. "And let's not forget that there's more in Earth orbital space than Earth and Luna," the statuesque, black-haired Martian pointed out. "The various colonies and stations around the L4 and L5 points are spread out across volumes much larger than the Earth itself, meaning that the odds of at least one of them being struck are commensurately greater. Not to mention that the 'margin of error' you pointed out, Lawrence, might be wide enough to encompass Mars's orbit."

"The risk of that is even slighter, Margaret," Styles insisted. "And in any case, it's only a short-term concern. Eventually whatever's paging backward through this woman's biography will run out of chapters, and the flares will stop. Maybe all at once, if S'rrel is right."

"So what are you saying?" S'rrel demanded. "That we just do nothing about the risk of injury and death?"

"How much greater will the risk be if people panic? The public is still reeling from the Naazh crisis and that hullabaloo around the New Humans. They're getting stirred up by fearmongers about Arcturian Augment shock troops, or whatever they're claiming they are this week, being let into the Academy. They've lost enough faith in Starfleet's ability to protect them. We don't want to lose more face by admitting weakness.

"Sure, we could mobilize some massive emergency force here in the heart of the Federation, but that would just call attention to the fact that we have no plan beyond trying to clean up after the fact. And if that's the best we can do anyway, then it makes little difference whether we mobilize or not."

"It makes plenty of difference, Captain!" Cartwright's fierce exclamation silenced Styles quite effectively. "Don't be a fool. You know as well as anyone that lives depend on the speed and effectiveness of the response in the wake of a disaster.

"You're concerned with Starfleet's image? How good will we look after the fact if we failed to prepare for a threat we *knew* was coming? It'd be V'Ger all over again. Days of advance notice, and we couldn't mobilize more than one capital ship to defend the heart of the Federation!" He shook his head. "We waited too long to rebuild the fleet after the Klingon Wars. We trusted too much in Earth's defense grid to protect us, and V'Ger shut it down effortlessly.

"This time, we have weeks of advance warning. And we have more ships on hand in the home system now. So let's use them the way they're meant to be used."

Chekov winced at the reminder of V'Ger. The admiral declined to mention that the powerful artificial intelligence had stolen the planetary defense grid's shutdown codes from the *Enterprise*'s computer—a massive breach of security on Chekov's first mission as that ship's security chief. No matter how many people assured him that nobody could have prevented an entity of V'Ger's immense power from doing what it wanted, his pride had never fully recovered.

Worse, it was a reminder that he felt just as helpless in the current crisis. As mysterious as V'Ger had been, at least they could see it and track its movements. At least it had been possible to confront it before it reached Earth and find some way to stop it. The vacuum flares were a more inchoate threat. After all these weeks, they were still stuck with reacting rather than anticipating.

Not that Styles was right, of course. It was still worthwhile to be ready—to assign local Starfleet and civilian assets to patrol Solar space for rapid response, and to coordinate with civilian authorities to effect evacuation and relief plans. But it chafed Chekov to have to settle for cleaning up after the fact.

He prayed that Uhura's search for answers would pay off soon. There was no telling how much time the Sol system had left before the flares began—or how bad they would get once they came.

Kaferia (Tau Ceti III)

Kaferia was a good place for an intelligence operative to retire. The Kaferians may have resembled humanoid ants, but they were anything but a hive culture, prizing individual freedom and privacy rights. Anyone who wished to elude attention and drop out from interstellar life could easily do so here.

Luckily, Conrad Reppert had not sought to disappear completely—merely to find a quiet, welcoming place to live out his days. Admiral Cartwright had been able to provide Spock with his contact information, and the *Enterprise* captain and Uhura had received an affirmative answer to their request to beam down to Reppert's dwelling.

Getting this far, however, had been the easy part.

Reppert's nurse, a gold-carapaced Kaferian male whose name translated as Morning Nectar, led Spock and Uhura to the rear deck of the commodore's home. It was a small but well-appointed abode surrounded by wide lawns and well-kept gardens, with a substantial grove of Kaferian apple trees beyond the low rear fence of the backyard. Reppert sat in the center of an outdoor loveseat, the space to either side occupied by cushions and book slates, suggesting that it habitually hosted only one occupant. He gazed out at the apple grove, seemingly oblivious to the new arrivals.

"Commodore?" The nurse leaned over him and laid a foreclaw gently on his shoulder. A rapid, clicking stridulation came from the nurse's mouthparts, interpreted into English by the voder he wore. "It's me, Nurse Morning Nectar. There are some people here from Starfleet. They'd like to talk to you, if you feel up to it."

"Starfleet?" Reppert murmured. "Of course they're from Starfleet. Tell them I'm not ready to beam back up. Still have two days' leave."

"Commodore, you're at your home, here on Kaferia. You have guests."

"Guests?" He seemed to snap out of his haze, turning to take in the visitors. Grinning, he rose to his feet and strode over to Spock and Uhura with unexpected vigor. "Welcome, welcome! Conrad Reppert, pleased to meet you. I get so few visitors from Starfleet anymore." He frowned at their red-jacketed uniforms and turtleneck collars. "I'm sorry, I don't recognize your division. Damn quartermasters never could make up their minds."

"Commodore, I am Captain Spock of the *U.S.S. Enterprise.* This is Commander Nyota Uhura."

"Spock, Spock. I've heard of a Spock. But no, he's a lieutenant on Chris Pike's ship. *Discovery*, wasn't it? No, it'll come to me."

Uhura stared at the commodore, recognizing a kindred spirit. Several months before her encounter with *Nomad*, right at the start of the brief Federation-Klingon War of 2267, Reppert had been captured on an intelligence mission in Klingon space and subjected to the experimental memory probe that they called the "mind-sifter." Uhura knew that Spock had endured the same probe on Organia, protected from its effects by his Vulcan mental discipline. Starfleet Intelligence trained its members to resist mental probes as well, but Reppert had been in Klingon hands for over a week and had endured repeated sessions under the mind-sifter at its highest setting, far beyond what Spock had experienced. The device had stripped his memories from his mind and left little behind. It had been much like what *Nomad* had done to her, but what *Nomad* had excised with cool, surgical thoroughness, the mind-sifter had ripped out with bare claws, leaving stray fragments behind but doing too much damage to the underlying substrate to allow Reppert to recover as Uhura had.

She felt ashamed of feeling so sorry for herself. She had lost memory but not function, allowing her to rebuild and resume her career with minimal difficulty. Reppert had been left a shell of his former self, damaged beyond repair and forced to retire decades early. For the first time, she felt that she had been the fortunate one.

Except that Reppert was their only lead to her past, and his memory was in ruins. What hope was there of recovering anything?

Uhura cut short that line of thought. She'd believed her own memories were just as irretrievable, until her family had proven her wrong.

She took the commodore's hands, drawing his attention. "Commodore Reppert . . . do you recognize me? We may have met when we were younger. I was a cadet at Starfleet Academy, early in my fourth year. I wore my hair long and straight then."

"Academy?" Reppert shook his head, giving a gallant smile. "If I'd had a classmate as pretty as you, dear, I'd remember."

"No, sir, you were working for Starfleet Intelligence. I was a student. I believe you came to speak with me about some research I was doing. Something involving subspace communications and the quantum vacuum."

"I studied communications at the Academy. Yes. Signal intercepts . . . decryption . . . They wanted to know our decryption codes . . . I wouldn't tell them. They put me in the chair . . ."

He was growing agitated now, and the nurse stepped in. "Conrad, it's all right. You're safe with us. You're here on Kaferia. Do you smell the trees? Do you hear the fruit drakes chirping?" The nurse laid both pairs of foreclaws on the commodore's arms and shoulders, gently massaging them and turning him outward to look at the apple grove.

Reppert's anxiety subsided, and soon he was nodding and smiling. "Yes . . . such a pretty song they have. Have you heard it?" He turned. "Oh! Morning Nectar, we have guests. I'd better make some iced tea."

He moved inside, and Uhura looked after him with concern. "Will he be all right?"

The nurse turned his antlike head toward her. "Making tea? He's fine with a well-practiced activity like that. He might not remember why he made it, though."

Spock folded his hands before him, seeming hesitant to speak. Uhura could predict what he was about to say. "Nurse Morning Nectar . . . normally I would not make this suggestion, but our need for information is urgent, a matter of Federation security. Are you familiar with the Vulcan mind-meld?"

The nurse's bright mandibles blurred. "The commodore's doctors did consult with Vulcan healers years ago. They advised against telepathic intervention, due to the risk to the practitioner. To enter a mind so badly damaged and confused . . . you might not find your way out again. Or you might experience the same horrors the Klingons inflicted on him."

"In fact, Nurse, I already have. I was subjected to the Klingon mind-sifter during the same conflict as the commodore, though not as extensively. My mental disciplines allowed me to protect myself. As I am already familiar with the impact of the process upon the mind, I believe I could evade any harmful effects. I may even be able to ameliorate some of the damage the commodore suffered."

Morning Nectar spread all four arms. "Well, if you're sure, then I can't object. It's the commodore's decision, of course." Uhura reminded herself of the Kaferians' strong belief in individual freedom.

Spock stepped closer to Uhura. "Commander, assuming the commodore is amenable, he and I will require solitude. Aside from the extremely . . . intimate nature of the meld, there is the risk that he may inadvertently vocalize some fragment of classified information."

"I understand, Captain." She touched his arm, ever so briefly. "Sir . . . how likely is it that you can retrieve what we need to know? Is it worth the risk to you?"

Spock held her gaze evenly. "The likelihood that he retains a specific memory of his single meeting with you more than two decades ago is slim. However, we have no better options at this time." His features eased, the mask of command falling for a moment. "At the very least, I may be able to bring some comfort and aid to a fellow subject of the Klingon mind-sifter. For that alone, it would be worth the attempt."

She smiled up at him with deep fondness. "I should've expected nothing less, sir."

Uhura passed the time in Morning Nectar's company, drinking iced tea (which was really very good, sweetened with crystallized fruit drake honey) and discussing Kaferian linguistics. Even to her ear, the swift clicks the Kaferians' bright-hued mandibles produced, blurring together into a cicada-like drone, went by too quickly to discern much in the way of meaningful patterns. After a while, she gave up, with apologies to her host. It was starting to remind her too much of her research into the vacuum flare patterns, and of the fruitlessness of this investigation into her past.

When Spock emerged with the commodore, Morning Nectar moved to check on his patient. "Were you able to assist him, Captain?"

"Only to a limited extent, I fear. Perhaps his lucid periods will be slightly longer now. But most of what I could do to circumvent the damage has already been done by his brain's natural healing processes, and presumably by prior treatment. The point of diminishing returns has already been crossed.

"However, I have done what I could to seal away his memories of the trauma he endured in captivity. It may prevent further panic attacks, or at least ease them."

"Thank you, Captain Spock." The Kaferian understood that anything else Spock had uncovered was none of his business. He invited the commodore to the kitchen to help him prepare lunch.

Once they were alone, Uhura turned to her friend. She wanted to throw her arms around him and thank him for his compassion toward the old man, but she knew that even now, with his greater acceptance of emotion in the wake of V'Ger, Spock was still a very reserved individual who would find such a display uncomfortable. So she kept her tone professional. "Anything, sir?"

A small shake of his head. "No. While Commander Kor evidently exaggerated when he claimed the mind-sifter's maximum setting would reduce the subject to a vegetative state, he was truthful enough when he said that it emptied the mind of the memories it read. What remains are only fragments of a life.

"When I focused on his memories pertaining to Starfleet Academy, I did receive some sensory flashes that may have been connected to you—the shimmer of dark hair, the perception of a pleasant voice. But they were too difficult to distinguish from other sensory impressions. I do not know the commodore's mind well enough to organize and separate the impressions. Normally in a meld, the partner's mind guides one's own in interpreting their unique web of associations. But Commodore Reppert's mind is too disorganized for that."

Uhura sighed. "I understand, sir. We knew it was a long shot."

Spock studied her. "Still, you experience the disappointment that comes when a slim hope of success gives way to certainty of failure."

He really did understand emotion better now. "I just don't know where we can turn next. We're all out of leads."

"We have believed ourselves to have no leads before. Further investigation has produced new ones."

"Which have all gone nowhere."

"That is not predictive of future outcomes."

She laughed. "You know, Doctor McCoy is wrong. Your logic can be very comforting at times."

"Logic is meant for utility, Commander. We seek answers, not comfort. To that end, I suggest we return to the *Enterprise* and plan our next move."

"Yes, sir. Let me say goodbye to the commodore and Morning Nectar."

"Certainly."

She moved into the kitchen, where the commodore and the nurse were preparing something that resembled cucumber sandwiches. "Ah, there you are," Reppert said. "Would you like to stay for lunch? I . . . I'm sorry, I can't recall your name."

She stared at him for a brief moment. "It's Uhura, sir. And no, it looks lovely, but we don't have the time."

"Oh, too bad. I'm sorry I couldn't help you with your . . . the thing you wanted to know. I'm afraid it's all classified, you see." He tapped his forehead. "Couldn't tell you even if I wanted to. Locked up so tight even I can't find it. Sorry." He chuckled in evident good humor.

"I understand, sir. We appreciate your willingness to make the attempt."

"That's all right, dear. You always were passionate about recovering lost knowledge."

Uhura stared at him, shocked. "Sir? What do you mean by that?"

"Now, where did I leave the brown mustard?" The commodore turned away and toddled around the kitchen. None of Uhura's further entreaties distracted him from his quest for condiments.

What could he have meant—assuming he had even been thinking of Nyota Uhura, not someone else she had momentarily reminded him of? The one time they had met was long before *Nomad*, so what lost knowledge could she have sought back then? Lost by whom, and when? Where had she been seeking it? And what could it possibly have to do with the vacuum flares?

"Ah, there it is!" Reppert held up the mustard jar triumphantly. Uhura was grateful that at least someone was able to find what they were looking for.

Starfleet Medical

Leonard McCoy leaned back in his office chair and stretched his limbs, letting out a yawn. He'd lost track of the time he'd spent coordinating with Starfleet and civilian emergency teams and cataloguing medical supplies as part of Admiral Cartwright's vacuum flare preparation effort.

He would have preferred to spend the evening with Ashley Janith-Lau, as he had been spending the majority of his evenings and mornings lately. But she'd had to postpone their plans, for she'd finally convinced Commander Rakatheema to agree to another meeting to discuss her concerns about his goals for the Warborn. Since he'd resisted for so long, there was no room in his formal schedule, so they would be meeting after hours at his home.

The hell of it was, McCoy realized that he didn't particularly mind having the opportunity to work overtime on flare readiness and other lingering responsibilities. "I'm turning into as much of a workaholic as Jim and Spock," he muttered. Quirking a brow at himself, he added, "And now I really *have* ended up talking to myself."

Then again, he realized, Janith-Lau was no less committed to her own calling, as evidenced by this evening meeting with the commander. He supposed a light, casual romance was the best thing for both of them. It was certainly safer, given his disastrous track record with serious relationships.

"Yes, that's for the best," he murmured. "Keep things fun and breezy. No angst, no drama."

The comm signaled, indicating an outside channel whose code he didn't recognize, but which had a Starfleet signature. He hit the activation switch. "Starfleet Medical. Leonard McCoy here."

"Len!" It was Janith-Lau's voice, sounding highly distressed. He sat up abruptly. *"You have to get over here, now. Please hurry!"*

"Ashley? Calm down, what's going on? Where are you?"

"At Rakatheema's. Please, Len, come right away! I think he's dead!"

Chapter Thirteen

Rakatheema residence
Presidio Heights, San Francisco

Captain Asakeph sh'Deslar peered intently at Ashley Janith-Lau, her antennae curling forward inquisitively. "All right, tell me again, from the beginning," the tall Andorian instructed.

McCoy put a supportive hand on Janith-Lau's shoulder as she sighed and gathered herself. It must have been hard on her, still being in the room where she had discovered Rakatheema's body, but the Starfleet Security captain had insisted that she and McCoy remain on the scene while her team finished their inspection. McCoy had told Janith-Lau to call the local police once he'd gotten off comms with her, but Rakatheema had been with Starfleet Security, and apparently Admiral Cartwright had pulled some strings to ensure his people would investigate the murder of one of their own.

"I arrived for our meeting and found the door ajar," Janith-Lau said. "I didn't think that was suspicious; nobody really needs to lock their doors on Earth, and I knew he was expecting me.

"But when I reached the study, I spotted Rakatheema on the floor beside his desk. I rushed to his side and felt for a pulse. I couldn't find one, but his body was still warm, and I'm not familiar enough with Arcturian anatomy to be sure I knew where to find a pulse. So I tried to administer CPR, but he was unresponsive."

"It didn't occur to you that handling the body might disturb the evidence?"

"I didn't know it was a crime scene. For all I knew, he'd had an accident or a stroke or something."

"So once you found him unresponsive, you called Doctor McCoy." Sh'Deslar's eyes and antennae shifted their scrutiny to him. "Rather than notify the police, you contacted your romantic partner."

"He's a Starfleet doctor with decades of space experience. I'm a pediatrician. I figured he'd be more qualified to help—if there was any chance the commander could be helped at all."

"And what did Doctor McCoy say?"

McCoy held his tongue. Sh'Deslar had already gotten his account, and no doubt she wanted to hear Janith-Lau's side to compare their stories. Still, there was something he didn't like about the *shen*'s tone.

"He told me to calm down—which was good advice. My practice doesn't bring me into contact with death very often, thankfully, so I was pretty shaken up. He said he'd be right here, and told me to call the police.

"About a minute later, he beamed in." She threw him a grateful glance. She was aware of his hatred of being transported, and what it meant that he'd chosen to brave it anyway to reach her side as quickly as possible. "He examined the body and confirmed that Rakatheema was dead beyond revival. Apparently Arcturians cool down more slowly than humans after death, what with their thick, insulating skin. He'd died at least fifteen minutes before I arrived."

"Before you *say* you arrived. So far, none of the commander's neighbors can confirm they saw or heard you."

"I'm small, and I prefer soft-soled shoes. I don't make much noise when I walk."

"And since you did walk rather than taking public transit or transporter, we can't yet confirm your arrival time that way either."

McCoy stared at her. "Captain, just what are you insinuating?"

"I'm doing my job, Commander. Doctor Janith-Lau claims to have discovered the body. Her DNA is all over it and vice versa, and our scans identify no other unambiguous DNA traces besides Commander Rakatheema's." Her antennae thrust forward aggressively. "There are multiple eyewitness accounts of an altercation between her and the commander three days ago."

He scoffed. "Because she's a *peace* activist who was worried he was pushing Starfleet in a militaristic direction! Are you seriously proposing pacifism as a motive for murder?"

"You'd be amazed what people can rationalize, Doctor."

"My God, Captain, Rakatheema's windpipe was crushed by a single blow! Does she look strong enough to do that?"

"On an Arcturian, if the blow is struck at just the right weak point, in just the right way—and it was—then great strength is not required. Someone with the knowledge and dexterity of a medical doctor could pull it off."

"She told you she doesn't know Arcturian anatomy!"

"She *told* me." Her brows lifted, driving home the point.

"Why, of all the—"

He broke off as Janith-Lau grasped his shoulder. "It's all right, Len. Like the captain said, she's doing her job. I'm a plausible suspect—the only one she has at the moment. I can't blame her for thinking that under the circumstances. She's only doing her due diligence. The best way to deal with it is to cooperate with her investigation. Surely it'll turn up evidence to clear me, or to identify the real killer."

"You're too trusting, Ashley." McCoy peered suspiciously at sh'Deslar. "Don't forget, Rakatheema was one of her own. And you know how Andorians are about vengeance. How objective do you think she can be?"

The captain kept her stony calm, but her antennae stiffened angrily. "For your information, Doctor McCoy, I was born and raised in Cincinnati. I'd appreciate it if you'd keep your stereotyped assumptions to yourself." McCoy flushed, feeling ashamed of himself. "And yes, he was Security, but I never met the man. I can do my duty fairly. I want to make sure I find the *right* killer, whoever that may be. That's the only way to get justice."

Sh'Deslar turned back to Ashley. "But you're right, Doctor Janith-Lau—at the moment, you're a definite suspect. Under the circumstances, I have no choice but to detain you for further questioning."

Janith-Lau nodded bravely. "I understand."

McCoy stared at her. "You're just gonna stand for this? Call your lawyer! Call Jim! We can fight this!"

She clasped his hands. "It's all right, Len. I know the truth will set me free soon enough." She smiled. "Besides, getting arrested is a badge of honor for a peace activist. Although usually not under these circumstances. I'll be fine."

McCoy kept his silence as sh'Deslar formally arrested Janith-Lau and escorted her away—but he wasn't about to take this lying down.

Kirk would know what to do.

Starfleet Headquarters

"Admiral, this whole thing is ridiculous! Ashley Janith-Lau is no murderer!"

Admiral Cartwright threw an impatient glare at Kirk as the two flag officers strode briskly through the halls of the Headquarters complex. "Based on, what, two weeks' acquaintance?"

"Doctor McCoy has known her for years. I trust his judgment."

"And I trust Captain sh'Deslar's judgment. I recommend you

let her do her job and focus on doing yours." Cartwright grimaced. "We're stretched thin already with vacuum flare preparations. The last thing we need is a murder to contend with!"

"All the more reason you should let me assist in the investigation, Lance. At least let McCoy handle the autopsy. The sooner we get this resolved—"

"Enough, Jim. You *and* McCoy clearly have a personal stake in this."

"I can compartmentalize my emotions, and I trust Bones to do the same. We both had to do so often enough on the *Enterprise*. I'm sure you did too. You know the rules as well as I do."

Kirk recalled a time or two when those rules had worked against him—such as the Ben Finney court-martial, where his own old flame Areel Shaw had been assigned to prosecute him. In a civilian court, their relationship would have required her recusal, but under military law, an inability to follow orders due to personal attachment would be dereliction of duty.

Cartwright was unswayed. "That may be the case on a starship out in deep space, where there's no other authority to turn to. A captain or CMO *has* to take responsibility despite personal attachment, because there's no one else. Here on Earth, that doesn't apply. I don't doubt your ability to compartmentalize when you need to, Jim—but you *don't* need to in this case. There's no good reason for you to be involved besides your personal interest in the suspect."

The senior admiral stopped and turned to face him, obliging Kirk to do the same. "You're still thinking like a frontier captain, assuming you have to take sole responsibility for everything that happens. You've got to accept that your situation is different now. You're part of a larger whole, and you can't just barge in and take charge of every situation. You need to learn that before you end up turning into some kind of maverick."

Kirk held his gaze evenly. "You give me too little credit, Lance. There's more at stake here than one person. The Warborn cadets have struggled to gain acceptance from the start, and they've just lost their primary advocate. With Rakatheema gone, that leaves you and me as the strongest proponents of their presence in Starfleet. We have a responsibility to see that this tragedy doesn't ruin their chances."

Cartwright's expression wavered as he considered Kirk's words. "That's a valid point. Still, you're too close to this. Besides, your responsibility is to the students—the Warborn and everyone else. They'll need your attention to get them through this hard time."

"That's fair." Kirk thought for a moment. "At least let me assign Commander Chekov to assist Captain sh'Deslar."

The senior admiral shook his head firmly. "I need Chekov for the flare task force. He's the closest thing we have to an expert on the damn things. He's currently out on the *Amazon*, patrolling local space."

"Sulu, then. He has some training in security." That was a slight overstatement; it was merely one of multiple disciplines Sulu had experimented with briefly in his early years in Starfleet. But it had been sufficient to let him double up as the *Enterprise*'s weapons officer on his first five-year tour aboard her, and to lead the occasional armed landing party. For what it was worth, Sulu's parallel counterpart in the alternate universe of the Terran Empire had been the *I.S.S. Enterprise*'s security chief, implying an innate aptitude for the role.

"He's had little contact with Doctor Janith-Lau," Kirk went on. "And as a faculty member, Sulu is under Professor Blune's authority, not mine."

After a further second, Cartwright nodded curtly and resumed walking toward the Major Missions Room. "Very well. *If* Captain sh'Deslar agrees. And if you agree to stay the hell out of her way and mine. Focus on your own job, Jim."

"Yes, sir. Thank you, sir."

He split off from the admiral at the next intersection, heading for the exit and from there to the Academy to speak to Sulu. He counted this as a win, but it was more of a compromise than he preferred.

Cartwright has a point, Kirk realized. *I can't do it all myself. I don't need to—there are plenty of others here who know their jobs better than I do.*

I need to learn to delegate. Trust in Spock and Uhura to handle the flares; trust in Sulu to handle the investigation. It's the students who need my attention now.

"Radiation signature detected!"

Admiral Cartwright spun away from the windows overlooking San Francisco Bay. His eyes swept across the three large screens that dominated the opposite wall of the Major Missions Room, showing status graphics of the ongoing monitor effort and patrol distribution across the Sol system. Indeed, the center screen was showing a graph of a radiation signature that had become familiar to Cartwright by now.

He cursed silently. He'd been monitoring the situation for over eight hours and had just been thinking of getting dinner. He supposed he'd just have to grab a ration pack when he could.

Lieutenant Kexas, the Edoan who had called out the alert, was shuffling around the "pool table," the double-hexagon console at the center of the room, working its controls with all three of her arms. "Confirming. It is a vacuum flare signature."

"Location?" As Cartwright moved in alongside her, he hoped this third flare event would be like the previous two that had struck the Sol system over the past fifty-two hours. Both flares had lasted nearly five hours and had grown to encompass a volume larger than the Earth itself, yet both had appeared in empty space, in keeping with the probabilities. The first affected zone had contained nothing of note besides a navigational buoy and a small Earth-crossing asteroid. The second flare had been in the path of an Earth-Mars shuttle with nearly two hundred passengers aboard, but far enough ahead that they were able to decelerate and avoid it; the only casualties had been a few missed appointments. Mercifully, Admiral S'rrel's fear of all the flares appearing at once had not come to pass. But that meant the threat would continue to hang over Earth and its neighbors for an unknown time to come. How long before their luck ran out?

Not long at all, he thought as he saw the location marker appear on the system overview display on the rightmost wall screen. Kexas spoke, confirming and adding detail to the display. "Flare zone is in the orbital path of the L5 Lagrangian community. Projecting growth rate and longevity . . . estimating sixty-two minutes before the first L5 facilities enter flare zone. Estimate fourteen percent of L5 facilities at risk of direct flare contact."

Commodore Song had called it. The L4 and L5 Lagrangian points—islands of gravitational stability leading and trailing Earth in its orbital path by sixty degrees—were natural places to locate space stations. The first wave of L5 habitats in the twenty-first century had tragically been lost in one of the early warp experiments, but the Lagrangian points had been too valuable to leave unoccupied for long, and thus they had eventually filled up again with asteroidal ore-processing facilities, repair and refueling stations, research outposts, and the like. Over the past two centuries, they had grown up into sizable space-based communities, orbital cities in their own right comprising numerous space stations spread out in wide orbits around the Lagrangian points like satellites around invisible planets. Given how wide a volume they occupied, it was no surprise that they would be the first targets hit.

"That fourteen percent. What's their total estimated population?"

A Zaranite ensign answered through his breathing mask. "Two hundred eighty-four thousand, Admiral."

And barely an hour to evacuate them. "Order all available ships to converge on L5. Ground all civilian traffic, and authorize in-system warp travel for the task force. Alert medical facilities to prep for incoming casualties."

The control room personnel moved briskly to comply with Cartwright's orders. This was what they'd spent the past few days preparing for, and they had it down cold. Cartwright was sure the captains and crews of the task force ships were equally ready.

But how well would the civilians of L5 cope with what was now bearing down on them?

U.S.S. *Amazon* NCC-1975

Pavel Chekov double-checked the sensor reading on his science station, praying it wasn't actually showing what he thought it was showing. With *Reliant* still under repair at Denobula, he had found himself assigned to the *Amazon*, a *Soyuz*-class ship very similar to *Reliant* in design. The bridge science console was a near-perfect match for his station aboard *Reliant*, but he hoped there was some subtle difference he had overlooked, leading him to misread its displays.

But the error check confirmed the result. Mizuki City, the massive L5 habitat that the *Amazon* had been assigned to evacuate, was moments away from being engulfed by a new surge of vacuum flare microbursts that had just erupted from subspace directly in its orbital path.

When Chekov announced this, Captain Jangura spun to face him, blinking his bulbous red eyes. "Damn. That's sooner than expected." The greenish-brown Saurian turned to his helm officer. "Merck, increase speed. Get us back there!" As the lieutenant acknowledged the order, Jangura turned to his first officer. "Randolph, how many people are left to evacuate?"

"Over four thousand, sir," Commander Joel Randolph answered in a lilting Indian accent. "But we'll have trouble punching transporter beams through that interference."

"Can you and Chekov make it any less troublesome, Commander?"

The handsome, dark-complexioned young officer traded a look with Chekov and nodded. "We can try, sir."

Chekov smiled briefly at his old Academy classmate. It was good to be working together again, though he was still getting used to thinking of Joel by his married name—and trying not to be too envious that Randolph had managed to find a spouse *and* become a first officer before Chekov did.

The two of them fell readily back into their old rhythms as they applied themselves to the transporter problem. It wasn't so different from the tests and simulations they had gone through at the Academy, aside from the stakes being much higher. Joel had always had a knack for outside-the-box solutions, though it had often fallen to Chekov to point out the practical problems he overlooked.

". . . So this lets us narrow the confinement beam and tighten the focus. It'll pierce the interference more effectively."

"But it will slow the transmission of the matter stream by nearly fifty percent, Joel. Which doubles the risk of a microflare emerging within or near the beam. It could blow the beam wide open and we'd lose the evacuees."

"They'd be at less risk as moving targets than sitting ducks, Pavel. Remember those tennis lessons I gave you? Always keep moving."

Ensign Rider at communications spoke up. "Damage report from Mizuki, Captain. Main power compromised. Several outer compartments breached to vacuum. Multiple fires ignited by microflares. Casualty list too, sir. Their hospitals are filling rapidly."

"And at just as much risk as the rest of the city," Jangura hissed. "Gentlemen, get those transporters working!"

But another problem was almost immediately heralded by an alert from Chekov's energy sensors. "A transport docked to the city is leaking gamma radiation! Looks like warp reactor damage. Containment fields weakening."

"Confirming distress signal," Rider added. "They're unable to shut down or jettison the reactor. They're evacuating back into the city."

"It won't save them if that reactor goes," Randolph said, striding forward. "Merck, get us in there! Rider, have them release the docking clamps once the ship's empty. I'll tractor it away." He took his position at gravity control.

Chekov kept working on the transporter problem, reorienting the targeting scanners to focus on the dock facility to which the ship's crew was evacuating. They were the ones in most urgent need of rescue. Clenching his teeth, he went ahead and made Randolph's proposed modification, hoping his old classmate was right about the odds.

"The ship is evacuated," Rider reported, "but docking clamps are frozen!"

Jangura turned to the tactical station. "Chu, target phasers on the ship's docking port. Blast it free."

"Twenty seconds to core breach," Chekov announced, even as he forwarded his final computations down to the transporter chief below. "Energizing all transporters now."

"Phasers locked," announced Molly Chu. "Firing!"

Chekov glanced at the main viewscreen, which Rider had focused on the transport ship and the adjoining docking module of Mizuki City. Both were engulfed in the fierce, eruptive sparkle of the vacuum flare, occasionally spitting out small jets of vaporized hull material or emitting brief, blinding flashes from inside their windows. A phaser beam sliced through the docking connector at the prow of the transport, and the blast of decompressing atmosphere, spent in a fraction of a second, pushed the ship into a slow, tumbling drift away from the station.

That tumble worried Chekov for a moment, but Randolph soon reminded him why he'd been the Academy's top tennis star three years running. He snagged the ship in the tractor beam with flawless aim and flung it deftly away from the dock.

Even so, it barely made it a kilometer before it blew. Anyone left in the docking module would have taken an instantly lethal dose of radiation. Jangura turned to the science station. "Transport status?"

Chekov smiled at the report from the transporter room. "Module evacuated, sir. All passengers now aboard."

"Very good, Commander. You think we can find room for a few hundred more?"

"As many as we can fit, sir."

He glanced over at Randolph, who gave him a thumbs-up. He returned it, but his celebration was guarded. This was one small victory in a larger crisis—one whose duration he could not predict.

Even a pro like Joel couldn't win every game.

U.S.S. *Prospero* NCC-1801

Malcolm Uhura slumped on the couch in the break room of the *Prospero's* sprawling sickbay. "Eighteen hours straight," he gasped. "I haven't had a shift like this since my residency."

The fatalities from the flare strike on Mizuki City and the other L5 colonies had mercifully been few, no more than several dozen, thanks to the advance preparations and the quick response of the emergency fleet. It would have been a considerably larger death toll if not for the hard work of the fleet's medical teams.

Malcolm had been struck by all the different ways the tiny, searing wormholes could injure people. Only a few had suffered internal punctures or burns from microflares manifesting inside them or passing through them. Many had suffered thermal or radiation burns from their proximity, or had their organs damaged by the overpressure shock from flares bursting in small, enclosed compartments, instantly superheating and expanding the air. Many had ruptured eardrums or retinal burns. Quite a few had been poisoned by noxious gases leaking from blown conduits or toxic compounds from vaporized structural materials. There had been a fair share of straightforward cases of thermal burns and smoke inhalation when leaking fluids had been ignited by microflares or by sparks from damaged electrical circuits. And inevitably, some had been crushed or trampled by crowds too panicked to follow instructions for an orderly evacuation.

Most of the injuries had been well within the means of modern medicine to cope with. Individually, they would have been fairly simple. But there had been so *many* of them all at once. Sometimes the difference between life and death came down to the brutal question of whether doctors had the time or resources to devote to a patient. Malcolm was grateful he had not had to make that kind of triage decision today. It had been arduous enough as it was.

"You did well, though." Doctor Christine Chapel sat beside him and handed him a cup of coffee, which he grasped as a lifeline. "You're a hard worker, like your sister."

He let out a small chuckle. "Ironic. Just a week or so ago, I considered my sister a lost cause, a nonfactor in my life. Now I'm the one being treated as an extension of *her* life."

Not that he hadn't been thinking in similar terms when he'd volunteered for the emergency program Starfleet was organizing in the Sol system to prepare for the vacuum flares. If this crisis was somehow connected to his sister, or aimed *at* her, then it was a matter of an elder brother's pride to stand against it. So it had been as Nyota Uhura's brother that he had signed on. He should not have been surprised that a colleague of hers had spotted his name and requested his assistance aboard her hospital ship. But it had been surprising to hear the glowing terms in which Doctor Chapel described his sister's brilliance and dedication, as well as her warmth and kindness. It wasn't normal for an eldest child to think of his annoying second-born sibling in such terms, even without twelve years of estrangement.

"So what's it like?" Chapel asked. "Finally getting to see your sister's world?"

He sighed. "It's . . . intense. Your world. Bizarre and stressful, compared to my cozy research lab back in Kampala." He gave Chapel an appraising look. "But it clearly forges powerful bonds among its members. I'm grateful that Nyota found *some* family in the wake of her memory loss."

Chapel held his gaze. "I was the one who did the bulk of the work re-educating Nyota after *Nomad*. I really came to feel a sense of responsibility for her. And even though her memory had been effectively reset to zero, I felt I got to know her better than ever before. Her keen mind, her eagerness to learn. Her love of music, her warmth, her playfulness. The things that remained intrinsic parts of her even without her memories."

He studied her. "Why did you keep her aboard the ship? Why not send her home to recuperate?"

She sighed. "We were out in deep space. *Nomad* damaged us, and by the time we were able to limp toward a starbase, another emergency came up and we had to divert. By then, Uhura was already back on duty, because she learned so fast. She was given the option of a medical leave . . ."

He nodded. "But she refused. She didn't want to face us."

Chapel touched his hand. "She didn't want to be reminded of what she'd lost. Remember, she only lost episodic memories, not emotional bonds. She could bear facing her crewmates more than her family, because losing her memories of her crewmates didn't hurt as much."

Malcolm thought that over in silence for a time. It was a good, soothing thought.

The next thing he knew, he was waking up on the couch hours later with a blanket draped over him. He smiled. Christine Chapel was good to the Uhura family.

Chapter Fourteen

Starfleet Security Headquarters

"Free Ashley! Free Ashley! Free Ashley!"

Vekal stood with Targeemos on the periphery of the group of protestors standing outside Starfleet Security Headquarters. The two cadets did not join in their chant, but they offered tacit support with their proximity. Vekal saw little logic in the idea that repeatedly restating a demand would increase the likelihood of it being granted, but apparently it had a symbolic value for these emotional beings, and Vekal wished to express his support for the peace movement's goals. His concern about Starfleet's intentions for the Warborn had only been exacerbated by the events of the peace activists' recent visit, and upon learning that Targeemos shared his concerns, he had suggested approaching the activists and offering their support.

Beside him, the natural-born Arcturian shifted her weight and looked around nervously, betraying a level of conviction rather weaker than Vekal's. "Are you sure it's okay to be out with them in public?" she asked, a variation on an inquiry she had posed several times already.

"Starfleet has always respected the rights of free speech and protest," Vekal told her, "and the freedom of its members to question and dissent, within the bounds of duty." He set his jaw. "If that has changed, then our concerns at the evolution of Starfleet will be borne out, and whatever response we may provoke will serve as evidence for our cause."

"I'm all for making my voice heard, but my parents would be furious if I got kicked out of the Academy in my first month."

"Whereas mine would be disappointed if I continued to pursue membership in an organization that did not comport with my principles."

"Great. Then I can come live at your house when I get kicked out of mine."

Further badinage was interrupted by the cheering of the protestors as Doctor Janith-Lau emerged from the building at last, accompanied by her attorney. The reporters on the scene moved forward, but the attorney intercepted them and advised them that the doctor would not be making a statement at this time. Instead, she hurried over to meet with the other activist leaders at the head of the group, the slightly built Vulcan woman T'Sena and the heavyset Argelian man Rogo. The other activists circled around the three leaders to cordon them off from the reporters and escort them toward their private air tram, which granted Vekal sufficient proximity to overhear their conversation.

"I've just been released on my own recognizance," Janith-Lau told them. "They still consider me a suspect." She pulled back her right sleeve to reveal a tattoo-like imprint on her forearm. "It's a passive sensor tag—it'll trigger an alert if I try to leave the city."

Rogo stared at the temporary imprint sorrowfully, as if it were a grave injury. "Outrageous. To impose such restrictions on your freedom when you've done nothing."

Janith-Lau showed far more equanimity. "Until they find evidence to exonerate me or identify the real killer, they have to consider me a suspect. I don't blame them for following procedure."

"You're far too trusting, Ashley. I wouldn't put it past them to have killed this Arcturian just to discredit our movement."

T'Sena gave him a look of strained toleration. "That is hardly logical, Rogo. The victim was one of the primary advocates for the increased militarization we object to."

"All the more reason it makes us look guilty! Just because he was the public face of it doesn't mean he wasn't answering to higher masters. This brings sympathy to their cause by making them look like the victims."

Janith-Lau touched his arm. "Starfleet isn't the enemy here, Rogo. We want to reform them, to remind them of their professed principles before they drift too far from them."

She widened her attention and raised her voice to address the group. "This is a distressing time for us all, but that's why it's important to keep calm and not lose focus. Let's just get back to our offices, regroup, reflect, and talk about what comes next. You're all welcome to join us."

As the activists filed into their tram, Targeemos hesitated and turned to Vekal. "Does that include us?"

"The word 'all' is unambiguous in English."

She glared. "I mean, *should* it include us?"

"Our classes are done for the day. And given the sentiments Rogo expressed, it might be of value to have Starfleet representatives included in the group to provide balance."

"We're a few years from being full-fledged Starfleet. If we don't get kicked out just for being here."

"Then that should make it easier for those with Rogo's sensibilities to accept us."

The young Arcturian still looked unsure of herself. "I don't even know how I feel about Rakatheema. I mean, I never wanted him to be murdered . . . but without him pushing for it, maybe we don't have to worry about the Warborn being misused anymore."

Vekal's expression hardened. "As long as the Warborn are present, the temptation for their misuse exists—both among their superiors and among the Warborn themselves." He stepped toward the tram. "Which is why this group's efforts are still needed, and why I am accompanying them. Are you coming?"

After a few more moments' hesitation, Targeemos rushed inside the tram just before the doors closed.

Presidio Heights, San Francisco

Hikaru Sulu hoped that solving Commander Rakatheema's murder would be easier than persuading Captain sh'Deslar to accept his help.

He had welcomed Admiral Kirk's decision to assign him to assist in the murder investigation. Not only was he concerned at what Rakatheema's death might mean for the Warborn cadets he had championed, but he was intrigued by the opportunity to explore the role of a detective, a persona he had only infrequently had occasion to adopt in the course of his career. But sh'Deslar had been reluctant to grant him the opportunity, even under orders from Admiral Cartwright.

"I know you," she'd told him when he'd reported for duty the day before. "Part of Admiral Kirk's special clique. He thinks he can use his influence to get me to drop the case against Doctor McCoy's girlfriend."

Sulu had put on his most charming, self-effacing manner. "Honestly, I've barely even met Doctor Janith-Lau. I'm more concerned about the Warborn cadets."

The captain had looked at him skeptically, adopting an interrogatory tone. "How so?"

"I've gotten to know a couple of them in my piloting class. I like them. I think they have a lot of potential. And I'm concerned what their sponsor's murder will mean for their future at the Academy. I figure there's a good chance it was done to hurt them."

Sh'Deslar had not softened. "It's reckless to presume a motive going in. It can bias the investigation."

Sulu had smiled. "'It is a capital mistake to theorize before one has data. Insensibly one begins to twist facts to suit theories, instead of theories to suit facts.'" He had shrugged at her stare. "Captain Spock likes to quote Sherlock Holmes."

She had crossed her arms. "So you're only concerned with seeing justice done for Rakatheema?"

"I wouldn't be here otherwise."

The captain had bent enough to let Sulu assist in the investigation, but only on a peripheral level. That was what had brought him out onto the streets of Presidio Heights on this brisk October morning, going door to door to canvass Rakatheema's neighbors for any information they might recall about the comings and goings around his apartment building on the night of his murder. On a safe planet like Earth, there was little need for widespread surveillance, so eyewitness accounts were their best option. Sh'Deslar had gotten no luck interviewing the fellow tenants of Rakatheema's building; none of them had seen or heard a visitor prior to the point when Janith-Lau had called for help. But there was a chance that the killer had been more careless before reaching the building—or after leaving it, presuming that Janith-Lau was innocent.

Presidio Heights was a quiet residential district in easy walking distance from Starfleet Headquarters and the Academy, a popular neighborhood for Starfleet personnel stationed in San Francisco, and not far from his and Demora's residence in Lower Pacific Heights. It was a nice neighborhood to walk through, with lots of elegant, lovingly maintained pre–World War III buildings coexisting alongside more modern ones. It had its share of steep, hilly streets, but that was no bother for a native like Sulu. If sh'Deslar had hoped to tire him out with busywork, she'd find that it had backfired. The chance to meet and converse with dozens of his fellow San Franciscans, a number of whom were current or former Starfleet members or the families thereof, was no hardship for the gregarious Sulu.

Eventually, his canvass bore fruit in a more practical way. A married foursome of Rigelians had been out on their balcony having a barbecue on the evening of the murder, and two of them recalled seeing an Arcturian in an Academy cadet jumpsuit coming from the direction of Rakatheema's building around the time of his murder.

"You're sure it was an Arcturian?" Sulu asked the two witnesses, the endomale and exomale members of the family.

"Oh, yes," said the pale, craggy-faced exomale. "We've seen the commander around the neighborhood often enough."

"They're rather distinctive, don't you think?" the smaller, silver-skinned endomale said. "All that loose, drooping skin. Hard to mistake for any other species."

"But this definitely wasn't the commander. Wrong uniform, and the build was different. Taller, leaner. There was something about their movement that seemed . . . dangerous. Like you wouldn't want to be in their way."

"Oh, do you think they killed the commander?" the endomale asked, clasping his husband's hand for comfort. "I've heard about these warrior clones on the nets. There's no telling what they're capable of."

"We can't say anything for sure yet," Sulu said. "We're just interested in talking to anyone who might have been in the vicinity. Can you give me any more details about the cadet you saw? Anything distinctive about their uniform?" He knew there was little chance the witnesses could have noticed anything distinctive about a Warborn Arcturian's face or build from such a distance.

The exomale snapped his fingers. "They had some kind of metallic epaulets, and a, a sort of tube wrapped around their chest and shoulder."

"Did you notice any color patterns on them?"

"Hmm, maybe. I'm not sure I remember specifically."

Sulu worked his data slate to call up personnel files of the Warborn cadets, setting it to display their identifying epaulet and bandolier patterns without showing their faces or other identifying information. He asked the couple to look through them for any familiar patterns. The Rigelians did their best, but they were only able to narrow it down to five patterns with common elements.

Still, their description of the cadet's path let him narrow his canvass, and before much longer, he turned up another witness, a black-haired human ballerina who'd been returning from an evening dance recital. She described spotting the cadet coming down the sidewalk toward her, freezing for a moment as if surprised to see her, and then turning off at the intersection between them. "They were nowhere to be seen by the time I got to the corner," she said.

"Did you get a good look at the cadet?"

She nodded. "They were right under a streetlight. I'm not sure I could tell them apart from another Arcturian, though."

"Can you describe what this person was wearing?"

The ballerina mentioned the epaulets and bandolier, and this time, when Sulu showed her the patterns on her slate, she was able to narrow it down decisively. "It's this one. The gold and black with the red diagonal stripe between them."

"Are you positive?"

"Honey, my father's a fashion designer. I grew up learning the business before I decided I loved dance more. I can't look at a piece of clothing without deconstructing its design and tailoring. I *wish* I could unlearn that."

Sulu smiled at her. "Hey, you gotta go with your dream. I appreciate your help. We may contact you later."

Despite his surface friendliness, though, Sulu's heart sank at her description of the cadet's bandolier markings. He was fairly sure he found it familiar himself. When he took back the pad and opened the full personnel file associated with the image, he winced as he read the name of the cadet who might very well have murdered her own Academy sponsor.

Portia.

Starfleet Security Headquarters

Kirk would have been pleased that Captain sh'Deslar's investigation had shifted away from Ashley Janith-Lau, if only it hadn't shifted toward one of the cadets he was responsible for. He would have preferred to keep the students out of this—especially the Warborn, who were grieving the loss of their strongest advocate. But the evidence sh'Deslar and Sulu had gathered could not be denied.

Thus it was that Kirk now stood in the observation room, whose one-way mirrored wall let him watch as sh'Deslar interviewed the Warborn one by one to gather further corroboration for her findings. To avoid leading the witnesses, the Andorian captain kept her questions general, along the lines of "Did you ever hear anyone at the Academy—a faculty member or a fellow cadet, say—express animosity toward Commander Rakatheema?"

"Too many to count," said the female Warborn named Viola. "Toward him, or toward us. A lot of people are unhappy having us here. That Vulcan, Vekal? His people are supposed to be unemotional, but I don't see that when he looks at us."

The Warborn resisted speaking ill of any of their own, their unit solidarity kicking in. The big one, Bertram, showed little interest in cooperating at all. "Rakatheema was a fool. We don't belong in Starfleet. We don't belong anywhere. Maybe now they'll send us back home and freeze us again. Best thing for everyone."

Sh'Deslar had little luck penetrating their group loyalty—until she spoke to the boyish Benedick. "I want to help any way

I can, Captain, really," he said. "But I can't believe any of my fellow students would've done harm to the commander."

"Then the more information you share with us, the more easily we can clear them as suspects. If they're innocent, surely the evidence will show that. Simply telling us what they said won't make the difference—it's just one piece of data to consider."

Benedick fidgeted. "Oh, naturally a number of cadets trash-talk their professors or even their sponsors. It's just . . . what's the human expression? Blowing off steam. It's just the way some people are."

"Some people?"

"Well, like Portia. She's got a temper and she's not afraid to express it. She was really angry when we found out Rakatheema wanted us to fight for Starfleet. Said he was as bad as the Arcturians who exploited the Warborn of the past. But I didn't take her seriously. It's just the way she talks. They say it's good to talk about your feelings, right? That it's a healthier way to work through them than acting on them. Or so they said in psych class."

When Horatio's turn came, his concern was for Janith-Lau. "There is no way that woman is a killer, Captain. You should stop wasting time pursuing her and find the real culprit."

Sh'Deslar took in his gentle urgency. "What makes you so sure?"

"She is a woman of peace. It defines every thought she expresses, every action she takes. The very reason she opposed Rakatheema's advocacy of us was her fear that we might be exploited for martial ends. It would be contradictory for her to commit violence in the name of peace."

"But isn't that your whole purpose? The Warborn? To fight to preserve the peace of Arcturus?"

"To preserve the life and safety of Arcturians through our sacrifice. And yes, when necessary, through violence. That is the compromise of our existence. But Doctor Janith-Lau walks another path. A narrower, more difficult path, but one she is as firmly committed to as I am to mine. Of that, I am certain."

"In that case, can you think of anyone else who might have been hostile to Rakatheema? Perhaps even a fellow cadet?"

"I cannot believe that of anyone who seeks to join Starfleet. To choose that calling is to commit to the highest ideals."

Sh'Deslar cocked her head, her antennae shifting. "Some of your fellow Warborn seem less comfortable with that choice than others. Perhaps they aren't as committed to those ideals."

"I can't believe any of them would turn on a fellow Arcturian."

"Even one they saw as a threat? An exploiter, perhaps?"

"Our mission is to battle threats to Arcturus, not to ourselves."

"And none of you have questioned that mission?"

Horatio sighed. "I suppose some of the students must have told you about Portia's outburst a couple of weeks ago. All right—I can't deny it. I'm sure she won't either. She's very . . . forthright. Well . . . when it suits her to be."

"What do you mean by that?"

The soft-spoken Arcturian hesitated. "She can be very private too. We're used to living and working communally; even though we now reside in separate dorm rooms, we tend to congregate together between classes. But Portia has been prone to wander off by herself at times, increasingly of late. When we ask where she's been, she tells us to mind our own business." He chuckled. "I suspect she might be experimenting with sexuality. It's not something we normally contend with, but our whole purpose here is to expand our horizons, and she's the most daring of us. But I don't know who she might be doing it with. You'd have to ask her."

The captain leaned forward. "Do you remember if she 'wandered off' two nights ago?"

Horatio stiffened. "I'd really rather not confirm that, Captain."

"Shall I make it an order, Cadet?"

He sighed and spoke reluctantly. "Yes. She was absent for some time."

Finally the time came to speak to Portia, and this time, sh'Deslar saw no need to be circumspect. Indeed, she asked Kirk to join her in the room; as commandant of cadets, he should be on hand for whatever was to come next.

The security officer got right to the point. "Where were you two nights ago, Cadet Portia?"

The cadet stared back angrily. Kirk was struck by how physically similar she, Horatio, and most of the others were, yet there was no mistaking the intensity in her eyes or the raptorlike alertness in her body language. "I was by myself. Walking along the shore."

"Can anyone corroborate that?"

Portia bristled. "Why should they need to? Isn't my word good enough?"

"Just answer the question."

"No."

"Excuse me?"

Portia grimaced. "I mean that no one can corroborate it. I go out there to be alone. Get away from everyone looking at me like I'm about to snap and kill someone."

Sh'Deslar's antennae darted forward at her choice of words. She activated a data slate and pushed it over. Portia glanced down at the video file it played. "What's this supposed to be?"

"Don't you recognize the person in that file?"

"It looks like me. I'm walking across campus. So what? I do a lot of that."

"This was taken by a surveillance imager at the edge of the Academy campus two nights ago—the night you claim to have been down by the shore. It shows you leaving campus in the other direction—toward Presidio Heights."

"Impossible. I wasn't there."

"You just said that was you."

"I said it *looks* like me. Most of us look like me."

"The bandolier pattern matches yours."

"Must be a trick of the light."

"It isn't. Image analysis confirms it. What's more, gait analysis shows it to be consistent with your movements."

Portia leaned forward and spoke insistently. "It wasn't me. Your computers are wrong."

"We also have eyewitnesses confirming the presence of an Arcturian cadet wearing your bandolier in the vicinity of Rakatheema's apartment."

"Then they're lying. What is this, some kind of plot to discredit us? Prove we're as savage as they say we are?" She looked up at Kirk. "How are you part of this, Admiral? You said you were our advocate."

Sh'Deslar went on relentlessly. "We also looked more closely at the DNA evidence from the murder scene. Arcturian genetics are . . . complex, but once we filtered out Rakatheema's own DNA, we found genetic traces consistent with an Arcturian female, with the epigenetic configuration unique to the Warborn. The only female Warborn cadet whose recorded DNA profile is consistent with those traces is you, Portia."

The young Arcturian's eyes widened in disbelief. "That's impossible."

"Do you deny that you're capable of killing?"

Portia glared. "Of course I can kill. That's what I was designed to do. But I wasn't there."

"Eyewitnesses say you resented Rakatheema. That you believed he wanted to exploit the Warborn."

"He did. He as good as admitted it."

"So he was a threat to you and yours. And as you said, you were designed to eliminate threats to Arcturians."

"You're twisting it!" Portia took a deep breath, gathering her wits. After a moment, she spoke more carefully. "I may not have approved of all of Rakatheema's goals for us, but his support still benefitted us. I didn't have to like him in order to go through the doors he opened. He got us off Arcturus, worked to convince people to give us a chance to be more than just cannon fodder."

She looked up at Kirk with a touch of pleading in her eyes. "I've enjoyed that chance, Admiral. I've only just started to explore the freedom to become who I choose to be. I don't want to lose that. You know the first thing I thought when I heard the commander had died? That we might not get to stay at the Academy without his advocacy. That all the new possibilities I've discovered could be taken away.

"If people think one of *us* killed him, that will just strengthen their belief that we're too dangerous to be in Starfleet—or even to be let out of our cryopods. His murder could cost us everything we've gained. I'd have to be crazy to kill him. Any of us would be."

Kirk wanted to believe her. As strong as the evidence appeared to be, he recognized the mentality of a soldier in Portia. She was capable of violence, he was sure, but in a disciplined, directed way, with purpose and precision. It was a tool to her, one to be wielded where it would do the most good.

Still, the case sh'Deslar and Sulu had built was too strong to ignore. "I'm sorry, Cadet Portia. But I can't deny the evidence."

She met his eyes with betrayal in hers, then turned to sh'Deslar. "Am I under arrest?"

"You're not a civilian. You're still bound to perform your duties as assigned by your commanding officer." She looked to Kirk.

"However," the admiral told Portia, "you are to be held subject to certain restrictions pending an official hearing. You're forbidden to leave Academy grounds except under official supervision. You're to report to me on a daily basis. And you're not to be allowed any access to weapons or to pilot any vehicles."

That last part seemed to be the one that hurt Portia the most. Kirk recalled Sulu telling him how well she had taken to flying.

Still, she quickly gathered herself and met his eyes again. "Fine, sir. The sooner I get to make my case at that hearing, the better. Whoever killed Rakatheema is targeting us. I won't let that happen without a fight."

As he met her gaze, Kirk had no doubt she was up for any fight that came her way. But would that free her or convict her? And would the rest of the Warborn share her fate?

Chapter Fifteen

U.S.S. *Enterprise*

Less than a day after the flare strike on the L5 community, the *Enterprise* had received a transmission from Rajendra Shastri of the Penthara IV colony, addressed to Nyota Uhura. "*When you contacted me earlier, I knew it had to be connected to these flares, but I ignored it anyway. I let my . . . my personal feelings blind me to how serious the problem was. Now, after Denobula and L5 . . . I can't pretend anymore. I'm ready to talk.*"

As it happened, the *Enterprise* had already been en route to Penthara IV in hopes of locating Shastri, their sole remaining lead. Captain Spock arranged with the colony's leaders to place Shastri on their fastest interstellar craft, on course to rendezvous with the *Enterprise*. Twenty-nine hours later, Spock and Uhura stood in the transporter room and watched as Commander Scott beamed the man aboard. Uhura was still confused but no longer surprised by the surge of complex, intense feelings she experienced at the sight of Shastri, the same feelings that every mention of his name had evoked. She hoped his presence would resolve that mystery as well as the other, greater ones.

Rajendra Shastri was not a particularly striking presence—a

man about her age, average in height, with features consistent with the South Asian origin of his name. Those features were pleasant enough, but not compelling to her. Whatever lay beneath these powerful emotions was nothing so superficial.

In the briefing room, once Spock and Uhura had explained the entire situation and their reasons for seeking him out, Shastri shifted uneasily in his seat as he absorbed it. He had trouble meeting Uhura's eyes. "So you really did lose your memory," he finally said.

"I had no reason to lie about that," Uhura told him, unable to keep a touch of resentment out of her voice. "Did I?"

He wrung his hands together. "I didn't . . . I didn't know what to think. It was such a . . . so hard to believe. And coming so soon after everything that happened on Argelius . . ." He was visibly wrestling with deep emotions of his own. Finally he met her eyes. "I guess I was afraid it was too good to be true. That you'd had second thoughts and . . . and gave me a feeble excuse for breaking things off with me."

Uhura was stunned. It explained everything she felt, yet it fit none of the facts. "We were lovers?"

Shastri winced and let out a painful laugh. "Well . . . only barely. We'd only just started. I mean . . ." He took a deep breath. "At the Academy, and afterward, we were just good friends. I certainly thought you were beautiful, I would've been open to that, but you were always seeing someone else. Or I was, or we were both so caught up in exams and simulations and field training that we didn't have time for personal lives."

"So what *did* we do together, Rajendra? What did we work on at the Academy? And what's the connection to Argelius and the other planets?"

He shook his head. "So strange to hear you use my full name. To see you look at me like a stranger."

"Mister Shastri," Spock interposed, "there will be time to

process your emotions later. For now, it is urgent that you tell us what you can about your researches with Commander Uhura."

"Of course, Captain. I'm sorry—I left Starfleet discipline behind a long time ago."

He took a breath and straightened his shoulders, then began again, turning to Uhura. "You and I bonded over the fact that we were both subspace hams in our youths."

She nodded. "My family told me. It's how we found you."

"Did they tell you about the musical patterns you thought you heard in the subspace noise?"

"Yes. But they said I abandoned it because I realized so many signals from random points in space couldn't share a common origin."

"You did, but . . ." He let out a nervous laugh. "So strange to be telling *you* about your own words. You never forgot anything!"

"Please, Rajendra."

"Right, right. Sorry. What you told me was that you knew intellectually that it didn't make sense, but you could never completely shake the feeling that there'd been something there. You were embarrassed about having so much trouble letting go of a—of what you thought was a childhood daydream."

"You make it sound as though it wasn't."

A brief, convulsive grin. "You always wanted to rush through a good story, Nyota. I'll get there.

"What I told you was that I trusted your instincts. If you felt there was really something there, you shouldn't have given up on it. And you'd gotten me curious as well. I wanted to hear this . . . this music of the spheres for myself.

"Anyway, you agreed, but you were still a little embarrassed about it. You were so driven then. Trying to live up to a family of overachievers. So you swore me to secrecy. You didn't want anyone to know if it turned out to be nothing.

"We had to find some . . . creative ways to get time on the

Academy's subspace equipment." Shastri spread his hands and shook his head at the looks on the officers' faces. "Nothing larcenous, just allocating an hour or two of buffer time here and there when we requested the equipment for our formal studies. You mastered things so fast anyway that you usually had plenty of time to spare.

"Before long, you were able to track down more of the signals—or at least what you believed were signals. I wasn't as convinced I could make out patterns in the noise as you were, but I never had your ear. Still, with Starfleet equipment, we were able to verify a nonrandom structure to the patterns. Elements of rhythm, harmony, recurring motifs . . . like music, as you always said. Or like math—the kind of fundamental mathematics often used to establish a translation baseline starting from first principles.

"We tried sending replies on the same frequencies, to test whether there was really an intelligence behind the signals, something that might react to our response. If there was someone there, we wanted them to know they were being heard and that we wished to communicate. When we analyzed the patterns that followed, we did extract more information—hints of linguistic structure, densely packed, but too fragmentary, too alien, for the translators to parse. But we weren't sure if we were getting results because they were actually responding to us, or just because our decryption algorithms were improving.

"As we analyzed the emissions, we determined they had attributes consistent with quantum wormholes. The kind that pop up naturally out of the quantum vacuum all the time."

Spock and Uhura traded a look. Finally, this was starting to connect. Still, Uhura was puzzled. "Natural quantum wormholes come and go almost instantaneously. To persist long enough to transmit meaningful information . . ."

"Yes. We knew how unlikely it was, but that made it a mystery worth pursuing—as well as one we were both determined to keep to ourselves until we could be sure we weren't missing some embarrassingly obvious explanation.

"After all, your original reason for giving up on the search was still there: How could the same signal come from so many unconnected points?"

Spock leaned forward. "If I may interpose, Mister Shastri . . . I presume you both considered the fact that wormholes' points of exit can be quite distant from their points of origin. Thus, a single source could transmit wormholes to any number of widely distributed coordinates."

"Naturally, Captain Spock. That was the first thing we looked at. But the wormhole signatures didn't fit. The spatial gradients, the EPR tensors, the transkinetic vectors . . . at least, the ones they'd have to have to match what we were reading . . . they didn't converge in any number of dimensions. If anything, the signatures suggested that each individual quantum wormhole spanned hardly any distance in space."

Spock's brow lifted. "You stress 'in space.'"

Shastri nodded heavily. "As opposed to time. Yes. Eventually Nyota and I realized there was only one explanation for how signals from all over space could have a common origin: because the whole universe had a common origin."

Uhura's eyes widened. "The Big Bang."

"Or just after it. When all the matter and energy of our universe—even the very space of our universe—was still compressed into a single impossibly dense, hot mass. Under such intense energy conditions, quantum wormholes would've been spontaneously forming all the time—and with such intense energies driving them, the wormholes' other ends could come out anywhere in space and time. Including our time."

"But that's . . . that's incredible. How could anything alive or sentient have existed in those conditions? Or for such a brief time?"

Shastri chuckled. "You asked that exact question back at the

Academy. Fortunately, there are a lot of professors at an academy. We posed it as a hypothetical question to our astrophysics instructor. You remember Doctor Sitko, right? Lanky guy with a beard and—" He broke off. "Oh . . . sorry."

"I understand."

He cleared his throat. "Anyway, Doctor Sitko explained that, due to the far greater density and energy of particles at the time, there had been more particle interactions—more *events*—in the first few minutes of the universe's existence than in the thirteen-plus billion years since. See, because all the particles were so much closer together, moving with so much energy, they interacted far faster, and far more often. Like how ten people in a turbolift will touch each other far more often than ten people wandering the Sahara Desert, and any one of them will need far less time to pass a rumor to the other nine. So it was like time was accelerated compared to now.

"Most people don't realize it, but most of the history of the universe, most of the interactions and transformations and upheavals it's ever gone through, happened in less than the first *second* of its existence—the four fundamental forces splitting apart, the inflationary epoch, quarks combining into protons and neutrons, matter and antimatter annihilating each other until the small excess of matter remained to make up the universe we know."

"Yet the primordial universe was in a state of thermal equilibrium," Spock pointed out. "Matter and energy were too uniformly distributed for complex patterns such as life or intelligence to form."

"That was true to begin with, Captain Spock. But for a window of about two, three minutes as the first atomic nuclei began to form, that equilibrium broke down. We tend to talk about the primordial plasma as being uniform, and overall, it was. But on a local scale, assuming it didn't all break down at once, then there could've been turbulent, dynamic interactions as things began to change. Like the smooth ice atop a frozen lake cracking into chunks as it starts to melt."

Uhura smiled to herself. Shastri may have left Starfleet years ago, but he was still practiced at that science-officer trick of devising mundane metaphors to explain complex science to non-science officers. The effort was unnecessary for Spock's benefit, but she appreciated the analogies. Her mind was already roiling enough from trying to assimilate the facts of her own past, without the added complication of recalling cosmological theory.

Shastri's hands, which had waved over the table to illustrate a smooth sheet of ice, now turned upward into a shrug of sorts. "It was a brief transitional period in the grand scale of things, granted. But at the accelerated pace of the newborn universe, those couple of minutes were like billions of years today. There's no telling what kind of complex patterns could've emerged from that turbulence."

"Fascinating." Spock steepled his fingers. "As we have traveled the galaxy, we have discovered that life and intelligence can be formed from any number of substrates beyond our own. We have encountered intelligences in the form of minerals, gaseous compounds, even self-sustaining electromagnetic and psionic matrices. In any substrate where patterns of sufficient complexity can form, consciousness can arise. Given the profound energy density and reaction rate of the Big Bang nucleosynthesis era, the complexity of the interactions that arose could have been . . . beyond anything we have encountered in our era."

Shastri nodded. "Countless civilizations could've arisen, thrived, and died out in the primordial plasma in less time than it's taken me to explain the theory. More civilizations than there are in the entire cosmos today."

His eyes were haunted when they turned back to Uhura. "Doctor Sitko saw it as a purely theoretical exercise, of course. But you and I realized that we might have been witness to a . . . a profound tragedy. We might be hearing messages from ancient, long-dead civilizations—countless species that thrived for subjective eons, but were doomed to extinction by the inevitable expansion and cooling of the universe, its transition into a state where their kind of life could no longer exist.

"Not only that, but what they were sending us was . . . eclectic. We were sure of it by then. Math and science, music, dense information that might've been written records, history, literature, art. Why would they send such a range of information types into the far future? It couldn't just be some kind of accidental wormhole spillage. It was too consistent, too *per*sistent over years.

"So we realized—what if the signals were an attempt to leave a legacy? To make sure their knowledge, their culture . . . even their music was remembered by the universe that came after them? It was the only explanation that made any sense to us."

Even Spock was stunned to silence for a few moments. At length, he spoke. "If true, this represented an astonishing discovery."

"We knew that, Captain." Shastri turned back to Uhura. "We talked it over for hours, and you decided that it was time we told people what we were doing. We wrote up a formal report and submitted it to our faculty advisor. We were hoping we could convince Starfleet that this was worth applying its full resources to—even if it did come from a couple of cadets."

He paused to take a sip of water. "We didn't hear anything for a couple of days. Then we were called in to a meeting with an officer from Starfleet Intelligence—Rupert or something."

"Conrad Reppert," Uhura supplied.

"That's right. He made it very clear to us that we were forbidden to pursue our project any further. Apparently Starfleet got pretty nervous about research involving time travel or communication with the past. They were afraid that if we sent messages back the other way, it might change things in the past—maybe even wipe out our own history." He scoffed. "Bizarre, right? Can you believe that?"

Shastri sobered at the serious look that passed between the two officers. "Oh. I . . . see Reppert wasn't the only one who thought that way." He blinked. "I'll . . . take your word for that."

"Hm. Well. At the time, Nyota, you didn't react the way you did just now. You and I were on the same page then. We argued that these plasma beings, as we'd started to call them—or, well, as I called them and you put up with—anyway, we insisted they were so far in the past that they might as well have been in an entirely separate universe. Nothing they could have done in the fireball universe could have prevented it from ending and producing the universe we know.

"But Reppert said the opposite might be true. The state of the universe today was shaped by its initial conditions in that fireball, so even the slightest change to those conditions could wipe out whole galaxies. The way he and Starfleet saw it, there was no telling whether the vast gulf of intervening time would damp out any alterations to nothing . . . or amplify them into an avalanche.

"So Reppert laid down the law: we were forbidden to conduct any further attempts at communication with the plasma beings, on pain of expulsion from Starfleet. All our work on the project was redacted and classified, and we were forbidden to speak of it to anyone. Even our faculty advisor." He lowered his eyes. "She was lost on the *Exeter* years later, I heard."

Uhura studied him. "But obviously that wasn't the end of it."

Shastri sighed. "It was for a few years. For myself, I was disillusioned by Starfleet's hidebound reaction to our work. I thought I was joining an organization where any kind of exploration was encouraged. After Reppert, the uniform started to feel restrictive. I stuck with it long enough to graduate, and to complete my minimum term in service, but I mustered out at the first opportunity.

"As for you, well, you seemed to be okay with it. You were still committed to your path in life, despite that setback." He smiled at her. "I'm the kind of person who'd walk away from an organization that didn't fulfill my expectations; you're the kind who'd commit to rising through the ranks so you could change it from within.

"Still, we stayed in touch after graduation, and though we never talked openly about the fireball universe, I could tell you were still haunted by the songs we'd heard. You felt their legacy deserved to be remembered—that it would be too great a tragedy if they had passed from the universe without any record that they ever existed.

"Of course, you were still under orders not to tell anyone about your research, and you wouldn't disobey. But I already knew—and after a couple of years, I was no longer in Starfleet anyway.

"Eventually, we started to collaborate privately on renewed attempts at contact—with whatever safeguards we could devise to minimize any risk of timeline contamination or whatever. You were traveling all over space on your ships, but I was a pretty active traveler too. When you had the opportunity to take shore leave on a civilized world with the right facilities and equipment, you'd let me know, and if possible, I'd meet you there. Sometimes you had to work without me, but I joined you as often as I could.

"We spent years trying to tease the signals out of the noise. We sent messages out to reassure them we were still listening, and to encourage them to focus their efforts on us so we could get a clearer, more complete signal, not just fragments. Sometimes the wormhole signals reacted to us, changing in response, intensifying. Sometimes they seemed to echo back traces of what we sent them, as if to confirm our message had been received. But it was tenuous, fragmentary at best—never enough to open clear communication. The quantum foam was too intermittent a medium for that. Everything we sent through, everything we got back, it was like it went through a blender in between. We could never quite build the right algorithms to reconstruct it, not with the way the quantum vacuum constantly shifted. But there were enough hints of progress that it inspired us to keep striving."

Shastri fell silent for a moment. Then he smiled, blushed, and continued a bit more hesitantly. "It was just the two of us, meeting privately, having our little scientific trysts and hoping nobody would find out. It was exciting. Romantic. And as you tried to contact the plasma beings—well, you sang to them. You'd always thought of their signals as music, from the first time you picked up traces of them, so that was how you signaled back. And having such an extraordinary audience . . . it inspired you. You'd never sung so beautifully.

"As we kept up the research on and off for several years . . . well, I found my friendship for you turning into love. I had no idea if you felt the same way, though. And I didn't want to risk ruining what we had—either the friendship or the research."

He paused. "Finally, on Argelius, things came to a head. We made a breakthrough—finally, a coherent two-way communication with the plasma beings, signaling our presence and getting an acknowledgment beamed back, an unambiguous echo of the song you'd sung to them."

He grinned, still blushing. "We were thrilled, overjoyed. After years of teasing and frustration, we finally had fulfillment. And . . . well, we were on a planet of free-love hedonists. When in Rome . . ." He cleared his throat. "We fell into each other's arms and . . . well . . ." He finally met her eyes again, though his emotions remained guarded. "I discovered that my feelings for you were mutual. You told me you loved me too. That you could share things with me that you couldn't with anyone else. By the time your leave ended . . . our friendship had become something more. You made it clear to me that you wanted it to continue."

Blinking away tears, Shastri lowered his gaze. "But then, just a few weeks later, you suddenly fell silent. I sent messages, but got no reply for nearly a month. I was panicking and fearing the worst even before I got your message. That . . . that cold, distant message, as if from a stranger, telling me that you had . . . no *memory* of me." He winced. "It was devastating. How could I believe such an outrageous claim? And how little must I have meant to you, that you'd toy with my affections like that and not even give me the courtesy of a credible excuse for dumping me? It felt like you were insulting me on purpose, and I couldn't for the life of me understand why."

Shastri rose from the table, unable to sit still anymore. He ran his fingers through his short black hair as he gathered himself. "Long story short—too late—I dealt with my pain by moving to Penthara, throwing myself into the work of building a new colony. I tried to forget my old life, to start over." A smile began to return to his features. "And I did. Build a new life, that is. I made new friends . . . eventually fell in love and settled down."

He pulled a small holo-imager from his pocket and activated it, displaying the image of a striking, purple-haired Catullan woman and a small boy blending her features and Shastri's. "My wife, Sudo. Our son, Kiran."

Uhura smiled at the picture, blinking away tears of her own. "They're lovely. I'm glad things turned out well for you." She hesitated. "I hope . . . now that you understand I was never lying to you . . . that we can . . ."

His tone sharpened. "What? Put it all behind us? Go back to the way we were? It's too late for that, Nyota. What happened on Argelius—it changed everything. Nothing could go back to the way it was before. Nothing *should*."

"But what we almost had—what we had for one brief shining moment—you cast that aside forever."

"I couldn't help it," she protested. "I couldn't remember."

"But you could have *tried*!" Glancing at Spock, he took a deep breath to calm himself. "Yes, I was furious. I thought you were lying. I sent you that angry letter saying I never wanted to speak to you again. But you *accepted* that. You . . . you told me just now that you felt a powerful surge of emotion when you saw my name. You could've acted on that. Ignored my angry letter, tracked me down, made me understand."

Shastri drew in several deep, slow breaths. "Instead, you gave up at the first obstacle. That's nothing like the Nyota I knew. She would *never* have given up on trying to communicate.

"But she's gone now. She's as good as dead. And the woman who took her place . . . you didn't have the courage to face me, to understand what I was to you or what you'd done to me. And so you never rediscovered the work we'd done. You abandoned the plasma beings as completely as you abandoned me.

"That's what's going on now, Nyota! Don't you get it?" He flung out an arm, gesturing toward the universe beyond. "It's the plasma beings. A dying civilization, calling out for someone to remember them. They got one brief answer, raising their hopes—and then nothing.

"So they've been boosting their gain, trying to push a signal through. Pouring more and more energy into their quantum wormholes, aiming at the star systems where they picked up our earlier, fragmentary attempts at contact."

Spock's brows rose in alarm. "The energy of the primordial plasma is effectively limitless by our standards. With more of it being applied at each attempt . . . there is no telling how destructive the vacuum flares may become."

Shastri's gaze still bored into Uhura, though. "If you had tried harder, if you'd tracked me down and confronted me . . . I would've reminded you of your research. I don't know if I could've still done it with you, but at least you would have *known*. You would've resumed contact with them long ago. And none of this would be happening now.

"That's not because some killer robot wiped your memory. That's because you turned away from getting it back." He leaned forward, resting his palms on the table. "Because you gave up on your past. You gave up on me. And so you gave up on them—on a dying civilization crying out for your help.

"Just look what's resulted."

Spock had the good grace to look disapprovingly at Shastri on Uhura's behalf. But it was more than she deserved. Shastri was right—she had succumbed to her fear and taken the easy way out, avoiding her past rather than facing the pain it caused. She had deprived her family, and herself, of twelve years together. She had thrown away a chance at a lasting love.

All of which paled in comparison to the greater catastrophe she was responsible for.

Chapter Sixteen

U.S.S. Enterprise

"So now we know the source of the vacuum flares." Spock addressed the briefing room screen like a professor before his class as he summarized Rajendra Shastri's revelations. His audience consisted of Admirals Morrow and Cartwright as well as Federation president Chab jav Lorg, who had joined them in Starfleet Headquarters' Major Missions Room for this briefing. Uhura stood alongside Spock, with Montgomery Scott on her other side. The subspace signal was clear enough for mutual comprehension, but it was overlaid with both visual and aural static that made Uhura's fingers twitch, reflexively seeking a console she could use to clean up the signal.

"The entities existing in the primordial universe—which we have provisionally designated 'plasma beings'—lost their line of communication almost immediately after opening it. We surmise that they have been attempting to reestablish that link by sending more and more intense quantum wormhole probes to those approximate locations where they made partial contact with Commander Uhura before."

Uhura stayed quiet. She was still wrestling with the emotional impact of what Shastri had told her. She thought she had worked through her grief and anger long ago, but here was one more precious thing that *Nomad* had stolen from her, and the pain was as fresh as the discovery. Her mind reeled at the lost possibilities, the life she might have had if only she hadn't been humming to herself on the bridge that day.

The personal blow of discovering a forgotten love was painful enough—but beyond it was a far more profound sense of loss. *Nomad* had not only stolen her love; it had stolen her life's work, and with it the hope of an unimaginably ancient and alien civilization to pass along its legacy. In their desperation to renew contact, the plasma beings had unknowingly killed or injured hundreds of innocent people. Her personal loss had snowballed into a far greater tragedy.

"But why start now, twelve years later?" Cartwright asked. *"And why track backward through prior contacts?"*

Spock had clearly anticipated the question, given the readiness of his reply. "The early universe operated on a profoundly different time scale from our own, Admiral. As the wormholes are temporal to begin with, the relative passage of time at the different ends need not align. I would hypothesize that their first successful attempt to restore contact at Argelius simply happened to manifest a dozen years later in our time frame—an infinitesimal margin of error compared to the billions of years of separation between their era and ours. Subsequent attempts were presumably calibrated to follow its parameters and thus have occurred near the same time.

"As for the reversal of the sequence, they could be systematically backtracking through their prior contacts—or there could have been some form of temporal inversion in the original transmissions Uhura and Shastri sent to them. Again, the relation between our time flow and theirs is arbitrary."

President Lorg wrinkled his snout in puzzlement. *"But why choose* our *time to focus on?"* the middle-aged Tellarite asked in his folksy Martian accent. *"If they were trying to contact beings in the later universe, they could have done it with any number of other civilizations over billions of past and future years."*

"They, or others like them, may indeed have done so, Mister President," Spock replied. "It is quite possible that more civilizations—if that term can be meaningfully used for societies of such a profoundly alien physical nature—rose and fell within the several minutes of the nucleosynthesis era than have existed in the subsequent thirteen point seven eight billion years of the far cooler, more diffuse universe we occupy. Many such species throughout space and time may have made similar contacts in the past, or may do so with other primordial plasma civilizations in the future."

Uhura was finally compelled to speak. "Which doesn't diminish the importance of preserving *this* civilization's distinct culture and history, if we can renew contact." She paused, glancing apologetically between Spock and the dignitaries on the wall screen. "I'm sorry, sirs. But if there's one thing recent events have made clear to me, it's that no one deserves to be forgotten. In the end, how we're remembered—or whether—is all we have. These beings are pleading with us to be heard, Mister President. We owe it to them to listen."

Morrow and Lorg looked sympathetic, but Cartwright's steely gaze didn't waver. *"That's all well and good, Commander, but it's hardly our priority right now. The flares in the Sol system are still coming, growing larger and more frequent. The last two have struck in empty space, but the second missed engulfing Luna by only a couple of million kilometers. We're relying on luck here—we still haven't found a way to modify deflector shields to keep the damned wormholes out."*

Commander Scott shook his head. "That's a futile effort, sir. They pop right out of the fabric of space itself, anywhere they like, even inside a ship and its shields."

"We know that, Mister Scott, but what else do we have?"

The burly, gray-haired engineer narrowed his eyes in that thoughtful way he had. "I've been thinking about that, Admiral. Maybe we need to be thinking less about walls and more about oil on the water."

Cartwright frowned, but it was Morrow who answered. *"Oil, Commander?"*

"Aye, you know. Mariners as far back as Aristotle knew you could calm a turbulent patch of water by spreading oil over the surface. The surface elasticity of the oil helps dissipate the wave energy—"

"Yes, yes, we know, Commander. I take it this is an analogy for something relevant?"

"Certainly, sir. The micro-wormholes in the vacuum flares—they're basically churned up by the turbulence created in the quantum foam on our end when those plasma folks pour energy into it from their end. So if we could permeate that volume of space with something like, oh, a dense field of polarized verterons . . . it might overwhelm the fluctuations creating the turbulence, damp them down like spreading oil on stormy water."

Spock was nodding now. "Yes. While the analogy is crude—no oleaginous wordplay intended—the principle is sound. It would be unlikely to *prevent* the flares, not at their current level of intensity, but it could ameliorate the intensity of a flare outburst, with fewer, less energetic microflares emerging in the affected area."

President Lorg snapped his thick fingers. *"Verterons. Back about a century ago, the early Martian colonists used verteron arrays to divert comets to Mars for terraforming. If there are still some of those around, could they create a big enough field to protect a planet?"*

"Doubtful," Spock said. "Any protective effect would be limited in range and efficacy; the wider the field, the weaker the damping."

"*Still, any damping is better than nothing,*" Cartwright said. "*At least we could try to protect vital areas, like the capital and Starfleet Headquarters.*"

Scott spoke up. "I think I can rig the *Enterprise*'s warp reactor to generate a verteron field inside the ship." He shook his head unhappily. "I don't like what it'd do to the warp coils, though."

"Mister Scott," Spock pointed out, "if we were in the midst of a vacuum flare, we could not engage a warp field in any case."

"We might not be able to afterward either, Captain." He sighed. "But if Earth is to be our last stand, I suppose it doesn't matter."

On the screen, Cartwright straightened. "*Transmit your engine modifications once you've computed them, Mister Scott. Hopefully they'll let the patrol ships last longer if they have to fly into a flare for rescue ops.*"

"Aye, sir!" Scott's eyes gleamed in a way Uhura knew very well.

"*This is encouraging news,*" Admiral Morrow put in. "*But there's one more serious problem we need to address. Our physicists have detected some alarming effects on local subspace as the flares have gotten larger. Instabilities are forming, as if subspace is being eroded by the flares. If they continue to grow and get more energetic, the damage could become great enough to tear open rifts in the fabric of space. Not unlike what happened about a decade ago with Professor Kettaract's botched experiment in the Lantaru sector. You were there, weren't you, Captain?*"

Spock nodded. "Indeed. Such a permanent disruption of subspace could render warp travel, subspace communication, and transporters unusable within the affected portions of the Sol system.

"Worse: If the rifts are created by quantum wormholes transmitted from the primordial plasma, they could allow that plasma to emerge directly into Solar space. A plasma denser than neutronium with a temperature of billions of degrees.

It would be tantamount to a supernova occurring within the system. Not only would all life on Sol's planets and moons be destroyed, but the radiation could eventually endanger Alpha Centauri, Procyon, and perhaps other core Federation systems."

Cartwright turned to Lorg. *"Mister President, I insist you evacuate to a safe location."*

"Now, let's have none of that, Lance. I didn't get where I am by backing down from an argument. We can do something about this, right? Now that we know the cause, we're that much closer to a solution. We just need to contact these plasma creatures, reassure them that we can hear them, and ask them to kindly stop shouting."

"I'm afraid it's not that simple, Mister President," Uhura said. "Shastri and I were working in secret, so we didn't keep written records. We relied on my eidetic memory—if you'll forgive the irony. I've forgotten *how* we compensated for the scattering effect of the quantum foam to reconstruct a coherent signal—while Shastri has spent the past dozen years trying to forget. The signal reconstruction protocols were more my department than his anyway; he mainly helped to configure the equipment."

The president and the admiral exchanged worried looks. Spock turned to Uhura. "Nonetheless, Commander, you were able to contact them once—to deduce their very existence from nothing but a nigh-undetectable pattern in the noise. That scientific ability is still within you, even without your memories. And you are beginning at a more advanced stage. You know what you are trying to contact, and you know that contact can be achieved. You have been studying the signals for weeks now, no doubt recapitulating much of your original work.

"More fundamentally, we simply do not have any other options. You and Rajendra Shastri are the only ones alive with the necessary knowledge to make contact with the plasma lifeforms. You must try."

Uhura held his gaze and nodded. "Aye, Captain. I'll do my best."

"Then I am confident we will succeed."

She smiled, appreciating his praise, even as she doubted it. The work itself would be challenging enough—re-creating years of research under the pressure of a time bomb counting down. But having to work with Rajendra Shastri added further complications. The rift between them was deep—and she no longer knew him well enough to have any idea how to mend it. Was there any chance they could recover the rapport they had once had?

Or would picking at those old scars create a rupture as explosive as the one they were trying to prevent?

McCoy residence
San Francisco

Leonard McCoy smiled across the dining room table at Ashley Janith-Lau. He'd invited her over for a private dinner to celebrate her exoneration, and to introduce her to some Southern cooking, insofar as he could manage between his limited culinary skills and her strict vegetarianism. The meal was mediocre, but the company was exquisite.

"You must be relieved," he said. "I know how it feels to be accused of a crime you didn't commit. Once on Dramia— Well, never mind." It was not the best example, since he had feared he might actually have been guilty of gross malpractice and homicidal negligence until Spock had proven him innocent. He didn't want to make the conversation about his own past anxieties; he was here to support Ashley. "Let's just say that spending time with Jim and Spock tends to get a fellow thrown in an inordinate number of prison cells. I guess some of that rubbed off on you too."

She chuckled. "Give me some credit, Len. I've led protests on a dozen planets in my time. I've probably been jailed more often than you have. It's a good sign that you're making the right people uncomfortable."

"Most of those were Federation worlds, weren't they?"

"The Federation isn't perfect. We're better than most, but we only got that way because of past generations of protestors who pushed for a better world. And we do backslide now and then—our leaders get complacent and lazy and need a kick in the pants to remind them what we stand for."

McCoy nodded. "Good point. There have certainly been times when I needed to remind Jim what he stood for when he got blinded by duty or pride or whatever. Everyone needs a kick in the pants from their friends sometimes."

She grinned wider. "Did Jim ever throw you in the brig for arguing with him?"

"No, but I'm sure he was tempted." They both laughed.

Janith-Lau tilted her head thoughtfully. "Of course, it's different on a starship. There, the captain has supreme authority. Here, the people do—at least when they remember that they do. It's easy for people to lower their guard and trust their leaders to take care of the decisions for them. But leaders make mistakes, and people need to be aware of them. Seeing protestors get arrested when we stand up for what should be basic Federation values . . . it's an effective way to get the public to notice when the authorities lose their way."

"Well, that's another thing to be grateful for. You've pretty much been proven right about the Warborn. Their own patron . . ." He shook his head.

His dinner companion looked anything but satisfied. "I never wanted Rakatheema's agenda to end this way. I wanted us to find a reasonable solution together."

"Of course—I didn't mean to suggest otherwise."

She barely seemed to hear him. "And Portia . . . I don't know.

She's aggressive, to be sure, but there was something about her . . . a sincerity, even a vulnerability." Her eyes focused on his again. "But also a, a clarity. Intelligence too. It's hard to believe she'd do something so . . . chaotic, so self-defeating."

McCoy pondered her words as he took a bite of his grits. "I've found over the years that people with a mind to do violence can create all sorts of rationalizations that seem sensible in their own heads. We like to think we're rational creatures, but much of what we do is just animal instinct that we invent justifications for after the fact."

Her lips twisted at the sourness of his words. "I prefer to think people are better than that."

He shrugged. "Before we can get better, we have to admit our flaws to ourselves. It's like Jim says—we know we're killers, but we decide we won't kill today."

"Then Jim is cynical too. It's not that simple. Most humanoids evolved cooperation as their primary survival strategy. It's how we have complex language and the ability to organize into societies, pass down knowledge, build civilizations. The idea that we're innately savages with a thin veneer of self-control was discredited centuries ago. Cooperative, selfless behavior is every bit as innate to us as aggression."

McCoy tilted his head. "For us, maybe. But can you really say the same about the Warborn? A people literally bred to be nothing but killers?"

"I don't accept that they're so fundamentally different from other Arcturians. The differences are more epigenetic, hormonal."

"Epigenetics can have a profound influence on brain development. You know that."

"But given how differently they're raised, how can we know what's nature and what's nurture? Len, the Warborn I've met and spoken to are as diverse and individual and complicated as anyone else. I *liked* them. Including Portia. I just can't believe she's a murderer."

He furrowed his brow. "What other explanation is there? Who else has a motive to kill Rakatheema? Or the ability to frame Portia for it?"

She sighed. "I don't know. I just know I want to believe in her."

McCoy reached over and touched her hand. "You want to believe in everyone. It's a wonderful quality. But it means you're bound to be disappointed sometimes."

After a moment, she pursed her lips and tilted her head. "Well, I guess you're right. For instance, I believed you'd be a better cook than this."

He feigned offense. "My dear lady, I am a doctor, not a restaurateur."

Starfleet Academy

"Did you kill him?"

A moment after Bertram asked the question, Portia had him forced against the wall of Horatio's dorm room, where the Warborn had gathered to discuss matters in private. The others showed little reaction, for clashes between the two most aggressive members of the group were not uncommon. But Bertram merely spread his hands and gave a casual shrug, as well as he could with Portia's hand around his throat. "Just asking. I'm fine with it if you did."

Portia gave his neck one last angry squeeze, then jerked away. Bertram folded his arms and relaxed against the wall as if he'd wanted to be there all along. His careless manner disgusted her. "No," she insisted to the group as a whole. "I didn't kill Rakatheema. That would ruin all our chances of a real life."

Viola frowned. "But he wanted to use us for the Federation's battles."

"As an advocate, he could be countered. As a martyr, he's a

far greater threat to us." Portia hissed through her teeth. "And Starfleet's as good as abandoned us already. Even Kirk wouldn't stand up for me when I told them I didn't do it. Nobody's going to question the false evidence."

Viola and several others muttered in sympathetic anger. But Horatio put a calming hand on her shoulder. "Give them a chance, Portia. They have to follow procedure. If you didn't do this, they won't be able to prove you did."

She stared at him, jerking away from his touch. "'*If*'? You don't believe me?"

"I want to believe you. But you *have* said you wanted to fight for your own goals."

"Not like they say I did! If I choose to start a fight, it will be one I believe in, one I'm proud of. One I have no reason to deny."

"That's laudable. But it will be your word against the evidence, unless you can provide something more solid. An alibi, an eyewitness."

"I was alone. I wanted to be. You know I was always the best at stealth."

Horatio tilted his head. "You understand why that won't be seen as a point in your favor."

"Nothing will! Don't you get it? They've feared the worst from us all along. They were eager to have their suspicions confirmed. Proven or not, even the insinuation will harden people against us. We'll never be allowed to remain."

She smacked her fist into her palm. "This has got to be Janith-Lau's work. Her people have been against us from the start. Killing Rakatheema and making us look responsible for it solves all their problems."

Benedick looked confused. "But . . . they arrested her. Why would she frame herself?"

"She must have been sloppy when she framed me. She got caught in her own trap at first."

Horatio shook his head. "Listen to yourself, Portia. Practitioners of nonviolence using murder to advance their cause? That's contradictory."

Portia held his gaze evenly. "No, Horatio. It's hypocritical. Not everyone's as pure in their ideals as you."

He took a breath. "I'm just saying it's best to avoid these rash accusations. If you're concerned about what people think of us, then it's best not to play into their expectations."

"Forget that," she said over the end of his sentence. "I'm done caring what other people think of me or intend for me. If Starfleet won't trust me, if it won't accept me, then I want no more part of it. I'm leaving."

Horatio caught her arm, and she glared at him dangerously. "Where will you go? You're under restriction."

"Like I said—I'm good at stealth." She looked around. "We all are. We're trained in infiltration and survival in hostile territory. Plus we have the sensor and comms interference from these vacuum flares in our favor."

Benedick still appeared lost. "But the Federation isn't our enemy."

"If they think we're the enemy, it's the same principle. We need liberty to act. To gather intelligence and strategize the defeat of our real enemies. We can't do that if we stay here."

He considered for a moment, then straightened. "I *like* it here, Portia. I have friends here."

Horatio nodded, placing a supportive hand on Benedick's shoulder. "Many of us do. We are not without support. We should rely on that support, win more allies—not risk alienating the friends we have, sacrificing their trust by going renegade."

"You do that, Horatio. You're good at that." Portia shook her head. "I'm not. I need to fight to survive. It's what we are at the core, whether we like it or not. At least we can make it our own."

She looked around at the others. "These two are obviously staying here. Who's coming with me?"

Bertram shrugged and stepped forward from the wall where he'd been leaning distractedly this whole time. "I'll come. Why not? I never wanted this Starfleet thing anyway. You have a battle for me, I'll fight it. At least if we get caught, they'll ship us back to Arcturus where we belong."

With a sigh, Viola stepped forward too. "I'll join you. I've tried to become what they want me to be, but I can't change my instincts. It was simpler before all this."

Titus moved to join her, then Caliban. Benedick stood with Horatio, and they were soon joined by Rosalind, Lysander, and the rest. It was not quite an even split—seven to five in Horatio's favor.

But it would do. A small team was best for infiltration anyway. And peace activists would not be formidable opponents.

"Let's go," she told her four.

But Horatio moved to block their exit. "Please reconsider this, Portia. This would be reckless enough at any time, but especially now, in the midst of the vacuum flare crisis. This planet needs everyone working together for its protection. Protecting civilians is our innate purpose. Let us show them that."

Bertram scoffed. "Haven't you heard? There is no protection. The things can strike anywhere, even inside people." He squinted, no doubt from the strain of thinking. "Wonder what'd happen if one appeared inside your brain. Would your head explode?" Mercifully, everyone ignored him.

Portia held Horatio's gaze unflinchingly. "The more distracted Starfleet and the Earth authorities are, the better for us. And five soldiers more or less won't make any difference to Earth's defense. You handle that, Horatio. We have our own mission."

After another moment, Horatio sighed and stepped aside. "You have the right to choose for yourselves. I'm just sorry you didn't make a better choice."

Portia started for the door, then paused alongside Horatio

and turned to him. "They left us no better choices to make, comrade."

U.S.S. *Enterprise*

"You're kidding." Rajendra Shastri gestured around himself at the *Enterprise* communications lab, staring in disbelief at Captain Spock. "You want me to work in here, alone, with *her?*" His last gesture was toward Uhura, who again stood alongside Spock and Commander Scott.

The captain met his agitation with unwavering calm. "You agreed, Mister Shastri, to offer whatever assistance you could to resolve this crisis."

"I've told you everything I remember about how we made contact. The rest was in Uhura's head, and that means it's gone now."

Uhura took a step forward. "Not necessarily. At home, I discovered that some lingering imprint of my memories is still there—like a palimpsest in an ancient parchment. With a strong enough sensory stimulus as a reminder, the residual neural connections were revived, and I recovered partial memories. So . . ."

She faltered, so Spock took over. "Thus, our best option is to reconstruct the environmental stimuli surrounding your breakthrough at Argelius. It would take too long to travel there, but this laboratory is a reasonable approximation of the private facility you say you and Commander Uhura engaged."

"Reasonable?" Commander Scott made an offended face. "It's a damn sight better. Still, we can knock it down to their standards if we have to. Just tell me everything you remember about how their lab was set up, laddie, and my cadets and I will whip it into shape. Or out of shape, as need be."

"So you set the stage, and then what?" Shastri shook his head and paced the lab for a moment before continuing. "Uhura and

I were in there for two days. Working, talking, joking around. And finally . . . things . . . happened."

Uhura blushed and looked away. Spock retained his poise and spoke with delicacy. "It should not be necessary to concern ourselves with what occurred *after* the primordial contact. Recreating the state of affairs before that point is all we should require."

Shastri tensed, then spoke carefully. "But even that . . . it's not like that first kiss came out of nowhere. We were already close, comfortable, physically affectionate. We gave each other shoulder rubs when we got tense or tired. We had an easy rapport, teasing and joking. We knew each other so well . . . there was a shorthand between us. We hardly had to finish a sentence before the other knew what we wanted. Sometimes just a glance was enough.

"Now . . ." Shastri's eyes focused on Uhura for a moment, then turned away. "No offense, Captain, but I'm not sure you can understand how hard it is for humans to get over a broken heart."

Spock looked back evenly. "I am more familiar with the human response to loss and grief than you imagine, Mister Shastri. I am aware of the personal difficulty of what we ask—not only for you, but for Commander Uhura, whom I consider a friend as well as a colleague. Yet the current situation—"

Uhura touched Spock's arm briefly to halt him, offering a grateful smile. She then stepped closer to Shastri. "Rajendra . . . this will be hard for both of us. But you were Starfleet once. You were willing to set aside personal needs and face hardships for the greater good."

"I walked away from that a long time ago."

"*Because* of your principles. Your belief in what's right.

"That's why I stayed on the *Enterprise* after I lost my memory. I was offered a medical discharge so I could focus on my recovery . . . but even without my memory, I felt a need to serve.

To make a difference for others, help them as my colleagues on the *Enterprise* helped me when I was lost and empty. That's what draws us all to Starfleet: the need to make a difference in people's lives." Her voice grew wistful. "No matter what we have to sacrifice along the way."

Shastri held her gaze for longer than he had since beaming aboard. Uhura realized that he really did have beautiful, soulful eyes.

Finally, he cleared his throat. "Okay. I'm sorry, I guess this is just as hard for both of us. I'll . . . I'll help any way I can."

She took his hand in hers. "Thank you, Jen." He jerked as if he'd received a static shock, but allowed the contact.

It only lasted a moment before he tugged his hand away and retreated, moving off toward Scott. "Okay, first off, there was a holo-table in the middle of the room. The Argelians love their sensory displays. It was circular. And the lighting was softer, more indirect . . ."

Uhura sighed. It was a start.

Chapter Seventeen

Starfleet Headquarters
Major Missions Room

Admiral Cartwright breathed a sigh of relief when the latest flare subsided with no serious damage. "Final duration and diameter?" he asked.

Lieutenant Kexas answered crisply. "Six point eight three hours, sir. Zero point seven six astronomical units."

Cartwright traded a look with President Lorg. "At that diameter, the next one has roughly one chance in eight of engulfing Earth. And a not insignificant chance of engulfing Mars."

Lorg absorbed the prospect of harm to his birth planet stoically. Cartwright knew the president took pride in his heritage as a member of Mars's small Tellarite community, which had played an often overlooked role in the planet's colonial history. But he was also a second-term Federation president, responsible for far more worlds than just his own. Cartwright had been by Lorg's side in enough crises to know that.

"How go the verteron arrays?" the president asked.

The admiral let out a grim sigh. "They're an antiquated technology. There aren't many left—we had to haul some out of the terraforming museum on Mars. Morrow's got the Corps of Engineers working round the clock to repair the ones we have and whip together some modern equivalent for the rest. One of our SCE team heads, Commander al-Khaled, has proposed a way to modify a starship deflector dish to create a similar verteron beam—projected outward, unlike Mister Scott's idea for a verteron field inside the ship. If we rig enough ships in time, they could form an orbital cordon to help cushion the blow on Earth or Mars, to an extent."

"Well, that's something." Lorg did not appear any less worried, though. "What does the subspace damage look like?"

Cartwright turned to Kexas, who fielded the question. "Local subspace permeability is up fourteen percent from baseline, sirs. Subspace interference is increasing, even between flare events. Even old-style radio communication is growing unreliable. We've had to switch to laser communication as a backup."

The Edoan furrowed her heavy brow ridges as she called up data and simulation results on the master situation table with all three of her orange-skinned hands. "The intervals between flares are growing shorter as well, sir. They're lasting longer, but the time between their respective midpoints is also decreasing. I believe the greater subspace permeability is making it easier for the plasma beings to punch wormholes through. Or perhaps as the barrier between our time and their more accelerated time erodes, the temporal differential is decreasing, so they appear to come faster."

"Damn." Cartwright grimaced. "Which makes it a matter of even *less* time before Earth or Mars is hit. Get me Captain Spock."

The Zaranite, Ensign Kozim, shook his bulbous, masked head after a moment. "Too much interference, Admiral. We can't get through anymore."

Lorg clenched his fists. "Then we just have to wait and hope they come up with an answer before our luck runs out."

San Francisco

Ashley Janith-Lau stood at the front of the office, looking around at her fellow activists. Their number had been growing since the Warborn controversy began, and the group assembled here included both veterans and newcomers, among them the Starfleet cadets Vekal and Targeemos.

"I want to thank you all for coming in today," she told them. "It wasn't easy to arrange with the comms interference, and it's understandable that a number of us chose to stay with our loved ones at this uncertain time."

"You are a loved one to us, Doctor," Rogo proclaimed exaggeratedly, provoking chuckling from the group. "Which is why we must demand Starfleet make amends for falsely accusing you. Now that the Warborn have proven that their bloodlust cannot be tamed, it's time to insist on expelling them from the Academy!"

Janith-Lau held up her hands to settle down Rogo and the others who seemed inclined to follow his lead. "This isn't the right time to address that, my friends. All of Earth—make that the whole Solar system—is facing a crisis, and all of us, Starfleet included, need to work together to protect the public. Remember, it's not Starfleet itself we object to, just its trend toward militarization. When it comes to disaster response and rescue, we're on the same side.

"So what we're here to do is discuss the ways we can assist in the crisis. Figure out what resources we can bring to bear, what community and personal connections we can draw on, how best to coordinate our actions in the absence of reliable communication. I've already reached out to the city's disaster response teams and—"

The door burst open, startling her into silence and a number of her listeners into outcries. A group of Arcturians rushed in, brandishing phasers. Janith-Lau recognized the big one who'd kicked the door in as Bertram. The others, four in all, were harder to tell apart, but she was fairly sure she recognized the one who stepped past Bertram to lead the group as they spread out and covered the room's occupants with their weapons. "Nobody move!" the leader cried, her voice confirming that she was Portia.

T'Sena was the first to recover her wits. "What is the meaning of this?"

Portia answered the diminutive Vulcan, but her head turned to take in the whole group. "Call it intelligence gathering. We're here to confirm who really killed Commander Rakatheema."

T'Sena looked down her nose on the cadet. "Your actions would appear to verify your own guilt."

"I'm not the one who had a motive to get rid of him, and the rest of us with him."

"This is absurd!" Rogo cried. "Ashley was the one who was framed."

"A convenient way to allay suspicion, isn't it?"

Janith-Lau stepped forward slowly, her manner placating. "Portia . . . let's just talk about this, okay? We've both been accused of this crime—that gives us common ground. We're willing to hear you out, but not if you come like this, waving phasers around and frightening people."

Portia stepped closer, keeping the phaser's emitter pointed at Janith-Lau. "Your pacifist act is unconvincing. Rakatheema's dead. I didn't do it. You're the only other ones who have a reason."

"To oppose him, yes. To challenge him. But we do not believe violence solves problems. It just makes it harder to find solutions."

"That's what it comes down to, isn't it? We were made to solve problems with violence. It's the whole reason we exist. So you reject our right to exist."

"We believe you don't have to be bound by your origins. You can choose to be more."

"And what if we choose to fight? For Starfleet, for ourselves, it doesn't matter which. If *we* get to choose, then you don't get to tell us which choice is right."

Out of the corner of her eye, Janith-Lau saw Vekal spring into motion. She had a brief impression of his hand reaching for Portia's shoulder, poised for a Vulcan nerve pinch. But before he reached her, she spun, grabbed his wrist, and threw him to the floor.

"You!" she cried, pinning him down. "You've had it in for us from the first day."

"And you are proving my concerns warranted through your actions," Vekal gasped. "You are too innately aggressive to be in Starfleet."

"Warborn are not aggressors. We defend." She dragged him to his feet and shoved him into Bertram's grip. The big Arcturian held the leaner Vulcan effortlessly. "I'm entitled to defend myself against a false charge of murder. I'm entitled to hunt down the real killers."

Vekal only grew haughtier. "You are delusional. These people are pacifists. Rakatheema was an experienced Starfleet Security officer. Even if they had the inclination to murder him, they would not have the skill."

Portia peered at him. "But you would, wouldn't you? You peace-loving Vulcans certainly put a lot of effort into martial-arts training."

"It is a way to discipline our minds and bodies."

"And it gives you the precision you'd need to crush an Arcturian's windpipe. That Vulcan strength wouldn't hurt either."

"You merely attempt to obfuscate the evidence pointing to your own guilt. The fact that you do so in the midst of committing a violent crime makes it less than convincing."

The Warborn cadet bit back her response, pausing for a

moment. "I have never needed your approval, Vekal. It's irrelevant to me." Turning away, she shifted her attention—and her phaser—back toward Janith-Lau. "You, though—you're the leader here, the one behind the strategies. Anything this group does is on your orders or with your consent."

Portia grabbed Janith-Lau's hair, yanked her head back, and stuck the phaser's nozzle against her neck. "So you're the one I want to have a conversation with."

Janith-Lau strove to manage her fear. "We can talk. But I can't tell you anything but the truth. I found Rakatheema dead. That's all I know."

Bertram stepped forward, cracking his knuckles. "Give her to me, Portia. I'll have her talking soon enough."

Portia's eyes widened, as if she were shocked by her own actions. She relaxed her grip, lessened the pressure of the phaser barrel on Janith-Lau's neck. "No. No, remember your training, Bertram. Intelligence extracted through torture is never reliable."

"It would be satisfying, though."

With a disgusted look, Portia shoved Janith-Lau back into an empty chair. "We're not thugs! That's what they want people to think we are. We're soldiers! We're professionals! We have standards."

Bertram shook his head. "I don't understand you, Portia. You say you hate our makers and everything they made us for. Yet you embrace what they made us to be."

Portia scoffed. "And you keep saying we're wrong to question their design for us, but you're the first to suggest defying their standards. And Horatio worships their code but uses it to justify abandoning our warrior nature entirely.

"Maybe none of us really know who we are or what we want. We weren't given a choice. Which is why we need to fight for the space to figure it out for ourselves—not let them damn us as berserkers. We're here to exact the truth, not revenge."

Janith-Lau dared to stand and take a single tentative step toward Portia, catching her attention. She tried to focus on Portia's eyes rather than the phaser barrel that recentered on her chest. "I want to believe that, Portia. But please . . . what will it take to convince you that we were not behind Rakatheema's death, or your framing?"

The bright-eyed Warborn youth struggled with the question. "I will question everyone here. You will tell me of your actions, your whereabouts on that night. We will see if there are any discrepancies, or if certain questions make you nervous."

"This whole situation makes us terrified. How can you distinguish that from dishonesty?"

"We'll just have to see, won't we?"

"Let us go, Portia. Let me talk to Captain sh'Deslar, even Admiral Kirk. They can reexamine the evidence, see if—"

"Sh'Deslar wouldn't hear me before! She swallowed every lie! And Kirk just went along with her."

Portia closed in on Janith-Lau once more, grabbing her arm and brandishing the phaser. "But he cares about you, doesn't he? Maybe now he'll have no choice but to listen to us."

"You don't know Jim Kirk very well if you think he'll back down in the face of a threat."

"I know the leader he *used* to be. Now I just see another bureaucrat behind a desk."

Janith-Lau tilted her chin back defiantly. For all her love of peace, she didn't resist her confrontational urge this time. "Do you really want to test that?"

After a moment's thought, Portia smiled. "Actually, I do. Finally, for the first time in my life, I'm fighting a real battle. Nobody goes into a battle knowing they'll win. But that's the point, isn't it? To test yourself against the odds?"

Her smile widening, Portia drew nearer, almost sensually. "I don't know if we can win this fight. But at last, I truly feel alive."

Starfleet Academy

Zirani Kayros and Michael Ashrafi waylaid Horatio and Benedick outside of April Hall as they headed for class. "Did you hear?" Kayros asked. She and Ashrafi filled them in on the hostage situation, or what they'd been able to discern of it from static-laden, distorted news broadcasts and scuttlebutt.

Benedick shook his head, eyes wide. "I can't believe even Portia would do something this reckless."

"Reckless?" Ashrafi scoffed. "Reckless is trying to smuggle Romulan ale into your dorm, or not studying for your physics test. This is out-and-out berserk."

Horatio looked down at the pavement. "I feared something like this. She turned away from our commitment, our discipline, to fight only for Arcturus. She was ready to fight for anything—I fear she now fights purely to fight."

Kayros didn't want to believe that. As difficult as Portia could be, there was a pride and integrity to her that Kayros respected. She even dared to consider Portia a friend.

She caught Horatio's arm. "You have to go to her. Convince them to let you negotiate with her. If anyone can get her to calm down and talk this through . . ."

The soft-spoken Arcturian sighed heavily. "We have already tried. I urged her to stay in the Academy, to do nothing to confirm people's fears of us. Instead, she's chosen to reinforce them."

"Horatio, you can't just abandon her!"

He held her gaze. "I have a responsibility to those of us who remain. More fundamentally, I have a responsibility to Arcturus. As long as the Warborn are on Arcturus, we are a threat to its peace and stability. We *must* find an alternate path offworld, and I believe Starfleet is our best hope. Portia and the others have jeopardized that, so those of us who remain must counter her actions by proving that we are peaceful, loyal, and obedient. If we cannot, then we are a threat to the Federation as well.

"I am sorry, Zirani, but I cannot help her." He moved past her, toward the hall.

"So that's it?" Ashrafi cried, spreading his arms. "You just walk away from your sister-in-arms, or whatever?"

Horatio stiffened at his words. After a moment, he relaxed and spoke over his shoulder. "She walked away from us. There's a difference."

As he moved on, Kayros turned to Benedick, clasping his arm. "You're okay with this?"

To be fair, he hardly seemed to be. "Sorry, Zirani. I wish I could help. But Horatio understands these things better than I do. I trust him." He gave Zirani a brief, tentative hug, muttered an apology, and moved on.

Ashrafi called out after the receding group. "Yeah, well . . . there are more things in heaven and earth than you knew well, Horatio! Or however that goes!"

Kayros sighed. "Don't be too hard on him. You know he always puts his duty to Arcturus first."

Her human friend grimaced. "Yeah, and peace this and gentleness that. I'm all for peace, but it's not the same as passivity."

Ashrafi checked his data slate for updates, but it still displayed little more than interference. "Damn these flares! As if the first time wasn't bad enough! It's like the damn things followed us here. Are we cursed, do you think? Are curses a thing?"

She rolled her eyes. His frivolity was wearing thin. "I heard a rumor that they're connected to Starfleet ship movements somehow. When it comes to Starfleet, all roads lead to Earth sooner or later."

He glared at her. "And who convinced me to stick with Starfleet when I almost quit, Zirani?"

She paused. "Actually, it was Vekal."

He was uncharacteristically silent for a few moments. "Do

you think he and Targeemos were in there when the Warborn showed up?"

"We haven't heard from them. I have to think they were."

"Do you think maybe Vekal can use his Vulcan logic and talk the hostage-takers into laying down their arms?"

They exchanged a horrified stare. "No, you're right," Ashrafi said in response to her wordless response. "He'll probably make it even worse."

U.S.S. *Enterprise*

Rajendra Shastri paced the confines of the communications lab like a caged animal. Uhura, who sat at the main console with her favorite receiver nestled comfortably in her ear, couldn't help noticing that the arc of his pacing tended to keep as much distance between them as possible.

"How long before we get to Earth?" Shastri asked to break the uncomfortable silence.

"About six hours. But we're not supposed to be thinking about that." She said it to remind herself as much as him.

"I know, I know. We're gambling on re-creating Argelius to trigger some memory fragment left over in your brain. Well, forgive me for being skeptical about that." He circled the central holo-table, tweaking its display parameters for the hundredth time as he peered at the multiaxial subspace spectral analysis graph hovering above it. "We might have a better chance of making contact once we get to their target area. They're trying to get through to us anyway, so it makes sense to put ourselves where they're already looking."

"The flares won't let us get close enough." She tried to keep the irritation out of her voice. "And our position won't matter if the signal configuration and data reconstruction protocols are wrong."

"That's what I'm saying! If we can read their transmissions directly—in real time, not just recorded data—it would better our chances of deciphering those things."

Uhura turned to glare at him. "Even if that's true, it won't get us to the Sol system any faster. We still have six hours to do everything we can to recover some fraction of my memory. It won't *hurt* to keep this up, and there isn't anything else we can do in the meantime!"

"Well—" Shastri broke off, unable to counter her argument. He gave a frustrated sigh and resumed pacing the lab.

I wanted strong emotions, she thought wryly. Following that thought, she spoke again, tentatively. "Did we . . . That is, when we were friends . . . did we have fights like this?"

He stared in surprise. "Not like this. Not at the slightest provocation." He barked out a laugh. "You were certainly passionate about what you believed in. You didn't take any crap from anyone. When I said something stupid, you put me in my place. But it was never malicious, never . . . bitter. There was trust there. Trust earned over years.

"Sometimes . . . we didn't even have to talk. We could sit together in silence for hours while we studied, while we worked on making contact. But not *this* silence, not . . . avoidance." His voice softened as his focus turned inward. "Just the opposite. The kind where two people are so much in sync that it's like being with another part of yourself. Nothing *needs* to be said. It just feels so right to be together—it doesn't have to be justified by saying something or doing something. It just *is.*"

He blinked moist eyes, and she could see his grief at what he had lost. "So no, Nyota. It won't be that easy for you."

"What won't?"

"Asking if it was like this, here and now. You're looking for a shortcut. An easy answer to get past this block of yours. If it were that bloody easy, don't you think you'd have done it by now?"

"I'm open to trying anything at this point!"

"But your first impulse is to go for the easy answer. The least painful one. The one that doesn't require you to think about who you used to be any more than you have to. You're too afraid to face it!"

"What would be the point?" she cried, rising to her feet. "I can't reconstruct who I was. Even if I recover some fragments of it now, I can never find a protocol to put them together the same way. And I've grown so much since then. Learned so much, formed new friendships."

"*Work* friendships! All you have anymore is Starfleet. No family, no romance . . . you're a fragment of who you once were! These officers who put you back together again, they just taught you the parts that were useful to them!"

Her voice rose with her anger. "You have no idea, Shastri. They did *everything* to encourage me to become my full self again. My life isn't incomplete just because *you* aren't in it."

"And your family? You hid from them too, let them think they were dead to you, until your *work* forced you to treat them as a resource!" He gestured sharply at her. "This is what I'm saying. You cling to duty and responsibility and Starfleet discipline because they're what was around you when they put Humpty Dumpty together again. They're your safe space. And for a dozen years, you've hid in it and wouldn't let anyone in from your old life. Maybe you were afraid your new self wouldn't measure up!"

Uhura gaped at him. "That's rich! Maybe you're forgetting that I *did* reach out to you after *Nomad*. I was still lost, fragile, looking for answers, and you were so cruel. You called me a liar, met me with such fury that I couldn't understand. How the hell was I supposed to reach out to you after that? How could you expect me to trust you?"

He opened his mouth to riposte, but she wouldn't let him. "You don't have the right to act like the wronged party, Shastri. You got mad because you thought your new girlfriend had dumped you. Oh, the horror.

"I had just lost *everything*! I woke up surrounded by strangers—none more so than the face in my own mirror! All I had were feelings of familiarity I couldn't understand, bursts of emotion I couldn't contextualize. I couldn't trust my own reactions. I felt I could instinctively trust the people around me, but how could I be sure that was genuine? It was a relief when they proved it through their actions."

She moved closer, circling the table to confront him without the holograms in the way. "Then I got a message from you. Another stranger, but the name filled me with such warmth, such assurance. With the same kind of trust I felt for my crewmates, but there was . . . joy as well. So I reached out, trusting you with my plight, expecting you to be as understanding as everyone around me had.

"Your rejection was the first breach of trust I remembered *in my life*. It shattered my innocence. You tear into me for not having the courage to reach out to my family, my friends. Well, *whose fault do you think that was?!*"

He stared at her for long moments, stunned—or shamed—into silence. Uhura allowed herself to take satisfaction in that. "You can't know," she told him, more softly but relentlessly. "You can't possibly know what it's like to lose everything."

After a long, loaded silence, he lowered his gaze and spoke very softly. "Yes . . . in a way, I can." He met her eyes again, not without difficulty. "Because I lost you.

"For years, Nyota, you *were* my life. You were the best of my friends, and that's always been a short list. I've always been an introvert, but you invited me in. You were patient with me, unjudging. You . . . you gave me the confidence to be the person you saw when you looked at me."

Uhura stared back, startled by his words. They sparked a memory—not of her life before *Nomad*, but a more recent time, when she had worked with Willard Decker on a program to increase Starfleet's diversity by promoting nonhuman recruitment. So many of her recruits had told her how grateful they were for the encouragement she gave them, for the sense of acceptance she created. She had believed that she had done it to pay forward what the *Enterprise* crew had done for her after Maluria—making Starfleet feel welcoming, familial, and accepting despite any impediments. It had never occurred to her that she might have done the same even before the memory wipe— that she had merely continued being the person she had always been.

Shastri went on in an elegiac tone. "I loved you before I even realized it. It just felt so natural, so comfortable, that I never noticed a moment when it started. It just *became*, without me even putting it into words in my mind."

His voice shook with emotion as he continued. "Why do you think I was so happy to drop whatever I was doing and fly across sectors to meet up with you on your shore leaves, all to help you in your mad quixotic quest? That was your passion. Mine was to help you fulfill it. All I wanted was to see the joy light up in your eyes, to see that blinding smile when your dream finally came true. All I needed for myself was to know I'd been there for you, to help you pull it off."

Uhura's emotions roiled. The warmth his words evoked in her was uncomfortable, unwelcome in the midst of her anger, her pain. *How dare he say these things?* But her own emotions in response were so confused that she was paralyzed, unable to know how to react.

He blinked away tears. "Then, at Argelius, you finally caught up with your impossible dream—and right after that, so did I. When you told me you loved me too . . . I couldn't believe it. I feared it was too good to be true.

"So when the very next message I got was you telling me you didn't even recognize my *name* . . ."

Shastri fell silent, aside from several deep, shuddering breaths. The silence boiled between them like the quantum vacuum, until his next words finally resolved from out of so many possibilities.

"I know I had no right to be so cruel, Nyota. It was petty and unfair, no matter how hurt I was. And knowing now how much harm I did you . . . I'm ashamed.

"That's what I hope you can understand. What I'm not sure I really faced until just now. My bitterness at having all this dredged up again . . . It's not the same resentment or insecurity I felt before. I . . . I came through that all right. I rebuilt, the same as you. I met Sudo, we built a life, had a son . . . I'm happy with what I have."

She felt a pang at his words. Of jealousy? Of envy? Of loss?

He went on regardless. "So the anger I feel is not . . . it's not toward you. What makes me so upset is that . . . that I couldn't be there for you when everything had been taken away. All I ever wanted was to be there for you. And when you needed me most . . . you didn't remember me. And that felt like a failure and a rejection and . . . I refused to believe it because it broke my heart either way, so if my heart was going to be broken anyway, I decided I should at least be mad about it." He wept freely now. "I got so mad at you because the alternative would hurt too much. But all I did was hurt you more."

Shastri moved convulsively, wiping away tears with his sleeve, then turning around to take in the room. "All of this . . . it's so screwed up. When we were there, on Argelius, we were in sync like never before. We both felt we were on the brink, and all we could think about was working together to cross the finish line. Nothing could come between us and that goal, or each other. And I would've done anything to help you achieve it."

He shook his head. "How can we ever hope to get that back now? With so many scars in the way?"

Uhura struggled to sort through the quantum foam of emotions within her, jostling between different states, unable to decohere into a single understanding. "Tell me. Jen. What happened between us? After the breakthrough? When we . . . what did we say? What did we do?"

He gave a convulsive laugh. "You want me to go into graphic detail? I'd rather not go there. I've tried not to think about it much. And I'm happily married now."

"Not . . . that part. I mean . . . what did I say, about what I felt for you? What did we talk about afterward?"

Shastri struggled with the words—or with the associated memories. "You . . . we were so happy, we just fell into each other's arms, and the rest came so naturally, like we were already together. Like I said before, maybe being on Argelius gave us permission. There was no doubt, no hesitation . . . we were best friends, we trusted each other implicitly, and we just . . . didn't see any reason not to do as the Argelians did.

"So we did. And I told you I loved you, that I'd loved you for years. And you said . . . not to sound vain, but you said you were relieved to hear it, because you felt love for me too and weren't sure if I returned it. I was so shy about expressing it—I didn't want to distract you from your quest, or risk our friendship.

"You told me that nothing—" His voice hitched. He cleared his throat before going on. "You said nothing could hurt our friendship. That becoming lovers was a natural outgrowth of it, a deepening of the bond we'd shared for so long. That it should've happened sooner. I agreed wholeheartedly.

"But you said we'd have plenty of time to make up for it. That you intended to make up for it, that you . . . wanted to build a future with me. Maybe take a ground post at a Starfleet research institute once we went public with our work." He chuckled. "Or at a university somewhere if they kicked you out of Starfleet. But the important things were that we'd continue refining contact with the plasma beings . . . and that we'd do it together."

Uhura realized they'd been drawing closer to each other as he spoke. It wasn't out of desire, but from a different kind of need. His words made her realize that *Nomad* had not only taken her past from her—it had stolen her future as well. A future she'd never had the chance to mourn, for she'd never known she'd lost it until now. And that knowledge clarified a feeling of loss that had been looming over her mind since she had first heard Shastri's name.

The new solidity of that feeling hit hard, and she burst into tears.

Weeping openly along with her, Shastri took her into his arms. As he held her, a rush of emotions flooded through her, and with them a jumble of sensory impressions. Countless touches—friendly hugs, jovial backslaps, mutual shoulder massages in cram sessions. Jen clasping her hand, stroking her hair as she wept herself to sleep after hearing of her father's death.

And there was more. The press of his lips, the warmth of his bare chest against hers. The joyous exhaustion as they lay together after trying to make up for years of inaction in a single night. The comfortable ease with which they'd begun their romance, in the afterglow of a triumph that made them feel all things were possible for the two of them as a team.

She resisted the impulse to kiss him, to stroke his hair. That option was far behind them. And it didn't matter. What mattered was the older, deeper bond that their passion had grown from. The bond that had enabled them to pierce the veil of time and make a childhood dream into reality, against all odds and obstacles.

"Jen," she sighed, hugging him tighter. "I remember you now, my dear friend."

He pulled back, eyes goggling. "You—you remember? How much?"

She winced, chiding herself for giving him false hope. "Not much. Moments, emotions, sensations. But I remember how it felt to be here with—to be in the lab with you on Argelius. I'm finally there. No technical details yet . . . but I think the channel's open now. We just need to tease out the signal."

His smile was still reserved, but warmer and more genuine than before. "Then we should get back to work . . . old friend."

Chapter Eighteen

San Francisco

On hearing the news about the hostage situation, Sulu rushed to Admiral Kirk's Academy office, where he found the admiral on the way out alongside a worried-looking Doctor McCoy. "Oh, good, I didn't miss you."

"You've heard, Commander?" Kirk moved past without slowing down, and Sulu fell in behind him.

"About the hostages, yes, sir. I wanted to ask if I could come with you to the scene."

McCoy looked at him with mixed feelings. "I'm grateful for your support, Mister Sulu, but what's your interest? You don't know Ashley."

"But I know Portia. She's one of my best students. I like her. She reminds me of Demora." He lowered his head. "And I found the eyewitnesses who identified her. I feel responsible for what's happened. I'm hoping if I can talk to her, build on our connection—such as it is—maybe I can stop her from making a huge mistake."

"Huger than murdering her own sponsor?"

"That's for the courts to decide. Until then, I'm willing to believe her."

"Very well, Mister Sulu," Kirk said. "You're with us."

On reaching the scene, they found Captain sh'Deslar coordinating with the SFPD's tactical team, although both groups seemed understaffed. "They chose an ideal time for this, from their point of view," sh'Deslar reported to the admiral once they'd touched base. "Emergency responders are already spread thin preparing for vacuum flares, and the subspace interference is hampering comms, security systems, and transporters. That must be how they got past security in the Academy armory to steal those phasers."

"I take it beaming the hostages out isn't an option, then?" Kirk asked.

"It'd be risky enough just from the flare interference, but they've sprayed the walls and windows with a refractory coating of some kind. Keeps us from seeing inside with eyes or sensors."

"Have you made contact with the hostage-takers?"

She held up a communicator. "I spoke briefly to Portia. She said I was 'in on it,' that she had nothing to say to me."

Sulu took a step forward to get her attention. "Let me try talking to her, Captain. She's one of my students. I think I can get her to trust me."

The security captain sighed. "Well, you convinced me not to kick you out of my office. If you can pull that off, anything's possible. But it's up to her whether you get anywhere."

She handed Sulu her communicator. "Frequency's already open. Still works at short range, but it's best if you speak up."

He flipped up the lid and took a breath to compose himself. "Portia? This is Commander Sulu. I'd like to come up and speak with you, if that's okay."

It was several moments before she responded. *"You're unarmed?"*

He took off his maroon jacket, exposing the gold turtleneck underneath—not so different, he sometimes thought, from the uniform he'd worn when he first served aboard the *Enterprise* nearly a decade and a half before. He stepped forward a few paces, slowly, and spread his arms, turning around. The cadets may have opaqued the windows, but he assumed they had some way to see out.

He raised the communicator again. "I just want to hear your side of all this, Cadet. Just have a conversation, like we did in the cockpit."

This time, the silence was longer. *"Just you. Come to the door and wait."*

He complied, and soon one of the Arcturian cadets—he believed it was Titus—swiftly opened the door and pulled him inside, then scanned him and patted him down for weapons. Satisfied, the cadet gestured with his phaser for Sulu to climb the stairs ahead of him.

Portia met him in the hallway outside the office. Sulu met her gaze evenly. "I'd like to see the hostages, if that's all right."

After a moment, she opened the office door and nodded to someone inside. A moment later, that someone—Bertram—appeared with Ashley Janith-Lau in tow. She looked healthy but distraught. "Are you and the hostages all right?"

"We're intact, Commander, but frightened. They haven't hurt us, but they've threatened us, interrogated us. They believe we—"

"Enough!" Portia cried. "It's my grievance to air." She nodded to Bertram again, and he none too gently guided Janith-Lau back inside.

Portia closed the door. "Satisfied?"

"I'm concerned, Portia. What led you to this?"

She spelled out her case in terse sentences—how she believed the peace activists had somehow framed her for murdering Commander Rakatheema. Sulu took it in and thought carefully about how to respond.

"How do you think they could have done that?" he asked. "Falsified your appearance, your DNA at the scene?"

"We've been under constant media scrutiny since we arrived.

Anyone could study my appearance and body language, collect some shed skin cells from where I've been. And creating prosthetic disguises isn't that hard."

"Even if someone in there did what you say, how does holding them hostage help? No court in the Federation will accept a confession made under duress."

"You think I care about courts? About laws and institutions and systems? It was the *system* that created us to die in others' wars. The hell with the system. *I* want to know. I want to look my betrayer in the eye and hear them say they did it."

"And what if it's not anybody in that room? You can't know for certain that it was."

"But as long as we hold them, *you* have a motivation to reexamine the evidence." She shrugged. "I'm willing to play fair. If you review the case properly this time, if you find proof that I was framed and identify who did it—and *if* you can prove to me that it's genuine and not a ploy—then I'll let the hostages go. If not, then I'll keep questioning them until the guilty one breaks, or one of the others exposes them to save themselves."

"And then what? How can you or any of the others hope to get back into the Academy after doing this?"

Portia sighed. "Look. Nothing against you. You were good to me, and I liked flying with you. But I don't care about the Academy. None of us felt at home there. Rakatheema didn't deserve to die, but he was wrong to make us go there. It would never have worked."

"Then what is it that you hope for?"

She let out a tired laugh. "I don't really know, Mister Sulu. I just want the freedom to search for it. To find my own purpose to fight for, instead of someone else's agenda."

Sulu gestured toward the room. "How do you expect *this* to lead to that, Portia? Think about it. Remember what I taught you. Consider the path ahead of you carefully. See the best way to reach your destination." He shook his head. "Can you see *any* way this path you're on will end up with you anywhere but in a penal colony? Or worse?"

"Maybe not," she admitted. "But this is all I have left, thanks to the ones who framed me. No one will ever trust the Warborn now. So if we have nothing left to lose, then at least we can choose to fall on our own terms, fighting our own battle. I would be happy with that."

When Sulu reported back to Kirk and sh'Deslar, he finished by saying, "Admiral, I don't think Portia killed Commander Rakatheema. Doing this . . . it doesn't make sense if she's trying to cover up her guilt. It just makes things worse for her and the others."

The admiral nodded. "I'm inclined to agree. This isn't the action of a guilty woman."

"Unless she's just psychotic," sh'Deslar pointed out.

"She isn't," Sulu insisted. "I've seen madness—more times than I care to think about. Portia's totally lucid. And she sincerely believes she's the wronged party."

"It's possible that someone disguised themselves as her," McCoy observed. "Hell, it could even have been one of the other Warborn. They are hard to tell apart at a distance, and one of them could've faked her ID colors."

Kirk didn't seem pleased by McCoy's suggestion. "One Warborn or another—it's just as bad for the program either way."

"With all due respect, sir," Sulu said, "I'm not as concerned for the program as I am for Portia—and for the hostages. If she really was framed—"

The admiral nodded. "Then proving who really did it would be the best way to resolve the situation without violence."

Kirk took in Sulu and McCoy with his gaze. "I want you both to go over all the evidence again. Look for signs that Portia was framed, and if so, who could have done it."

McCoy stared at him. "Jim, Ashley's up there! I should be here for her."

"Bones, you can do the most for her by solving this case. I've seen you crack tougher mysteries."

"I'm hardly an unbiased researcher in this case. How do I know I can trust my own findings? I'll grasp at any straw if I think it'll satisfy Portia and save Ashley."

Kirk smiled, amazed at his friend's humility and wisdom. Spock often accused the doctor of being blinded by his emotions, but McCoy had just demonstrated that he was keenly aware of their potential impact on his work as a scientist. But the very fact that he asked the question—as his first impulse, no less—provided its answer.

"Doctor, I have complete faith in your medical judgment. You were a scientist long before you met her. That's what brought you together." Kirk clasped his shoulders. "So be a scientist now. Find the truth. Let your personal stakes be a motivator rather than an impediment."

McCoy set his jaw and nodded. Captain sh'Deslar looked skeptical, but let out a resigned sigh. "Report to Security HQ. I'll have my people give you access to the case files."

Sulu nodded to her. "Thank you, Captain."

McCoy paused to give Kirk one last intense look. "You make damn sure Ashley stays safe, you hear?"

"I promise, Bones. You and Sulu do the same."

Starfleet Headquarters
Major Missions Room

"This is it," Lieutenant Kexas said as she, Admiral Cartwright, and President Lorg watched the newest vacuum flare grow on the central wall screen—less than half an astronomical unit ahead of Earth in its orbit. The screens were already suffused with static and data dropouts as the interference mounted.

"Given its projected size and duration," Kexas went on, "it will grow large enough to engulf Earth in approximately three hours, forty-one minutes. Our orbital path will be close to the periphery of the flare zone, but still, expected duration of passage is . . . probably as long as the flare lasts. At least another two to three hours." She turned her elongated, skull-like head toward the admiral and the president. "The concentration of microflares should be lower toward the periphery, but over that long a time, they will add up."

Cartwright grimaced. "And we'll have no more than five working verteron arrays and maybe fourteen ships ready to pour Mister Scott's 'oil' on the water by the time it hits. Estimated coverage?"

Kexas shook her head. "No more than twenty, twenty-five percent, planetwide."

"And that will only reduce the number and size of the wormholes, not stop them," the admiral grated. "We'll still have microflares forming inside buildings, people, power plants . . . subspace disruptions affecting safety force fields and warp reactors . . . how many could we lose? How much of our infrastructure could be ruined?"

Kexas tilted her head. "And that's assuming there's no subspace rupture this time. The erosion is already accelerating."

Lorg sighed heavily. "I should go."

The admiral peered at him. "You're finally taking my advice? Evacuating?"

The president snorted and gestured at the flickering screens. "Would it even be safe to attempt now, with all this subspace disruption? No, Lance. I need to go address the people of Earth. Prepare them however I can for . . . what's to come."

Cartwright briefly touched his sleeve. "There's still the *Enterprise*. They've come through for us again and again."

Lorg threw him a skeptical look. He may have been Martian-born, but he still had a Tellarite's love of argument. "That was with James Kirk in command. Oh, I know how vital Captain Spock was to those successes. But take it from someone who knows—your perspective changes a great deal once you're the one on top. And it can take a while to adjust to that change. You don't want to know the blunders I almost made in my first year in office."

He shook his head. "I wonder if sticking Kirk in the Academy is really the best use of his talents. Oh, I know, I know, he has his flagship and his occasional 'special missions.' But you folks chose a hell of a time to keep him on the bench."

U.S.S. *Enterprise*
Entering Sol system

The *Enterprise* dropped out of warp just inside the Main Aster-oid Belt. The subspace instability would let it come no closer to the raging vacuum-energy storm—a storm that the bridge viewscreen's tactical display showed expanding directly in Earth's orbital path. "It's no more than two hours from inter-cept," Jason Nadel reported from the science station.

"Unable to reach Starfleet Command," Cadet Ferat reported from communications, worry in her voice. "Even at this range!"

"Not unexpected, Cadet. Continue monitoring." Spock kept his tone calm and matter-of-fact, in hopes of encouraging the same response from the cadet crew. "Helm, proceed toward the flare zone at full impulse."

"Aye, sir," T'Lara replied, maintaining her calm more success-fully than the others.

Spock worked the intercom control on his chair arm to con-tact main engineering. "Mister Scott, how quickly can you rig the main reactor to generate the verteron field?"

"*I began the reprogramming the moment we dropped out of warp, sir,*" Scott reported a few moments later, the unevenness in his voice suggesting he was pacing briskly around the engineering complex as he spoke. "*But the circuit reconfiguration, the emitter realignments . . . at least twenty minutes to do the physical work, up to half an hour for testing and calibration.*"

"We shall need to bypass full testing, Mister Scott, as we do not have adequate time."

"*Aye, when do we ever?*" A hint of reluctance entered the engineer's voice as he continued in a more hushed tone, his vocal timbre altering as though he were leaning in close to the audio pickup. "*Sir . . . this is a cadet crew. We didn't expect to demand this much from them when we set out. If it were a seasoned team . . .*"

"Mister Scott. On any Starfleet mission, one must anticipate that unforeseen difficulties could arise. I would not have taken the *Enterprise* out with this crew aboard if my confidence in the cadets' abilities had not been equal to my confidence in their instructors' abilities."

Again, Scott's vocal timbre changed, this time commensurately with a straightened spine and a proud smile. "*Aye, Captain. We'll prove ourselves worthy of your faith, sir. Scott out.*"

Spock noted similar sentiments on the faces of the bridge personnel as they glanced over their shoulders toward him. T'Lara was the exception, but even her hands had briefly slowed in their movements across the helm controls. "Attend to your posts," he instructed.

As they complied, he opened a new channel on the command chair's comm panel. "Bridge to communications lab. We are in-system, and a sizable vacuum flare is underway and less than two hours from engulfing Earth. I recommend alacrity."

Uhura's voice as she replied was calm and professional, but not without fatigue. "*Acknowledged, Captain. We're making progress. Shastri and I have reconstructed much of our work on Argelius, but even there, it took more than a day to perfect the calibrations."*

"Understood, but my ability to affect the pace of events is negligible."

A pause. *"Is Scotty's verteron field ready to go?"*

"Preparations are underway. I expect it to be in operation once we reach the field perimeter."

"Sir, I think we need to get much closer than that. Jen was right about one thing: our chances of making contact are best if we're as close as possible to the heart of the storm."

Spock raised a brow, weighing the ramifications. "You understand the risks that would entail. The field would only diminish the microflares' frequency and intensity within the ship. The interference to ship systems would also be considerable."

"I understand, sir, but the closer our alignment with their transmission vector, the better the chance that they'll read our reply."

"Acknowledged, Commander. We shall proceed as you advise."

"And we'll redouble our efforts here. We'll have something for you by the time we get there."

"I trust that you shall. Spock out."

The captain turned back to the viewscreen, observing the growing volume of microflare activity depicted along Earth's orbital path. This situation—the *Enterprise* preparing to fly into a vast cloud of energy in hopes of communicating with the intelligence generating it, in order to protect Earth—contained elements that created a certain sense of familiarity. Doctor McCoy would most likely refer to it, inaccurately, as *déjà vu.*

Spock dismissed it as a matter of mere happenstance. One could find certain parallels between any number of unrelated situations if one selected the points of comparison arbitrarily enough. For instance, the V'Ger incident bore certain parallels, not only to this current situation, but to the encounter with *Nomad* a dozen years ago and to the rescue of the Mantilles colony from consumption by a sapient cloudlike cosmozoan a decade ago. It was in the nature of the intelligent mind to seek patterns and connections, but the process was prone to generate false positives that a rational thinker must disregard as irrelevant.

Yet another side of Spock—the side that his mother had instilled from childhood with an appreciation for art and literature—could not help but be struck by the resonance of his thoughts being drawn back to *Nomad* at the climax of a crisis indirectly precipitated by that probe's assault on Nyota Uhura. That act, as traumatic as it had been for Uhura, had appeared at the time to be peripheral to the threat *Nomad* had posed, a minor atrocity compared to its planetary genocide in the Malurian system. Yet it had been that seemingly incidental act that now, through an unpredictable chain of circumstance, came close to fulfilling *Nomad*'s ultimate aim of wreaking destruction upon Earth.

It proved what Surak had taught: No life was incidental. The death of a foot soldier or an innocent bystander could have consequences greater than the death of a king or a general, for all lives were interconnected in intricate and unpredictable ways.

His thoughts turned to the Arcturian Warborn—a people created to be disposable, now seeking to discover their own value. Already, in their short time at Starfleet Academy, they had made a difference in many lives, for better or worse. Yet the value of their lives—of their participation in others' lives, which came down to much the same thing—continued to be questioned, even by the Warborn themselves. One life had already been lost as a result, and there was no way to anticipate what further harm that loss could do in years to come, as its consequences rippled through the web of causality. Spock hoped that

Admiral Kirk would succeed in resolving that conflict before more lives were ended.

For now, though, his own purpose was to ensure that the admiral had that chance. Even on separate missions, he and Kirk were still connected.

As we have been, and always shall be.

Chapter Nineteen

Starfleet Medical

Sulu closed his communicator and came back over to McCoy, who was running every analysis he could think of on the Arcturian DNA sample from the murder scene. "That was Admiral Kirk," the younger man said. "Portia still hasn't budged. I had to tell him we haven't made any progress."

"Jim should know by now just to let me get on with my goddamn work. I'll tell him if and when we find something." McCoy banged the side of the analyzer, aware that it was little more than a theatrical gesture. "This damn interference isn't helping any. Tell Jim to bug Spock about getting *that* fixed!"

"Everyone's doing all they can, Doctor. But I'm afraid I'm out of ideas."

McCoy looked up at him, finally registering what he'd said. "You couldn't find anything fishy about the security video?"

Sulu shook his head. "There's no evidence the image was digitally altered. Spectroscopic analysis of the face is consistent with Arcturian tissues—no sign of prosthetic appliances or synthskin. And skeletal proportions and kinesics match someone raised under Arcturian gravity. That's hard to fake."

McCoy sighed. "Which means the killer is either an Arcturian, or someone who grew up on Arcturus, or someone from a planet with the same gravity as Arcturus. Doesn't narrow it down that much."

Sulu's expression grew heavy. "I hate to say it, but could it have been one of the other Warborn? Aside from Bertram, just about any of them could be mistaken for Portia in the dark. And they're trained martial artists—they could learn to imitate Portia's movements."

"It could be. But there are hundreds of other Arcturians on Earth. The killer could be someone from Rakatheema's past—I don't know, a vengeful ex-lover or something. There's no way to narrow it down."

"Doesn't it at least have to be someone with access to Portia, so they could steal a sample of her DNA?"

"Not necessarily. The samples taken from Rakatheema's home were degraded, contaminated. There's enough of an allele match to Portia to support the other evidence against her, but not enough to conclusively rule out any other Arcturian. It could be from someone genetically similar, like a family member."

Sulu perked up. "Warborn are always multiple births. Four to six at a time, sometimes more." His face sank. "But they don't raise them as siblings. They're just mixed in with the whole population, raised in a group crèche. And their parentage is anonymous, so the 'donors' don't form attachments."

McCoy grimaced. "Barbaric process. Dehumanizing—well, depersonalizing the poor devils so nobody cares if they live or die."

"You don't have to tell me. The point is, there's no way to identify who else Portia might be related to. What are the odds that one of the other few female Warborn here, picked randomly out of thousands, just happens to be Portia's sister?"

McCoy shrugged. "It wasn't random. They had to pass all the Starfleet entrance exams. You know how tough that is. If one batch of Warborn babies happened to be of particularly clever and adaptable stock, it's possible more than one of them ended up here—even though they wouldn't know they were related."

Sulu grew excited again. "Then we just need permission to access their DNA records!"

The doctor bristled. "It's not that simple, Sulu! They still have rights in the eyes of the law, even if their creators didn't think so. We can't just open up someone's private genetic records without probable cause."

"Oh. And we can't get probable cause without the genetic data. It's a vicious circle."

McCoy thought it over. "There is one possibility. If we assume we're looking for a female Warborn besides Portia, that narrows it down to Rosalind, Viola, and Kate. What I could try is to run a developmental simulation on the DNA sample. Project a range of possible physiognomies based on different possibilities for the missing alleles and epigenetic variations. If any of them match one of the other three, that could give us the probable cause we need."

"Great! How long will that take?"

"Not long, with Starfleet Medical's main computer working on it. Fifteen minutes—well, maybe twenty, with this interference. It's even more powerful than the *Enterprise* computer."

Sulu grinned. "I won't tell Captain Spock you said that."

"Oh, please do." McCoy's grin in return was wicked. He was finally starting to feel optimistic.

Twenty minutes later, his hopes were dashed. Not one of thousands of simulated facial and bodily structures was close enough to any of the three suspects, even given the superficial similarity of Warborn features. And a fair number of them were better than fifty percent matches to Portia's facial structure.

Still, something nagged at McCoy. It was like there was something he'd noticed unconsciously and forgotten before it percolated to the surface. *Probably just my anxiety about Ashley. Jim had better be keeping her safe.*

"I really thought we were onto something," Sulu said. "The reasoning all added up."

"Oh, it was perfectly logical, Mister Sulu. That's why I keep telling Spock you can't rely on logic alone. A chain of argument can fit together perfectly and still be completely wrong. Logic is only as good as the assumptions you start out with. Make the wrong assumption and—"

He broke off, eyes going wide. Sulu peered at him. "Doc? You okay?"

McCoy snapped his fingers. "Assumptions! My friend, you and I have been making one of the biggest assumptions in the book. One we human men, myself included, are far too quick to make."

"Which is?"

"That men and women are fundamentally different. That we're binary and opposite. The biological fact is, we're just slight variations on a common theme. The same biology given different tweaks by the hormones in our mothers' wombs. That's why some people are nonbinary or transgender. There are different genetic and epigenetic factors that balance out to make us develop one way or the other, and sometimes they land somewhere in the middle instead, or the genes shape the brain one way while the hormones shape the body the other way."

"Sure, I know that. My second cousin Mako changes pronouns almost as often as hairstyles. But what's your point?"

"Well, think about it, Sulu. You were the one telling me about Warborn procreation. They're parthenogenetic, right?"

"Right. A special hormone injection triggers self-fertilization in Arcturian females."

"But that means there's no male parent. No counterpart for the human Y chromosome in the Warborn's DNA. Don't you get it? Genetically, *every* Warborn is a hundred percent female! It's only the epigenetics, the hormonal influences in the womb, that determine if their anatomy comes out male, female, or in between."

Sulu's eyes widened. "So we were assuming the female markers in the DNA sample narrowed it down to the four female Warborn . . . but it could be one of the men too!"

"Exactly!" McCoy turned back to the computer. "This time I'm going to run the simulations projecting for masculine development. Let's see what we get."

Just moments after he started entering the parameters, the lights, screens, and ventilation fans cut out for several seconds, then snapped back on again. The computer displayed multiple error messages, and McCoy had to wait while the simulator program shut down and restarted.

"Blast it! We don't have time for this!" He prayed he could get a result—and use it to get a warrant—before Portia's patience ran out, or a vacuum flare struck Earth.

At the moment, he wasn't sure which of those outcomes frightened him more.

U.S.S. Enterprise

Cadet T'Lara flinched as the actinic streak of a microflare pierced the attitude control panel centimeters from her left hand, causing it to spark and flicker. Spock winced from the loud whipcrack sound it made as it superheated the air around it. Noting the pinpoint burn it had created just underneath the main viewscreen, he glanced back to confirm that it had pierced the lower portside status monitor of the internal security station.

"Status, Cadet?" he asked over the ringing in his ears, aware that hers was no doubt greater. As a full Vulcan, as well as a much younger adult, T'Lara most likely had aural sensitivity exceeding his own.

"Minimal damage, sir," the cadet replied. "Stabilizing pitch control."

Spock reflected that matters could be far worse. Thanks to Commander Scott's verteron field, only four microflares had penetrated the bridge in the seventeen minutes since entry into the flare field, and all had been relatively mild. They had also been nearly instantaneous, for Spock had ordered T'Lara to dive into the flare field at high impulse. The theory was that the microflares would be able to do less damage to any compartment, apparatus, or crew member they passed through if they only intersected it for a few hundred nanoseconds. The fact that such near-instantaneous passages still generated such heat and noise was a testament to the intensity of the primordial energy leaking through the micro-wormholes, even with the verteron field damping their frequency and average intensity. Indeed, the visible streaks of light came not from the microflares themselves, which were present too briefly for the eye to register, but from the incandescent, ionized atmosphere they left in their wake.

With this in mind, Spock had ordered the ship's internal air pressure reduced to minimum safe levels to lessen atmospheric transmission of shock and thermal damage, not to mention acoustic effects. Were the bridge at normal pressure, Spock and T'Lara would probably be deaf in their left ears by now.

The one place he had left at full pressurization was the communications lab, so as not to alter the conditions Commander Uhura relied on for memory assistance. Still, that was a gamble, for the lab was no more immune to microflare penetration than anywhere else on the ship. This would not be a good time for Uhura to suffer impairment of her exceptional hearing, or an injury should a microflare pierce her directly.

He had ordered all nonessential personnel to lie on the decks with their feet pointing toward the bow, to minimize the profile they presented to the oncoming microflares (or rather, the stationary microflares that the *Enterprise* passed through). This mission had a fairly small crew complement, though, so few were nonessential. It was only a matter of time, statistically speaking, before someone in the crew sustained a direct hit.

A proximity alert sounded. "A sizable cluster is forming in

our path," T'Lara reported, her voice raising only slightly. "Diverting . . . insufficient time to clear it."

Spock opened the shipwide channel. "All personnel, brace for microflare cluster." He leaned forward in the command chair, and the other bridge personnel hunkered down as best they could. It seemed almost quaint to defend against a subspatial quantum phenomenon using the same methods primitive Vulcans would have used to face a sandstorm or a hail of arrows. But the mathematics of probability and surface area were universal.

As the *Enterprise* passed through the cluster, Spock listened for system breach alerts from the damage control station. Several minor ones sounded over the first minute, accompanied by a single thunder crack of a flare passage through the bridge, well over the crew's lowered heads. Yet before long, a major alarm sounded, after which the rate of breaches began to increase.

"*Scott to bridge! One o' those hailstones from Hell struck the field regulator. The verteron field's gone down. It'll take at least ten minutes to re-rig it—*" A loud crack and a cry sounded behind him. "*Oh, no . . . Lieutenant Kwan's been hit! I need a medical team down here!*"

Spock nodded to Ferat, who relayed the order to sickbay. "On their way, Mister Scott. Repair the verteron field as quickly as possible."

"*Easier said than done when we're under fire!*"

"Sir!" That was Cadet Nadel at the science station. "Another ship is closing on our course. Just now picked it up through the static. It's . . . it's taking position directly in front of us!"

In moments, the barrage of microflares began to ease. Spock straightened in his seat, raising a brow. As far as he could discern through the static on the viewscreen, the vessel in whose wake they now flew was of the *Miranda* class.

"They're hailing, sir," called Ferat. "I think . . . yes, it's a laser-pulse communication. Just a moment . . ."

Though the Cygnian cadet was inexperienced with the alternative communication protocol, she nonetheless reconfigured her station with respectable alacrity. A moment later, a reasonably clear signal came through from the other bridge—the occupants of which were all unexpectedly attired in EV suits. Spock noted that the transmission was devoid of the normal background sounds of bridge equipment.

The captain, clad in an orange-and-brown EV suit, spoke through his helmet microphone. *"This is Captain Clark Terrell of the* U.S.S. Reliant. *You look like you could use a hand, Captain Spock."*

Spock tugged on the hem of his uniform jacket. "Your arrival is timely, Captain. I presume you have a working verteron field?"

"That's right. And we've depressurized to minimize the blast damage—and protect our ears."

"We have done the same, though to a less drastic degree."

"Understandable—your people have a lot of work to do. You need your freedom of movement." He gestured around his bridge. *"Whereas we're just here to run interference. I figured you'd be better off with a second verteron field leading the way."* He smiled inside his helmet. *"That is, if you hadn't lost the first."*

"Indeed. But your arrival should facilitate the repair of our field. Your proposal is sound, provided we maintain a minimum separation. At this speed, that entails a degree of risk."

"Being here at all is a risk, Captain. Yet here we are."

Spock decided that Commander Chekov's assessments of his new captain were not exaggerated. "Then I believe the proper vernacular is, 'After you.'"

San Francisco

After listening to President Lorg's static-laden speech to the people of Earth—solemnly advising them of the impending disaster and the limited defenses the planet had at its disposal, yet urging the people to be resolute and stand ready to assist their neighbors in need—Kirk decided that waiting out Portia and the Warborn hostage-takers was no longer an option. He strode out toward the building and called out, not bothering with a communicator. "Portia! This is Admiral Kirk. It's urgent that we talk!"

Captain sh'Deslar hurried forward and caught his arm. "Admiral, is it wise to take an aggressive tone?"

He glanced over his shoulder at her. "A passive approach hasn't worked. These are soldiers, Captain. Warriors born and bred. I have a feeling they'll respond to strength and boldness."

He moved farther forward, leaving her behind. Soon, a warning shot from a phaser struck the pavement near his feet, emanating from a small crack in one office window. He ignored it, stepping right over the burn mark in the pavement. "I'm here to parley! Are you afraid of a conversation?"

He kept walking. By the time he reached the door, it was pulled open from within, and Titus drew him inside and searched him. Soon, he was brought upstairs to where Portia waited in the hall.

"Do you have an answer for me, Admiral? Have you found the real killer? Or bothered to look?"

"Commander Sulu and Doctor McCoy are pursuing a lead. But that's not why I'm here. Did you hear the president's speech? Do you know what's about to hit Earth in less than an hour?"

Portia shrugged. "I heard. What of it? Of all the places on Earth the flares could hit, the odds that they'd be here are low enough. And I'm sure San Francisco is under one of those verteron shields."

"Those will only limit the size and frequency of the microflares. It won't block them altogether. And low probability isn't zero probability. You're putting these people in danger by not giving them the freedom to move if a flare burst does hit here."

He sharpened his tone. "More than that—you're putting others in danger by not letting these people help them. Your hostages were working on a plan to coordinate with flare relief teams when you captured them, did you know that? Not to mention the police officers and Starfleet security personnel who had to be pulled off flare duty to respond to your actions."

"Fewer than would have come otherwise. That was the idea."

"But at what cost? Look at what you're doing, Portia. You talk about wanting the freedom to be a fighter, a warrior. I respect that."

She scoffed. "Do you?"

"Yes, I do. I think of myself as a military man. I know it's in my nature to fight, to be aggressive—even to kill if I have to. I accepted that side of myself long ago."

"But aren't you the great paragon of Starfleet's diplomacy? There are textbooks about you already. The captain who came to peaceful terms with the First Federation, the Hortas, the Gorn, the Kelvans. The face of the Organian Peace Treaty."

Kirk chuckled in spite of himself. "Every one of those peaceful resolutions came at the end of a fight. In several of them, I was slow to open myself to the possibility. My first impulse was to destroy the threat, to protect my crew and my nation. There were other times when I did have to use force, when there was no other way." He glanced briefly downward. "On Organia, I had peace forced on me over my vocal objections. I had to learn to support it."

Portia's keen eyes narrowed. "Tell me truthfully, Admiral. Did you agree with Rakatheema that the Warborn should fight for Starfleet? That we should be its shock troops against the Klingons or Romulans?"

Kirk thought it over, striving to answer honestly. "I believed it was a possibility worth exploring. But not to exploit you. You deserved the dignity of making that choice for yourselves, the same as any other Starfleet officer.

"To be a soldier, Portia, is to put everything that you are on the line. To place your duty, your purpose, above your own life—and over others' lives, if necessary. In some ways, that's an even greater sacrifice—a more difficult responsibility to bear. It's a burden that should never be imposed on anyone who isn't fully committed to it."

She stood there absorbing his words for several moments. "All I want is to find my own purpose to fight. To have something worth fighting for."

"I understand that. I hoped Starfleet could give you that."

Portia's wrinkled brow furrowed further. "Nobody can agree on what Starfleet is! Some tell me it's meant for peace. Others push me to fight for it. How do you reconcile it all?"

Kirk pondered the question, reflecting on many years' worth of debates with Spock and McCoy, and a few more recent ones with Ashley Janith-Lau. "I've been trying to figure that out for most of my life. But I think I have a pretty good idea of the answer by now."

Her eyes shone with need. "Tell me."

"The answer is that there is no conflict between those goals—because peace is the only thing worth fighting for. The act of destruction only serves a purpose if it brings about some net positive result." He gestured with a hand, symbolically reaching toward her. "The Arcturians realized that when they stopped using the Warborn to fight one another, and redefined your purpose as the protection of Arcturus."

"I couldn't care less what they made us for. We were just their tools, to be discarded when they didn't want us anymore."

"What your ancestors did was terrible, yes. But step by step, through fits and starts, the Arcturians have tried to make it better. To turn something that began destructively toward a more beneficial goal. At first, it was for the benefit of Arcturus. Now, at least, they're trying to find a solution that benefits you. It's not perfect, but they're trying.

"Progress often comes in small steps. Instead of rejecting the next step because it isn't large enough, we should take it, then use it as a foundation to climb up to the next step, and the next, building momentum as we go."

She snorted. "Philosophical nonsense."

"No. It's the mentality of a soldier. Advance one step at a time, however you can. Hold what ground you can and push forward. If you fall back, gird your loins and push forward again. Never give up the fight as long as you draw breath. Because if you let up, the universe pushes you back."

He took a step closer. "We fight to bring order to the chaos, not just to create more chaos. If the fight becomes the end in itself, then it has no purpose.

"Portia . . . the Warborn may have been created to do battle, but that is not the sole purpose of your existence. It's the means toward becoming what you can truly be."

The lights flickered, no doubt from the growing flare interference. Kirk gestured toward the door, toward the hostages beyond. "This is your chance, Portia. You say you've been looking for something to fight for? Well, that fight is happening. The fight to protect life. My crew is fighting up in space right now to protect this planet. McCoy and Sulu are fighting to save the hostages—and just maybe to save you."

He reached out a hand again, no longer as mere symbolism. "You can join the fight too, Cadet. Come with me—and we'll fight together to protect whomever we can."

Kirk could see that Portia was waging her own battle within. At last, she sagged, letting out a heavy breath. "To be honest, I didn't know what my endgame would be. I realized this was a bad plan hours ago, but I couldn't see a way out."

She peered at him. "If I help you, will you advocate for leniency toward my people?"

He kept his own gaze steely. "Should that matter, soldier? We don't fight because it's free of consequences."

The corner of her mouth turned up slightly. "What's that line of yours they quote? 'Risk is our business'?"

He rolled his eyes. "It sounded better before it got overused."

Portia gave him a nod of understanding and respect, then turned and opened the door. Kirk stood unthreateningly just outside the doorway as she huddled with the other four and informed them of her decision to stand down. Bertram started to argue, but she slapped him down with a few words, and the others quickly fell in line. Then she turned to the hostages. "You're free to go. There are people out there who'll need your help soon."

The activists sighed and wept with relief, all except the two Vulcans, T'Sena and Vekal. The latter merely stared at Portia as if realizing something about her for the first time.

Ashley Janith-Lau rushed to Kirk and embraced him. "Thank you, Jim. I knew you could find a peaceful resolution."

He smiled down at her. "Don't tell your fellow pacifists, but I did it by appealing to her as one soldier to another."

She stared back. "I . . . guess we have a lot to talk about."

"Later. Right now we should get you all out of the building. Probably best to be mobile if the microflares hit."

No sooner did they get outside than Kirk spotted McCoy and Sulu headed his way. Janith-Lau flew into McCoy's arms and gave him a rather more enthusiastic greeting than she'd given Kirk. He traded a few murmured words with her, then led her over to the admiral, while Sulu touched base with Captain sh'Deslar.

McCoy's eyes widened briefly in surprise as he saw Portia coming out behind Kirk, but he quickly gathered himself. "Good, you're here. You'll both want to hear this. You too, Ashley."

As sh'Deslar's people came forward to take the Warborn into custody, Kirk held out a hand to hold them back. "Go ahead, Bones."

The doctor explained his epiphany about the Warborn being genetically female, and the computer extrapolation he'd performed. "When I projected for masculine development, several of the simulation runs produced close matches for one cadet. That was enough to be granted access to that cadet's DNA profile, and I've confirmed it's a match." He held out a data slate. "Here's our new top suspect for the murder of Rakatheema."

Portia gasped at the face displayed on the slate, alongside the computer simulations that matched it in various parameters. "Horatio? It can't be!"

"I hate to break the news under such circumstances. But he's your biological brother."

She waved his words away. "That means nothing. How could he be a killer? He's the one who's most pious about peace and nonviolence. He sounds the same as these fools." She gestured toward the activists.

Janith-Lau cleared her throat pointedly. "You seemed pretty convinced *we* were capable of murder."

Kirk spoke before they could continue the argument. "We'll find the answer when we find Horatio. Let me handle that. For now, we have more urgent worries."

He looked up at the city skyline and its flickering lights. Even the weather seemed to be changing, a cold wind picking up. His thoughts went out to Spock, Uhura, and Scotty on the *Enterprise*, to Chekov with the defense fleet. If anyone could find the answer before the Earth was engulfed, it was his old crew.

He knew he was needed here—that he had made a difference here tonight. Yet his eyes lifted to the sky, and he wished he could be out there with the *Enterprise*—even as it flew into the heart of the storm.

Chapter Twenty

United States of Africa

M'Umbha Uhura walked among the elephants, trying to keep them calm. It was the wee hours here, shortly before sunrise, but elephants in their natural habitat slept only a couple of hours a night as a rule, and only when conditions were calm and the temperature, wind, and the like were just right. Now, with a distant flicker in the western sky and the very air feeling charged and agitated, the elephants were in much the same mood.

At a time like this, M'Umbha would have liked to be back home in Nairobi, with Omar and her friends and neighbors. But the elephants were her community too, and they needed someone here to watch out for them. So she had come to them and explained as best she could through her universal translator. The device could allow near-perfect comprehension between civilized humanoids, but elephants were different in many ways and led simpler, more basic lives. For all their raw intelligence, they lacked the context to understand the situation fully.

What she could try to offer instead was comfort and reassurance. She had advised them that the faint, flickering haze growing larger and brighter in the starry sky was an oncoming storm, a different kind than they had seen before, but one that could hurt like lightning if it hit them. She did not have to explain that there was no shelter; to elephants, that was a given with any storm, any threat from predators. They did not have the luxury of civilized beings to feel entitled to exemption from nature's hazards; they merely endured them as best they could, and supported one another to ease their pain afterward. M'Umbha had promised that she would do the same for them; she and her team stood ready to offer medical aid if any of the herds were struck.

The matriarch of the herd had asked a question: *Is this another pain humans have brought onto us?*

There had been no accusation in the question, merely a resigned acceptance of reality. It had been generations since the age when humans had routinely enslaved, abused, and killed these magnificent giants, but the clichés about their memory were not exaggerated, and even now their trust was provisional at best.

Still, M'Umbha had not known how to answer the query. Though she did not fully understand the origin of the phenomenon, she knew it was connected to Nyota's efforts to communicate with some unseen intelligence out in the universe. The last thing she wanted the elephants to think was that her own daughter had brought down this threat upon them. Certainly there was no way Nyota could have known her efforts would provoke this.

She would not say, then, that humans had caused this crisis. But some intelligence, some technology out there, probably had. Someone had caused this through conscious action, probably with no awareness of the damage they were inflicting upon others in the pursuit of their own goals. That would be very familiar to the elephants. Would they care about the distinction between human and nonhuman civilizations?

Instead of dwelling on such questions, M'Umbha thought about her family. She thought of Malcolm volunteering to leave his cozy research hospital, working tirelessly out in space to heal the victims of the flares. She thought of Omar back home in Nairobi, no doubt sitting with their neighbors and cooking for them and telling silly jokes and anecdotes to keep them calm as they waited for a disaster they could not hide from. Most of all, she thought of Nyota bravely rushing forth on the *Enterprise* to take responsibility for the consequences of her past, and to try to save everyone—the elephants included—from having that pain brought down upon them.

This is what Uhuras do, she thought. *We connect people. We build bonds of understanding.* M'Umbha knew that somehow, somewhere out there, her daughter was doing just that—trying to make the connection that would let the flares' creators understand the harm they did, and convince them to stop.

After a time, she finally gave the matriarch her answer, knowing she would not have forgotten the question. "This is a pain that humans are doing their very best to prevent. My own daughter, Nyota, is leading them in that fight. So I believe they will succeed."

The matriarch flicked her ears skeptically. *Nothing can convince a storm not to strike.*

M'Umbha smiled. "You don't know my daughter like I do."

U.S.S. Enterprise

It had been several minutes now since any microflares had shot through the communications lab. Apparently the restored verteron field, in combination with *Reliant*'s field in the vanguard, had given Uhura and Shastri the grace period they needed to finalize their preparations. Nonetheless, their headaches and the lingering ringing in their ears helped them keep the urgency of the situation in mind.

Finally, Uhura leaned back from the main console, turning her head to give its display screens one more going over. "I think that's it. We're ready to transmit."

"Great!" Shastri paused, then turned to her. "So why aren't we?"

She flushed. "I don't know what to say. There's no chance they'd understand our speech. Autotranslation could never work with minds that alien." Not only minds, she realized; the plasma beings' whole physical universe was so different from hers that there could be few points of commonality for a translation matrix to latch onto.

Shastri smiled. "Who said anything about speech? You already discovered our common language with them decades ago."

Uhura stared at him. "I sang to them?"

"Every time. Didn't I mention that?"

"Yes, but I thought . . . never mind, I don't know what I thought." She searched her memory, but that well seemed to have run dry. "What did I sing?"

Shastri blinked multiple times. "I don't remember. I never really paid attention to the words. I just loved the sound of your voice."

"All right, then." She cleared her throat. "How about 'Two Moons'?"

He stared. "You hated that song! You made fun of the lyrics every time I listened to it."

"Did I? I have a recording of it in my voice in my personal database. It's the song that first tipped me off to the vacuum flare connection, when I found similar acoustic patterns in their emissions."

"You *kept* that? I convinced you to sing it once, so you could listen to it in your own voice and see if you liked it more." He chuckled. "You didn't. Though I thought it was a real improvement."

She smiled and touched his hand. "Perhaps that's why I kept

it. Anyway, I think the lyrics are fitting here, even if they are a bit corny."

"Well, I'm game if you are."

Uhura triple-checked her adjustments, then opened an intercom channel. "Comms lab to bridge. We are ready to attempt contact."

"Acknowledged, Commander. Proceed."

Closing that channel, she nodded at Shastri, who laid his hands on his own control panel, ready to refine the parameters of their transmission in response to their signal feedback. He nodded his readiness in return.

Taking a deep breath, Uhura called up the lyrics to the old Martian love song from memory and began to sing:

It seems like we've known each other forever.
It feels like a billion years and a day.
It seems so right that we should come together,
So what is this force that keeps us pulling away?

I meet your eyes and I gaze in a mirror.
The love and the fear are reflections of me.
We know each other's hearts and yet we keep our distance
Two close and loving strangers feels like all we can be.

Two moons racing through the sky.
Hard to come together, but we have to try.
Fear and panic keep us on the run.
If we overcome them, then the two can join as one.

She raised her eyebrows at Shastri: *Anything?* Checking the readings, he shook his head, then twirled his finger in the universal gesture for "Keep going." Hoping she wasn't making a cosmic fool of herself, Uhura took a breath and launched into the next verse:

I reach out my hand and draw it back again
Like some cosmic forces pull it away . . .

"Maintain course, Cadet," Spock advised T'Lara as he studied the plot on the celestial hemisphere display at the base of the helm/navigation console. The *Enterprise* and *Reliant* were maintaining a forced orbit around the flare epicenter, remaining at high velocity to minimize microflare damage while also maintaining proximity to the plasma beings' signal source. "We must remain in *Reliant's* wake."

"Understood, sir," the young Vulcan said. "However, the gravimetric distortion is making it difficult."

"Same here, Captain Spock," Terrell reported from *Reliant*. Even with laser transmission, his voice was growing difficult to discern through the rising interference. *"This kind of gravitational turbulence with no mass . . . we might be on the verge of a subspace rift. Whatever your people are doing, they'd better make it fast."*

"They are aware of the urgency, Captain Terrell."

The ship shook briefly, and the damage control display showed a new microflare breach in the starboard nacelle. Spock reflected that it was fortunate the warp drive was useless under these conditions in any case. However, the turbulence was making it difficult for the two ships to remain in perfect formation—and the microflare impact rate was rising again as the growing subspace instability began to exceed even two verteron fields' damping ability.

Through the digital flicker and dropouts on the screen, the EV-suited Terrell met Spock's eyes solemnly. *"I trust you also know that if a rift forms while we're this close, we'll never get clear in time."*

"That has always been a given, Captain Terrell. You are under no obligation to remain if you wish to save your crew."

"Are you kidding, Spock? They'd never forgive me if I forced them to miss out on the final play." He chuckled. *"You can rely on us, Captain. It's right there in the name of the ship."*

U.S.S. *Amazon*
Earth orbit

Captain Jangura stared at the vast field of flickering light that filled the main viewscreen entirely now. "Time to intercept?"

Chekov answered heavily. "Approximately six minutes, sir." It was difficult to be more precise. Earth's own orbital motion hurtled it inexorably closer to the fringe of the field at thirty kilometers per second, but the field continued to expand at an increasing rate, and there was no way to define an exact boundary for it as new microflare clusters erupted on its fringes unpredictably.

"Status of the verteron beams?"

"All functioning beams at maximum spread," Joel Randolph reported, touching the earpiece receiver he was using to monitor reports from the other ships and stations participating in Earth's orbital defense. "But the coverage is no more than twenty-eight percent."

Jangura let out a short, hissing breath, blinking his bulbous eyes. "Nobody's thought of a last-minute miracle for improving that?"

"This is as good as it gets, sir."

"Then make sure we maintain it, Commander."

"Aye, sir."

Randolph circled the bridge, checking the stations and giving nods and words of support to the crew. When he reached the science station, Chekov spoke to him softly. "Too bad we can't make an inboard verteron *field* and an outboard verteron *beam* at the same time. We may protect people down on Earth, but it'll be rough up here."

The first officer sighed. "You haven't changed, Pavel. Always the pessimistic Russian. How do you live with so little faith in the universe?"

Chekov thought about Uhura, Scotty, and Spock, and what they were attempting right now at the heart of the storm. "By having faith in my comrades."

U.S.S. *Enterprise*

"I'm getting something!" Shastri called. "Compiling now . . . They're pinging back, trying to confirm, but it's hard to lock on through the interference! Keep going! *Aahh!*"

His cry was in response to the deafening crack of a microflare passage, the second in as many minutes. The console sparked and a display screen blinked out, but for now all the vital status lights remained green. Uhura knew that wouldn't last long, though. At this rate, either the equipment would be struck or one of them would.

So she did her best to ignore it, like a true performer, and focus only on finishing the song.

Oh, we can defeat our fear.
All we need is with us right here.
No panic withstands if we just join our hands,
Yes, my dear . . .
Drawing near . . .
A-and we're . . .
Finally here!

Shastri ducked another microflare, then grinned and gave her a thumbs-up as she belted out the final refrain:

Two moons racing for the stars;
If we chase them long enough they could be ours.

No more fear or panic, just the force of our love.
The sky belongs to us—we are the two moons up above!

Even as she sang, the screens lit up with new data streams and subspace spectrographs. Finally, they had connected!

As soon as she finished, Shastri checked his board and crowed in confirmation. "This is it! A two-way channel, just like we had on Argelius! Signal is pouring through from their end!"

He leaped from his seat and they fell into each other's arms, laughing and pounding each other on the back. After a few moments, concern penetrated Uhura's euphoria. "But is it enough?" she asked, a bit hoarsely. "Now that they've connected, will they stop trying to force the signal through? Or will they ramp it up even more?"

They stared at each other wide-eyed. But in moments, the screens provided the answer. "Subspace interference subsiding," Shastri reported. "Vacuum energy levels too. Signal's still coming through, but tighter, clearer." He grinned at her. "They've stopped shouting—now they're just talking."

"At last."

"*Bridge to communications lab,*" came Spock's voice. "*The flare has begun to dissipate. Subspace erosion has leveled off. Have you made contact?*"

Uhura grinned and opened the return channel. "Affirmative, Captain! We're now receiving them loud and clear."

She clasped Shastri's hand and smiled at him. "And this time, we won't lose the connection."

Starfleet Academy

As soon as the interference cleared and Kirk got the report that the *Enterprise* had succeeded in stopping the vacuum flares, the admiral contacted Academy Security and ordered them to detain Horatio at once. The reply he soon received made it clear that that might be unnecessary.

He arrived at Horatio's dorm room with McCoy, Janith-Lau, and Portia in tow, as they were no longer needed for flare relief. Perhaps that task would have been easier for them to endure than what they found within, once Kirk nodded at the guards outside and led his party through the door.

All seven of the Warborn who had not gone with Portia were here, sprawled on the floor. From their orientation, they had been seated together, arrayed around Horatio, who was cross-legged and slumped against the wall at their head. The only other occupant of the room was Zirani Kayros, who sat with Benedick's head cradled in her lap. The Tiburonian cadet looked up at Kirk and the others, weeping freely. "Sir . . . I found them like this. Most of them were already . . . But Benedick . . ."

McCoy checked several of them for life signs by hand, then used his medical scanner on the rest to confirm it. He looked up grimly at the admiral. "Dead, Jim. All but Horatio, and he's slipping fast. Some kind of poison." He moved to the ringleader's side to do what he could, while Portia and Janith-Lau looked on in dumb shock.

"Benedick said . . ." Kayros gulped and gathered her breath before continuing. "He seemed so content. Said he finally got to sacrifice for Arcturus . . . that he was sorry he had to leave us, b-but Horatio said it was the only way. He said . . . Horatio *let* him hand out the poison!" She sobbed, and Janith-Lau moved to comfort her.

"Jim!" McCoy waved him closer to Horatio, who was moving slowly, moaning and cracking his eyes open.

Portia reached her brother's side before Kirk did, but there was nothing sororal in her as she confronted Horatio. "*Why?!* To kill your own comrades! Frame your sister! You knew, didn't you?"

Horatio gave her a faint smile that seemed absolving, as

backward as that was. "You . . . always said I was nosy. But . . . didn't . . . matter. Only . . . defending Arcturus. Our sacred purpose."

"We can be more than that! More than what they made us!"

His gaze became pitying. "Most beings . . . go their whole lives . . . not knowing their purpose. We are blessed to know from birth. We exist . . . to protect Arcturus. From ourselves if necessary."

Kirk knelt before him. "Horatio. How does any of this protect Arcturus?"

"Our mission . . . our purpose must remain pure. To fight for our world and no other. Rakatheema threatened that. Wanted us to fight for others." He refocused on Portia. "You threatened that. Wanted to fight for yourselves." He sighed. "I am sorry, sister . . . but it seemed an elegant strategy. To remove both threats in one act. It was . . . blessed fortune . . . that my DNA could be so easily mistaken for yours.

"I gave him a chance. Went to him . . . tried to convince him. Wouldn't bend. Insisted . . . dogma had to adapt to change. I . . . disagreed."

He let out a shuddering sigh. "Thought my plan . . . so elegant. But no plan . . . survives contact with the enemy." A faint laugh. "Should've known . . . not to go against you . . . sister. You are . . . a superior enemy.

"Once framing you failed . . . only one option left. Ensure we would not be exploited . . . for unholy purpose."

McCoy looked up at Kirk and shook his head, wearing an expression Kirk had seen far too often over the years. There was nothing he could do to save Horatio.

But the cadet—the murderer—smiled beatifically. "They all understood. All . . . good soldiers. We were created . . . to die for the good of Arcturus. We . . . succeeded in our mission. I gave them that. Please, sister . . . comrade . . . make sure the rest of us . . . die too. All of us. For . . . Arcturus."

Portia's face was stony as she gently took Horatio's head in her hands and lowered him onto her lap, paralleling Kayros with Benedick. Kirk peered past the heavy folds of skin into her piercing eyes, trying to understand what was going on behind them.

With a heavy sigh, Portia looked down at the brother she had grown up with but never known. "Good night, sweet prince," she said . . .

. . . then snapped his neck.

Her face remained just as stony as the security guards led her away moments later. Kirk doubted he would ever know whether she had acted out of mercy or revenge.

Epilogue

Starfleet Academy

After a brief hearing, Starfleet decided not to pursue homicide charges against Portia, for Horatio had been moments from death in any case. As for her actions against the peace activists, Janith-Lau had convinced her people not to press charges, and the city's authorities agreed to place the surviving Warborn's discipline in Starfleet hands, so that they could focus on repairing the damage caused by the flares' interference. Kirk wondered if, perhaps, they had also felt the five survivors had been punished enough.

Even so, there had to be consequences, as Admiral Chandra spelled out in a meeting in his office with Kirk, Professor Blune, and the five surviving Warborn. "Commander Rakatheema's dream was that Starfleet Academy could offer you a path to build full and rewarding lives for yourselves in roles beyond combat," the superintendent told them. "It is clear now that we failed in that effort.

"After what the five of you have done, you would have been expelled from the Academy in any case. There is no coming back from the line you crossed. Yet it may be that this is for the best. Perhaps Starfleet simply cannot offer you what you need to build the lives you deserve."

Portia appeared guardedly appreciative of his words. "I think you're right about that, sir. The commander felt your balance of military discipline and peaceful goals would be a transitional path for us. But I think the military side of Starfleet only reinforced our conditioning.

"Doctor Janith-Lau has offered to take us to a monastery on Vulcan, to help us explore a path of peace and self-discipline. I've . . . come to the conclusion that it may be the best thing for us. The others agree." Next to her, Bertram shifted in his chair, looking reluctant, but said nothing. "If it works out, the other Warborn will follow us there."

Kirk stared at Portia, surprised by her uncharacteristic words. "I thought that what you wanted was the freedom to embrace your warrior side. To find a cause to fight for."

She lowered her eyes. "I do, Admiral. But after the last few days . . . I think we have seen enough death. Enough loss. It has no appeal." She fidgeted in her seat. "I am Horatio's genetic twin. We share the same potentials—the same basic nature. And what he became . . ." She shuddered. "I don't want to lose myself to that. To become a threat to others—maybe even to my own comrades. That was never what I wanted to fight for.

"And you and Doctor Janith-Lau have helped me to see . . . that there are other ways to fight. That perhaps the worthiest battle is the one we wage with ourselves." On the table before her, her fists clenched. "Horatio . . . lost that battle. He surrendered too easily to blind faith . . . to a narrow definition of what we were allowed to be. I don't want to make that same mistake, sir. I don't want to surrender to my own assumptions."

Kirk smiled at her. "I respect your choice, Portia, and I wish you well. But I still feel it's Starfleet's loss. You are far more than most people expected of you."

She nodded. "Most . . . except Rakatheema. I may not have trusted his intentions . . . but he saw that we could be more. He fought to give us that chance . . . and he died for it. We owe it to him to achieve the spirit of what he sought for us, if not the specifics."

"I'm sure he would be proud to see that."

Bertram looked unsure of himself. "That play Horatio loved . . . that he took his name from . . . there was that man who said, 'This above all—to thine own self be true.'" He shook his head. "That's all I ever wanted to do. Just be what I was born to be. But now I think . . . maybe Shakespeare was wrong?"

Kirk smiled. "Shakespeare wrote that man, Polonius, as a fool. That speech showed his shallowness, his obliviousness in giving advice that he didn't understand or follow." He chuckled. "A friend of mine, Rhenas Sherev, once told me that she thought Polonius's fatal mistake was that he was a character in a tragedy who believed he was in a comedy. He thought Hamlet was mad with unrequited love rather than grief and vengeance, and so he died because he failed to understand his world and his role within it."

Bertram was still confused. "So . . . what does that mean?"

"It means that . . . you *should* strive to be true to yourself . . . but you shouldn't assume you already know who you really are, or how you fit into the world around you. It's through the striving that you discover your true self."

Portia turned to take in Kirk and Chandra. "That goes for you too, you know. Starfleet. You need to figure some things out about what you truly are—peacemakers, warriors, or something in between."

Kirk returned her gaze, acknowledging her insight. "I've been seeking that answer for most of my life. I still haven't found the answer. I think maybe it has to change as the galaxy we live in changes."

She considered that for a moment. "Maybe. But maybe it's by making the right or wrong choices that we change the galaxy."

He smiled at Portia. "It just may be at that."

Starfleet Headquarters

Three days following the last vacuum flare, the stream of data flowing through the cross-temporal wormhole link with the primordial plasma remained unabated. Uhura had needed to dump it to Starfleet's central science database as quickly as possible to avoid using up all the memory in the *Enterprise*'s library computer. And still the transmissions continued.

"But what have we really gained from it?" Admiral Cartwright asked. He sat at the head of the table in Headquarters' conference room, accompanied by Admiral Kirk, Captain Spock, Commanders Scott and Uhura, and Rajendra Shastri. "Our translators haven't been able to make heads or tails of it, aside from the common mathematics and physics. The rest is too alien to even begin to comprehend."

"For now, perhaps, Admiral," Spock replied. "But in the attempt, we may make other unanticipated discoveries about physics and the nature of the universe. Eventually we will find a basis for interpreting the knowledge the primordial civilization has sent us. It may be the work of generations to decipher the sheer volume of information. But that is true of many scientific endeavors. There is still much we do not know about the prehistory of Earth or Vulcan. There remain many gaps and unanswered questions. But every answer we do find is valued.

"This contact is an extraordinary discovery in itself: proof that intelligent life existed in the primordial minutes of the universe, a time when we had hitherto assumed no life or complexity could exist. That knowledge alone will refine our understanding of physics in ways that may lead to new technologies in the decades or centuries to come."

"But was it worth the cost, Captain Spock?" Cartwright

asked. "In their attempts to be heard, these plasma beings caused hundreds of deaths. They almost devastated the Earth, the whole Solar system."

"There have been many disasters resulting from botched first contacts," Admiral Kirk put in. "The Xindi, the Partnership, the Sagara, the Horta, the Gorn. That risk of fatal misunderstanding is always there, Lance. That's why it's so important to embrace understanding going forward, so that the same mistakes don't happen again.

"It's not about whether it was worth it. It happened. We have to live with it—and try to profit from its lessons. That's all we can do." Kirk's somber tone suggested that he was contemplating his own recent failure with the Warborn.

Seeking to ease the dark mood, Uhura leaned forward. "There's no point in trying to lay blame here, Admiral Cartwright. This was a tragic misfortune for everyone involved. A chain of accidents that grew out of all predictable control." She traded a look with Scott. "I can't even bring myself to blame *Nomad* for setting all this in motion. Even it was created in an accident, from two probes sent out on benevolent, scientific missions. In its own way, it suffered from a loss of memory just as much as I did."

She looked around the table. "If I've learned anything lately, it's the importance of memory. Without knowing our history, our context, we're incomplete. Adrift. We lose the connections that guide us, that keep us on the right path. We're blinded to the consequences of our actions . . ." Her gaze landed on Shastri. "And our inaction.

"That's what we've really gained from this. We've recovered the memory of a lost era of the universe. Even if we don't understand it, we've ensured that it lives on. That was what the plasma beings needed more than anything else, what drove them to strive so desperately to make contact. All they wanted, in the end, was to be remembered. What else do any of us ultimately have?"

Cartwright cleared his throat. "Yes, well, I'm still not pleased that you and Mister Shastri defied Starfleet orders in the name of that noble philosophy. However, I've been in consultation with Director Simok of the Department of Temporal Investigations. According to their Doctor T'Viss, Commodore Reppert's fears of disruption to the timeline were in error. As Simok explained it to me, with so many interactions and events occurring in those first few accelerated minutes, so many species evolving and going extinct, any change to the history of one or two such civilizations would have been infinitesimal on the scale of the entire universe."

"Logical," Spock said. "After all, we had previously believed the universe to be in thermal equilibrium in that era, uniform and lacking in the dynamism necessary for life and activity. Therefore, whatever changes occurred in that era must have evened out to insignificance on the cosmic scale."

"In any case," Cartwright went on, "since the basis for that order was in error, Starfleet will not be penalizing either of you for violating it. It would look bad after you both saved the Earth." He met both their eyes sternly. "On the other hand, none of this would've happened to begin with if you *had* followed Reppert's orders and halted your research at the Academy. So it cancels out. Don't expect any commendations for this."

Once Cartwright dismissed the briefing, Uhura and Shastri walked out hand in hand, splitting off from Kirk, Spock, and Scott as they discussed repairs to the *Enterprise*. "So," Shastri ventured, "we basically saved the galaxy. Does that happen a lot in Starfleet?"

She smiled. "Not as often as the vid dramas suggest. But often enough that it sometimes keeps me awake at night."

"Hmm. I was right to become a civilian, then. There are

much more enjoyable ways to be kept awake at night." Realizing what he'd said, he cleared his throat and let go of her hand.

But Uhura laughed. "Jen, don't be embarrassed that our friendship includes a taste of intimacy. It's over now, but it happened. It meant a great deal to both of us at the time, and there was nothing about it that we should regret or be ashamed of." She took his hand again. "I've learned that we should honor our memories. Celebrate them, cherish them, not hide from them."

He smiled and nodded, clasping her hand in both of his. "You're right, Nyota. God, it's good to have you back. Even if you're not quite the Nyota I knew. But then, I'm not the Jen I was."

"I'm proud to know the Jen you are now. You really came through when it counted."

They emerged onto the grounds of Headquarters, gazing up at the clear sky. The world felt normal again, like all the pieces were mostly put back into place. Everyday life was resuming, as it always did.

Shastri turned back to Uhura. "Speaking of cherishing our memories, I need to go back home and make some new memories with Sudo and Kiran. This is the longest I've been away from them since Kiran was born."

"I understand."

"So what about you?"

She smiled, understanding what he was nudging her to do. She still remembered only fragments of the events they had experienced together as friends, but she recognized every nuance in his voice, every unspoken sentiment and implication, as if they'd never been apart. It was immensely comforting.

"Yes," she said in answer to his tacit suggestion. "I've got a few weeks of leave saved up. It's about time I used them properly. I'm going home, to be with my family.

"It's time for me to build some new memories of my own."

Starfleet Academy

"Do you really have to go?"

McCoy walked alongside Ashley Janith-Lau through the Academy gardens, watching the students as they passed by—some jogging or doing *t'ai chi*, others chatting and laughing as they caught a quick lunch between classes, others studying under the shade of the same elm tree that McCoy remembered as a popular study spot from his own day. Perhaps the students were more subdued than usual, still absorbing the tragic events of the past week, but their lives and their studies had to go on regardless. At least, they would for most of the students.

"I mean, we've only been dating a few weeks," he went on. "I was just getting the hang of it again."

"Oh, I think you did fine from the start," she teased, tousling his hair. "Believe me, I'm not crazy about it either."

"Then why does it have to be you? I agree the Warborn deserve someone to offer them support and guidance, someone to speak for them now that Rakatheema's gone. But there are others in your organization who could do it."

Janith-Lau looked at him skeptically. "I've heard your *Enterprise* stories, Len. You, Jim, and Spock are all extraordinarily terrible at delegating responsibility. So don't act so surprised that I want to do this myself."

"I suppose you do have a point," McCoy muttered.

"But seriously . . . if I'm truly committed to peace, I can't limit myself to speeches and rallies and protests. Sometimes it's about individuals. Those five survivors—especially Portia—have a real need for some kind of peace in their minds, their hearts." She shrugged. "Even if it's peace with being a soldier, a warrior. But they need to find it first, to build it within themselves.

"I saw how lost they were when they took us hostage. It wasn't an act of hate or bullying, but of desperation. They didn't know how to cope with a crisis beyond using force. They knew it was a bad idea, but it was all they had." She smiled and shrugged. "I felt that, in a weird way, they were hoping we could give them answers. I mean, I know they wanted answers about the murder, but it felt like that was just the excuse. They needed guidance. Not on how to be a Starfleet officer, but on how to be themselves. That has to come first. And their prior upbringing didn't provide it."

McCoy pursed his lips, thinking it over. "I suppose that's a worthy challenge for a pediatrician, as well as a peacemaker."

She hugged him. "Don't worry. Vulcan isn't that far. We can still see each other from time to time." She pulled back and smiled. "That is, if someone else doesn't snatch you up first. I won't demand you be faithful to me or anything."

"We never really got that far anyway." He met her eyes with regret. "But I *was* open to the possibility."

She gave him a long valedictory kiss. "Maybe someday."

Once she went on her way, McCoy started back toward the main campus, spotting Kirk waiting for him along the path. "Too bad," the admiral said. "I was rooting for the two of you."

The doctor glowered at him. "You were just getting revenge for me trying to play matchmaker with you."

"I don't deny it."

He sighed. "I dunno, maybe it's for the best if we just focus on our careers from now on. We're both getting a bit too long in the tooth for our fancies to turn to thoughts of love."

Kirk grew contemplative. "I don't know, Bones. Ashley came into your life when you weren't even looking. Maybe we should just live our lives without expectations and be open to the opportunities that come our way."

McCoy looked around them at the students passing by. "I suppose even here, there are new things to discover."

"That's what an academy is for, Doctor. It may not be the *Enterprise*, but it's still an adventure."

Acknowledgments

Uhura's storyline in this book builds out of *Star Trek*: "The Changeling" written by John Meredyth Lucas. *Nomad*'s erasure of Uhura's memory in that episode was treated as an afterthought, with the personal consequences to Uhura completely glossed over, so I felt this was a story that was overdue to be told. I know of two prior stories that explored the aftermath of Uhura's memory loss: "See No Evil" by Jill Sherwin in the prose anthology *Star Trek: Constellations* and "Communications Breakdown" by Christine Boylan and Bettina M. Kurkoski in the comics anthology *Star Trek: The Manga—Kakan ni Shinkou*. Both those stories focused on Uhura's professional recovery, leaving room for me to examine the more personal consequences of her memory loss. *Living Memory* is consistent with both stories, though there are a few slight inconsistencies between the two (the ship is in greater need of repair in "Breakdown," and both stories claim to be Uhura's first away mission after *Nomad*).

Little has been established about Uhura's family and personal life over the years. I've drawn on bits and pieces from various sources to build her biography and family, though I've assembled the ingredients in my own way. Uhura's mother, M'Umbha, was named in a deleted scene from "The Man Trap" written by George Clayton Johnson and referenced in *The Star Trek Concordance* by Bjo Trimble. Her name appears to be a variant spelling of the Zambian name Mumba. Her father's name, Alhamisi, (Swahili for Thursday, presumably the day he was born) and her grandfather's name Uchawi (Swahili for sorcery or witchcraft, perhaps a nickname) both come from *Star Trek Log Ten* by Alan Dean Foster. Foster also established that her birthplace was Kitui, Kenya, and that her brother was a doctor at "Makere" [sic] University Hospital, though his name was given there as David. The name Malcolm for Uhura's brother comes from *Star Trek II Biographies* by William Rotsler, the source of Uhura's first name, Nyota. Rotsler also established Uhura's younger sister, though he named her Uaekundu, a name I could find no real-world origin for, so I went instead with Samara, the first name given to Lieutenant Uhura by the FASA *Star Trek* role-playing games in the 1980s. Rotsler proposed Damu Pua as Uhura's father's name, but as that apparently means "Bloody Nose" in Swahili, I treated it as a nickname.

Rotsler gave Uhura's birthplace as Nairobi, and several other sources have established it as her home. *Star Trek: The Lost Era—Catalyst of Sorrows* by Margaret Wander Bonanno established that she lived in Mombasa as a child and vacationed with her grandfather in the country. I've tried to reconcile these different origins. Mombasa is a major port city (and home to a space elevator terminus in the *HALO* game universe), so it made sense to establish it as a center of interstellar travel and commerce.

The premise that Uhura's father was lost in space when she was twenty comes from the 1978 Bantam *Star Trek* novel *The Starless World* by Gordon Eklund, though I have disregarded other elements from that novel (such as her father later turning up alive at the center of the galaxy). Uncle Raheem was established in the untitled issue 18 of IDW Publishing's *Star Trek Ongoing* by Ryan Parrott and Claudia Balboni; though that series was set in the Kelvin Timeline, Raheem would have been born well before the timeline split and thus should exist in both realities. Ironically, in Kelvin, he was the one lost in space.

Of Uhura's previous starship postings, the *Azrael* comes from Rotsler, the *Ahriman* from *Tears of the Singers* by Melinda Snodgrass, and the *Potemkin* from the video game *Star Trek: Starship Creator*. The starbase posting is my own innovation, just to mix things up.

M'Umbha Uhura's job as a legal advocate for elephants was loosely influenced by the Afrofuturist novel *Blue Remembered Earth* by Alastair Reynolds, as well as by the growing scientific evidence that elephants are conscious, intelligent beings. *Star Trek* has shown us the sentience of humpback whales in *The Voyage Home* and alluded to dolphin personnel on starships in *The Next Generation* and *Lower Decks*, so it stands to reason that the Federation would also do its best to respect elephant personhood and rights.

The ancestor who changed the Kenyan family name Uhuru to Uhura to "soften" it is an allusion to how Gene Roddenberry and Nichelle Nichols devised the character name, according to various sources. I tried to come up with a more Afrocentric justification for the vowel change, but there's no basis for such a thing in Swahili as far as I could determine.

The Earth colony on Altair VI was established in *Star Trek: Enterprise—Kobayashi Maru* by Michael A. Martin & Andy Mangels. The native population on Altair III was alluded to in *Star Trek: The Next Generation*: "Encounter at Farpoint" and depicted (vaguely, as robed and hooded humanoids) in DC Comics' *Star Trek: The Next Generation* issues 67–70 by Michael Jan Friedman and Deryl Skelton. I've attempted to reconcile them with the mention in "Amok Time" of a peace settlement at Altair that would send ripples as far as the Klingon Empire.

Cadet Peter Preston was played by Ike Eisenmann in *Star Trek II: The Wrath of Khan*, established in that film's script and director's cut as Montgomery Scott's nephew. Scott's dislike for Peter Preston's father was established in DC Comics' *Star Trek* (Volume 1) Annual #3, "Retrospect," by Peter David and

Curt Swan. Peter's adventures bear a certain resemblance to the experiences of Eisenmann's character in the short-lived 1977 NBC television series *The Fantastic Journey*, story-edited by *Star Trek*'s D. C. Fontana.

My placement of the tractor beam control on the movie-era bridge is conjectural. The original set plans show that it was intended to be a fold-out console adjacent to the engineering station, but this was never built. The forward starboard station is labeled on the set as "gravity control," and its console is repurposed from what was meant to be a bridge transporter station, with controls for aiming and operating a beam. Thus, it seemed a logical place for the tractor beam control. Thanks to Donny Versiga for his detailed digital reconstructions of the movie sets, which have been of invaluable assistance for the bridge scenes in my past two novels.

The song "Two Moons" is my own composition, written in the late 1990s for an early iteration of the Troubleshooter universe featured in my novel *Only Superhuman* and various short stories. It was conceived as a colonial Martian pop song using the orbital dynamics of Mars's moons Phobos and Deimos as an extended metaphor. As Uhura said, the lyrics seemed appropriate here.

S'rrel is the name the Decipher role-playing games proposed for the brown-furred Caitian counselor from *Star Trek IV: The Voyage Home*. Joel Randolph is the name given in that film's script to the *Yorktown* captain ultimately played by tennis star Vijay Amritraj. The Starfleet Headquarters set seen in that film was called the major missions room (uncapitalized) in Vonda N. McIntyre's novelization.

The (apparent) destruction of the original Solar L5 colonies was depicted in *The Lost Era: The Sundered* by Michael A. Martin and Andy Mangels. Mizuki City is named for the director of the Vanguard L5 colony from that novel.

The physics of the primordial universe, vacuum energy, and

quantum wormholes depicted herein is largely grounded in reality. However, theory tells us that the primordial plasma was in thermal equilibrium, too uniform for anything like life to emerge. I've fudged things a bit to suggest that the transition out of that phase was turbulent enough to allow complexity.

My portrayal of Arcturians is based on their depiction in *Star Trek: The Motion Picture*. Costume designer Robert Fletcher's notes on the species described them as a race of identical clones that could be bred swiftly and used as Federation infantry. This is incompatible with later depictions of the Federation and too similar to the Jem'Hadar (as well as the Clone Troopers in *Star Wars*), so I revamped the idea into something more distinctive. I originally intended to feature the Arcturians in my *Star Trek: Enterprise—Rise of the Federation* series, hence their historical connection to Captain Shumar of the *Essex* and the conquests of Maltuvis.

Admiral Chandra appeared as a captain in *Star Trek*: "Court Martial" and *The Captain's Oath*. His first name, Nensi, comes from his Kelvin Timeline counterpart, glimpsed as a member of a Starfleet Academy panel in the 2009 film.

The fan wiki Starbase 118 provided inspiration for the structure of the curriculum at Starfleet Academy. Other aspects of Academy operations and administrative structure were based on the United States Naval Academy (for instance, having a civilian academic dean). Some of the professors mentioned were nods to my own favorite college instructors, while others were borrowed from a *Wrath of Khan* set graphic.

Greg Cox's novel *To Reign in Hell: The Exile of Khan Noonien Singh* established that the presence of Khan's people on Ceti Alpha V was classified by Starfleet, explaining why the *Reliant* crew was unaware of their presence in the system.

I'd also like to thank the fans who once again helped me through a serious financial crisis with their donations, in return for which I've included various vessel, planet, institution, and characters names that a number of my donors suggested. Thanks to Byron Bailey, John Ballard, Eli Berg-Maas, Kimberly Blackwell, William Craig, "E D," Ricarda Dormeyer, Kelli Fitzpatrick, Robert Greene, Ensley Guffey, Dominik Patrick Hug, Casey Lance, Cooper Long, K McCann, Ronald Mallory, Brad Murray, Christopher Nelson, Danielle Pajak, Linn Payne, Alexander Perry, Scott Saslow, Darryl Schnell, Adam Selvidge, Gavin Sheedy, Jeffrey Singer, Benjamin Wert, Mybrid Wonderful, Paolo Andrea Zaccheddu, Robert Ziegler, and anyone else I've left out.

Finally, I extend thanks and remembrance to my uncle Clarence Preston Bennett (1929–2021), who asked me to name a "good, kind, wonderful" character in memory of his long-departed wife, Janith Ashley. I regret that he never got the chance to see the result.

About the Author

Christopher L. Bennett is a lifelong resident of Cincinnati, Ohio, with bachelor's degrees in physics and history from the University of Cincinnati. He has written such critically acclaimed *Star Trek* novels as *The Captain's Oath*, *Ex Machina*, *The Buried Age*, the *Titan* novels *Orion's Hounds* and *Over a Torrent Sea*, the *Department of Temporal Investigations* series including the novels *Watching the Clock* and *Forgotten History*, and the *Star Trek: Enterprise—Rise of the Federation* series. His shorter works include stories in the anniversary anthologies *Constellations*, *The Sky's the Limit*, *Prophecy and Change*, and *Distant Shores*. Beyond *Star Trek*, he has penned the novels *X-Men: Watchers on the Walls* and *Spider-Man: Drowned in Thunder*. His original work includes the hard science fiction superhero novel *Only Superhuman* from Tor Books and the duology *Arachne's Crime* and *Arachne's Exile* from eSpec Books, as well as various works of short fiction in *Analog* and other magazines, most of which have been collected in the volumes *Among the Wild Cybers: Tales Beyond the Superhuman*, *Hub Space: Tales from the Greater Galaxy*, and *Crimes of the Hub*. More information, ordering links, annotations, and the author's blog can be found at christopherlbennett.wordpress.com.